THE UNWANTEDS

Island of Dragons

Also by Lisa McMann

» » « «

The Unwanteds

Island of Silence

Island of Fire

Island of Legends

Island of Shipwrecks

Island of Graves

» » « «

FOR OLDER READERS:

Don't Close Your Eyes

Visions

Cryer's Cross

Dead to You

LISA McMANN

THE UNWANTEDS

Island of Dragons

Aladdin

NEW YORK   LONDON   TORONTO   SYDNEY   NEW DELHI

ALADDIN

An imprint of Simon & Schuster Children's Publishing Division

1230 Avenue of the Americas, New York, New York 10020

First Aladdin hardcover edition April 2016

Text copyright © 2016 by Lisa McMann

Jacket illustration copyright © 2016 by Owen Richardson

For information about special discounts for bulk purchases, please contact Simon & Schuster Special Sales at

1-866-506-1949 or business@simonandschuster.com.

The Simon & Schuster Speakers Bureau can bring authors to your live event. For more information

or to book an event, contact the Simon & Schuster Speakers Bureau at 1-866-248-3049

or visit our website at www.simonspeakers.com.

Book designed by Karin Paprocki

The text of this book was set in Truesdell.

Manufactured in the United States of America 1219 FFG

4 6 8 10 9 7 5 3

This book has been cataloged with the Library of Congress.

ISBN 978-1-4424-9337-7 (hc)

ISBN 978-1-4424-9339-1 (eBook)

Contents

For my editor, Liesa Abrams, who said yes.
This series, these characters, and all the islands
became real because of you. From the depths of
my heart, I thank you.

DEATH BE NOT PROUD

JOHN DONNE

Death be not proud, though some have callèd thee

Mighty and dreadfull, for, thou art not so,

For, those, whom thou think'st, thou dost overthrow,

Die not, poore death, nor yet canst thou kill me.

From rest and sleepe, which but thy pictures bee,

Much pleasure, then from thee, much more must flow,

And soonest our best men with thee doe goe,

Rest of their bones, and soules deliverie.

Thou art slave to Fate, Chance, kings, and desperate men,

And dost with poyson, warre, and sicknesse dwell,

And poppie, or charmes can make us sleepe as well,

And better than thy stroake; why swell'st thou then;

One short sleepe past, wee wake eternally,

And death shall be no more; death, thou shalt die.

THE UNWANTEDS
Island of Dragons

Fire

The desert land of Quill was no more.

Even though Aaron Stowe had implanted the fatal scatterclip into Gondoleery Rattrapp's forehead and cried out the words "Die a thousand deaths!" that ended her terroristic reign, the old woman's weapons had hit many unintended targets. The fireballs continued doing damage long after her demise.

The Artiméans limped home after the battle past dozens of small fires that burned throughout Quill. Fanned by the sea breeze and fed by the dry, brittle wood houses, the fires grew out of control. Soon every quadrant in Quill was engulfed in

LISA McMANN

flames. Frantic Wanteds and Necessaries were forced to abandon their homes and flee for the only part of the island that wasn't burning: Artimé.

"Let's keep the Quillens moving!" shouted Alex Stowe, the head mage of the magical land of Artimé, as the people passed through the invisible weather barrier to safety. "All the way to the shore and the edge of the jungle, so there's room for everyone!" In the confusion, he turned to two of his closest friends, Lani Haluki and Samheed Burkesh. "Try to convince them that it's safe to go inside the mansion, will you? I'm afraid we'll run out of space out here."

"We'll try," said Lani, "but it's not going to be easy." The lawn was tightly packed with Wanteds and Necessaries. Lani and Samheed did their best to spread the word, while Alex hurried inside the mansion to expand the upstairs living quarters so they could house the refugees who agreed to come inside.

But it was a lot of work trying to convince the stubborn-minded, fearful people of Quill that they wouldn't accidentally get any magic on them if they decided to take a room in the mansion until things could be sorted out.

Alex overheard an exasperated Samheed talking to an old

Quillen man. "Trust me," he said. "There's absolutely no way you are going to become magical just by sleeping in a nice bed for once in your life. Just come inside and I'll show you to your room."

When the stubborn man refused and instead sat down behind a bush outside the mansion, Samheed threw his hands in the air. "Fine," he said. "Sleep there forever, then. I'm sure I don't care." He went grumbling back through the crowd toward the weather barrier to try to direct some injured Quillens to the hospital ward.

Simber flew overhead, occasionally sweeping over the burning part of the island from a safe height, looking to rescue anyone who might be trapped. The orange flames weren't hot enough to harm him—not much, anyway. It had been the white- and blue-hot flames of Gondoleery's fireballs that had done him in. Nevertheless, the giant stone cheetah was especially wary after what he'd gone through. Simber knew that if Alex's twin brother Aaron hadn't acted so quickly to restore him, his sandy remains would still be on the road near the palace right now, burning with the rest of Quill.

Artimé owed Aaron a debt of gratitude, though a few were

LISA McMANN

having a hard time accepting that fact after all Aaron had done in the past to hurt the magical world. Alex was among the most grateful, though, for Aaron had done something that Alex couldn't do—he'd brought Simber back to life. While Alex sometimes struggled with the complexities of magic, Aaron's newfound abilities appeared almost effortless. Was there any limit to what Aaron could do? Alex was starting to wonder.

Needless to say, Aaron Stowe—former Everything, current Nothing—had earned a lot of respect from those who'd witnessed his unselfish actions. But he channeled his inner Ishibashi, kept his head down, and worked alongside the Artiméans to help with the injured and displaced people. And, being the closest thing to a leader of Quill, he found himself having to solve a whole new series of problems that came along with a community devastated by fire.

Once the fleeing Wanteds and Necessaries arrived in Artimé, they had no choice but to stay. Covered in soot and carrying what little they could salvage, they sought safety in the magical world they hated and feared. Some arrived defeated, some defiant, some overwhelmed, and some finally digging deep inside themselves and discovering their anger a little too late. And a few—mostly children—arrived with a tiny hint of excitement stirring in their hearts, for they had heard whispers about the happenings in Artimé, and they were not quite dead inside.

The heavy black smoke traveled westward with the wind, and it didn't take long for Queen Eagala and the hook-handed pirate, Captain Baldhead, to hear reports that something was amiss. After their meeting on Warbler, they sent out spies to see if the entire island of Quill was destroyed.

But Alex's magical weather barrier around Artimé proved to be one of the best spells the head mage had ever put in place. Soon the leaders of Warbler and Pirate Islands received word that the southern part of the island of Quill remained completely unharmed by fire and was filled with people. So they redoubled their efforts and continued planning the ultimate attack to destroy the magical land.

Alex and his people had other things on their minds.

The fires raged and settled and raged and settled again for weeks until there was nothing left to burn. During that time, Alex and his friends did whatever they could to assure their new visitors that they were safe now. Some of them, comforted by seeing Aaron safe and sound in Artimé, eased into their new lives a little at a time, trying to get used to the strange surroundings. Others chose to stay far away from the Unwanteds' mansion, sleeping on the lawn at the border between the two worlds, waiting until they could go back home. With no trained ability to imagine things, they couldn't fathom that Quill would look very different than it had before. But they'd soon discover there would be no home to go to.

When at last the fires burned out and it was safe to venture into Quill, all could see for themselves that nothing of worth remained. With no resources to rebuild, it seemed the Wanteds and Necessaries would be forced to stay in Artimé.

The annual day of the Purge came and went, unnoticed and obsolete.

The Island of Artimé

But the people of Quill didn't want to stay in the magical land. Wanteds and Necessaries went into Quill multiple times over the following weeks to consider ways to rebuild. Sometimes they brought creative-minded Artiméans with them in hopes of someone coming up with a plan. But with no resources, there were no solutions, and the groups returned day after day covered in soot and feeling desperate for their old familiar land. Frustrations ran high. Soon even the most stubborn of the Quillens had to admit there was nothing they could do to rebuild their awful world.

With the long-term outlook seeming quite grim, Alex

LISA McMANN

called a formal meeting on the lawn for all the Wanteds and Necessaries to attend so they could talk about what to do next. He even borrowed a podium from Mr. Appleblossom to stand behind so that it would feel familiar to the people of Quill. It was a subtle gesture that was unfortunately lost on the dull-witted Quillens.

After greeting the crowd, Alex laid out the situation. "I've talked with my advisors, including my brother Aaron," he said. He pointed to Aaron next to him, since his brother's presence seemed to give the Quillens some sort of comfort. "Because there's nothing salvageable left in Quill, and because it would take years to remove all of the soot and embers and burned-out structures from the island, you are stuck in Artimé whether you like it or not. But I have an idea. With your permission, we'd like to expand our magical world to cover the ugliness."

The crowd, more vocal than it had ever been, began to murmur and complain.

Alex waited, then went on. "Once the magic of Artimé covers the entire island, I can make individual homes for you like you had before. And . . . ," he said, cringing, "I can make the land as bland as you want it to be."

Claire Morning and Florence, the giant ebony warrior statue, were standing at the back of the crowd, and they exchanged wry grins. It was hard for anyone in Artimé to believe that there were people who would purposely choose to have a bland world. But Aaron had suggested the option be offered, and it seemed to quiet the complaints a little.

"In fact," Alex said, bolstered by the reaction, "I can give you a similar layout to what you had before. I can even number the houses exactly the same, and just add some trees—and grass, if you want it—and schedule some occasional rain, which will help your living situations a lot. That way you won't have to limit yourselves to two buckets of water a week. Your gardens and farms will flourish, and you and your livestock and chickens will have plenty to eat and drink."

Mr. Appleblossom, who had been in charge of rescuing the livestock and chickens that had run from the fire into Artimé, nodded and smiled as the Quillens talked among themselves about this new development. Once Mr. Appleblossom had put all the farm animals in one place, he'd set up a nice corral behind the mansion where they wouldn't be bothered or frightened by the owlbats, platyprots, and other strange creatures that roamed freely in Artimé. The Quillen animals were flourishing on the food, water, and care that Mr. Appleblossom and his helpers had been giving them.

Kaylee Jones, the American sailor whom Alex, Aaron, and Sky had rescued from the saber-toothed-gorilla-infested Island of Graves, had found a bit of comfort in the sight of animals that actually seemed normal to her, so she had joined Mr. Appleblossom's team. She'd set up a petting zoo for the children from both worlds to enjoy, which was something she remembered loving from her own childhood. Carina's son Seth and the younger set of Stowe twins, Thisbe and Fifer, were frequent visitors.

Now Kaylee stood off to one side with Sky, Samheed, and Lani, looking decidedly healthier than she'd been at the time of her rescue. Upon her arrival, she'd been shocked by the gray, desert land of Quill—perhaps more shocked by it than by Artimé—and wondered how anyone could turn down the opportunity to have enough fresh water to drink. Yet before her eyes, a small group of Wanteds stubbornly argued and shook their heads, complaining about ridiculous things. She marveled at the stark difference between the two kinds of people on this island, and was infinitely glad that her rescuers had come from Artimé.

As the crowd grew louder in their discussion over whether grass should be allowed, and whether they wanted it to rain more, Alex leaned toward his brother. "Now what do I do?" he whispered.

Aaron put a hand on the podium. "You want me to step in?" he asked quietly.

Alex frowned. "No, I can do it. Just tell me what to say to them, because I have no idea right now."

One corner of Aaron's mouth turned up slightly. "Tell them that if they try having grass in their yards and they don't like it, we can always remove it so they can have dirt yards like before."

Alex sighed. "But I don't want to create dirt yards."

"Think of all the drawing they can do in the dirt when it rains," Aaron said, almost mischievously.

The look on Aaron's face caught Alex by surprise, as so many things had in the past few months. His brother was a different person now, thanks to his time on the Island of Shipwrecks with the three old scientists: Ishibashi, Ito, and

LISA McMANN

Sato. Alex still wasn't sure if Aaron had gotten whacked on the head a little too hard when the pirates had kidnapped him—that's how big his transformation was. But Aaron insisted he had still been an awful person when he'd first regained consciousness in the stone shelter, and Ishibashi had been quick to agree.

Alex smiled. "All right," he said. His insides felt complete now that he had his brother beside him. The two of them standing together with the same goals in mind was a dream Alex never thought could come true. Not like this. Not as friends, anyway.

Alex stepped back to the podium and lifted his hand in the air for silence, which came quickly. The Quillens were nothing if not militant about letting the person at the podium speak—even if he was someone they didn't trust. "We can always give it a try with the grass yards," Alex said amicably, "and if it turns out you don't like this luscious stuff massaging your bare feet every day, I will give you a dirt yard as before. Aaron will see to it."

Aaron nodded his promise to the people, and that calmed them immediately.

"Leave it at that," Aaron said under his breath. "Finish up—you're about to lose them."

Alex nodded. "Thank you, people of Quill. All in favor of having your own magical homes right where the old ones used to be, raise your hand."

The Wanteds and Necessaries had never been asked to vote on anything before. They looked at one another, confused.

"Just go ahead and put your hand in the air like I'm doing," Alex said, "if you want me to extend the magical world in order to give you your homes back. And if most of you agree, I'll do it."

Samheed stared from the audience and made a face at Alex. Alex ignored him.

Aaron raised his hand as well to show the people. But no one wanted to be the first in the audience to do it.

"Okay, then," Alex said, hesitating a bit, trying to figure out what to do next. "How about this: Everyone who would like to have their own home back as I proposed, just keep standing there with no hands in the air."

No one moved.

"Good!" said Alex. "Excellent. That's all of you. I'll begin

LISA McMANN

working on it right away. If everything goes well, we should have the first new homes ready in a matter of days. Thank you for coming!"

The people didn't move.

"And now you may go," said Alex, with a grand flourish that made Lani crack up and have to hide her face.

Alex stepped back from the podium and turned to Aaron as the Wanteds and Necessaries began to disperse. Only a few small groups stayed around to voice complaints. "Whew," he said. "Tough crowd."

"Yes," Aaron said. "That was pretty clever how you did that, though."

A group of five or six Wanteds approached Aaron.

"We don't want to live in the magical world," one said grumpily. "We want nothing to do with that Unwanteds magic."

Aaron and Alex exchanged a worried glance. "But . . . ," said Aaron, "there's nowhere else for you to live."

"We don't care," said the spokesperson.

Alex scratched his head, perplexed. How was he going to satisfy everybody?

But Aaron took hold of the situation. "No problem," he said. He turned to Alex. "Can you leave a small portion of Quill untouched by magic for these fine Wanteds?"

"I—" Alex began, then hesitated. "Well, sure, I *can*, but . . ."

"Very good," Aaron said smoothly. "Our problem is solved. Give them a bit of barren, burned-out land to live on." He thought about what Ishibashi might say, and added, "And make it as far away from here as possible."

Aaron Longs for Home

I t had been a crazy few years for Aaron Stowe. He went from Wanted, to university student, to assistant to the secretary of the high priest, to leader of the Restorers, to high priest of Quill. He'd killed a kind magician; nearly killed his brother; sent his father to the Ancients Sector and made his only friend, Secretary, get him back; and sent Secretary to the Ancients Sector only to watch her die because he stupidly set loose a wild creature upon a group of innocent children.

That was a lot of horrible deeds to deal with, and Aaron would be lying if he said he didn't think about them often. He spent hours roaming the smoldering ruins of Quill alone, contemplating. He stood where the portcullis had been, and looked at the charred remains of the palace—his former home. Yet there was nothing he could think of that he missed about the place. Nothing had made that cold, gray palace feel as cozy as his cot on a rock floor in the middle of a hurricane.

Thinking back upon his life in Quill made Aaron feel numb inside. Everything he had once lived for was gone. He smiled ruefully, wondering what sort of metaphor Ishibashi would make from it. He missed the old man, sometimes desperately.

Every now and then Aaron thought about what it would be like if the pirates hadn't mistaken him for his brother—if they'd captured Alex instead, and Aaron had remained in power. Would he still be high priest, or would Gondoleery have ousted or even killed him by now? Would he still sneak to the jungle to be in the one place he felt at ease, among the misfits . . . the misunderstoods? Would he have eventually confided in Liam that he was so terribly uncertain about what he was doing? Or would he have kept it all in, as always? As one is expected to do in Quill?

And would he be raising his sisters to be bad like him? Thisbe and Fifer were almost two years old. When he looked at them, he couldn't imagine them growing up in that horrible, stark palace.

One quiet morning he sat on the lawn with his sisters, watching them play in the sand, making sure they didn't venture too far into the water. They were learning to swim, but it was the current that worried Aaron the most, knowing they could be swept off their little feet and pulled out to the sea.

Aaron could swim a little now. Not like Alex and Sky and the others, but at least he wasn't terrified anymore. Not really, anyway, though he still had nightmares about the little pirate boat and the hurricane. But he also had good dreams about returning to the Island of Shipwrecks.

Carina Holiday and her son, Seth, walked up to the beach. Seth ran over to the girls, and Carina sat down next to Aaron.

Some of Alex's friends had begun to trust Aaron by now. Simber, for sure, and Sky, of course. But Carina had kept her distance, watching him—he saw her and others, too, like Claire Morning and Samheed Burkesh, always, always watching him. And while Aaron knew their skepticism was deserved, it was hard to take, and it didn't feel very good. He wondered why Carina chose the spot next to him to sit.

"Good morning," Aaron said.

"Good morning," she replied, crossing her ankles and pulling her knees up. She sipped from a steaming mug.

Aaron watched his sisters shriek with joy when they saw Seth, who was a year or so older than them. They had become fast friends—most of the time anyway. As good friends as two- and three-year-olds could be, he supposed. "The girls really love Seth," he said to break the silence.

"He adores them, too," Carina said. "And I am rather enjoying this quiet morning."

"It'll be even quieter when the Quillens are gone," said Aaron. "Alex is going to start expanding the magical world soon."

"I was at the meeting," Carina said.

"Of course," said Aaron, feeling awkward. "Sorry I didn't see you."

If Carina noticed Aaron's awkwardness, she didn't indicate it. "I would imagine the Wanteds and Necessaries can't wait to go home," she mused.

Aaron nodded. He understood the feeling.

Seth started to pile and pack sand into a large mound. Thisbe waited until he was almost done and pushed it over. But Seth didn't get mad; he just started building it up again. Fifer played quietly by herself, singing a nonsensical made-up song.

"I guess she's like me," Aaron said, more to himself than to Carina. He looked up. "Thisbe, I mean. The one in red." Suddenly he felt strange for saying it, as if he were admitting something that made him very vulnerable. He still had a hard time with that, especially with people he didn't know well. Perhaps he always would.

Carina smiled. "Can you see their personalities emerging?"

"Yes. It's interesting. They're quite different from each other once you get to know them," Aaron said. "Thisbe plays hard and sleeps hard. She puts all her energy into everything she does—see?" He pointed as she knocked Seth's sand tower down again with her whole body, landing on the boy. Seth fell back, surprised, and laughed with Thisbe when she laughed. They got to their feet.

"Again?" Seth said to her.

"Again," Thisbe agreed. Seth started piling sand.

"And Fifer," Aaron said, shaking his head. "She's very gentle and . . . I don't know. Intensely musical, and thoughtful, I guess. Can a two-year-old be thoughtful?"

"I think so," Carina said. "Seth is that way too."

"Yet he puts up with Thisbe's games so well."

Carina nodded. "And the girls love each other, don't they? They seem inseparable."

"They are," Aaron said, thinking about so much more than just his sisters. "They're best friends. They couldn't live without each other."

Carina sipped her drink and watched the kids quietly. "You know," she said after a while, "I used to think that twins were trouble. Marcus and Justine. You and Alex." She swung her head to give Aaron a look of raw honesty. "Because it was really difficult with you for a long time, you know?"

"Of course." Aaron dropped his gaze. "I know."

"But you're proving that it doesn't have to be that way," said Carina. "You're showing your sisters something important, I think."

Aaron pursed his lips. He hadn't thought about that before. "Somebody wise told me that just because Alex was good, that didn't mean I had to be bad in order to be distinct from him. I could be a different kind of good."

"The man from the Island of Shipwrecks?" asked Carina.

"Yes." A spear of longing passed through Aaron. He looked

left, to the east, as if that would bring Ishibashi's island closer. But then he turned his gaze back to the girls, his face clouding over. He'd miss them. A lot. "Once we have the Wanteds and Necessaries settled, I guess I'll be free to go back there."

"Is that what you want to do?"

"It doesn't really matter what I want," Aaron said. "It was part of the deal. Alex found me, brought me here, and I did my job. I was never meant to stay."

Carina reached out, putting her hand over Aaron's, and gave it a gentle squeeze. "Thank you for helping us," she said. "You're an incredible mage—I have no idea how you were able to do so much without training. And I can't believe I'm saying this, but I'm very glad you came back. At least for a little while. If you decide to stay, well, I certainly wouldn't mind. You're all right, Aaron."

Aaron stared at her hand on his. He wondered if he'd ever get used to people being kind to him.

Later, when Aaron was alone and thinking about the responsibilities he had to attend to here on this island before he could leave, he found his mind turning to Panther. He went inside the mansion, past Simber and Florence, whose broken leg was restored. He climbed the stairs to the balcony and slipped down the not-even-a-faint-secret of a hallway. He went past all the doors, not knowing where some of them led, and into the kitchenette.

He stood for a moment in front of the tube, feeling guilty. One thing he hadn't told anyone about was his past visits to the jungle. He'd tell his brother eventually. He had to, so Alex could take care of the creatures once Aaron was gone. But he knew that when that happened, he'd have to confess to the rock and to Panther that he'd been lying to them. He'd have to tell them that he wasn't Alex.

The thought pained him, and the longer it lingered, the more painful it became. Maybe he would ask Alex to confess for him . . . but that made Aaron feel like a coward. A feeling he knew all too well.

For now, Aaron decided as he stepped inside the tube, *the jungle is my secret.* It was the only thing left that truly belonged to him. And he wasn't ready to give it up. He desperately needed one place to go where nobody stared at him or wondered if he was still evil inside.

LISA McMANN

House After House

Alex had never spent so much time working on his concentration and spells as he was spending now. Once he'd found Mr. Today's journal that detailed how he created the world in the first place, Alex designed his own spell that would expand the existing boundaries of Artimé to cover almost the entire island.

It didn't all happen at once, unfortunately. He had to go bit by bit, section by section. Each section fell into place a little like how the hospital ward did whenever Alex had to expand that. As he pressed the invisible boundary outward, grass dropped down to mark his progress.

Once Alex had extended Artimé to cover up all but one small section of the charred remains of Quill, which he left for the cranky group of Wanteds as promised, he began working on the infrastructure, putting in a paved road where the dirt one used to be and laying down walking paths throughout the community. He widened the stream and had Ms. Octavia create a bubbling freshwater fountain in the Commons like the one she'd made for the *Claire*, so that the community could come and draw water from it whenever they needed it. Things were taking shape. Alex was careful to hold back so he wouldn't accidentally make Quill too beautiful. The restraint was almost painful.

Then Alex took to his office to work on a house component. He asked Aaron to help design the layout, and Alex created a prototype for the first house and tried it out in the vast open space in the Museum of Large. After a few tweaks, Aaron approved, and Alex had the design exactly the way the Quillens would want it.

The head mage called Samheed, Lani, Carina, and Sean Ranger to help make replicas of the component. The group spread out their supplies and tools in the Museum of Large, below the outstretched trunk and huge sharp tusks of Ol' Tater, the mastodon statue.

The new magical houses looked more like Wanted houses than Necessary ones, not just because the design was simple enough to replicate, but because Alex thought the Necessaries—who had been on the cusp of helping Artimé take out Gondoleery—deserved nicer houses than the ones they'd had. And it was easier to design and replicate one spell component than two, so Alex chose to do it as such. He decided that if any Necessary came to him demanding a smaller, less equipped home, he would gladly oblige.

When Alex finally had enough components for all the Quillen households, he began installing the houses one at a time in nearly the same layout as Quill had previously had, doing his best to work from memory and getting guidance from some of the older Necessaries who had known every inch of Quill.

By this time, the Wanteds and Necessaries were more than anxious to go back to their familiar-looking, yet slightly more colorful and less ugly world. Dozens of Wanteds and Necessaries moved into their new homes every day as Alex worked long and hard to re-create their world. Most of the recipients knew very little about how to express their thanks for a gift so huge, but some of them managed, which felt like progress to Alex. And a thank you now and then for the hardworking head mage of Artimé was very much appreciated.

The small group of cranky Wanteds who wanted nothing to do with magic settled in the charcoaled remains just beyond the Ancients Sector, across the island from Artimé. They were so blinded by their opposition to magic that they were willing to sleep in soot and scrounge for food and water just to make a point. Alex wasn't quite sure what that point was, but he didn't really care, either, as long as they didn't bother him.

And Aaron worked with some of the more reasonable Wanteds and Necessaries to try to make the Ancients Sector into something much more humane than it once was. He pointed out the willingness of the Ancients to help fight Gondoleery, thus proving their usefulness, and suggested the Ancients Sector be a place of respite for the elderly to go to on their own accord, where they could enjoy their last days without fear or chains, and be among friends.

Needless to say, Alex "forgot" to build the sleep chamber, and no one seemed upset about that.

As for the palace, Alex decided not to build one at all, and instead put a lighthouse with a lookout tower in its place on the top of the hill. For the time being, he appointed Gunnar Haluki to watch over the new annex, reassign jobs to all the people instead of just the Necessaries, and make sure the farms and animals were being nurtured properly. Gunnar asked Claire Morning to teach the Quillens how to make the most of their new situation, and she began by showing them how to funnel rainwater off their roofs into barrels so they wouldn't have to travel to the fountain to get it. They'd always have more than enough water to go around for people, plants, and animals.

With only a little grumbling, the people of Quill settled in to their new Artiméan-made homes, and life returned to almost normal.

Henry Finds a Purpose

Back in Artimé, the last of the injured had recovered from the battle against Gondoleery, and the hospital ward stood empty. Henry Haluki had been a permanent fixture there over the past months, and was often regarded as the go-to healer since he was seen there the most, though he still took orders from Ms. Morning and Carina. But just because there was no one for Henry to heal didn't mean he had nothing to do. He used his free time to work with plants from his greenhouse, experimenting with their medicinal properties and creating new, more potent strains that would make his healing serums more effective.

And every day he painstakingly added to his store of proven medicines so they'd never be in short supply again.

He spent a little time with other people—the nurses sometimes helped him bottle up the medicine—but he was often lost in thought these days. He hadn't quite forgiven himself for not saving Meghan Ranger. Yet whenever he thought about giving her the glowing seaweed he'd gotten from Ishibashi, which would've extended her life indefinitely, he knew that he'd done the only thing he could. He'd obeyed Ishibashi's command: Never use it on any human without their permission. Meghan had been near death by the time Henry saw her—perhaps she was dead already. But Henry never had the opportunity to ask her, and so he'd stood there, holding the seaweed, looking on helplessly at her still body.

Alex had unwittingly helped Henry come to terms with his guilt after the fact. And now Henry knew that if he was forced into the same predicament with the head mage's life hanging in the balance, he didn't have to agonize over it. He'd asked Alex a hypothetical question about having the chance to live indefinitely, and Alex had told him point blank that he wouldn't ever want to have his life significantly extended by unnatural means. It was a relief to know.

And now that their world was finally at peace, Henry was extremely glad he didn't have to worry about it anymore.

But even though they were at peace, Florence started up Magical Warrior Training again, knowing Artimé could never be too prepared. One day, Henry was outside cutting some leaves from his greenhouse plants that Ishibashi had given him. He paused now and then in his work to watch the training, and felt almost wistful.

On the end nearest him was Thatcher, a young teen from Warbler who was about Henry's age, perhaps a year older. He had black curly hair and dark brown skin, and orange eyes like all the Warbler children. He wasn't intimidated by the instructors, and he liked chatting with them. His obvious ease with more authoritative figures was striking. But the blond-haired Warbler girl next to him, Scarlet, was all seriousness, especially in her attempts to mess Thatcher up without him noticing. Henry watched Scarlet for a moment, and then his eyes strayed back to Thatcher, and he observed the Warbler boy's carefree spirit and sense of humor when he joked with Florence and Ms. Morning.

At one point Thatcher caught Henry staring and smiled at

him, raising a hand in greeting. Henry smiled back and quickly looked down at his cuttings. "I might need to take a class soon," he said to nobody in particular. He gathered up his cuttings, and then walked in a wide circle around the students to keep from getting accidentally struck by a poor throw.

On the day after Alex finished expanding the world, he walked past the hospital ward on his way to the kitchen to get a snack and noticed that every bed was empty for the first time in a long time. He paused, then went in, seeing Henry working alone at the laboratory table with something bubbling merrily in a beaker nearby.

"Congratulations, Henry," Alex said. "Empty beds. Now that's an accomplishment!"

Henry looked up. "Thanks. The last one checked out a couple days ago. Did you finish the expansion in Quill? Anybody give you trouble?"

"Yes, it's done," Alex said. "No real trouble to speak of, but I'm whipped. Do you have anything that'll help my sore shoulders feel better? Those were some long, hard days of spell casting. More than I've ever done in one stretch before."

Henry reached up and pulled a small container of herbal lotion from a shelf. "This should do the trick. Find a nice girl to rub some of this on your shoulders. It'll feel better in no time."

"Because of the lotion?" Alex teased. "Or because of the girl?"

"It doesn't really matter, does it?"

"I guess not," Alex said. "Are you speaking from experience? Do you have a girl rubbing lotion on your shoulders that I don't know about?"

Henry grinned. "I'm not really into girls. But no."

Alex returned the grin and patted Henry on the back. "Thanks," he said, taking the lotion. "Do you want me to make this room smaller again? Or do you like it all big and empty like this?"

"I wouldn't want to tax your poor aching muscles," Henry said.

"Why, Henry Haluki," Alex said, "I think you're mocking me. You used to be such a serious and respectful young lad."

Henry shrugged. "I guess I've been jaded by all the battles you've dragged me into," he said brightly. "You can leave the

LISA McMANN

room big. I like it like this. It gives me lots of room to spread out my plant cuttings to dry."

"All right," Alex said. He turned to go, and then paused and looked over his shoulder. "You should go outside and get some fresh air sometime, you know? Try some new spells. Swim. Have fun."

Henry looked up from his work again. "This is fun," he said. He got up from his chair. "But I do need to go outside, actually, to get some more roots."

"Great. I'll tag along. Maybe you can teach me something."

"Doubtful," Henry said with a smile, "but I'll try."

The two headed outside past Simber and Florence and strolled over the lawn toward Henry's greenhouse area. But they didn't get far before Alex noticed Spike Furious circling just offshore.

"Hmm," Alex said, narrowing his eyes. "One second, Henry." Alex jogged to the water's edge. "Is everything all right, Spike?" he called out to the whale.

"The Alex!" shouted Spike. "I have been waiting for you with important news!"

Henry joined Alex.

"News from whom?" asked Alex.

"It is from Pan, the coiled water dragon who rules the sea!"

"Really?" Alex said. "She came to you? What did she say?"

Spike trumpeted water from her blowhole. "She said these words exactly: 'Tell Alex that Karkinos the crab is gravely ill and rapidly losing strength, and he has begun drifting westward. Have you found a way to save him? There isn't much time.'"

"Oh no," muttered Alex. "He's headed toward the waterfall." He took a few steps into the water, muttering something unintelligible. And then he called out, "How much time does Karkinos have to live?"

"Only days," Spike said. "I can feel his approaching death in the water."

"Cripes," muttered Alex.

"Alex," Henry asked, "what's this all about? Lani mentioned once that Karkinos was sick, but I didn't know it was this bad."

Alex turned and waded back to shore. "It . . . well, to be perfectly honest, Karkinos hasn't exactly been my top priority with everything else going on. But Pan told me he was getting

LISA McMANN

worse a few months ago when we rescued Kaylee and Aaron."
Alex shoved his hands in his pockets, feeling helpless. He gave
Henry an imploring look. "How much medicine have you got
on hand?"

"It depends," said Henry. "What kind do you need? What's
wrong with him?"

"Nobody really knows," said Alex. "But if he drifts over the
waterfall, he might not be the only one who dies. We have to
do something."

Henry looked perplexed. "Karkinos is enormous," he said.
"Even if I knew what kind of medicine he needed, I wouldn't
have enough."

Alex shook his head. "Islands aren't supposed to die," he
muttered. Quickly he went through his options. If they couldn't
save Karkinos, they had to at least save Talon, Lhasa, Bock . . .
He began listing off the inhabitants to see if they all would somehow fit in the magical white boat. But Talon was likely as heavy
as Florence, and then add to that all the hundreds of dropbears
and the hibagon and Vido the rooster . . . He shook his head.
Even if Talon could fly the whole way, there was no way they
could fit even a small percentage of the others on the boat.

"We'd have to take the pirate ship to rescue them," Alex said, looking at the patched but seaworthy vessel standing in the lagoon. "But it would take days to get there in that thing. There's not enough time!"

Henry racked his brain, mentally going over all the medicinal stores. He had quite a lot now, but what a waste it would be if they used it all on Karkinos and it didn't work. Plus, after all Artimé had been through, Henry didn't ever like being without enough medicine. But if it could somehow save the crab's life . . .

Henry's eyes widened, and he sucked in a breath. "Wait a second," he said. His hand went to his component vest, to the special pocket with a spell-protected lock, and felt the container that he'd kept there ever since Ishibashi had given it to him.

"Alex," Henry said, his voice measured, "what's the absolute fastest way to get a single person to the Island of Legends?"

Alex frowned, thinking of all the options. "Either Simber or Spike would be faster than the boat or the ship."

Henry tapped the container through his vest thoughtfully. "And Spike can talk to all species, right?"

"Right," said Alex. "But neither one of them can carry all the creatures here to Artimé, so we need a boat. Why?"

Henry set his jaw and nodded firmly. "We don't need a boat. Get Spike ready."

"What? I don't understand," said Alex.

Henry's eyes gleamed. "I'm saying I've got the right medicine, Alex. I can keep Karkinos alive . . . but only if I can get there in time."

Planning a Journey

That's an awfully long ride on the back of a whale," Alex said to Henry. "And what if the medicine doesn't work? You wouldn't be able to save everyone."

Henry stared out over the sea, thinking fast. Was the small container of seaweed enough to save such a large creature as Karkinos? Ishibashi had only used the tiniest pinch of it to heal a sea turtle. Henry's container was packed full. He wouldn't have time to go all the way to the Island of Shipwrecks for more . . . but he didn't think he'd need to.

"Henry?" Alex prompted.

"What?"

LISA McMANN

"What if it doesn't work?" Alex said again. "You wouldn't be able to save Talon and the others."

"Well, do you have any other options?" Henry asked impatiently. "You said the pirate ship can't get there in time. If Karkinos is drifting toward the waterfall, all the inhabitants are going to get pulled down it and their lives will be in danger if they can't get everyone tied down in time. To stop that from happening, we need speed first of all. And I'm telling you I've got the right medicine. I'm sure of it! I just need to get there." He jiggled his foot, ready to spring into action as soon as Alex gave the word.

Alex studied the young man. Henry had grown up fast by necessity. He was one of the most responsible and selfless people Alex knew. He'd been by Alex's side in the gray shack when all was lost, and he'd stayed loyal and focused ever since.

"All right," Alex said. "I believe you. But you and Spike aren't going alone. Let's go talk to Florence and see what she recommends."

"Great!" said Henry. He started toward the mansion while Alex thanked Spike and told her what was happening. "I need you to swim as fast as possible. Can you do that?"

"I can swim like a bullet, the Alex!" said Spike, sounding extremely happy to be chosen as the fastest ride in Artimé. "I will go tell Pan and return shortly to take Henry to the Island of Legends."

Alex watched the whale swish through the water in search of Pan. He'd never witnessed her top speed before, but it was true—he'd instilled great speed in her when he'd brought her to life. Now it would come in handy.

He jogged to the mansion, finding Henry and Florence deep in conversation, with Simber standing silently by.

Florence's face wore a pained expression. "I want to go," she said softly. "I have to." She and Talon had grown very fond of one another during their visit to Karkinos, and had made plans to see each other again once life in Artimé settled down. And now she feared she might never see Talon again if Henry's plan was unsuccessful.

Henry looked to Alex for help.

"Hi, Florence," Alex said, coming up next to Simber. "You heard?"

"Yes," said Florence.

"Obviously Henry can't go alone with Spike," said Alex.

"I want to go," Florence said again.

Alex pressed his lips together, perplexed. "I know," he said, his voice gentle but firm. "I'm sorry, Florence. I just can't see how that's possible without slowing Spike down considerably. And speed is of the utmost importance."

Florence lifted her chin and looked away, trying to hide her feelings. Her heavy ebony body had been a benefit in so many ways, but it had its drawbacks, too. She knew what Alex said was true. But how she wished there was a way. She blinked and looked at Simber. "If only I could borrow your wings, my friend," she said.

"Talon has wings," Simber reminded her. "He doesn't need to go down the waterrrfall with the rrrest of the island."

Florence laughed bitterly. "Do you really think he'd stay back and watch everyone go over the edge?"

Simber looked down. "No. Of courrrse he'll stay with them, just as Alex chose to do with ourrr ship."

"If we don't hurry . . . ," Henry prodded. He was ready to jump on the whale's back and go at a moment's notice.

A flash of light through the window caught Henry's eye. "Spike is out there circling again," he said. He moved to the window and his eyes opened wide. "Wow—what the stink is *that* thing next to her?" he breathed.

Alex rushed to his side to look. Coming up out of the water and walking onto the shore with her oversized dragon head, snakelike body, and four stocky legs growing from the thickest part of her trunk, was Pan herself. Her long, whiplike tail snapped and curled like a lasso behind her, her clawed feet dug divots into the lawn and shot bits of grass into the air behind her, and the plume of scales that burst from her head sparkled a myriad of colors in the sunlight.

"It's Pan," Alex said. "Come and meet her." He rushed to open the door and ran outside, the others following.

Alex greeted the dragon, his heart pounding from being so close to the great beast. She seemed immensely larger on land than she'd seemed in the open sea. Her sprawling body made Simber look small.

Simber stood back, wary of the dragon's potential fiery breath.

Alex introduced Florence, Henry, and Simber.

"Greetings," said Pan. "I have seen you from afar. It is good to meet friends of the sea in these dark times." She eyed Florence. "You are the one Talon speaks of."

Florence's face grew hot. "Is he well?" she asked.

"He is lonely," said Pan.

"Oh my," said Florence, looking completely lost for words.

Simber rescued her. "How is it that we haven't seen you beforrre?" he asked Pan.

The dragon stretched out her neck to look across the island. "With pirates in my waters capturing and selling sea creatures these many years," she said warily, "it has been in my best interest to stay hidden."

Florence, Simber, and Alex exchanged glances, all of them realizing the same thing. The pirates weren't just capturing sea creatures. They intended to sell them! But to whom?

"We understand," Florence said. "We're pleased you trust us enough to venture on land."

Alex spoke up, anxious to get to the point. "Pan," he said, "our healer, Henry, believes he has something that will help Karkinos. He'll travel to the Island of Legends on Spike's back. We're deciding who else to send with him now, and they'll be on their way shortly."

"I will accompany them to Karkinos," Pan said, "to make sure they arrive safely. There is danger everywhere."

Henry's eyes widened. Now he had two very large creatures to spend time with, and he had no idea what to expect from the dragon or if she was safe. He shot a pleading glance at Florence.

Florence looked up at the dragon. "You're aware we killed the sea eel, of course?"

"I am also aware of other eels," said Pan.

"Ah, so therrre *is* morrre than one," said Simber, eyes narrowing. "That concerrrns me grrreatly."

"Yes," said Pan. "As I said before, I am in the business of hiding. Do not fear for your boy and your whale with me."

Alex looked up at the dragon's face. "Thank you . . . for the information. We'll need a little time to organize."

The dragon nodded once. She turned and glided into the water, her tail swirling constantly, making shapes in the air.

Alex turned to Henry. "Find Aaron and Sky and ask them to quickly construct a seat for you that we can strap to Spike."

"Right," said Henry. He dashed into the mansion.

Alex looked at Simber and Florence. "I'd feel more comfortable if we sent someone with Henry."

Pan stopped in the water and swung her head back toward them, her plume of scales shimmering. "I do not wish to pry, but is there a reason you don't want to go, Florence? I would have thought you'd be the first to volunteer. But perhaps your feelings for Talon have changed. If so, he should be told."

Florence looked up. "Oh no," she said. "That's not it at all. It's just—I'm carved of ebony, too heavy for Spike to carry at full speed. And speed is of the essence now, I'm afraid." She hesitated. "My heart belongs to Talon. If you wish to tell him that, I'd be grateful. . . ." She looked down, embarrassed and sad all over again.

Pan's tail weaved through the water as she floated a short distance from shore. "You might slow down a whale," she said, "but nothing can slow down a dragon. If your presence here can be spared, you must ride on my back and tell him yourself."

Strange Company

A short time later Spike sat in the lagoon, waiting to depart. Sky came flying out of the mansion with Aaron right behind, carrying a makeshift cocoonlike chair-bed that they'd weaved from strips of lightweight but sturdy cloth. A harness was attached.

Sky swam with it to Spike and hoisted the chair onto the whale's back. As she secured the harness around the great whale, Henry and Alex exited the mansion carrying a waterproof crate of supplies to attach to it, and Samheed and Lani came walking toward the shore from the new land of Quill.

LISA McMANN

"What's going on?" Lani asked, watching Alex and Henry head into the water.

Aaron turned. "Henry is going to Karkinos with medicine, so Sky and I made a chair for him." He'd never met the crab island or any of its inhabitants, but he knew that much about what was happening.

"He's doing what?" Lani asked. "I'll go with him."

Samheed nodded. "Me too."

"Um," Aaron said, "I guess there's something about having to leave immediately, and too much weight will slow Spike down . . . or something." He still felt apprehensive about talking with his former classmates, especially Samheed, who'd had a special hatred for Aaron.

Samheed frowned. "Hey, Al!" he shouted. "Lani and I want to go too."

Alex glanced over his shoulder as he and Henry climbed on Spike's back with the crate.

"Nope," Alex said, attaching the crate to the cocoon harness. "We're all set."

Samheed scowled. "Too late again," he said.

Lani slumped. "We're losing our touch, Burkesh," she said.

Sky waded to shore with Alex and Henry not far behind her. Henry ran up to his sister and gave her a quick wet hug. "Bye," he said.

"How long will you be gone?" she asked.

"I don't know. I'll need to stay long enough to make sure Karkinos is healing properly. He's floating west toward the waterfall—did you hear?"

Lani's eyes widened in fear. "Oh no! Do you think you can save them?"

Henry gave his sister a solemn look. "I don't know. But I'm going to try."

"Be careful," Lani said, ruffling his hair.

As Alex joined them, Sky pointed out over the water. "Look," she said. The coiled water dragon emerged from under the water and floated quickly into the lagoon.

"Yikes," said Lani. "That thing is huge. Is that the water dragon you met?"

Sky nodded. "Her name is Pan."

Henry patted his component vest, making sure he had his

LISA McMANN

seaweed and other spells. When the mansion door opened and Simber and Florence filed out, Henry took a deep breath. "Time to go," he said.

"Stay safe," said Alex, giving Henry a hug and a clap on his back. "I thought about sending Charlie with you, but neither you nor Florence speaks sign language, so he wouldn't be much use. He'd probably just get seasick, anyway." He handed Henry a painted pebble. "But here's this in case you need to send a seek spell. And I put a few extra sacks of components in the crate, just in case you need them."

"If I need a few sacks' worth, I'll be in big trouble." Henry took the pebble and slid it into his pocket, then waved awkwardly at Samheed, Aaron, and Lani, and headed out to Spike's back.

"You be safe too," Alex told Florence, and hugged her.

Florence couldn't stop smiling. "I will," she said. She scratched Simber's stony head, and then she waded into the water toward Pan.

"Wait. Florence is going too?" Lani said, incredulous. She looked at Aaron. "I thought you said something about too much weight."

Aaron shrugged. "Don't ask me. I'm not in charge here." He watched the strange-looking entourage as Florence mounted the dragon's back.

Pan spoke quietly to Alex. "Once I've delivered them, I'll check in on them from time to time to see if they are ready to go home."

"Oh," said Alex, concerned. "You won't be staying with them?"

"I'm afraid I cannot," Pan said. "I have other things to attend to." She gave a wistful glance in the direction of the cylindrical island.

"I hope everything is all right," Alex said, remembering for the first time in months her request for wings.

"It has to be," said the dragon. With a regal nod to the Artiméans, Pan called for Spike to lead the way at her top speed, and she would match it.

Spike set off with Henry, and soon Pan and Florence, propelled by Pan's extraordinary tail, pulled up beside the whale in the sea, heading west at an astounding clip.

Talking Dragons

When Henry and Florence and their unusual rides were growing small in the distance, Alex, Sky, and Aaron sat on the lawn to contemplate the fate of the giant crab island. Soon Samheed and Lani joined them, and Kaylee meandered over as well.

They talked for a while about Pan, and Alex and Sky relayed the whole story of how they first met her at the cylindrical island to the east of Artimé.

"Who do you think she was catching fish for?" Sky asked Alex. "She doesn't live on that island, does she?"

LISA McMANN

"I don't know if she lives anywhere," Alex mused. "She's a water creature who rules the sea. I wouldn't think she lives on land at all. Maybe someone helpless lives on top of the island and she provides food for him."

"Could that be the one she wants the wings for?" asked Lani. "I mean, what kind of wings does she need?"

Samheed raised an eyebrow. "Are you sure the wings aren't for her?"

Alex shrugged. "She said she was asking for someone else. Besides, I don't think it would be possible to make wings for a dragon. Dragons are real creatures."

Kaylee cleared her throat. "Um, news flash, Mr. Head Mage: No, they're not. Not in my world anyway."

"What a boring world," Samheed remarked. Aaron frowned at him, and Lani poked him with her elbow.

"You really have no idea what you're talking about, Samheed," Kaylee said lightly.

"That's very likely true," Samheed admitted.

"I mean that dragons are born," Alex went on, "like people and nonmagical animals. "They're not created out of materials, or sculptures brought to life."

LISA McMANN

"So?" asked Lani. "Does that matter?"

Alex knit his brow, trying to figure out how to explain what he meant. "It's like with you, Lani. Say you decided you just couldn't live another moment without a third arm. Could I make a human arm for you and attach it and have it become part of you?"

Lani frowned. "Why would I want a third arm?"

"That's not the point," said Alex.

"Why would *anyone* want a third arm?" Lani went on. "Where would you put it? On your back? You'd always be uncomfortable sleeping, and I doubt it would be all that useful."

"Ms. Octavia makes it work with eight," Kaylee said. "She's very efficient."

"But she's not human shaped," Lani said. She thought for a moment. "I wonder how she sleeps? With all the arms splayed out, do you think?"

Alex sighed. He glanced at Aaron, who was lying on his back looking at the sky, content to listen to the conversation. Aaron noticed Alex looking at him and winked.

"The point is," Samheed said, "you don't know what or

who Pan wants wings for. That cylinder could be an island filled with statues just like ours. Mr. Today probably had a whole secret world next door that he never bothered to mention to anybody."

Aaron turned his head and glanced at the jungle. "Like that one?" he almost said. But he wasn't sure Alex and the others knew about all the creatures in the jungle. Some of them must have seen Panther coming from it firsthand. Had none of them ever tried to go there? He doubted it, because the rock certainly would have mentioned it the other day when Aaron had paid them a visit.

"I wonder what other business Pan has to attend to that would force her to come back here so soon," said Sky. "Maybe the wingless inhabitant of the cylindrical island is dependent on her. After all, she was feeding him."

Alex nodded, then stared out over the water, lost in thought. "Is it even possible?" he mused after a bit. "The wings?"

Aaron had been thinking about that as well. Attaching wings to a creature and making them come alive couldn't be all that different from turning a vine into a tail. "Sure it is," he said softly.

Alex looked curiously at his brother. Aaron seemed so confident—it was almost disconcerting. "How do you know?" Alex asked.

"Yes," added Lani. "How would you know?"

Aaron sat up on his elbows, but remained silent for a time. "It's just . . . it's logical," he said, sounding a bit off. "I could make wings work." The others just looked at him.

"You're so sure," prodded Alex. "But you're not answering the question. How do you know? Because I admit I don't."

Aaron flashed Alex a quizzical glance. "Well, how do you *not* know?" he asked. "I try things, and they just . . . happen. But you should know—you're the head mage. You can do anything."

"That's not exactly how it works," Alex said, sounding defensive. "I mean, obviously things come more naturally to you. Like—like accidentally turning a scatterclip into a lethal weapon and nearly killing me with it, remember that one? Or being able to see out of the secret hallway from the moment you first stepped into it. Or killing Gondoleery when none of us could do it, or putting Simber back together from a giant pile of sand . . ." He trailed off. Impatiently he batted at a lock

LISA McMANN

of hair that had fallen into his face. "But apparently the rest of us have to actually learn things, okay? From instructors and books. Or by experimenting. And we don't get it right every time."

Aaron was sitting up now. "Okay, okay. Sorry," he said. He wasn't ready to explain how he knew the wings would work. And he didn't feel like arguing that magic *didn't* always come naturally to him—he'd worried and failed plenty of times, but Alex hadn't witnessed those moments. "Beginner's luck, I guess," he said lightly. "I probably don't know what I'm talking about."

"Quite right, you don't," said Samheed.

The air prickled uncomfortably.

Aaron looked down. "I didn't mean to upset anyone," he said. "I'm sorry."

Alex sighed. "No, it's all right." But something in the conversation wouldn't leave him alone. When he'd listed all of Aaron's seemingly effortless feats of magic like that, he'd realized the increasingly broadening scope of things Aaron could do. And it was beginning to dawn on him that perhaps Aaron was actually much more magical than anyone knew . . . more

LISA McMANN

magical than Alex was. The thought made Alex's insides hurt a little. He shifted, adjusting the robe that fastened at his neck.

The group grew silent again.

After a while, Aaron excused himself and went inside the mansion, past Simber and up the staircase to the balcony. He entered the not secret hallway and walked to the end of it, then turned into the kitchenette and got inside the tube. He pushed all the buttons at once and found himself in the jungle.

He sucked in a deep breath of the familiar, musky jungle scent, and let it out. Panther bounded over and screamed in his face, and the rock rumbled and rolled into sight.

"Panther has been very anxious to play stay and attack with you again," said the rock in its deep voice. "None of us have heard the end of it."

"Is that right?" Aaron smiled, and his shoulders relaxed. "I can help with that." He picked up a stretch of vine and began shaping it into a spider. It was good to be with friends.

The Big Map

As the afternoon wore on, Lani and Kaylee went off to the library together to look for maps, and Samheed left to talk with Mr. Appleblossom about a play he'd started writing. Alex and Sky stayed in the grass, lying on their backs and watching a wisp of a cloud pass by slowly overhead. They hadn't had much time alone together in months.

But Alex was distracted, bothered at first by the conversation with Aaron, but then his thoughts turned sharply back to the looming situation with Karkinos. "I hope Henry's all right," he said. "Maybe I should have gone with them."

Sky stared at him. "Alex, please. Florence is there. Who

LISA McMANN

could possibly offer more protection than Florence?"

"She's great as long as she doesn't get snagged by an eel. Did you hear? Multiple eels in these waters, according to the ruler of the sea."

Sky smiled. "That's such a great title," she said. "Ruler of the sea."

"It's even greater when Spike says it," said Alex.

"Spike is a seriously awesome creature. You really did a good job with her. I'm glad Pan is there to help her and the other sea creatures."

"Sounds like Pan has got as many problems as we do," said Alex, "with those eels working for the pirates and capturing her people."

"Her *people*?"

Alex laughed and rolled on his side toward Sky. "Her sea people. Creatures."

"People of the sea," said Sky, rolling to face Alex.

They shared a kiss.

"I'm really liking this whole peace thing," Alex said, lightly bumping his forehead against hers. "And having time to be with you."

"Me too," said Sky. "Both of those. And mostly I'm glad you stopped being ridiculous about us being together."

"I am dumb; you are smart," said Alex with a laugh. "At least I'm learning."

Sky grinned. "At least there's that," she agreed.

They spent hours being lazy, then went to the dining room for a snack. There they found Lani and Kaylee standing over a large map that they had spread out over one of the tables.

Lani looked up excitedly. "Kaylee found this map up on the third floor of the library—she said her land of America is on it! Come over here and see."

Alex and Sky exchanged quizzical glances and hurried over.

"This map is huge," said Alex. "Look at all the land."

"And the water," said Sky. "Where is your America, Kaylee?"

"That's it," Kaylee said wistfully. She outlined a portion of land on the left half of the enormous map. "It's this section of the continent of North America, called the United States." She moved her finger to the right. "And I live here, along the east coast."

"Is that where you ran into the hurricane?" Sky asked.

"Oh no," said Kaylee. "I was far from home. You see," she said, "I'm not sure if you know this, but the world is like a ball. This side of the map connects to the other side. It's just lying flat on this paper."

"Okay," Lani said, sounding skeptical.

"I was in a race—a solo race around the world," said Kaylee. "All the water in the word is connected, you see. It's kind of like sailing from island to island here, only on a much larger scale.

"The race started in Newport, Rhode Island. From there I headed east across the Atlantic Ocean to the coast of Spain." She pointed to it and traced her route. "Then I sailed south around Cape Town, South Africa. Then up to Abu Dhabi, and then around India and Singapore and the Philippine Islands to South Korea. I had just left there and was on my way to New Zealand when the storms hit."

"That's an incredible distance," marveled Lani, who was using the map's key to figure it out. "You were very far from home."

"I was at sea for months," said Kaylee, "except for restocking supplies in the ports. I was the youngest sailor to ever attempt this race alone."

"You didn't have anybody with you at all?" exclaimed Alex. "We'd never do that here. Too dangerous."

"My instructor and team were in a boat nearby most of the time, following me in case anything went wrong. But the rules stated that I had to do everything alone." Kaylee studied the map and shook her head. "I was doing fine. I don't know what went wrong, exactly. The storm came out of nowhere, and I got separated from my team. But I'd been in lots of storms before. It wasn't a big deal."

"Where were you on this map?" asked Sky. "Maybe we can find our island."

Kaylee gave a grim smile. "South of Japan, northwest of the Philippines," she said, and touched the spot on the map. "I realize all these place-names don't mean anything to you. But Japan—that's where the scientists are from." She hesitated, then added, "This area of the sea is also where the circus ship had been when it hit a storm. Before it ran ashore on the Island of Graves, I mean. I read about it in the ship's log."

Alex took a closer look and pointed to some dots on the map. "There are islands there, right? See? Could this cluster be us?"

Kaylee laid her hand on Alex's shoulder, realizing he wanted Artimé to be on her map almost as much as she did. "Those are islands, yes," she said gently. "But they're not your islands."

Alex frowned. "How do you know?"

"They're labeled, see?"

Alex looked at all of the land around the dots, reading the unfamiliar names aloud.

Sky gave Kaylee a solemn look. "So, have you figured out where we are if we're not on your map?"

Kaylee shoved her hands in her pockets and sighed. "Yeah, I have, actually. It's been in the back of my mind since the storm, but I didn't want to believe it. However, after reading the ship's logs I started to reconsider. And finding out that a dragon not only exists here, but is the actual ruler of the sea? That pretty much solidified it in my mind."

Alex and Lani looked up from the map. "Where are we, then?" asked Alex.

"Well," Kaylee said, pointing to a triangular shape made of faint, dotted lines on the map, "I'm afraid we're lost about a hundred miles south of Tokyo in the Devil's Sea. Also known— quite fearfully by sailors, I'm afraid—as the Dragon's Triangle."

Trouble at Sea

Henry was glad for the cocoon, which was more like a giant wind sock than a chair, because it allowed him to stretch out and relax without fear of flying off Spike's back. He had never gone so fast in his life. His eyes watered in the wind, and after a while he just curled up and put his arms over his face to shield them.

"Are you okay?" Florence called out to him.

He nodded and gave Florence a thumbs-up.

Before dark, Warbler Island was growing large off to their left. Pan and Spike decided to go around the island at a bit of a distance to keep from being noticed by anyone there.

LISA McMANN

Spike slowed and cleared her blowhole, drenching Henry, though he was wet anyway from the sea spray. "Something is not right at Warbler," she said.

Pan slowed as well and swung her head around to look at the silent island. Florence and Henry looked too.

Pan's yellow eyes narrowed. "Ships," she said.

"In the water?" asked Florence. Neither she nor Henry could see them.

"Yes," said Pan. "Lined up around the east side. They've moved some of their fleet offshore, it appears."

Florence looked troubled. "I wonder why?" She thought about the Warbler children in Artimé.

No one had an answer.

"I'll take a closer look on my return," said Pan. "There are no people on board the ships that I can tell, so likely they won't be going anywhere tonight." They sped up again, anxious to get to their destination.

With Warbler behind them, the Island of Fire grew larger, and the Artiméans and Pan noticed more ships, this time sailing from the pirate island toward Warbler.

Florence pointed them out to Henry, and Spike and Pan

changed course to make sure their group wasn't detected.

"This doesn't look good," Florence said to Henry.

"It could be nothing," Henry said. "Or maybe the pirates are buying more slaves, like Copper."

"I doubt they would need multiple ships for that," Florence said. It was worrisome.

The party continued traveling swiftly as darkness fell. Henry curled up once more and fell asleep, and Florence sat quietly, thinking about seeing Talon again.

Deep into the night, Spike called out, "Something bad is coming."

"What is it, Spike?" asked Pan, her head darting around. "An eel?"

"Ye-e-s!" Spike yelled, her voice panicky. She jerked. A second later, something slithered around her tail. The whale twisted in the water, rousing Henry from a deep sleep, and then without warning she jumped into the air with the eel wrapped around her. Spike submerged with a giant splash and dove deep, trying to shake the eel. Henry hadn't had time to scream—or breathe.

"Henry!" yelled Florence, sitting up in alarm.

LISA McMANN

"Hold on tight, Florence!" Pan commanded. Florence leaned forward and held on to Pan's neck. Together they dove underwater to find him.

Startled, Henry sucked in seawater and choked as he was dragged inside his cocoon at full speed. His lungs and throat burned, and water pressed against him like a thousand-pound weight, forcing its way into his mouth and nose, pushing against his eardrums and eyeballs. Blind and disoriented, Henry wound one arm through the straps of the cocoon and desperately swung out with the other, trying to connect with whatever was dragging them down. *Don't breathe!* he told himself, but his body reacted in its own way.

With no air, Henry sucked in more water until his chest and head threatened to explode. Black spots wavered before his eyes. His thoughts became dull and jumbled. The pressure was daunting, and he felt himself slipping away. Knowing he was drowning, he tried to fight it, tried to strike out with his arm again, but he couldn't get his body to move. Soon both arms slacked and the thudding pressure of the water pounded the consciousness from him.

Under the surface of the water, Pan went for the eel's head.

The eel dodged and sent out an electric shock, but Pan narrowly avoided it. Then the dragon struck out, weaving and striking again, and finally grabbed the eel's face in her mighty jaws. The eel screamed. Pan clamped down hard, crushing its sparking head.

At the eel's other end, Spike flailed in the water, trying to escape from its grip. She saw Pan and Florence and spurred toward them, hoping to move closer so they could help her.

Florence leaned over Spike and hurriedly unwound the trapped eel from her tail. "Go!" she cried through the water when Spike was free. The whale shot to the surface as fast as she could.

Still gripping the eel's head between her teeth, Pan followed Spike to the surface so that Florence could help the boy, but the dragging tail of the eel thrashed and struck out. As Florence bent over Spike and saw that Henry wasn't moving, the eel slammed into her head with a mighty blow, knocking her off Pan's back. Florence yelled and made a desperate grab for Pan, trying not to sink all the way to the bottom of the sea. But Florence's slick hands against the dragon's slippery scales couldn't keep their grasp.

Pan's tail shot out like an arrow through the water. The dragon wrapped it around Florence's wrist as the eel writhed and churned nearby. It was hard to tell which was which in the dark water. Florence grabbed on to Pan's tail and pulled herself up hand over fist to the surface, desperate to see if Henry could be revived.

With a roar, Pan struck out with her claws and speared them through the eel's skin. She opened her jaws wide to get a better grip, exposing rows of sharp teeth, and with a sudden movement, she clamped down again and chomped off the eel's head, swallowing it whole. Its body dropped into the water, and with a few twists and splashes, it disappeared.

Florence made it to the surface and hoisted herself onto Pan's back once more. When she was safely steady, she leaned over and began wrestling with the cocoon to get Henry out. "Henry!" she shouted, afraid. Was it too late?

The boy didn't move.

A Close Call

Florence reached into the cocoon and pulled Henry out. His eyes were closed, and he flopped like a bundle of rags in her arms. She ripped off his component vest and threw it aside, then squeezed his abdomen and pressed on his chest and pounded his back, trying to get him to breathe. She had no breath of her own to lend him.

Pan worried over the scene as Florence tried everything she could think of to save Henry. But he didn't respond, and he didn't respond, and he didn't respond.

Finally the dragon spoke. "Let me try," she said. "Put him on his back and open his mouth."

LISA McMANN

Florence turned Henry over, supporting his head. His arms fell to his sides. She took his face in her hand and gently opened his mouth.

Pan turned her neck, bent down, and closed her eyes as if making a wish. She blew a slow breath into the boy's mouth.

Henry's chest rose. Pan kept blowing, and then she pulled away and opened her eyes, watching him carefully.

Without warning Henry reared up, coughing and choking, water spewing from his mouth. He twisted to one side, Florence supporting him, and gagged and gasped until he'd cleared most of the seawater from his lungs.

Florence looked like she could cry. She turned to Pan. "How did you do that?"

"I didn't know it would work," the ruler of the sea said softly. "But dragons can do things one wouldn't expect them to do."

Finally Henry stopped choking long enough to speak. "My vest!" he rasped. "Florence, where is it?" He coughed again.

Florence looked around. She'd flung it aside. Where was it? "It's gone now," she told him. "But there are extra components in the crate in case we need them."

Henry struggled mightily to sit up next to Florence on Pan's back. His eyes were bloodshot, and his hair stood on end. "No. You don't understand—I have to have it!" he cried. "The medicine for Karkinos is in there!"

"What?" cried Florence.

Alarmed, Spike wasted no time. She dove underwater in search of the vest, and Pan ducked her head below the surface to look around, letting her tremendously long tail slither through the water in search of it too.

"I didn't know that's where you kept the medicine," Florence said, distraught. "I'm sorry. I thought it was packed with the other supplies."

Henry stood on Pan's back, holding on to Florence's shoulder, peering anxiously at the water even though he could see very little in the darkness. "If we don't find it we'll have to go get more, but it comes from Ishibashi's island," he said. "We don't have time to go all the way back there!"

Florence put a hand to her forehead as she realized the severity of the consequences. "I thought you were dead," she said. "I wasn't thinking about the vest. I was thinking about you."

"Oh, Florence," Henry said, reaching out to her. "I'm not

blaming you. Thank you—you saved my life. I just hope . . ." He stared at the water in the darkness, waiting.

Minute after agonizing minute went by. Henry coughed now and then, still recovering. He drew strength from his fear and focused only on the water. How could Spike or Pan possibly find the vest in the vast, churning waters of the sea?

After a time, Florence detected a ripple in the water's surface a short distance away. "I hope that's not another eel," she muttered.

Henry looked up.

Pan lifted her head up out of the water as the ripple got closer, and soon the tip of Spike's spike was evident, coming toward them. When the whale reached Pan's side, she rose up, and there, hooked around the base of her spike, was the vest.

"Spike, you found it!" said Florence.

"Oh, thank goodness," Henry breathed. "You have no idea what this means."

Florence reached out to get the vest and handed it to Henry. Anxiously he checked the special pocket, and there he found the tin of seaweed, safe and sound. He slumped back in relief, then put the vest on and secured it.

"Well done, Spike," said Pan, like a queen to her favored subject.

Spike bowed to her, then turned to Henry. "I am terribly sorry I hurt you," she said.

Henry stroked the whale's forehead. "You couldn't help it," he said. "And I'm all right now. I would have been fine if I'd just taken a breath before we went under. I was just surprised."

"We all were," Pan said. "We're lucky Spike detected the eel coming at us when she did or we'd be in much more dire circumstances now."

Spike bowed her head humbly and sidled up to the dragon. "We must go," she said. "We have lost too much time."

"Are you fit to go again?" Florence asked Henry.

The boy nodded. His vest was in place and secured, with the container inside its pocket. That was all he needed.

Florence helped Henry climb from Pan's back onto Spike's. He slid into the cocoon, and when all was well again, the four continued their journey.

The Dragon's Triangle

As Kaylee gazed at the map on the table, Alex, Sky, and Lani looked curiously at her.

"The Dragon's Triangle?" Alex asked. "What's that?"

Kaylee gave him a grim smile. "It's a mythical place. Or at least that's what I used to think."

Sky and Lani exchanged a questioning glance. "We're not mythical," Lani said. "We're real."

Kaylee continued to explain. "There are a few places in the world—the world I came from, I mean—where ships and airplanes have been lost and never found. The Bermuda Triangle is one. The Dragon's Triangle is another." She pointed them out on the map. "In the old days sailors would avoid the mysterious waters in those places for fear of being lost for good." She pulled a dining chair out from the table and sat down heavily. "I remember studying it before I set out on my journey, knowing I'd be passing nearby. A fleet of Japanese military ships disappeared there—here, I mean—in the 1950s." She looked up. "When I saw the Quillitary vehicles on your island, I wondered if they'd come from those missing military ships."

Alex's eyes widened. "There's a whole shipload of them sunk off Ishibashi's island."

"I'm not surprised to hear that. Some scientists went in search of the missing fleet," Kaylee said. "But they went missing too."

"Ishibashi, Ito, and Sato?" guessed Lani.

"For sure," said Kaylee, nodding. "I forget the name of their ship, but it was well documented."

"Oh!" said Alex abruptly. "I saw the name. Some of the letters were missing. K-O something number five."

Kaylee looked sharply at him. "That's it! *Kaiyo Maru Number Five*. You saw it? It was Ishibashi's ship?"

"That's what Ishibashi told me," Alex said. "I transported it from under the water and put it on the shore so they could get their stuff if they wanted to."

"And they did," said Sky. "Remember the telescope Ishibashi showed us?"

Alex nodded.

Tears welled up in Kaylee's eyes for reasons she had trouble articulating. "No one has ever returned from a triangle," she said. "I guess . . ." She trailed off, gazing across the dining room deep in thought. "I guess I always thought the people had died. And the ships and planes that disappeared were at the bottom of the Devil's Sea, so deep they were unable to be recovered. I never imagined there was an actual place where people could survive . . . and thrive, even."

Sky frowned. "If the scientists are from your world, are you saying that it's possible we *all* came from there? That we were somehow swept into the Dragon's Triangle? Because I'm pretty sure I wasn't. I was born on Warbler. So was my mother."

"Not you specifically," Kaylee said. "But maybe your ancestors. Your grandparents or great-grandparents or who knows how many generations ago were lost at sea, succumbing to the grasp of the dreaded triangle. And instead of dying, they found themselves here."

"Like the people in the vessel?" Sky asked. "Several months ago a . . . a thing fell from the sky and landed in the water."

"An airplane," said Lani.

"Right," said Sky. "The people inside were dead, though."

Kaylee nodded. "I suspect they came from my world," she said. "If no one on all the seven islands you've visited manufactures or flies airplanes, they must come from somewhere else, right?"

"We have parts of airplanes upstairs in the Museum of Large," Alex said. "Mr. Appleblossom and Mr. Today kept them from years ago."

Kaylee looked at the others, puzzled. "But I don't understand something. Didn't anybody ever tell you stories about how they came to be here? Your grandparents or anyone?"

"Not in Quill," Lani said. "No storytelling allowed. Or writing things down."

Kaylee shook her head. "That's right," she muttered. "What a strange place." She looked at Sky. "How about you on your island?"

LISA McMANN

Sky pointed to the scars on her neck. "We didn't exactly have a chance to talk a lot, and we didn't have school like the children in Quill did—we just worked from the time we were able. But I know my mother and her parents were born on Warbler. You're the only one I know who just showed up here and survived."

"Well," Kaylee said, "there are the scientists, too."

"Oh yes," said Sky, "I forgot. They never told us, though—you did."

"And Talon, maybe," suggested Lani. "He said he didn't remember how he arrived on Karkinos, but he's been there for thousands of years."

"Well . . . ," Kaylee said, screwing up her face a little as she was about to object, but then didn't see the point in it.

"And Issie," Alex said, sitting up. "She's been looking for her lost baby for seven hundred years, remember? I wonder if she was swept into our world while she was looking?"

"And now maybe she'll never find her child," Sky said sadly.

They were silent and thoughtful for a long while as they contemplated the origins of everyone they'd met in their tiny, seven-island world.

Lani's interest returned to the map. "What's the name of your . . . of the place you came from?"

Kaylee found the spot for her. "My family is here in a city called Manchester-by-the-Sea. It's part of the state of Massachusetts." She glanced at Lani, who seemed enormously interested. She added, "But my ancestors are actually English—from here, across the Atlantic Ocean." She pointed to a piece of land to the right.

"I wonder where my ancestors lived," said Lani. "Do you think they were English too?"

Kaylee studied Lani. "Well, if I had to guess, I'd say you've got some Asian roots, or maybe Polynesian or Hawaiian. . . ." She shrugged, but then searched for and pointed out the locations she was mentioning.

Lani turned to look at Kaylee, incredulous. "How in the world would you know that?"

"Because of the way you look, I guess," said Kaylee, almost apologetically.

"No way. Seriously?" asked Lani.

Kaylee nodded.

This was a foreign concept to all the Artiméans.

"That is so cool!" said Lani. She brushed her fingers over the Hawaiian Islands, and then did the same to the tiny Polynesian islands below.

"So," interjected Alex, "people look different depending on where their ancestors came from?"

"Yeah, I guess," said Kaylee. She was shocked that there were intelligent humans who didn't understand this. But it was true that the people of Artimé didn't have a specific look about them—they had a variety of skin tones and hair and eye colors. Which made sense when she thought about how their ancestors must have come from all over the world.

"Where do you think my ancestors are from?" asked Alex, leaning over the map.

Kaylee frowned. "I'm not sure about you. You're sort of ambiguous. Maybe southern Europe, like Italy." She pointed out the area on the map. "But your sisters have different skin and eye color than you and Aaron."

"They look like our mother," said Alex.

Kaylee had never seen Alex's mother. "They definitely look more distinct with those black eyes, but I don't know—I'm not actually an expert on this or anything." She chuckled nervously, feeling weird about declaring people's heritages without having any information about them.

"Yes, but what do you *think*?" asked Alex. "It's not like we'll be mad at you if you're wrong. We're just curious."

"Well," said Kaylee, giving in, "maybe your mother's ancestors are from Tahiti or somewhere tropical. Or northern Africa, like Morocco." Kaylee soon realized Alex was right, and they'd probably never know the truth, so she began to take the whole topic a bit less seriously and started to have fun with her predictions. "I'd guess that Sean Ranger has Irish roots, and Carina looks Eastern European—maybe Russian. And Samheed has a pretty clear Middle Eastern look."

"What about my ancestors?" asked Sky.

"Mexico or South America," Kaylee guessed. She pointed the places out. "You know, there's a good chance all of you have ancestors from a bunch of different countries." She paused thoughtfully. "Most people in America are like that too, actually. People from a lot of different countries moved to America in the past few hundred years, so there are a lot of Americans today with combined heritages."

The friends began to imagine a similar scenario in their world—people from the seven islands meeting others on different islands and falling in love, and somehow they ended up in a silly conversation about what Florence and Talon's children might look like if they ever had any.

When the fun died down, Alex was quiet for a minute, and then he frowned and turned toward Kaylee. "You said no one ever returns to your world from the triangles. But your world is so huge—how would you know if one returned or not?"

"Oh," Kaylee said, "it would be all over the news channels and the Internet in about ten seconds. Nobody would be able to keep a secret like that for long."

"The Inter-what?" asked Alex.

Kaylee sighed, looking suddenly weary. "Nothing. Never mind. Nobody's ever returned—you'll just have to take my word for it."

Lani bit her lip. "So," she said softly, "now that we know where we are, and we know there's no way back to your world, what can we do to help you?"

Kaylee blinked hard and tried to appear brave. "I think you keep doing what you've been doing all along. We make the best world we can, wherever we are. Because the next person to end up here will definitely be just as sad as I am right now." She looked at the others. "But at least there's a chance they can be sad with friends."

Aaron's Last Secret

When Aaron returned through the tube after many hours spent in the jungle playing stay and attack with Panther, the kitchenette and hallway were dark. He stayed in the tube for a moment, looking at the buttons in the dim light from the window. Would the button to Haluki's house work now that the tube had been destroyed in the fire? What would happen if he tested it?

He was tempted to try them all out individually. Indeed if he had been feeling reckless, he might have. But now he had creatures and people counting on him. What if he pushed the button that led to the broken tube on Ishibashi's island and he got stuck somewhere in the invisible in-between? There weren't many things more frightening to Aaron than disappearing into thin air, never to be seen again.

He stepped out, thinking of his scientist friends. He was growing more and more anxious to go back. It seemed like a perfect time to leave now that the Quillens were settled in their little housing rows.

Aaron's footsteps echoed down the wide hallway. Seeing light streaming from under the door that led to Alex's living quarters, Aaron stopped and knocked.

"Come in," Alex called.

Aaron opened the door and stepped inside. "Hi," Aaron said. "Am I disturbing you?"

Alex looked up from the small desk, where books lay scattered about. On the floor were three or four tottering piles of them. "No, come in. Have a seat." Alex shoved the hair off his forehead and pushed his chair back. He wore the slightly dazed look of someone who had just returned to real life after having been lost in another world for hours.

Aaron's expression was similar. He sat on the bed. "Sorry about earlier."

LISA McMANN

"It's okay," said Alex. "It's actually really great that you're so naturally magical. I mean, I know I'd be dead if it weren't for you. You saved me. And Artimé. I shouldn't have gotten so defensive about it."

"Everybody fought hard," Aaron said, shrugging off the compliment. "I just got lucky."

"It's more than luck," Alex said. "I guess I'm a bit jealous that it comes so easily to you."

"It doesn't, actually, but whatever," said Aaron lightly. He changed the subject. "How's everything in the new Quill? Or are we calling everything Artimé now?"

"We'll keep it Quill, I think," said Alex. "It's confusing otherwise, isn't it?"

Aaron nodded. "Too confusing. Besides, the Quillens won't call it Artimé, so why fight them on it?"

"Good point. It's settled, then." Alex folded his hands in his lap and tipped his chair back to balance on two legs. "What other crises can we solve today?"

Aaron glanced around the room, catching his reflection in the large mirror on Alex's wall. Mirrors still startled Aaron at times, even in his own room, so he'd covered his up with paper. Now, though, he looked at his reflection and touched the scruff on his chin absently, studying it. There were some scratchy bits among the soft fuzz now, and he could see that the scratchy bits were as black as his sisters' eyes. "We look like our father," he said.

"Unfortunately," Alex said with a wry grin, but the humor was lost on Aaron.

Aaron turned abruptly. "I was wondering . . . The reason I've come . . . Well, um, *first*, is everything going as it should?"

"How do you mean?" asked Alex.

"With Quill. Have I fulfilled my end of the agreement?"

Alex let his chair rest on all four legs. He leaned forward. "Yes," he said. "Of course you have. More than."

Aaron studied his brother, and found it suddenly difficult to speak. "If it's all right with you, then, I'd like to go back to the Island of Shipwrecks," he said.

Alex's mouth twitched. He let out a sigh. "Oh," he said. "Well, sure." He stood abruptly and swung around to stand behind the chair, putting his hands on the back of it and leaning forward. "That is, if you really want to. You . . . you don't have to. You know that, right? I—we like having you here. Most of us, anyway."

Aaron dropped his gaze. "I know. I'd like to go, though. Ishibashi must be worried about me by now—it's been months. So if we could leave as soon as it's convenient for you to take me there, well, that would be good."

Alex was quiet. "Sure," he said. After a minute he nodded. "We can leave once we hear back from Pan to make sure Henry made it to the Island of Legends all right. Does that sound okay?"

Aaron gave a sharp nod. He stood up. "Thanks," he said. "It's been . . . nice. I mean, well, you know. Good spending time with you, anyway. And . . . and the girls." He cleared his throat. "But yes, it's time I go." He took a step toward the door.

"Okay," Alex said, his voice strangely hollow.

At the door, Aaron hesitated. He desperately wanted to tell Alex about the jungle, but at the same time he desperately wanted to wait until the last possible minute so that he would be long gone by the time Alex made his first visit there. Yes, it was cowardly leaving Alex to explain to Panther and the rock that the person they thought was Mr. Today's successor was really a fraud. But Aaron couldn't bear to do it. The more time he spent with his jungle friends, the more Aaron knew he could never tell them the truth.

"Is something wrong?" Alex asked.

Aaron closed his eyes briefly, pained. Then he met Alex's gaze once more and shook his head. "No, nothing. Good night, brother." He left the room, closing the door quietly behind him.

"Good night, friend," Alex said softly, and stared at the door, feeling empty. After a moment he sat down at the desk, turned back to his open book and closed it, and put out the light.

Return to the Island of Legends

The hours of the night passed smoothly. Before the sun rose, Spike could sense Karkinos's nearness in the waters. She adjusted her direction. "Karkinos is moving quickly toward the danger of the waterfall," said Spike in a worried voice. "He is far from where he is supposed to be."

"He is a long distance from where I saw him last," said Pan, lifting her head high in the air and straining her eyes. "We must move swiftly!"

Spike lowered her head and put all she had into increasing her speed. Pan stayed with her. Florence hung on and leaned forward in anticipation while Henry slept. Florence would wake him when it was time.

It wasn't long before they came upon the giant squid, which normally lived under the crab's protection, out in the open sea. He was agitated. Spike slowed for a moment to speak with the sea creature, and the animated conversation roused Henry. As soon as Spike finished talking, she sped up once more. The squid followed as quickly as he could, but fell behind.

"The crab no longer has strength to fight the current," Spike informed the others. "He is moving faster toward the waterfall. He is still alive, according to the squid."

Henry sat up and gripped the tin through the fabric of his vest. "We have to make it," he said. "We *have* to. Do they know what they are in for?"

Pan edged ahead of the whale. "When I discovered what happened to your ship, I informed Talon of the dangers."

"Let's hope they're anchoring everybody to the island," Florence muttered. She looked at Henry. "How long before the medicine works?"

"Fairly quickly . . . I think," said Henry, remembering the

LISA McMANN

sea turtle that Ishibashi had healed. "But it won't fully restore his strength immediately. It'll keep him from dying. Whether or not he'll be able to resist the current is something we'll have to find out."

"Pan, can you go any faster?" asked Florence.

"Perhaps a bit," said Pan.

Florence thought for a long moment. "Here's what we're going to do," she said. "Henry, crawl out of your cocoon and give me your hand. I'm going to pull you over here with me."

"Okay," said Henry, feeling a bit uncertain about jumping from one creature to another at this ridiculous speed. He began climbing out.

"Pan," Florence went on, "once Henry's over here, can you push yourself to your top speed? Then Spike can follow and meet us there."

"Your idea is wise," said Pan.

"I agree," said Spike. "I will try to hurry so that I can explain to Karkinos what is happening. I can go faster when fully submerged, so perhaps I will keep up all right."

"Perfect." Florence held her hand out to Henry. He grabbed

it tightly, closed his eyes, and jumped. Florence pulled him in front of her and he landed hard on the dragon's back. "Have you got the medicine?" she asked.

He tapped his vest. "I have it."

"Hit it, Pan!" Florence shouted.

Pan wasted no time. She pulled ahead, and soon they were speeding faster than before.

Spike disappeared under the water, but an occasional splash behind them assured Henry and Florence that the whale was nearby.

Finally, as the sun rose, Henry and Florence could see the island not far off. Pan put forth an extra burst of speed.

"Henry," said Florence, "go straight to Karkinos's mouth and give him the medicine. I'll try to help from land and explain everything to the others. I hope I can find them. . . ." She trailed off, worried, and peered around the side of the dragon to see if she could find the telltale glint of bronze coming from Talon's body. But he was not near the shore.

"Listen," Henry said as they approached the crab island's shore. "The waterfall. Can you hear it?"

Florence stood up on the dragon's back and looked beyond Karkinos. "I see it," she said. "Pan, do you feel the waters pulling you?"

"The sea is not too strong for the one who rules it," Pan said. She angled and pulled up alongside one of the twin reefs made by Karkinos's claws.

Florence and Henry exchanged a worried look. Simber, Spike, and the squirrelicorns pulling the ship's ropes couldn't stop their ship from tumbling over the waterfall at the edge of the world. How were the four of them supposed to save an entire island? They were dangerously close to disaster.

Florence reached down to help Henry stand so that as soon as Pan was close enough to the claw reef, he could jump off and run to Karkinos's head with the medicine. "Ready?" she asked.

Henry nodded. "Ready!" he said. And when Pan slowed and unfurled her tail, Henry ran down the length of it, slipping a bit but catching himself, all the way to the reef. He jumped off the dragon's tail when it grew too thin and sped up the claw to the mainland.

As he ran, he fumbled with his vest pocket, whispering the secret word that would unlock it. He pulled out the tin and held it tightly in his hand as he rounded the shell and came up to the crab's enormous eyeballs, perched on their eyestalks. A thin, sickly film covered them.

Florence was not far behind. "Talon!" she shouted. "Lhasa! Are you here?" There was no answer. "They must be trying to secure the others to the island," she said, worried. She walked to the edge of the wooded area and peered down a path.

Henry knelt near the crab's face. Karkinos's mouth was under water. "Karkinos, it's Henry from Artimé. I have medicine that can help you. Can you lift your head?"

The crab didn't move.

Henry turned to look over his shoulder. "Florence, we have a problem!" he called out. "He doesn't understand me. Pan, can you help?" And then he spotted Spike arriving. "Spike!" he cried. But Pan and Spike had other plans as they called for the help of Issie the sea monster and began to push against the moving island.

The rushing of the waterfall grew louder. Henry could see clouds of mist rising from it and feel its dampness on his skin. Florence hadn't heard him. She disappeared among the trees.

"Spike!" Henry called again.

LISA McMANN

The whale looked up.

"Can you talk to Karkinos? See if he can lift his mouth out of the water so the medicine doesn't wash away!"

Spike left Pan's side and disappeared under the water. A moment later Spike surfaced. "He is not responding," she said.

"But I need to ask him a very important question!" Henry shouted, beginning to panic. What was he to do if Karkinos wasn't able to respond? Forego the medicine and plunge over the waterfall with all the others? He thought about Ishibashi and the injured turtle on the Island of Shipwrecks. Ishibashi hadn't asked permission of the turtle. Was that because it was an animal? If so, did that mean Henry could administer the seaweed to Karkinos the crab for the same reason? Hadn't Ishibashi mentioned only needing permission from humans? He was quite sure that was the case. But Karkinos seemed almost human compared to the turtle.

Henry looked at the mist rising from the waterfall. He didn't know what to do—all he knew was that they were all counting on him. "Can you pry open his mouth?"

Spike nodded and turned around in the water, then tipped to one side and aimed her spike at the crab's mouth just under the surface of the water. Slowly she moved forward, her eyes nearly rolling back in her head as she strained to see what she was doing.

"That's it," said Henry. "Just a little more. Wiggle it a bit. Now angle your spike upward to pry his mouth open so I can climb in. Careful not to pierce him."

The whale obliged.

As the crab's jaws opened, Henry looked inside. Water flooded into the mouth. "How am I going to do this?" he muttered.

"We must hurry!" Pan called out. She strained against the crab's shell, her tail spinning like a propeller in the water. Issie pushed alongside her, but the two together could only slow down the island's progress—they needed to reverse it.

Henry looked inside the crab's mouth again. "Hold it open, Spike. I'm going inside."

Without another word, Henry slipped into the churning water, hanging on tightly to the edge of the crab's shell so the current wouldn't wash him away. He reached out and grabbed the bottom of Karkinos's mouth, trying to avoid cutting himself on the various chewing appendages. With a splash, he swung

LISA McMANN

himself inside. But with the crab's mouth propped open, water washed in and out. It could take the magic seaweed with it.

Henry's heart thundered inside his chest. He knew what he had to do.

"Let go, Spike," he said. "Let his mouth close. He won't swallow me. . . . I don't think so anyway. And when I yell, pry it open again. Okay?"

Spike didn't ask questions. "I will do that, Henry."

Before Henry knew it, the crab's mouth was closing around him. He sucked in a breath as his world grew dark, and when the jaw clamped shut, Henry sat inside, trying to get his bearings. The water sloshed around his shoulders, and the briny smell of impending death inside was horrid. Despite the bubble of air above the water, Henry began to panic.

Just take it easy, Henry told himself. *Get the job done*. He forced himself to stay calm. After a moment, he began feeling around the pod he was in, wondering if there was a way for him to get Karkinos to swallow some of the water so he could press the seaweed into the side of the crab's mouth. Cautiously he pushed down, half scooting, half swimming, toward the back of the crab's mouth, then pounded on his palate, trying to stimulate the swallowing mechanism. With one particularly sharp blow, Karkinos's head reared back, sending Henry tumbling and splashing toward his throat.

Henry gasped and reached out blindly, clinging by one hand to a section of teeth, nearly dropping the tin of seaweed, but managing to hang on. Water rushed past him, and when the crab's head settled, there was only a little bit of water remaining inside his mouth. As soon as Henry felt certain the crab wasn't going to swallow again, he dropped down and hurried to open the tin.

The seaweed glowed, shedding a tiny bit of light in the moist pod. Henry knelt down and felt around the briny sludge of the crab's mouth for a place to pack the medicine where it could be absorbed. He soon found a slippery fold of tissue near the crab's cheek . . . or whatever it was called. Quickly he pulled half of the glowing seaweed out of the tin and pushed it into the space, spreading it out for maximum exposure and packing it down as tightly into the fold as he could.

He felt his way over to the other side of the crab's mouth and did the same. "Come on, Karkinos," he breathed. He shook the tin upside down to get the remaining bits out, hoping it was enough for the enormous creature.

LISA McMANN

There was nothing more Henry could do but wish. And he could do that just as well outside of the giant crab's mouth. He shouted to Spike through a tiny space near the feeding appendages and waited. He could hear the churning water and the shouts of Pan and Florence outside. "Spike!" he cried out again. "Open up!" Now that he had done the job, he was more anxious than ever to get out of Karkinos's disgusting mouth.

"I am coming, Henry!" Spike shouted.

Henry jiggled impatiently.

"No, Spike!" Pan called out. "I need you! We must all push together now or we'll never get out of the waterfall's grasp. Hold on, Henry! Everyone, push to the northeast with all your might!"

Henry's heart sank at the words. "Okay," he managed to say. He slumped against the crab's mouth opening, watched the seaweed glow, and tried not to gag at the stench. He could feel the crab's mouth slime drip onto him from above. He hoped he wouldn't run out of air. More importantly, though, at the moment at least, was his hope that Karkinos wouldn't go sailing over the waterfall headfirst with Henry trapped inside his mouth.

There were so many things to worry about, and Henry sat there, helpless to do anything. He wished he could see. And then he remembered he had a highlighter right in his pocket. He lit it at half power and looked around at the algae on Karkinos's teeth and the sea worms crawling along the crab's cheek. His stomach gurgled. Quickly he put the light out again. "Disgusting," he muttered. "Really wish I hadn't seen that."

From outside he heard Florence shout. "Hang on, Henry!" she thundered. "We're going over the edge!"

Henry's heart flew to his throat.

And then the giant crab's mouth began to churn.

A Clattering Reunion

Henry froze as the crab's muscles rippled under him, sending the seaweed tin tumbling to the back of his mouth and Henry scrambling for a sharp upper tooth to hang on to. Then Karkinos opened his mouth, and water rushed in over Henry's head. He could barely hold on, and he couldn't escape. When the water rushed back out, Henry coughed and sputtered and looked out over the edge of the waterfall as he dangled above it from Karkinos's tooth.

"Aaaaaaah!" screamed Henry. "Help!"

Pan shouted unintelligibly, and the crab began shaking.

Spike was yelling too, and Issie and even the squid had joined them by now, everyone using all of their strength to stop the crab from plummeting over the waterfall. It inched forward, then somehow moved two inches backward. Then forward again. Then three inches backward, the crab's body beginning to hum. Karkinos was coming alive.

His claws snapped once, twice, and his body swiveled in the water, Henry swinging with it. Soon the crab was scooting backward, and with the help of all the other sea creatures, Karkinos began inching against the tremendous pressure of the current.

"He's doing it!" Henry shouted once he could catch a breath. "Karkinos is alive! And he's paddling! Everybody, don't give up—now's the moment! Give it everything you've got!"

With another giant rush of seawater coming into Karkinos's open mouth, Henry lost his grip on the crab's tooth. He dropped underwater and surfaced, trying to swim back to the tooth, but a wave struck him. Henry was washed outside of Karkinos's mouth and into the churning sea. The boy surfaced and sputtered, grabbing and grasping at anything he could reach, lest he be swept away.

Once Karkinos realized what it was that he'd just spat out, he picked Henry out of the water with his giant claw. Henry gratefully hung on to catch his breath, then climbed onto the reef and crawled his way to shore. When he looked up toward the center of the island, he saw Talon, wings engaged, flying above Vido the golden rooster's perch in the tallest tree. Talon pulled on a rope that was attached to the island.

Hearing Henry's news brought new life to the strange crew, and they dug in harder than ever, finding extra strength from the encouragement. With a shattering groan and a hearty grunt, Karkinos paddled and pushed with the bit of life he'd regained, and soon the entourage was making even more headway.

"You've got it!" Florence shouted, paddling with a tree trunk she'd pulled from the woods nearby. "Keep going! Due north will get you out of the pull of the current faster. Good work everybody!"

Henry found a big stick and started paddling too.

The island moved. And it moved. Foot by foot and yard by yard, Karkinos reached deep under the surface and swept his broad claws like enormous oars, his legs like gondoliers' *rèmos*, and pulled himself along with the help of his comrades and friends. One minute at a time they fought the current together, almost certain they could never make it, but pressing on all the same, until at last they had gained significant ground. Victory was in sight.

But was it in reach? The creatures were exhausted, and some of them fell away for a long moment to rest. Without the full crew, Karkinos strained and grew still, and the island slowed to a stop. "Come on!" cried Henry. "We can't stop now! We're almost there!"

The sea creatures rallied, and Karkinos stirred and began paddling again, and they all pressed on once more until they regained momentum. Finally the crab's inhabitants found themselves outside the realm of danger. A shout of victory rose up among the trees and from the sea.

Pan slipped away. The water rippled over her head as she sped back to Artimé alone. The remaining creatures continued to help Karkinos journey back to his usual spot in the sea.

When Talon was certain the island was safe, he dropped his rope and flew down to the center of the island to free the creatures he'd tied down for safety. Not long after, the shiny bronze man emerged from the forest looking awfully anxious. He was followed by Lhasa, Bock, and a handful of dropbears. There was also a strange blurry creature Florence had never seen before, bringing a nasty smell along with him, but he immediately dashed behind some brush and disappeared.

But Florence only had eyes for one.

When Talon caught sight of Florence, he faltered.

She dropped her tree oar into the water.

Talon ran to her. He picked her up in the air, or at least he tried to, for she was admittedly very heavy, and he swung her around, which, to be technical, was a bit more like dragging her feet through the sand. And then he dipped her low and leaned in, staggering slightly, and she wrapped her arms around his neck to keep from falling. And with a loud clank, Talon kissed Florence soundly on the lips for all the island and sea creatures to see.

A Night Journey

When Pan arrived on the shore of Artimé that evening, Alex, Simber, and Sky hurried to meet her and hear the news of Karkinos.

"Is everything all right?" Alex asked. "You're back so soon—are Florence and Henry okay?"

"Henry and Florence are well," said Pan, "and Karkinos appears to be reacting favorably to the medicine. He was able to help us when we needed him most. If Henry hadn't acted so quickly, all of us would have gone over the waterfall. It was a very close call."

"Oh no," said Sky. "How horrible! I'm so glad that didn't happen."

LISA McMANN

"Is the island back in safe waterrrs?" Simber asked.

"Yes," said Pan. "The inhabitants and sea creatures will continue to help Karkinos stay in his usual position in the sea over the next few days while Henry monitors the crab's health. I fear the crab may have strained himself with all the exertion."

Pan's tail curled and uncurled in the water behind her. "And I must tell you that we saw unmanned ships anchored in the water on the east side of Warbler Island, and some traveling from the Island of Fire to Warbler as well. On my return, nothing had changed at Warbler, and I saw no ships in transit. Perhaps there is some sort of trade going on between the two islands." She glanced over her shoulder at the sound of a splash in the water, but it was only a fish jumping. "It seemed odd," she went on, "but I didn't see a reason to suspect anything more at this time. I will keep an eye on them the next time I travel that way."

Alex looked concerned. "Warbler has given us a lot of trouble in the past. Thanks for watching out for us. Perhaps Simber will have to make a trip in that direction soon to have a look."

"It never hurts to be cautious," said Pan, but her mind was elsewhere. She glanced anxiously toward the east.

"Thank you, Pan," said Alex. "You've been such a great

help." He paused. "Now that we've done what we could for Karkinos, I'd like to help you. Perhaps you could tell me what sort of wings you need? I don't know if I can make them, but I'd like to try, at least."

Pan looked at the young man thoughtfully. "Magical wings, you mean?"

"Yes," said Alex.

Pan regarded Sky and Simber as if she were not quite sure she could trust them with a secret, and then she looked over her shoulder at the sea before leaning in toward Alex. "I must show you," she said softly. "Come with me. I will return you to this spot by daybreak."

Alex's eyes widened. Did he dare go off with the dragon alone without knowing where she was taking him? But why wouldn't he? She had helped them so generously, he couldn't say no. *Perhaps I should ask Aaron to join me,* he thought. But then he frowned—he was the head mage of Artimé. He didn't need Aaron's help. Alex looked at Simber, who of course had heard the conversation. The cat narrowed his eyes but nodded once. Sky nodded more vigorously.

"All right," Alex said to Pan, just as quietly. "How do you

LISA McMANN

want me to, ah . . . climb on, exactly?" he said, looking up at the dragon's back.

Pan's tail slithered around and picked up Alex, depositing him in a sitting position. "We shall return," Pan said to Sky and Simber. "Do not fear." She turned her head to regard Alex. "Hold on very tightly to the folds of skin at the base of my neck, where the scales are worn away," she said.

Alex did as he was told. He leaned forward as she began to move, and a moment later Pan was skating across the water, propelled by her tail. On the open sea, Pan sailed over the waves at a breathtaking speed that Alex had never experienced before. He pressed his face against the dragon's neck and hung on tightly, keeping his eyes closed as his skin rippled from the force of the wind. Before Alex could imagine they were anywhere close to the island, Pan slowed. Alex opened his eyes and saw the towering cylinder in front of him.

Pan's tail snaked under Alex's arms and encircled his chest, then lifted the mage into the air, suspending him above the water. She sank the claws of her front feet into the island wall, and in an awkward jerking fashion began to climb, holding Alex completely still in the air all the while.

"Whoa," he whispered as the height grew dizzying. He gripped Pan's tail around his chest.

"Do not be afraid," Pan said. "I'm going to set you on the top edge of the island between two spikes. Hold on and don't fall in, whatever you do."

"Or out, I suppose," Alex said weakly.

"That could be nearly as painful," Pan agreed. She clung to the side of the island and lifted her tail as high as it could go. She set Alex down on the rim of the crown. "All right?" she asked, loosening her hold on him but not letting go.

Alex grabbed on to the spiked crown and planted his feet. His knees quaked. "All right," he said.

"Don't worry about any noises you may hear," said Pan. "They can't get to you."

Alex gripped the wall tighter. "They?" he whispered. His heart thudded.

Swiftly Pan whipped her tail around another spike in the island's crown and took several large steps up the wall until she was halfway to the top. Then she sank her claws in and clung to the wall once more, letting her tail drop into the sea like she had done when Alex and Sky first met her. She pulled

LISA McMANN

up several fish and flung them over the top of the crown.

Alex turned his head to watch the fish sail overhead and into the island. He was still fearful, and he almost didn't want to know what sort of creatures Pan was feeding, but curiosity won out. As long as it wasn't a bunch of saber-toothed gorillas, he figured he could handle it. He turned his head and peered down as Pan fished some more.

The inside of the island was like a pit. Alex couldn't see very far down. In the darkness he could only make out a few strange shadows. But when the fish made a splash in the bottom of it, there was a mad scramble and several roars, followed by a few flashes of fire that disappeared immediately.

There's water inside the island? And fire, too? thought Alex. He glanced at Pan, and then back down into the island pit. *Could it be?*

Pan gathered up another tail full of fish and flung them into the pit, and the sounds followed as before. She repeated the act twice more, and then wrapped her tail around a crown point and pulled herself up to the top.

Alex looked at her, wide-eyed. "I'm sorry, Pan, but I have to ask—what horrible-sounding creature are you keeping down there that you want me to give the ability to fly?" he said. "Do you seriously want me to provide world access to a roaring beast like that? How can I? Wouldn't it put my people in danger?" He couldn't imagine that Pan would want to unleash anything horrible. Had he judged her wrongly after all?

Pan gave Alex the most heartfelt, sorrowful look he'd ever seen her express. And then she looked in all directions as if making sure no enemies were near. Satisfied, she turned her face up to the sky, opened her mouth, and blew fire into the air.

At first Alex didn't know what she was doing. But then he realized she was providing light for him. Slowly his eyes left hers and he leaned over the edge to look down inside the cylindrical island.

And when he focused on the scene below, he gasped and nearly lost his balance. "Oh my," he whispered. "What in the world do we have here?"

Pan's Sobering
Predicament

Alex stared into the cylinder. The water came up two-thirds of the way, and several large rocks broke through the surface. With the light flickering overhead and the long shadows falling all around, it took Alex a moment to understand what he was looking at. Things moved over the rocks.

The light went out. "These are my children," said Pan. Fire sparked again from below.

Alex looked up at her. "Your children?" he repeated. He looked down, fascinated as flashes of young dragon faces popped up and disappeared. "How many are there? Are they dangerous? How long have you—"

A low warning rumble came from Pan's throat.

Alex closed his mouth. "I'm sorry," he said, knowing Pan kept her secrets closely guarded. He imagined she would tell him as little as possible—and she didn't like to be asked.

The dragon shifted on the wall. Her tail snaked down into the pit and she gently caressed the dragons' faces with it. "No one must know about them."

"Why not?" Alex asked, even though he tried not to.

Pan looked at Alex sharply. "Because of the pirates."

Alex glanced down at the young creatures as he pieced the information together. The pirates had been caging and selling sea creatures . . . but to whom? And young coiled water dragons must be very valuable to them if Pan was afraid enough to keep them hidden inside this island.

Pan looked all around cautiously, then lit up the night again so Alex could see the dragons' features more clearly. Each was about the size of an adult human, and they sported a variety of hues. One was the color of flame, one the shade of a forest, one as icy blue as a wolf's eyes, and two were a deep purple like the sky before a rainstorm. One of the purple dragons had a golden stripe down its back. All five had iridescent scales that sparkled beautifully in the firelight.

"You want them to fly? All five of them?" Alex said, rubbing his chin. "Is that so they can escape from the pirates?"

Pan frowned and the rumble returned.

Alex shrank back. He couldn't seem to stop asking questions. "I'm sorry," he said again. He thought long and hard about what role he should play. Would he risk anyone's life by offering to make wings for the dragons? "Pan," he said cautiously, "before I can agree to give wings to these dragons, I have to know if they will harm anybody. I hope you can understand why I need to know this."

Pan bowed her head. "Yes, of course I do," she said quietly. "And I realize the strength and power my children carry. While I cannot predict their future actions, I have raised them to follow in my ways. They will not harm anyone who contains more good than evil."

More good than evil. What an interesting directive. Alex looked into Pan's eyes and saw the honesty within them. He marveled that dragons could possess the ability to sense a person's goodness or evilness. It seemed to Alex that creatures like this could be a real asset to the world.

"All right," he said. "I'll help you. You don't have to tell me anything else unless you wish to. I'm giving you my full trust."

"The less you know, the less you can reveal," said Pan. "My secrets are for your safety as well as mine and my children's." She paused and added, "Please—know that I am extremely grateful for your help, and . . . and it is quite humbling for the ruler of the sea to be in need of it." She bowed her head slightly, gazing down at the young dragons. "Would you like to meet them? They will not harm you."

"Oh." Alex's eyes flickered, and his heart pounded in his chest. "Yes, of course," he said. The words came out thin with a whoosh of air. "You'll pull me out if anything . . . happens?" He began to sweat, thinking of being stuck in that pit with five dragons. But then he banished the thought. He had to see them up close. There was no way he could make wings for a creature he hadn't seen or touched with his own hands.

"Nothing will happen," Pan said. "But I will keep a hold on you with my tail and I won't let you go."

Alex nodded and tried to take a deep breath, but his lungs weren't cooperating. "I'll need to see them up close," he said, "and touch their scales. Would that be all right?" Alex's hands automatically went to his pockets to see what sort of components he had with him, just in case something went horribly wrong.

"I expected that," said Pan. "Yes, you may touch them, but greet them first with a closed fist so they can smell you."

A sickening chill ran through Alex and both his fists closed reflexively, but he didn't dare ask Pan another question. He could only trust that she would keep him safe and not let them eat him.

"Climb on my back and hold on to my neck," said Pan. Alex obliged, and soon Pan began the awkward trek down the inside of the cylindrical island with Alex clinging to and swinging from her neck.

Soon she settled into the water with the young dragons, which climbed over her tail and blew tiny blasts of fire from their throats.

Alex dodged the fire and hung on tightly to Pan's neck, just out of the young dragons' reach. He lit a highlighter so he could study them—their structure and skin, their coloring, their proportions and center of balance, and the way they moved. He put the highlighter behind his ear to hold it steady, pulled out his notebook and produced a pencil from it, and eased over to a small rock ledge above Pan's back so he could sit and sketch.

While Alex carried out his job, Pan began to speak in a strange, soothing language that he didn't understand. But clearly the young dragons understood it, for they soon settled down and stopped their attempts at breathing fire.

After a while, Alex looked up from his notebook. "Could I see the orange one a bit closer, please?" he asked.

Pan called the orange dragon to her, and when the young thing drew near, Pan wrapped her tail around its legs, picked it up, and moved it to Alex's side. She looked at the mage. "She won't hurt you. Mind the spines, though. They're quite sharp."

Alex looked warily at the ridge of spikes that rippled down the dragon's back, and noted them in his sketch. "Hello," he said to it, and put his fist out, remembering to greet her first before doing anything else. "I'm, uh, I'm Alex." He tried not to tremble.

The orange dragon turned her oversized face toward Alex and tilted her head, bringing her nose nerve-wrackingly close to Alex's hand. After a moment she pulled away. Apparently she accepted Alex, or at least she didn't seem intent on eating him.

Alex stared at her, memorizing the landscape of her body and noting there was no plume of scales bursting from her head, like Pan had. The young dragon's scales didn't cover her body—instead they were found in large patches, with bare skin in between.

Alex strained his neck to look closer, and then glanced at Pan. "Is it all right . . . ?"

"It is," said Pan.

Tentatively Alex reached out to touch the dragon's side next to a patch of shimmering scales. The snakelike skin wasn't slimy like he'd expected. It was soft and pliable. Silky, but thickly so, and it hung a bit loose on the dragon's frame as if the dragon were still growing into it. A few scales dangled and came away in Alex's hand. Perhaps they would be useful. He glanced at Pan again. "May I take some scales from each dragon to use for their wings?" he asked Pan.

"You may."

"And will they . . . ," Alex began, then hesitated to ask Pan another question, but he needed to know the answer. "Will they grow to be as big as you?"

Pan hesitated. "Yes," she answered after a moment. "Eventually."

"Then their wings will have to grow along with them," Alex muttered, jotting down notes and then sizing up Pan in comparison to the young orange. "Perhaps twenty times over," he muttered, "or they won't be able to fly when they're bigger. Unless I make them oversized now. . . ." He shook his head. "No, no, no. They'll be too heavy, and the dragons won't be able to lift them." He turned to Pan. "How long before they are full grown?"

"A hundred years or so."

Alex wasn't too fazed. He was used to things living hundreds of years by now.

"And how long will the young dragons stay their current size?" he asked.

"Perhaps ten more years," said Pan. "And then they'll grow rapidly."

LISA McMANN

The task seemed nearly impossible. How was Alex supposed to make magical wings for nonmagical living creatures—wings that would automatically grow when the dragons grew? He understood how Simber's wings had grown with him when he was first made. It was because Simber was entirely magical. But these dragons had not been created by some human magician. They'd been born, and they existed without magic—at least without the kind of magic Alex knew. How could he possibly connect magical wings to the living, nonmagical creatures in such a way that the two parts would communicate with each other and grow in tandem without a mage stepping in to help? Alex couldn't figure out how to do that. He thought of Aaron, how sure he'd been that it could be done. Alex lifted his chin. "Of course it's possible," he muttered, trying to convince himself.

After a long time of sketching and thinking and sketching and worrying and sketching and agonizing, Alex wrapped his arms around the young orange and lifted it up, trying to see how heavy she was. The dragon squirmed, then licked Alex in the face.

Alex laughed and set the dragon down. He thanked her and petted her neck.

The orange dragon closed her eyes and rested her head on Alex's shoulder. A purrlike rumbling came from its throat.

"Aw," said Alex. "I think she likes me."

"Careful, Alex," Pan said. "Step back a moment."

Alex stepped back as a roar and a tiny burst of flames shot from the orange dragon's mouth. The dragon smiled sleepily at the mage, and he smiled back. Pan spoke to her, and she hopped back into the water with a splash.

In turn, Alex examined each dragon and drew elaborate sketches of it. He even drew one so perfectly and distinctly that it sprang from the page in 3-D and floated above the notebook, just like a 3-D doorway. He'd never done that before— he didn't even know it was possible. He couldn't wait to tell Ms. Octavia about it. It would make a great model for the preliminary design work.

When Alex had collected scales from each dragon and sketched and colored in everything he could, he pressed the 3-D drawing back into the notebook and closed it, and said good-bye to the five young dragons.

Pan brought him back up to the top of the island, and the two descended the other side. Once in the sea, Pan sped over the water with Alex on her back, both of them silent and contemplating. One sorrowful, one stumped, but both determined.

When Pan reached Artimé not long after dawn, Alex dismounted and stifled a yawn. "This is our first priority now," Alex promised her. "But I have to be completely honest with you about my abilities. I don't know if I can actually do this. And even if I can, I'm not sure I can make wings that will work for the dragons' entire lives. They may only be useful while they remain this size."

Pan bowed to Alex. "I am grateful for your efforts to help my family, even if you find no success at all," she said. "We will survive somehow. Dragons always do."

Magic All Around

While Alex slept and dreamed about dragon wings, the rest of Artimé was doing business as usual, or so it appeared. With the mention of ships at the neighboring island, Claire Morning decided it was important to continue Magical Warrior Training during Florence's absence as a precaution, and to keep the spell casters in the know about new spells. Today her class was made up of the more experienced fighters, including Warbler children Scarlet and Thatcher, who had by now graduated from their beginner's training.

Working alongside Claire was Lani Haluki, who was explaining

LISA McMANN

some of the most recent nonlethal spell components and how they worked. She also reminded the warriors of the two deadly spells: heart attack, which required three components to put an end to an average human-size enemy, and the single scatterclip, which was harmless on its own, but deadly when coupled with the right phrase. There would be no practicing for these two, and only those who wished to have that amount of power carried them. Lani reminded the class that it was Artimé's policy since the days of Mr. Today, that each person must think long and hard about whether she wanted to have that responsibility.

Observing the training today were Aaron and some non-magical friends: Kaylee, Sky, and Crow, who was looking after Thisbe and Fifer along the water's edge. Sky sat in a chair under a tree a short distance away, reading a book, while Aaron, Kaylee, and Crow all lay on their stomachs, elbows in the sand, hands cupping their chins. Aaron and Kaylee lounged together, and Crow was a few feet away, perched sideways so he could see the training and watch the twins at the same time.

Kaylee and Aaron, both feeling a bit like outsiders in Artimé, had fallen into a friendship of convenience. Aaron wasn't accustomed to having friends at all, so he was always awkward with people until he relaxed. And Kaylee was boisterous and playful—the complete opposite of Aaron, or so it seemed. Yet it was her large personality that relaxed him, and the two got along somehow.

Crow eyed them suspiciously from time to time, but they didn't seem to be romantically involved at all, which was a relief. He was tired of watching other people kissing, including his own sister. He preferred a more anonymous kind of admiration over outward displays of affection, and he was exercising that anonymous admiration now as he watched Scarlet. He studied the intense look on her face that never broke when she was casting spells. He appreciated her long blond hair swishing over her shoulders when she followed through on her spell casting.

Scarlet stood next to Thatcher, who had the tallest hair Crow had ever seen. Most of the time Scarlet stayed focused on her task. But once, between exercises, she and Thatcher laughed together at something Ms. Morning said to them, which Crow couldn't hear. Crow frowned, even though he knew Scarlet and Thatcher had been friends for a long time.

Near Crow's legs, Fifer piled up small, flat stones, one on top of another in a precarious stack, using extreme precision

LISA McMANN

for a child her age. Thisbe stood on the other side of Crow, entranced as she watched the magical warriors on the lawn. Every now and then she imitated their movements, saying "Dat!" or "Boom!" and casting imaginary spells of her own.

"Hey, Crow," Kaylee called. "Who's the dude with the righteous Afro?"

"The what?" asked Crow. Half the things Kaylee said made no sense to him.

"The boy next to Scarlet."

"Oh. That's Thatcher. He's one of the Warbler kids."

"I figured, due to the orange eyes and the scars on his neck."

"I forget about those things sometimes," Crow said. Orange eyes and neck scars were all too common to him.

"He's really good," Kaylee said.

Crow bristled. "Scarlet's better," he said in a quiet voice. He returned his gaze to Warbler girl.

Kaylee looked sideways at him and pressed her lips together to stifle a smile. "Yes, I totally agree," she said. "Scarlet rocks." She poked Aaron with her elbow.

Aaron startled. "What?"

Kaylee leaned in, her shoulder touching Aaron's shoulder

and her face dangerously close to his. He resisted the urge to shrink away, and she whispered in his ear, "Crow has a crush on Scarlet."

Her breath was warm as it caressed his skin and slipped down below his shirt collar. Aaron's ear tingled, and then his whole body tingled. His heart thudded in his chest. He didn't even register what she was saying. Instead of responding like a normal human, Aaron froze. He stared straight ahead and didn't move. He had no idea what to do. All he knew was that her shoulder was still touching his, and he wasn't sure if he wanted it to stay there or move away.

With Crow, Aaron, and Kaylee all momentarily occupied, and Sky reading intently under the tree, nobody actually paid much attention when Thisbe meandered over to where her sister was stacking stones. Thisbe took a warrior stance and pointed at the tower. "Boom!" she said.

The stones flew into the air of their own accord and pelted the sand around Fifer. Fifer stared, and then the twin girls began giggling hysterically. "Again!" cried Fifer.

"Again!" cried Thisbe.

Fifer began to pile the stones once more.

Contemplating Flight

Alex woke around noon feeling groggy and disoriented after having stayed up all night with Pan, but once he bathed and dressed, he was wide awake and ready to work. He found Ms. Octavia in her classroom and told her about the dragons and what had transpired overnight.

"That's quite a project," Ms. Octavia said, scratching her head with one of her tentacles. "I admit I have no idea how you're going to do it. I've only fixed existing appendages. I always left the creating of them up to Marcus."

"I know . . . I still have to figure that out. But," Alex said, his face growing excited, "I have something cool I need to show you."

"What is it?" asked Ms. Octavia.

Alex pulled his notebook from his pocket. It sprang open to the page with the 3-D dragon drawing. The drawing popped up and hovered a few inches above the page.

Ms. Octavia took in a sharp breath, and then carefully took the notebook from Alex and looked more closely at the dragon from all angles. She took off her latest pair of fake glasses from Mr. Appleblossom and studied it some more, turning the notebook in a circle. Then she looked at Alex. "I've never seen this happen before," she said, admiration in her voice. "I am very proud of you. Your drawing has continued to improve to near perfection over the years because you work so hard at it, and clearly this is your reward for that. Well done, Alex. Well done."

"I didn't mean to do it," he said modestly. "It just happened when I was drawing."

"You must have been perfectly precise," said the octogator, "or I'm sure it wouldn't have happened. This is really something to celebrate! I wish Marcus were here to see it."

LISA McMANN

Tears sprang to Alex's eyes at the mention of the wonderful old mage who had saved so many Unwanteds over the years. Alex longed for Mr. Today to see this accomplishment. "It's okay," Alex said, swallowing the lump in his throat. "Perhaps he knows somehow."

Together they brainstormed the predicament of putting magical wings on a nonmagically made creature.

"Was Jim the winged tortoise created from a real tortoise?" Alex asked.

"No, I'm afraid not," said Ms. Octavia. "He's like the rest of us."

"But what about you?" Alex said. "You're parts of two animals. Octopus and alligator. Those creatures are nonmagical, yet you exist magically."

"Ah, but you forget that I am not actually either of those animals, not even a little bit. I only look like a combination of them. I was created from items found in the sea—seaweed, shells, plant life."

"I remember that now," Alex said, thinking back to when all of Artimé was gone and Ms. Octavia's body had morphed into those materials. "So what exactly is the real dilemma here?

I think it's like I told Lani yesterday. I can't create a third arm and attach it to her, and expect it to work like the other two arms, can I? Because she was born a living human, and magic and human parts can't communicate. A third arm would need blood and muscle and bone connected to the rest of the body, and magic can't create that, can it?"

"No magic that I know," said Ms. Octavia. She tapped her snout thoughtfully as a second tentacle began jotting down notes and a third picked up her coffee mug and brought it to her mouth. She took a sip and swallowed.

As they sat thinking, there was a knock on the door. Aaron poked his head in.

"Am I interrupting?" he asked.

Alex frowned. He wanted to be the one who figured this out, not his freak prodigy brother. But then he reluctantly admitted it was silly of him to be acting so petty about Aaron's abilities. Alex needed Aaron, just like he needed his other friends for the various things they were good at. And then he remembered Aaron would be leaving soon, perhaps for good, and the empty feeling gnawed at him.

"No, you're not interrupting," said Alex. "We're talking

LISA McMANN

about dragon wings and . . . and I think maybe you can help us. Unless you can't stay, of course." Alex tried not to look hopeful.

"I was just looking for you to see if you were getting lunch," Aaron said. "Of course I'll stay, but I don't know what help I'll be."

"Okay. Great, then. We'll get something to eat afterward if you can wait," Alex said.

"If I can wait?" Aaron nearly laughed. "I'm from Quill. Of course I can wait for food. I'm just thrilled to know there is some. Also, I was wondering about Henry. Is there any news? And if it's all right for me to, you know, go home. To Ishibashi's, I mean."

"Ah, yes—sorry," Alex said. "I meant to tell you. I should be able to get you back to the Island of Shipwrecks very soon, but I was sort of hoping to finish the dragon project first. Then we can set off together, attach the wings, and continue on to the Island of Shipwrecks."

"Oh," Aaron said. "All right." He was only a little put off that Alex wasn't going to jump into the boat today to take him away. "Of course that's fine. I don't want to inconvenience you." He came and sat down with them. "What's going on?"

Alex filled Aaron in on the conversation so far.

Aaron listened intently, and when Alex reintroduced the third-arm scenario, he closed his eyes, a perplexed look on his face.

"What's wrong?" Alex asked.

Aaron didn't answer at first, and then he said, "So you're saying that you wouldn't be able to give Lani a third arm because you can't create human blood and bones and things like that, and for this same reason you can't make dragon wings." He opened his eyes and looked inquisitively at Alex.

"Right," said Alex. "I know you think you can do this, but—"

"I can," said Aaron. "You're making it too complicated."

Ms. Octavia nodded. "I think you may be right, Aaron. Why do the wings need to have dragon's blood and bones and muscles in them in order to work?"

"Because they have to grow with the body when it grows," Alex explained, feeling a bit exasperated. "See, the dragons are small. About my size right now. And Pan said they'll stay around this size for another ten years or so, but then they'll grow rapidly, and they'll continue growing until they're a hundred years old. And if the wings aren't made of actual dragon parts, then once the dragons start to grow, their magical wings won't grow with them. And they'll be useless because the dragons will be too heavy for the wings to support."

Aaron sighed, and Ms. Octavia looked at Alex. "I'm sorry, Alex," Ms. Octavia said, "but I don't think it's possible to provide the dragons with body parts that will grow with them. There are limits to our magic for good reason. And this is one of them. Don't you agree?"

Alex pushed his hair off his forehead thoughtfully. "I guess so," he said. "So what do I do? Make prosthetic magical wings that cease to be useful once they have their growth spurt?" He leaned forward and said quietly, "I think she wants to keep her children away from the pirates."

"By the time they grow, maybe they won't need to fly to get away from the pirates anymore," Ms. Octavia said. "They'll be big enough to fight them off."

"Yes, exactly," said Aaron. "So it's really a simple solution. It's no more difficult than using a vine to fix a—" He clamped his mouth shut.

"What?" asked Alex.

"Um, a rope," Aaron said lamely. "Or," he said, scrambling to come up with something, "no different from the heart attack spell. That spell has wings."

"That's true."

"It's probably going to be very easy," Aaron said, "like I've said all along. You always make things too complicated."

Alex's mouth dropped open. "I do not."

Aaron gave Ms. Octavia a side-eye glance. "He does, doesn't he?"

Ms. Octavia lifted her eyebrows and shrugged. "Yes," she said. "Sorry, Alex."

Alex just shook his head. "You two," he muttered. "So I guess the biggest question is what materials are we going to use to make this happen. Because we'll need a lot of them, and they'll have to be a big variety of colors in order to blend in properly. We don't want our dragon friends to look like our patch job on the ship. They'll be our artwork on display for all the world to see."

"Fair enough," declared Ms. Octavia. "Though we can easily just paint the wings to match the dragons if we can't find the right material. Why don't you work on designing a mini-model-size wing for your 3-D drawing that will be aerodynamic and strong enough to transport its weight, and then once the dimensions are perfected, you can move on to a full size pair of wings. Aaron can help me see about some materials that will suit the job."

Alex agreed. He showed the two his drawings to point out the various colors necessary. Aaron was appropriately impressed by the 3-D drawing that popped off the page, which made Alex feel a little more secure in his abilities. At least Aaron couldn't do *that*.

Once Ms. Octavia and Aaron had had a good look, they headed off together, and Alex sat in the classroom alone with his project. It was good to be doing the thing he did best and enjoyed most once again.

Old Friends and Traditions

With so much help from sea creatures, it didn't take much effort for Karkinos to stay afloat in his usual spot in the sea. He showed signs of tiredness from time to time, but Spike and the giant squid fed and monitored the crab to make sure he had everything he needed. Henry kept an eye on his health and strength, which improved little by little.

At first Henry worried that he hadn't given the crab enough seaweed, and even considered making a trip to the Island of Shipwrecks to get more. But after a few days of resting and eating, Karkinos began making great strides.

LISA McMANN

Indeed, he became almost playful as more time passed.

"He's acting like his old self again," Talon said one day as he and Henry stood at the edge of the island and watched the crab play tag with the squid and Issie. "He reminds me of the creature he was before he fell sick—which was well before your ship first landed here."

"I'm really glad to hear that," Henry said. It was a relief to know their efforts had paid off. Karkinos lurched to one side trying to tag Issie with his claw, and Henry grabbed on to Talon's arm to steady himself. "I think Karkinos has a long, healthy life ahead of him."

Talon put his bronze hand on the boy's shoulder and looked at Henry earnestly. "I cannot possibly thank you enough," he said. "You risked everything for us. I don't know what I would have done if you'd been hurt."

Henry could see the gratitude in Talon's eyes. "But I wasn't hurt," the boy said. "I'm really glad we could help. You and everybody here mean a lot to us. We talk about you all the time—about how much fun we had here. You are our friends." He grew quiet, thoughtful. Talon made him feel like he'd done something right. But there was one thing that had been

LISA McMANN

bothering Henry since the time they arrived. Something he couldn't quite shake from his conscience. He looked back to the playful water creatures and frowned.

"I've been meaning to do something," Henry said under his breath, and left Talon's side. "Spike!" he called out. He walked toward Karkinos's reefy claw.

The whale surfaced near Henry. "What is wrong?"

"Nothing's wrong," Henry said, crouching down near Spike's face. "I don't think so, anyway. But I need you to speak to Karkinos for me. Can you do that?"

"Yes, I can and will," said Spike.

"Tell him that I used a medicine on him that will extend his life indefinitely . . . perhaps even forever. And I should have asked his permission first, but he wasn't responding to you and we were about to go over the waterfall, and, well . . . there were so many lives at stake that I administered the medicine without asking him first. And I'm sorry. I hope he thinks I did the right thing."

Spike waited until he was sure Henry was done with his confession, and then disappeared under the water. A moment later Henry could see Spike talking earnestly to the crab.

The crab and Spike conversed for a moment, and then Spike swam back to Henry.

"Karkinos says he does not wish to be dead or stuck in a rotating waterfall, and he wants to live as long as Talon lives, which is likely forever, so you have done him a great favor. He is very happy."

Henry breathed a sigh of relief. "Oh good. Thank you, Spike. That's a big relief."

Spike left to go back to his hiding spot under the crab's body.

Henry stood up and went back to Talon's side.

"I couldn't help overhearing," Talon said. "Where did you get such incredibly powerful medicine?"

"It doesn't matter now," Henry said. "I'm actually glad I'm finally rid of it."

"I don't understand," Talon said. "Wouldn't every healer wish to have a large stock of such a medicine?"

Henry regarded the bronze giant. "You've lived thousands of years," he said. "Have you ever thought about what it would be like if you could die?"

"Many times in the past I've longed for such a thing," admitted Talon.

Henry nodded wisely. He had spent hours thinking about it since that day in Ishibashi's greenhouse when the scientist had given him the seaweed. "I don't like having the power to take away someone's death," said Henry. "It's too much responsibility. For me, at least. I worry about it a lot."

Talon nodded thoughtfully. "You are wise beyond your years, lad," he said. "I hope your worries subside now that you have so valiantly used up your supply."

Henry gazed out over the water. "I have a feeling I'll sleep all right tonight."

Florence approached with an armload of firewood and some sand chairs. She stoked the fire as Lhasa the snow lion came prancing out of the woods, not quite touching the ground as always. Behind her was Bock, silent and observant as ever.

Talon watched them settle around the fire. "I think this is our cue," he said to Henry. "Time for a story. I only wish Fox and Kitten were here to tell it."

Henry laughed. "I guess you'll have to tell one instead."

"I shall do it with pleasure," said Talon. "Whose story would you like to hear?" Talon and Henry walked over to the fire to join the others.

"The story of that smelly, blurry one, please," said Henry.

"Ah, the hibagon," Talon said.

"Yes, him."

They settled by the fire next to Florence, and Talon announced the Tale of the Hibagon.

"I wish there were a great long story about the hibagon," Talon began. "But Lhasa and I will tell you everything we know, won't we Lhasa?"

"We will!" said Lhasa, her voice ringing with laughter. "Start us off, please."

Talon smiled and began. "Not long ago, perhaps twenty years or so, a large bundle of logs bumped up against the side of Karkinos, just there," he said, pointing to a spot on the eastern shore. "The logs were the size of entire tall trees, taller and bigger around than any tree we have growing here."

Lhasa smiled dreamily. "I imagined they were trees from a giant forest that had never been found by anyone but the creatures living peacefully in it."

Talon nodded. "I wrestled the logs ashore, thinking we could use them for firewood once they dried out. But when I released the cords that enclosed the bundle and the logs rolled apart, a strange creature emerged. I admit it gave me a fright, for I wasn't expecting that. He was about as tall as you, Henry, covered in black bristles as stiff and sharp as pine needles. And he carried with him a rotten stench of death that could drop a human to his knees to beg for mercy."

Lhasa curled up her nose. "He walked upright like a man but hunched over, and darted about so jaggedly that he was hard to see clearly. And even when he stood still, which wasn't very often, he seemed blurry. Like his body had no true outline— his bristly coat faded away at the edges. I admit I couldn't stand to look at him."

"Which turned out to be good," Talon said, "because once I coaxed a name from the fellow he insisted I not look at him again, for stories were told in the land he came from about the dangers of looking too long at a hibagon."

Henry leaned forward, intrigued. "What are the dangers?" he asked.

"If you look at a hibagon, you'll fall in love with him." Lhasa tittered.

"Ugh!" cried Henry. "That would be horrible! Once you fall in love with him, does his stink go away?"

LISA McMANN

"I don't know," said Talon, "for I assure you I've never looked long at him again."

"Ah," said Florence, "but what an awful curse to have. Poor hibagon. He seemed kind enough to warn you."

"He is kind, indeed," said Talon. "But very uncomfortable around anyone. He soon dashed off into the woods, leaving us wondering about his origins. When I ran across him again some weeks later, he asked me about Issie. He said he knew of her from his world. She was as notorious as he."

Henry frowned. "He's from another world? And so is Issie?"

"So it seems, although Issie has never spoken enough to confirm it," said Talon. "It's a mystery to all of us. Both the hibagon and Issie are famous elsewhere, though we know not what for."

"Did you ever find out how the hibagon got here?" asked Florence.

Talon gazed at her. "Eventually. He told me about his home in a forest, which grew high in the mountains. It was much like Lhasa imagined it—a peaceful place unharmed by outsiders. Only the occasional hibagon hunters passed through, trying to catch him, but those instances were few, and years passed between them, so the hibagon felt safe in his land . . . that is, until one fateful day."

Henry's eyes widened. The fire crackled, making him jump.

Talon went on. "The hibagon heard strange noises in the distance, so he hid inside a hollow of an old dead tree as usual. But the noises grew louder, closer. Days passed, but the hibagon was comfortable, and he went out at night to eat, staying close to his tree.

"But soon animals began bounding past his hiding spot, fleeing. The noises grew even louder, and it was as if the hibagon could hear the trees crying out. He could stay hidden no longer—he had to see what was happening to cause such unrest in his peaceful land.

"That's when he discovered the humans. They weren't searching to capture him this time. Instead they were chopping down his trees, bundling them up, and loading them on huge moving machines, leaving an ugly scar on the forest bed. Horrified, the hibagon drew closer and closer to the human camp, hiding behind trees, until a human saw him and gave chase.

"The hibagon raced around the machines, and when he

was sure no one was watching, he dove into the nearest bundle of logs and squirmed deep inside, intending to wait until night-fall so he could escape. He listened to the humans laugh at the man who had claimed to see a hibagon, and then the work began again, with trees falling all around. The hibagon was devastated. Sickened! He had to get out of there.

"As the day wore on, the hibagon felt his bundle of logs move, and before he could do anything, he was being lifted high into the air. He crawled to the end of the bundle to get a better look at what was happening, but soon the end was pushed up against a hot metal surface, and the hibagon could no longer see. He couldn't turn around, and he couldn't risk backing out from between the logs during daylight, so he remained still. But soon the logs were moving once more, this time on a bumpy journey that lasted hours. When finally the journey seemed to end, the logs were lifted into the air once more and set down again.

"Able to see at last, the hibagon soon discovered that he'd been loaded onto a freighter. The ship left the docks and sailed for days, and the hibagon found very few moments through-out the journey where he could emerge from his hiding place and sneak food, for sailors patrolled the decks at all hours. He nearly died of thirst on the journey, and would have if it hadn't been for the rain. As the rain soaked the logs and dripped down, the hibagon drank every drop he could."

Talon paused. "Unfortunately, the rain turned into a violent storm. After many hours of rocking, and waves coming up over the deck, the ship went into a sharp spiral. The hibagon lost consciousness, and when he woke, the ship was gone. He was alone on the sea, trapped inside the bundle of logs. More days passed, and finally the hibagon's bundle of logs floated here." Talon folded his hands in his lap.

"Wow," said Henry. "What a story!"

"That's incredible," said Florence, shaking her head in awe.

"Yes it is," said Lhasa. "And now the hibagon lives peacefully here among the trees, away from the dropbears, of course. And away from Vido the golden rooster—the hibagon can't stand Vido and all his strange warnings and senseless proverbs."

"Can Vido fly?" asked Henry.

"I assume so," said Lhasa, with a musical laugh, "or he couldn't have made it to the tallest tree in the center of the island. But I have never seen him fly. Have you, Talon?"

"Not even once, Queen Lhasa. Perhaps he flies in secret."

"Ha-ha!" The snow lion rolled through the air and shook her mane. "Oh, I'm just so delighted to have visitors, and so grateful that Karkinos is feeling better. It's pure goodness to laugh again. How generous of you all to rescue us! We shall never forget the kindness of Artimé."

Making
Masterpieces

Back in Artimé, Ms. Octavia knew that wings for something as fierce and beautiful as a dragon had to be made of only the finest material, and when she ran into Crow with Thisbe and Fifer near the shore, she had her answer. For it happened that there was a garden of magical flowers on the lawn, and Thisbe loved to pluck their petals because new petals of different colors emerged immediately following. There was only one problem, and that was an abundance of flower petals to clean up. But Crow and the girls faithfully gathered the petals each time they were finished playing and brought them into the mansion's kitchen to be

LISA McMANN

used for table decorations and whatever else the chefs could think of.

But a surplus of petals had built up over the months since Thisbe first discovered the flowers, and because they were magical they didn't shrivel up and die. They kept their pristine beauty, and no one quite knew what to do with them all, until now.

"They're perfect for covering the dragon wings," Ms. Octavia declared. She ordered the surplus to be delivered to her classroom and sent Crow and the twin girls to pick more immediately, to their delight.

In Ms. Octavia's classroom, Alex had finished the official designs for all five sets of wings, and now Aaron, Samheed, and Lani were experimenting with different materials, trying to create the best "bones" for them.

Lani had a book of birds with full illustrations and diagrams that she and the others referred to. Alex sat alone at a table with the scales he'd taken from each of the young dragons, trying to replicate them magically so he'd have enough scales to match the patterns on the young dragon bodies. Sky was busy nearby, hand sewing sheets of canvas to cover the structures.

Samheed and Lani were working with various pipes and hoses that they'd found, but the pipes were too solid and the hoses too floppy to work. They needed something firm yet pliable, so when the wings were magically instilled with life, they would move and flow naturally and fold up when the dragons weren't in flight. They pondered other ideas for the bones, like tree branches and rope, but they ran into the same problems.

Aaron simply stared at the drawing for a long time. After a while he looked up and excused himself. "I'll be back soon," he said. None of the others really paid much attention to him, expecting little from him design-wise, at least, for they hadn't witnessed him in action. So his departure went largely unnoticed.

He returned a short time later with several long strands of vines hanging from his shoulders, the ends dragging on the floor. He coiled them on his worktable and began to shape one into an outline of a dragon's wing. When he got to outlining the joints of the wing, he doubled up the vine and used ribbon and glue to keep it in place, for that part needed to be a little firmer than the rest. Eventually he was satisfied that the shape was correct. But would it move properly? He put his hands on it and closed his eyes, and whispered, "Live."

The structure came to life, swishing gently on the table like Panther's tail. Aaron studied it, picturing the wing on a dragon and imagining the movements it would need to make in flight.

"Whoa!" said Lani when she noticed what Aaron was doing. "How'd you do that?" She dropped her sticks and went over to Aaron's table. "Vines! Where'd you get these? These are great." She picked up a vine from Aaron's desk. "May I try one?"

"Sure," said Aaron. "I brought enough for all the wings in case it actually worked. What do you think, Alex?"

Alex looked up from his project, and his eyes widened at the sight of the moving outline of a dragon's wing on Aaron's table. He stood up quickly, upsetting his chair in his rush to see what was going on, and hurried over. He studied the wing skeleton for a long moment, and then looked at Aaron. "It's great," he admitted. "And you just did this instinctively? First try?"

Aaron blushed and looked down at the table.

"Can I pick it up?" Alex asked.

"Sure," Aaron said again. "I'll help you."

Alex picked up the base of the wing in one hand and lifted

the first dart of the wing joint with his other. Aaron picked up the second wing-joint dart and the very tip of the wing. Together they held the wing loosely so it could continue to move as it wanted to.

"Hey, Samheed," said Alex. "Come over here. I need you to be a dragon for a minute."

Samheed frowned and put down his crafts, but once he saw what was happening, he came over willingly and turned his back to the brothers. "That's pretty cool," he said begrudgingly.

"I know," said Aaron, sounding a bit smug this time.

Alex stifled a laugh and pressed the base of the wing to Samheed's back. "Do you dare to let go of your end, Aaron? Or do you think it'll break without the added magic of the flying material?"

"It's pretty sturdy," said Aaron, "but it'll need some more reinforcement before it's finished. I'll let go for a few seconds, and we'll see where the weaknesses are."

Alex nodded, and Aaron let go of the tip of the wing, then the joint. The wing sagged slightly, but it continued to move in a swishing pattern that, with a little help from the cloth cover and the flower petals, would give the wings excellent movement and a great look. After a moment Aaron lifted the tip again and carefully bent the wing at the joints to make sure all of his measurements lined up and the movements were perfectly fluid.

"That's excellent!" Sky called out from her side of the room. "But how am I going to cover it with material while it's moving like that?"

Aaron pressed his lips together. "Um . . . I'm not sure," he said. He tried fully folding the wing and it became still, but it only stayed still if he was holding the dart, as if the wing could sense through his fingers that he wanted it to stop moving. As soon as he let go of it, it began moving again. He had no idea how to make the wing stop moving for good. He'd never done a spell like that before. What was he supposed to say—"Die"? He looked at his brother. "Alex, do you know how to make it stop?"

Alex squelched a grin. He certainly did know. "Why yes, I do," he said.

Aaron narrowed his eyes. "How?" he said, suspicious.

"You have to sing a song to take away the magic," said Alex, clearly delighted.

"What?" cried Aaron. "I can't do that."

"You have to. That's the only way you can get it to stop."

Samheed and Lani began to chuckle, and Sky looked on, eyes filled with merriment.

"Well, then, *you* do it," said Aaron. "I—I don't know how. I mean I wish I could sing. But I've never done it, actually."

"You may as well learn," said Alex. "Besides," he lied, "only *you* can stop the magic since you're the one who made it alive in the first place."

Sky almost called Alex out on the lie, but it was so entertaining to watch Aaron squirm that she held back.

Aaron gave Sky a pleading look. "Are you sure you can't attach the fabric when it's moving?"

Sky shook her head. "Nope. Sorry," she said.

Aaron glanced at Lani and Samheed. He knew he wouldn't get any help from them. Finally he sighed and gave up. "Fine. What do I have to sing?"

Alex wrote down the lines to Ol' Tater's song, changing a few words to make the spell work for the wing. He handed the spell to Aaron and then hummed the tune for him. Alex was slightly off-key, but it was the best he could do.

LISA McMANN

Aaron read the chant. "Are you serious? This is absolutely ridiculous," he said. "Who designed this spell?"

"Mr. Today, I think." Alex shrugged. "It's the only way to fix it."

"Well, it's a lot easier to make things come alive," muttered Aaron.

"And you're awfully good at that for having no training," said Alex, "so I'm sure you'll be great at this, too."

Aaron didn't answer. He opened his mouth, and then he closed it again and sighed. He cleared his throat. He shuffled his feet, and held the paper at different distances from his face to find what would feel most comfortable. Then he looked at the wing moving around on the table. He closed his eyes and shook his head.

The others watched silently, exchanging mischievous glances.

Finally Aaron opened his mouth again and croaked out the words:

Dragon wing, dragon wing,
Too much sadness, no repeats.

I am sorry, more than sorry,

But it's time for you to sleep.

The wing ceased to move. And the room exploded in laughter and applause for Aaron's terrible singing.

Aaron was surprised and confused by the outburst, and he felt his cheeks grow warm. He looked from one face to the next, at first thinking he was being ridiculed, and it reminded him of what things were like when he had been thrown out of the university long ago. But slowly it began to dawn on him that the people in this room were not acting mean-spirited. They were just plain spirited. And they had played a trick—no, not a trick, a joke—on Aaron.

The former high priest wasn't 100 percent sure what the joke was, but instead of yelling at them as he initially wanted to do, he sought out Sky to make sure this was supposed to be funny.

Sky smiled warmly at him. "It's okay," she mouthed.

Aaron glanced at his brother, who was laughing and coming toward him.

"This is a joke on me," Aaron said.

LISA McMANN

"It sure is," said Alex.

One corner of Aaron's mouth turned upward as Alex slapped him on the back. Aaron risked a glance at Lani, and then at Samheed, who wasn't sneering.

"You're a pretty good sport," Samheed said. "I'll give you that."

Aaron laughed a little. "Thanks," he said. "And the song worked. Maybe I'll take singing lessons since I'm so good at it."

The friends howled in laughter, and encouraged him to do so.

Aaron smiled. He still didn't know precisely what he'd done that was so funny, but he was enjoying this new feeling inside him—the feeling that he was not only useful, but also that he was finally a part of something good in Artimé.

Preparing to Fly

With such a competent group of mages working on the task, the five sets of wings were assembled, tested, and covered in canvas in a matter of days. All that was left to do was to line them with flower petals and scales before the rest of the magic would be added.

Sky, Samheed, and Aaron were the most skilled at attaching the delicate petals and scales without damaging them. Once they finished each wing, Alex used the preserve spell on it, then added a shimmer spell he'd invented to make the wings as beautiful and iridescent as the bodies of the dragons.

LISA McMANN

With a few final touches, the wings were perfect—lithe and beautiful and just the right dimensions.

At first Alex wasn't sure how he was going to attach the wings to the dragons, but he had a few ideas. He asked Samheed to make up a new variation on scatterclips and sticky-clips, called superclips, a permanent spell that would attach one thing to another thing without harming either one of them. But it was troublesome trying to get the wings to seal completely to anything, and it left the base joint stiff and unwieldy, so they gave up on that idea.

Lani came up with a melding spell by using a bit of soft eraser from Ms. Octavia's cupboard as a component. She stretched and kneaded the eraser into a wonderfully pliable material, then instilled magic in it that would meld the wings to the dragon, making them appear continuous and leaving them perfectly flexible.

Alex tested Lani's spell by melding a flowerpot to a large rock outside and moving it this way and that. Then he fired all sorts of elemental spells at it to make sure it could withstand fire, storms, salt water, heavy winds, and anything else he could think of that the dragons might come in contact with.

When he was satisfied with the results, he asked Lani to make up a large batch of melding components for him to bring along to the Island of Dragons. Finally they were ready to test out a pair of wings to see if they would really work.

"Do you want to test it?" Alex asked Aaron.

"Me?" asked Aaron nervously. "Oh, no thank you. I'm—I'm just fine here on the ground. And besides, I have a cooking lesson in the kitchen to get to."

Lani jumped up. "I'll do it."

"Sorry," said Alex. "You're not heavy enough. We have to simulate a real dragon."

"Drat!" said Lani, sitting back down. "Foiled again. I never get to do anything fun."

"I won't remind you about driving the Quillitary vehicle," said Alex.

"We agreed to never discuss that again, remember?" said Lani sweetly.

Samheed rolled his eyes and groaned. "Fine. I'll do it," he said.

"Thank you," said Alex.

They went out onto the lawn with one pair of wings. Alex

instructed Samheed to take his shirt off so the wings could adhere to Samheed's back. Samheed shucked off his shirt, and Alex melded the wings to him.

"That feels really weird," Samheed said. He shrugged his shoulders a few times.

"Does it hurt?" asked Alex. "Walk around a bit."

"No, it doesn't hurt. They're not even all that heavy." Samheed walked around and the wings, still folded, moved naturally with his stride. "It sort of feels like I have two extra arms."

"Can you move them?" asked Alex. "Think about flying—they should be intuitive to you, at least a little."

Samheed rotated his shoulders, experimenting with his new appendages and thinking about flying. After a minute he figured out the muscles he needed to move in order to make the wings unfold. He concentrated and flapped the wings in an awkward, jerky movement as he walked around. After several minutes, his motions grew smoother.

"Good," said Alex. "Now take a running leap and start flying."

"Yes, boss." Samheed did as he was instructed. He ran toward the jungle as fast as he could, wings flapping, and jumped into the air.

He soared straight up two or three yards, his wings flapping wildly. Then he faltered and crashed to the ground.

"Ouch," Samheed said. He spit grass from his mouth and pushed himself to his feet.

Alex frowned. "What did you do wrong?" he asked.

Samheed looked at Alex. "How should I know? You're the head mage." He noticed a grass stain on his knee and tried to wipe it clean.

Lani stood quietly, arms folded, and then she brought one hand to her chin as she studied Samheed. She tilted her head slightly, watching the wings move as he walked around. Samheed started running again, soared up into the air like before, and then spiraled down to the ground in another crash landing. "Oof," he said.

Samheed lay there for a minute, winded, then rolled to his side and got up again. "You know, I'm not sure how many more times I want to do this," he said.

Alex shook his head. "You're flapping your wings. I don't know why they won't keep you up, unless they're just not strong enough. In which case we're in trouble."

"They're definitely strong enough," said Lani. "I did all the

LISA McMANN

equations. That's not the problem." She continued to study Samheed, and then a thought struck her, and she began digging around in her component vest pockets.

After a moment Samheed started running again.

"Wait!" hollered Lani. "Don't try just yet." She pulled an origami fire-breathing dragon from her pocket and looked at it.

Samheed slowed, and both he and Alex turned to Lani. "What is it?" asked Alex. "Did you think of something?"

"Remember when we created these?" Lani said, holding up the origami dragon.

Alex nodded. "What about them?" He and Samheed walked over to where Lani was standing.

"Do you remember what happened when we tested them out?"

Samheed took the dragon and looked at it. "No. What happened?"

"Oh!" said Alex. "We had to give them eyes."

"Yes," said Lani.

"But Samheed already has eyes."

"Right, but then we had to tell it where to go," Lani said. "We had to give it directions."

Alex grimaced. "Of course. How are we possibly still alive after being so stupid?" He looked at Samheed. "You have to tell the wings where you want to go."

"Yeah, I picked up on that," said Samheed, shaking his head and walking away.

"We're nothing without you," Alex said to Lani as Samheed started running once more.

"It's true, I know," said Lani.

Samheed jumped into the air, shouting, "To the jungle!" And this time, the wings flapped and Samheed began flying forward instead of straight up. He hovered about ten feet off the ground, then gained altitude when he figured out how to pump his wings harder.

The scales caught the light, and the wings shimmered as Samheed worked them up and down. The ride was a bit jerky at first, but then it smoothed out into a beautiful, fluid motion, like the way Claire Morning conducted musicians.

Alex and Lani stood side by side and watched as Samheed flew toward the jungle with the wind rippling through his hair and a huge grin on his face. A few people on the lawn paused in their activities to watch as well.

"It's working great," said Alex.

Lani nodded. "I wonder how he'll land."

"Hmm," said Alex. "Good question. I hope he doesn't fall from *that* height."

"That would be tragic," Lani agreed. "Maybe we should get Simber out here." They couldn't take their eyes off Samheed.

"Nah," said Alex after a moment. "He'll be fine."

As Samheed neared the jungle, he began to lean to one side, making a wide turn. Soon he was flying toward Alex and Lani. He held his arms bent in front of him and moved his shoulders to keep the wings flapping.

"How am I supposed to land?" Samheed screeched when he drew near to Alex and Lani.

"Slow down your flapping!" Alex called out, though he had no idea if that would work.

Samheed slowed his movements and he lost altitude.

"That's working!" shouted Lani.

In fits and starts, Samheed dropped lower in the air, sometimes gut-wrenchingly fast, other times gently, as if he was starting to get the hang of it. He leaned again to curve around, stretching the wings out and soaring slowly, and then, narrowly missing his friends, he neared the ground, folded in his wings, and crash-landed a third time.

After he rolled to a stop, he looked at Alex. "Well, they work. I'm not so sure I'm the right person to have wings, but I imagine with a little practice, the water dragons will pick up the necessary skills better than I did."

"Not to mention," said Lani, "they'll likely land in the water, which is a bit softer than the ground." She reached out and helped Samheed to his feet, then planted a kiss on his cheek. "I'm glad you're not hurt."

"Had enough?" asked Alex.

"Definitely," said Samheed. "Get these things off me."

He turned around, and Alex released the meld spell that held the wings to Samheed's back. With a squeak and a whoosh, the wings' suction released, and Alex and Lani each pulled one off.

"Aaron really did a good job with these, you know," Lani said.

"Yes. He's surprisingly good at a lot of things," added Samheed generously. "He's all right."

Alex nodded. It was true, and he was genuinely proud of

LISA McMANN

Aaron, even if his natural ability was annoying at times. Alex was going to miss him. As the three friends walked back to the mansion and the regular activities on the lawn resumed, he grew melancholy. The wings were ready. "I guess Aaron and I will leave in the morning, then," he said. "We'll stop at the Island of Dragons to attach the wings, and then I'll deliver him to the Island of Shipwrecks."

Samheed didn't say anything, but Lani placed her hand on Alex's shoulder as they walked inside the mansion together, each of them with a dragon wing tucked under one arm. "It's probably for the best," Lani said. "It seems like he was really happy there."

Alex nodded. "I know," he said, feeling almost miserable about it. He and Lani put the wings in Ms. Octavia's classroom, and then Alex went to the kitchen to find Aaron and tell him he could finally go home.

When he walked into the bustling kitchen unnoticed, Alex observed the food designers discussing and admiring their beautiful presentations. He found his sisters and Crow by the tube delivering food and his brother wearing an apron and chef's hat, knife poised as he listened carefully to what the head chef of Artimé was explaining.

Alex watched as Aaron painstakingly perfected a recipe, and then he gazed at his sisters, absorbed in their task of placing the beautiful food creations into the delivery tube. It was a rare moment, all four Stowe siblings in the same room. And one that wouldn't happen again once Aaron was gone.

Alex felt a certain heaviness descend upon his shoulders and a loneliness rise to his throat, and instead of embracing the familial moment, he turned away, overwhelmed by it. With his head bowed, he stumbled past the dining room to the entry-way, past Simber and up the stairs to the once secret hallway, past the doorways to the last one on the left, where he went in. He sat down at his desk and lowered his head, resting it on his folded arms.

A few moments later, he got up, sent a message to Aaron's blackboard telling him they would leave the next day, and entered his private quarters to pack.

Warning Signs and Secret Good-byes

Early the next morning Alex found Simber in his usual spot by the front door to the mansion. Alex beckoned to the cheetah to go outside with him and take a walk. The cat followed the mage out the door, and the two strolled together along the shore.

"I had thought you could take Aaron and me to the Island of Dragons and then on to the Island of Shipwrecks," Alex said. "I would have liked that, but Aaron has requested we bring some supplies with us—mainly some fresh soil so he and the scientists can get some plants growing outside now that the storms are gone. I want to give them quite a lot since we have plenty to spare. But I don't think we'll be able to fit all the sacks of soil on your back along with the five pairs of dragon wings. And the two of us, of course."

"It's all rrright," said Simber. "The boat will be morrre comforrrtable forrr you anyway." He paused, sampling the air as he often did, and then gazing in the direction of Warbler Island to the west. "Besides, I'm mildly concerrrned about what's happening overrr therrre."

Alex followed the statue's gaze, but he couldn't see whatever Simber was able to see. "You mean the ships that Pan told us about?"

"Prrrecisely," said Simber. "Therrre's some activity happening that I'm not completely comforrrtable with—ships sailing between the pirrrate island and Warrrbler. It's out of the orrrdinary forrr them, which makes me suspicious."

"Of course it does," said Alex, reaching out and putting his hand on the cheetah's neck. "I wonder if the pirates are selling sea creatures to Warbler. I honestly can't figure it out—who else is there to buy them? Whenever I ask Pan, she gets quiet."

"I don't know," said Simber. "And I don't think Marrrcus knew, eitherrr, orrr I hope he would have told me." Simber

LISA McMANN

didn't sound like he had much faith in that, though. The original head mage of Artimé, Marcus Today, had kept many secrets that went to the grave with him.

Alex shrugged. "At least we freed the sea creatures—some of them, anyway."

Simber frowned. "The pirrrates neverrr came afterrr us. I admit I'm surrrprrrised by that."

"Ah, but they did—they just went to the palace by mistake and retaliated against the wrong guy," Alex reminded him.

"Trrrue," said Simber. "I wonderrr if they'll everrr rrrealize theirrr errror. With theirrr rrrelationship with Queen Eagala on Warrrblerrr, I imagine they will."

Alex shook his head. "Please, Sim. We're finally at peace. Give us a little chance to enjoy it before you go imagining other problems, will you? Besides, they would have attacked by now. It's been months."

The statue growled softly, but he let the conversation die. Soon they reached the edge of the jungle. They turned around and walked back toward the mansion. The lawn was beginning to fill up with residents of Artimé. Mr. Appleblossom held a fencing class there, where he had Kaylee teach some moves since she was well trained in the sport.

Ms. Morning was on the lawn meeting with Lani, who was showing off some new spell components she'd invented. And quite far away, Liam Healy, former governor to the former high priest Aaron and rescuer of Thisbe and Fifer, was standing near the front door of the mansion with Aaron himself. Both appeared to be scanning the lawn in search of someone.

Alex waved, and Aaron waved back. Alex climbed on Simber's back. "They look like they need something," he said.

"Let's go," said Simber. He began to run with Alex holding on around his neck. Soon they reached the mansion and Alex hopped off.

Aaron's face was anxious. "What time are we leaving?" he asked.

"I've decided we'll go around sundown," said Alex. "That way the boat will have us to the Island of Dragons by morning. We'll want to attach the wings during daylight, don't you agree?"

"I—well, yes, I should think," Aaron said, but he sounded

distracted. "Thanks, that's perfect. I was hoping we weren't heading out first thing. . . ." He trailed off, and then dashed back inside the mansion before Alex could say another word.

"What was that about?" Alex asked Liam.

"I d-don't know," said Liam, who often stammered when nervous. "But as I was telling Aaron, I've got the sacks of dirt ready to go. So, um . . . where . . . ?"

"That's great, Liam," Alex said. "Thank you. I'll help you load them on the boat."

While Alex and Liam loaded the *Claire* with hundreds of pounds of soil, Aaron was far away in the deepest part of the jungle, trying to be strong. He'd been here a lot in the past few days, always thinking it would be his last visit, but then finding a way to come back one more time.

Upon his arrival, Panther had come running, her sleek black body shimmering and her muscles rippling. Hanging from her jaws was one of the spiders made of vines that Aaron had constructed. Panther dropped it at Aaron's feet and batted it with her paw.

Aaron grinned and picked it up. "Stay," he said.

She sat obediently and rubbed her whiskers against Aaron's side. Aaron picked up the vine spider and threw it with all his might. Panther's body jerked, but she stayed in place, waiting for her cue.

"Attack!" Aaron shouted.

The panther leaped in the air and charged toward the spider. She slid to a stop on the jungle floor, picked it up and shook it, and then brought it back to Aaron.

"Well done!" Aaron praised.

They played the game for nearly an hour, until Aaron's arm grew tired. He sat down near a pile of vines and began constructing more spiders for Panther—he wanted to have enough for her to play with for a long time. He began piling them up on one side of him, while Panther lounged on the other side, her face pressed against Aaron's thigh and one paw resting possessively on his knee. She closed her eyes.

"I'm going away for a while," Aaron said softly. He reached out and petted Panther between the ears.

Panther turned to look at Aaron, her eyes wide and sad.

Aaron set down the spider he'd been working on. "You'll be okay without me." He frowned, and then he slipped his

LISA McMANN

arms around the panther's neck in an awkward hug.

Panther struggled to get up, and Aaron quickly got up too. He'd been here far too long. He needed to pack his things. "Good-bye," he said. "Tell the rock and the dog that I said good-bye. And I'll . . . I'll see you later. Sometime. Okay?"

Panther screamed in Aaron's face. Aaron gave the beast a long look, and then he swallowed hard and went inside the tube. "Keep your tail on," he said. "I'm not sure if Al . . . if anyone, I mean, knows how to fix those. Not like me, anyway."

Panther wagged her tail, and Aaron stood helplessly watching her. Finally he waved, trying not to break down, and then pressed the button that would take him back to Artimé.

In the kitchenette, Aaron stepped out of the tube, pinched the bridge of his nose, took in a deep breath and let it out, and then entered the hallway. He walked toward the balcony, stopping by Alex's living quarters. The door was open, and things were strewn about the room.

Alex stood at the bed, cramming clothes into a medium-size traveling bag.

"Hey," said Aaron.

Alex looked up. "Oh, hi," he said. "Are you packed?"

"Almost," Aaron said. He looked swiftly away. "I was wondering if you have an extra bag. It seems I've accumulated a few things that I don't want to leave behind, and I can't fit everything into my trunk. Just a small one will do."

"Yeah, sure," said Alex. He went to his closet and pulled out a cloth bag with handles, and handed it to Aaron.

"Thanks," said Aaron, taking it. He hesitated, and then expelled a sharp breath. "Okay, see you in a bit."

"Around sundown," Alex reminded him.

"Got it," said Aaron. "And, uh, don't forget to tell your blackboard that you're leaving this time."

Alex grinned. "Thank you for the reminder. I'll do that. Hey, Clive, you filthy beast, wake up! I'm going away for a few days and . . ."

Aaron stepped away. With his mind full of plans, he slipped down the hallway toward the balcony and headed for his room, never noticing Simber near the mansion's entrance, watching him curiously as he often did.

More Good-byes

At sunset the white boat was fully loaded with soil, wings, personal items, and Charlie the gargoyle, who was stationed in his favorite spot inside the cabin. Aaron looked at the crowd that had gathered to send him off. He was surprised and quite moved by the number of people and creatures who had come to say good-bye. While Alex stood quietly to one side, Aaron accepted hugs from Sky, Lani, and even Samheed, as well as Ms. Morning, Ms. Octavia, Carina, and Sean. When Kaylee stepped over to him, she hugged him for a split second longer than he expected, and then she kissed him lightly on the cheek, making his ears flame. "If you fix the tube," she whispered, "maybe I can see you again."

Aaron became immediately flustered, muttered something unintelligible, and quickly stepped back.

Kaylee grinned and shoved her hands in her pockets. "And Ishibashi, Ito, and Sato, of course," she added.

"Right. Sure," Aaron mumbled. His heart thudded in his chest as if he'd just run full speed across the lawn. He didn't understand his feelings. He only knew that whenever Kaylee whispered in his ear, it gave him a thrill he'd never felt before.

Quickly he turned away from her and bent down to pick up his sisters. He hoisted them up and gazed at each one's face. "Good-bye," he whispered to them, and tears sprang to his eyes. "Perhaps you can come to visit me now and then."

Alex stepped in and put a hand on Aaron's back. "We will," he said. "I'll make sure of it." He looked at the girls. "Can you say good-bye to Aaron?"

"Bye, Ay-on," said Thisbe.

"Bye, Ay-on," echoed Fifer, and then her face crumbled and she began to cry.

"Oh no," said Aaron. He tried to comfort her, but she only cried louder. "There. It's going to be okay." He looked around anxiously.

Crow stepped in and took Fifer, and Sky reached for Thisbe so the brothers could depart.

At last Aaron turned to Liam and shook his hand. "I'm very . . . I'm proud of you. Of us," he said, his voice cracking a bit. "Thank you for what you said that day in the palace . . . that day you asked me if I wished I was Unwanted. I . . . well, I won't ever forget that. And you took a huge risk. You're much braver than you think, Liam."

Liam, dumbstruck, just kept shaking Aaron's hand until the former high priest removed it from his grasp.

Alex looked at Aaron, and Aaron at Alex. "Let's go," they said together in one voice. The group around them tittered, and even Aaron managed to break a smile. With a last look over his shoulder, he caught Kaylee's eye, and the heat rushed to his head again.

The brothers struck out for the boat, and a few minutes later Alex was steering away from Artimé. Aaron stood at the stern, reminded that once upon a time he thought he'd never have another friend after Eva died. But now he watched a myriad of them grow small in the waning light, Fifer's cries taken away by the breeze. It very nearly broke his heart.

A Brother's Love

Alex commanded the white boat to go to the Island of Dragons, and the identical twin brothers began speeding eastward over the waves. Charlie stayed in the cabin, which he preferred over the water view, and the brothers remained in a melancholy silence until they were some distance away from Artimé.

When Aaron could no longer make out any faces in the dark, he sat down heavily in the seat across the aisle from Alex. "That was harder than I expected," he said.

Alex was quiet, nursing a giant lump in his throat as he looked out over the water. He was still trying to grasp it—these were his last few days with Aaron. Things had finally become good between them, and soon it would be over. "I'll bring the girls to see you now and then," he reminded Aaron, as well as himself.

"Thank you," said Aaron fervently. "That makes it easier."

"I can't wait to find out what new spells you discover," said Alex. He wanted to be sure Aaron knew that he was okay with his talent now.

"I don't expect I'll try to do much of anything magical, actually," said Aaron. "I kind of forgot about magic when I was there before. Never had a need for it."

"Oh," said Alex. "Well."

They fell back into silence.

After a while, Alex glanced at Aaron, thinking he might have fallen asleep, but Aaron was staring out over the waves. "What are you thinking about?" Alex asked.

Aaron didn't answer right away, but then he said truthfully, "I'm thinking about Kaylee."

Alex raised an eyebrow. "What about her?"

"She . . . well, she whispered in my ear, for one. It made me feel weird."

"Good weird? Or bad?"

Aaron thought about it. "I'm not sure. Good, I think."

Alex tried to hide the grin on his face. For a former ruler of an entire civilization, and a mage with astounding abilities, Aaron was definitely naive about a few things. But Alex supposed his brother had never had any real friends his age until now, and certainly no romantic relationships. "Hmm," said Alex. "Maybe she likes you."

"She's my friend, I think," said Aaron, though he sounded uncertain.

"Well, yes, I know that," said Alex. "But I mean maybe she, you know, likes you in a different way."

Aaron had a hard time imagining anybody liking him like that. He'd never pictured himself coupled with anyone romantically. In his imagination, he was always and forever alone. "I don't know," he said.

"Don't know what?"

But Aaron didn't know the answer to that question either. He shrugged and shook his head. "I don't want to talk about this. It doesn't matter anyway."

Alex understood the complex thoughts that were probably

going through Aaron's mind. "I get it," he said. He got up and unfolded his seat to make a bed.

Aaron did the same, and the two grabbed blankets and lay down under the stars.

The next morning Alex woke to a familiar sight: the cylindrical island jutting up in front of them. The boat was idling, slowly circling the island. Alex got up and started looking for Pan. Knowing she was probably hiding, Alex hoped they wouldn't have to wait long before she noticed them.

"Pan?" he called out a bit uncertainly. His voice woke Aaron, who sat up and looked slowly up the immense wall of rock before him. Charlie opened the door and peeked through the crack to see what was happening.

"How are we supposed to get up there?" Aaron asked.

"Pan will help us," said Alex. "I hope she's here."

It didn't take long before Pan's oversized head appeared above them, and soon she was climbing down the wall in her awkward way, using her tail as a rope and sinking her claws into the stone, dropping down one length at a time. When she

189 « Island of Dragons

neared the boat, she stopped and clung to the wall, looking all around warily.

"Do not call my name aloud again," she said in a low voice. "You're too trusting. You know the pirates are on the move."

Charlie quickly closed the door to the cabin, hiding inside.

"I'm sorry," Alex whispered. "I didn't think they had come all the way out here."

"They haven't—not yet, anyway," said Pan. "But we cannot be too cautious. Eventually they will notice that the storm is gone from the Island of Shipwrecks if they haven't already, and that will anger them as well. We must be very careful not to give them a reason to come this way."

Alex and Aaron nodded, Aaron's eyes wide with dread at the thought of the pirates making a stop at his future home. He hadn't thought about that—without the hurricane, anyone could approach the island and attack the scientists. It made Aaron even more eager to get there and check on them.

Pan continued to look all around, and when she was satisfied they were not being watched, she peered at the wings lying in the boat. Her face changed abruptly. "How beautiful," she crooned. She looked at Alex and Aaron with tears in her eyes. "You have matched my children perfectly. I could not have imagined it."

"I hope they work," Alex said.

Pan's eyes clouded. "As do I," she said.

"Let's give them a try. Which dragon shall we work with first?"

"Arabis the orange is the most mature," said Pan. "She will sit quietly while you work on her."

"Then we'll work on Arabis first," said Alex.

Aaron picked up a wing for the orange dragon and handed it to Alex, then went back for the second one. He gave a dubious look at the ruler of the sea, afraid to ask where they had to go, exactly, to find the orange dragon.

Pan gripped the side of the cylindrical island and dropped her tail, letting it slither around the boys. "We must hurry so no one notices your boat," she said.

Alex frowned, thinking Pan was acting a bit paranoid. "We'll go as fast as we can, but we want to get it right."

"Of course," said Pan. With her tail tightly wound around the boys' chests, she lifted them out of the boat.

Aaron clung to the wing and looked around anxiously as he

began to rise in the air next to Alex. "This is quite frightening, isn't it?" he whispered.

"A bit," Alex agreed. "But she won't let go of us."

"Let's hope not," said Aaron.

Pan climbed up the wall, her body moving jerkily but her tail remaining quite calm as she went. Soon she reached the top and swung the boys over and down into the core of the island.

In daylight, the dragons were much easier to spot in the shallow water. Aaron looked as if he were about to faint. He began to tremble and sweat profusely.

"They won't hurt us," Alex said. "I promise. Aren't they beautiful?"

Aaron had to admit they were, but his fear reminded him of the day he met Panther. A pang of guilt mingled with the fear. He still needed to tell Alex about the jungle animals.

Pan called to Arabis, the orange dragon, in a strange language. "They are learning to communicate in your language," said Pan. "But for safety we speak the language of the dragons." She continued to speak to Arabis the orange, coaxing her to climb up and sit on a rock ledge out of the water. Pan lowered the boys down next to her, and Arabis turned her attention to Aaron, sniffing him.

"Oh my," Aaron said, beyond uncomfortable. "Hi there." He shrank back and pressed against the wall, holding the wing in front of him like a shield. He gave himself a silent pep talk to build his confidence, knowing the dragon, like Panther, could probably sense his fear.

"Hold out your fist, like this," said Alex, showing him how to greet the dragons.

"Why?"

"So they can smell you and determine if you are more good than evil."

Aaron's face went gray. "You're joking."

"No," said Alex.

"What if . . . what if I'm . . . not?"

Alex shrugged. "You are."

"How do you know?"

Alex gave his brother a sympathetic look. "Just do it."

Aaron did it, trying not to shake. His eyes closed and he held his breath. Sweat beaded on his forehead.

Arabis sniffed Aaron's fist. Then she sniffed again, lingering over him for several moments as if trying to decide. Eventually she seemed satisfied with him and moved her head over to Alex to do the same thing. Alex greeted her.

Aaron opened one eye. "Is she done?" he whispered.

"You passed," said Alex. "Congratulations. You are more good than evil."

Aaron let out a deep breath. "I was worried."

One of the other young dragons blew a small blast of fire into the air nearby, making both boys jump.

Pan nodded at Alex. "She's ready."

Alex took a deep breath to calm his nerves. He plucked a meld component from his pocket and lifted the base of the first wing in the air. He pressed the wing against the dragon's back, moving it around, trying to find the exact best angle to secure it. Once he felt confident the wing was placed correctly, he applied the meld spell and watched as the base of the wing melded into the dragon's back, and the wing magically took on the exact sheen of the dragon's body. Alex stepped back and looked carefully at it from all directions, as Arabis turned her head curiously to see what had been attached to her.

Aaron handed Alex the second wing, and Alex did the same

with it on the other side of the dragon's back. Once attached, it also took on the magic sheen of the dragon's body. "Okay, Aaron," said Alex. "Can you bring them to life?"

Aaron nodded and gingerly stepped toward Arabis. The orange dragon's spiny back rippled as she tried to get used to the new appendages, and she shifted uncomfortably. Aaron put his hand out and touched the dragon's side. "Don't be afraid," Aaron whispered, partly to remind himself to calm down.

The dragon turned her face so she could see Aaron, and the two gazes connected. Arabis's trembling stopped, and Aaron smiled at the beast. "I'm going to make your new wings feel better," he said. He didn't know if the dragon could understand him, but she bowed her head as if she did.

After a moment, Aaron touched her right wing and concentrated on it, thinking about bringing it to life. "Live," he said softly.

The wing shimmered and began to move of its own accord. Aaron gently guided the wing into its folded position while Arabis craned her neck to see what was happening. Then Aaron moved around to her other side and did the same with the left.

LISA McMANN

Pan watched from a short distance away, her eyes shining.

When Aaron looked up, he said, "You'll want to give them some lessons before they are suited to fly long distances. We tested the wings at home and discovered that the wearer must command the wings to go to a certain place or to fly in a certain direction. And they must concentrate and think about flying."

"I will teach them the requirements," said Pan.

Alex looked up. "I've made the wings a little larger than necessary to accommodate small amounts of growth. Unfortunately, because the wings are magical and not real appendages, I was unable to give them the ability to grow along with the dragons. But you had mentioned that the young dragons would remain this size for about ten years before they begin to grow rapidly, so these wings should be sufficient to last them until then."

"It is long enough," said Pan humbly. "Thank you."

Alex bowed. "If you are able to bring the dragons back to me in Artimé when they've begun their growth spurt, we will happily make new wings to suit their larger size."

Pan bowed in return. "We shall never forget your kindness. Both of you."

Aaron cleared his throat. "We should probably finish the

job before you thank us," he said. "Which one is next?"

"Yarbeck, the purple and gold," said Pan. "And then Ivis, the green. Then we'll do the males, Hux and Drock, after the females are done. I'll help you bring the rest of the wings."

While Arabis the orange experimented with moving her wings, Pan wrapped her tail around the boys and went back to the boat, returning a short time later with the other four sets. Over the course of the morning, all five young dragons received their magical appendages, and Alex and Aaron finished up their work getting only a tiny bit singed by Drock, the dark purple dragon, who seemed the most temperamental of the entire cylinder of dragons.

The dragons were clever, and soon Arabis and Yarbeck were managing to take short, awkward flights around the inside of the island. Pan left them to their antics. She brought Alex and Aaron back outside of the island and delivered them to their boat.

As she set them gently into the *Claire* and thanked them once more, Charlie exited the cabin and began signing to Alex.

Alex concentrated, trying to decipher Charlie's sign language. "What is it?" he said. "Is something wrong? Slow down a bit, will you?"

Charlie began again, slower this time, and Alex followed along, mumbling a word or two under his breath. And then he relaxed a bit.

"What is it?" asked Aaron.

Pan's eyes blazed with concern. "What's happened?"

Alex put his hand in the air to reassure the dragon. "I don't think there's cause to worry," he said. "A visitor has arrived on the shores of Artimé."

Surprising News

What sort of visitor?" demanded Pan.

Charlie signed again.

When he finished, Alex looked up. "The unconscious sort," he said. "This isn't the first time it's happened. Charlie says the folks at home are certain she's an escapee from Warbler. She's wearing rags and a thorn necklace, just like Sky and Crow were when they arrived on a raft."

"I see," said Pan, settling down. "Is she expected to survive?"

"I hope so," said Alex. "Claire and Carina are working on her."

Pan blinked slowly. "I wish her the best. Perhaps she can shed some light on the recent activities on Warbler."

LISA McMANN

"We'll pass that on," said Alex. He turned to Charlie. "Did you get that?"

Charlie nodded.

Alex glanced at Aaron. "Ready?"

"Ready," said Aaron. His stomach fluttered with excitement. He lifted a hand in farewell to Pan.

"Thank you," Pan said to them. "You'll never know the depth of my gratitude."

"We're glad we could help," said Aaron.

Alex smiled at the dragon. "I'll stop back to see you on my way home in case there's news," he said. And with that, the brothers were on their way to the Island of Shipwrecks.

The rest of the journey was uneventful. Alex was tired and fell asleep early, and Aaron stared out over the water in front of them, fretting about Panther and the jungle. Finally he decided he'd confess right before Alex left the Island of Shipwrecks. That way Aaron wouldn't have to witness Alex's disappointment for long.

With his mind finally settled, Aaron slept. They passed the Island of Graves without incident, and by morning they awoke to the sight of shipwrecks.

Aaron jumped to his feet and combed his hair with his fingers. Alex offered him breakfast, but Aaron was too nervous to eat. He strained to see if there was any movement on the island. Were the scientists still alive and healthy?

His fears were soon assuaged when he saw them emerge from behind the rocks, moving swiftly toward the shore to greet them.

Aaron sighed with relief and bounced on his toes, leaning forward over the bow, as Ishibashi lifted a hand to his eyes to shield the sun.

Alex shoved his hands in his pockets and glared at the water, trying to swallow the lump in his throat, and let the boat steer itself carefully around the wrecks and rocks near the shore. Soon they were within spitting distance, floating close enough to walk across a handful of rocks to the island. Before the boat stopped, Aaron hopped out and rushed across the rocky path toward the scientists. He caught the old men in a giant group embrace, almost knocking them down.

Alex lagged behind on the boat, heaving two sacks of the dirt they'd transported and bringing them onto the shore, then going back for more. He wanted to give Aaron a moment

LISA McMANN

to catch up. He also selfishly wanted Aaron to feel sad about leaving him, but that didn't seem to be happening. Alex was miserable, and Aaron seemed actually . . . joyful.

Soon Ito broke away and rushed across the rocks to Alex's side. He grabbed the last sack of dirt, flung it over his shoulder and carried it to the pile, then pulled Alex by the arm to the others, talking excitedly in his native language. Alex smiled reluctantly and joined them.

"We are glad to see you both alive and well," Ishibashi said. "We've been worried these past months. He turned to Aaron. "And how is your applecorn?"

Aaron laughed. "It's intact," he said.

Alex looked puzzled, but no one explained.

"Are you here to visit? Or to stay?" asked Ishibashi.

"My job in Artimé is done, and I'm here to stay," said Aaron. "If you'll let me."

Ishibashi's grin grew wide. He turned to Ito and Sato and translated the news. The two older men clasped their hands together, expressing their happiness.

"And Alex-san?"

"Oh," said Alex, "I've got to go home."

"Will you stay for tea?" Ishibashi asked.

Alex didn't know how long he wanted to extend the agony. But it wouldn't be polite to say no. "Sure, I'd love that," he said. "Thank you."

Ishibashi spoke to Ito and Sato again, and soon the two hurried off toward the shelter.

Alex, Aaron, and Ishibashi remained on the shore, and while Aaron and Ishibashi talked excitedly, Alex looked on, feeling a bit lost. He watched his brother become alive and animated—a rare sight—and he knew Aaron was in the right place here. But it didn't make Alex feel much better.

Alex's sight blurred. "You forgot your bag," he said, turning abruptly. He crossed the rocks to the white boat, taking a few deep breaths to steady himself. It would be a lonely ride home, just him and Charlie.

Alex climbed into the boat and picked up Aaron's trunk and bag of belongings. They weren't heavy—Aaron hadn't acquired much in his time away from the Island of Shipwrecks. Alex carried them ashore and dropped them at Aaron's feet.

Aaron looked up. "Thank you," he said, sounding a bit guilty. "You didn't have to do that."

LISA McMANN

Alex waved him off, not trusting his voice. He attempted a smile, which came out a bit crooked.

Ishibashi put his hand on Alex's arm. "Thank you for bringing Aaron home to us. Perhaps we can convince you to stay the night?"

Alex shook his head. "No, thank you, Ishibashi-san. I've got to get back to Artimé and check on Henry. He's been out saving the giant crab island's life . . . somehow."

Ishibashi looked confused for a moment, but then his face cleared. "Ah, I see," he said knowingly. Then his eyes grew troubled. He looked from one boy to the other, but he remained silent.

Alex couldn't bear to look at Aaron. "Actually," he said abruptly, "I should probably skip tea and head out. I'm . . . I'm sorry for the trouble."

Ishibashi smiled sympathetically. "Tea is never trouble. But I understand."

Alex's face crumbled. He had to get out of there. Finally he looked at his brother. "Good-bye," he said.

Aaron reached out his arms and embraced Alex for a long moment. "I'll see you again soon." He patted Alex on the back, a bit harder than he intended, for he hadn't yet perfected the sort of touch one gives when one is going to miss someone. And then he remembered the jungle.

Aaron closed his eyes for a moment and sighed. "Before you go, there's something you should know," he said. He opened his eyes and looked out over Alex's shoulder at the white boat, where Charlie was waving and jumping up and down on one of the seat cushions. Aaron frowned and released Alex. "Oh my," he said. "Look. Charlie's waving, and I don't think he's just saying good-bye."

Alex turned quickly and squinted at the gargoyle, whose waving now turned to hand signals.

Aaron looked from Alex's face to Charlie's, and back again.

Alex strained to make out what Charlie was saying. After a minute, his hand rose to his chest. He clutched his robe and swore under his breath. Charlie finished signing and stood there in the boat, shoulders slumped.

"What is it?" asked Aaron anxiously. "What's happened?"

Alex turned to Aaron and Ishibashi. "I've got awful news," he said with agonizing slowness. "It appears Artimé is about to be obliterated."

LISA McMANN

Ishibashi's Secret

What?" cried Aaron. "Obliterated? By whom? Certainly not Quill. Not after everything you've done for them."

"No, it's not Quill this time," said Alex. "There's not a lot of information yet. The escapee from Warbler regained consciousness for a few moments—long enough to give a warning before collapsing again. She said that Queen Eagala and the pirates have been plotting the demise of Artimé for some time. And they are only days away from an attack." Alex turned back to Charlie. "Is there anything else?" he called.

Charlie shook his head. There was nothing else to tell.

"I have to go now," Alex said. "They need . . . me." He stared at Aaron, fear in his eyes.

Aaron searched his brother's face, and his heart fell into his stomach. He dropped his gaze and swallowed, then glanced at Ishibashi with a pleading look.

Ishibashi looked down.

Aaron let out a breath, cringed, and finally turned to Alex again. He shook his head, resigned. Then he bent down and grabbed his bag. "Come on," he said. "I'll go with you."

Alex's eyes flickered. "You don't have to do that."

"It's okay," Aaron said, lifting his chin stoically. "Let's go back to Artimé. Quickly now! We need time to prepare. Besides," he admitted, "I wouldn't be any good sitting here worrying. I'll be there with you through it all. You can take me back here after we win the battle."

Alex could only stare at his brother. There was no way for him to express how deeply he appreciated Aaron's willingness to sacrifice all plans to go back and help Artimé once more. "Thank you," he murmured.

Aaron turned to Ishibashi. "I'm sorry. I hope you understand why I have to go back."

LISA McMANN

The old man nodded, but his face was awash in agony. He was acting very strange.

Alex noticed the look on Ishibashi and regarded him with growing concern. "What's wrong, Ishibashi-san?"

Ishibashi gulped, then clung to Aaron's shirtsleeve, a battle raging behind his eyes.

Aaron became alarmed. "Is something the matter? Are you ill?"

The scientist shook his head. "I am ill with guilt," he whispered.

"What?" asked Alex.

Ishibashi let go of Aaron and covered his face for a moment. Then he looked up. "There is something I must confess to you before you go, Aaron. Something that may be crucial to you in battle."

The boys stared. "What is it?" Aaron asked.

"The medicine that Henry has for the giant crab—I know what it is. I gave it to him."

Alex shifted impatiently.

"Yes, and?" prompted Aaron.

"It's a magical seaweed that will allow Karkinos to live many years . . . perhaps even forever."

"That's great," said Alex. "But we really need to go. . . ."

"Shh," said Aaron, touching Alex's arm. He narrowed his eyes at Ishibashi. "Go on."

Ishibashi's look turned helpless. "I told Henry that whenever one uses that medicine on a human, he must have their full understanding and permission to do so."

"That makes sense," said Aaron.

Ishibashi nodded sorrowfully. "But I did not heed my own instructions."

Both boys were still now. Staring at the little man.

"When you landed on our shores, Aaron, I thought you were our new friend Alex. You were so near death—there was nothing we could do to save you . . . except for one thing."

Aaron's bag dropped to the sand with a thud. "What are you saying?" he said harshly.

Alex's stare moved from Ishibashi to Aaron as the truth came to him. "You gave him that?" he whispered. "So he's . . ."

Ishibashi nodded, and a tear slipped down his cheek.

"Unbeknownst to Aaron, and without his permission, I gave him the seaweed. And now he is like Ito, Sato, and me. Immortal."

Ishibashi faced Aaron. "I am very sorry I didn't tell you this news before. I was afraid to. But you deserve to know the truth."

Aaron just looked at him. "Immortal?" he breathed.

Ishibashi nodded. "Obviously we are not fully sure that we, and you, will live forever, because forever hasn't come to pass. So there is no way to test the theory. But from our best scientific deductions to date, we're quite certain. You won't die, Aaron."

The brothers were dazed, too blown away by this news to say anything.

Ishibashi touched their shoulders and spoke gently. "And now you must go. Take this news and ponder it. If you are angry, I am the one to blame."

Aaron put his hand to his head as if to stop it from spinning.

Alex recovered from the shock and gave Ishibashi a meaningful look. "Thank you for telling us," he said. "We'll talk it through on the ride home."

"Please tell no one, not even your friends, for we don't want word of the seaweed to get into the wrong hands. It could be very dangerous if that happens. The fewer people who know of it, the better." Ishibashi gripped Aaron's shoulder. "Are you all right?"

Aaron nodded dumbly. He reached out for the man and embraced him. "I'm okay," he said. He released the scientist and picked up his bag again.

"We will talk more when you return," said Ishibashi. He whisked away a tear. "If you are not too angry to return, that is."

Aaron just shook his head. "I don't feel anything right now," he said. "But this island is where I belong. This news doesn't change that. I don't think so, anyway." He nodded at Alex. "Let's go."

Alex hugged Ishibashi. "Thank you," he whispered to the scientist, though he wasn't sure why. Perhaps because it was he who Ishibashi initially intended to save.

Alex picked up Aaron's trunk and followed him to the white boat, both minds whirring. Ishibashi Junpei remained on the shore, wondering if he'd ever see them again.

Aaron Immortal

Can you believe it?" Alex asked Aaron once the boat was weaving through the rocks and on the way.

Aaron shook his head. He sat at the stern, watching Ishibashi grow small as the white boat flew across the waves at top speed. When the scientist was gone from sight, Aaron dropped his head in his hands.

Alex stayed in the captain's seat. He checked in with Charlie to see if there was anything more he could learn about the impending battle, but there was nothing new. "Has Florence returned?" he asked.

Charlie stood still a moment, then shook his head.

Alex frowned. "Okay. Thanks. You can go."

The head mage mulled over the battle predicament. He felt lost without Florence, and hoped Artimé was dealing with the news all right. He sighed, feeling helpless, and glanced over his shoulder at Aaron.

"Are you okay?" Alex asked gently. "Do you want to talk about it?"

Aaron looked up. His face was wan. "I wish I'd asked Ishibashi what exactly this means."

"Yes, me too," said Alex. "I'm not so sure he knows. I think he'd have told you more if he knew specifics. But it's all making sense now, isn't it? The fact that they are so old, and still so strong. And Henry being secretive about his medicine, but so sure it would work to heal Karkinos. Henry did great keeping their secret, that's for sure." He recalled the time Henry had asked him the hypothetical question about whether he'd want to live forever. Now he knew where that conversation had stemmed from.

Aaron shook his head, still overwhelmed. "But what if I don't want to be immortal?" The vastness of that prospect was something he couldn't digest. "Does it mean that if someone

LISA McMANN

were to hit me with three heart attack spells, I wouldn't die? Or run me through with a sword? Or chop my head off? Even then?"

"I don't know," said Alex. "I doubt Ishibashi knows, either, unless they've tried killing each other to test it out. But somehow I doubt they'd do that."

"What happens if I get a non-life-threatening injury?"

Alex smiled grimly. "I don't know. I can punch you in the face if you'd like. See what happens."

Aaron laughed. "I'll think about it," he said. He leaned his head back on the seat and ran his fingers through his hair. "Ugh," he groaned. "This is so weird."

They fell back into silence. As the day became night, Alex's mind returned to the more urgent matter: the pending attack and the unsettling word that the Warbler escapee had used. "Obliteration." What would they find when they reached home?

Alex urged the white boat to go faster, and he stayed near the controls late into the night as they sped past the Island of Graves.

Aaron dozed, and soon Alex was nodding off too. After a

time he got up, arranged the seat into a bed, and lay down, knowing he needed rest. But his nightmares were filled with frightening attacks on Artimé, and they ended with him being stabbed through the heart when he was just out of reach of Ishibashi, who was holding magical seaweed. In the dream, as Alex died, he saw Artimé's mansion and all of its vibrant color disappear before his eyes, leaving only a gray shack and a throng of angry, starving Unwanteds turning on each other, with enemies taking over the island.

The sun was bright overhead when Alex awoke. Aaron was shaking him.

"Hey!" said Aaron. "Wake up. You might want to slow down the boat. Pan's been chasing us for the past few minutes."

It took Alex a moment to process the strange request, but then he sat up and immediately commanded the boat to stop. He looked around, disoriented until he caught sight of the cylindrical island and Pan gliding up beside them in the water.

Pan swung her head to look at the boys as the waves splashed up against the side of the boat. "Have you any news?"

she asked. "Why is Aaron with you? Has something happened to the scientists?"

Alex had forgotten his promise to stop on his way back. "I'm so glad you saw us," he said. He explained what had happened with the escapee from Warbler and the coming attack, and told her that Aaron had returned with him to help fight.

Pan listened intently. Occasional angry bursts of smoke shot from her nostrils, making Alex and Aaron shrink back. She remained silent until Alex had finished speaking, then moved swiftly to the cylindrical island and climbed its wall halfway. She trained her gaze to the west. "I see no sign of movement yet," she said. "So you will beat them to Artimé. Perhaps that gives you some comfort."

"A little," said Alex. "I don't suppose you see Florence, Henry, and Spike returning by any chance, do you? I'm feeling nervous without Florence to lead us to battle."

"I'm sorry—I don't see them," said Pan. She climbed back down the side of the island and glided over to the boat. "Perhaps now is a good time for me to return the great favor I owe you. What can I do to help?"

Frantic
Preparations

A lex pressed his fingers to his temples, trying to organize his thoughts so he could utilize Pan's offer in the best possible way. "We desperately need Florence," he reiterated, thinking aloud. "And Henry for healing. And Spike . . ." He looked up at Pan. "Can you go to the Island of Legends as soon as possible? Let Henry, Spike, and Florence know that we need them home immediately if it's safe to leave Karkinos."

"Of course," said Pan. "I need a short time to prepare the children for my absence, but I'll arrive at the Island of Legends by late tonight."

LISA McMANN

"Thank you," said Alex. "That's a tremendous help."

"It's the least I can do." Immediately Pan began fishing with her tail as she'd done in the past, and soon she was launching large fish into the air so they'd land inside the island. "Safe travels, and take care," she said. "I'll see you upon my return." She flung another bunch.

Alex held his hand up. "Good-bye for now. Let me know if you have any trouble with the wings."

"Think no more about that," said Pan. "Luck be with you. You'll need it."

Alex nodded, his heart heavy knowing she was right. He started up the boat and turned to Charlie. "Let Claire know that we've made it to the Island of Dragons and should be home sometime after dark tonight. Tell her Pan is heading out shortly to the Island of Legends to alert Florence, Henry, and Spike."

Charlie nodded and went back into the cabin.

Alex directed the boat to go home, and soon the brothers were speeding over the waves.

With the boat magically piloting itself, Alex sat down heavily and put his face in his hands. "This is really happening," he whispered. His nightmare and the discussion with Pan had brought with it a sense of real doom and an intense fear of the unknown. What were they in for? If only Alex could have a glimpse of the future so he'd better know what to do. But there was no magic spell for that.

Aaron, who was rummaging around in the supplies, pulled out two lunches and brought one over to Alex.

Alex took it and sighed, feeling defeated. "I don't know what to do," he said.

"Try eating it," said Aaron.

"Not with the lunch. With the—wait. Was that another joke?"

Aaron shrugged and bit into the crust of a bulging savory pie.

"You're feeling better then, I take it," Alex said. He watched Aaron stuff his face, and then began eating too. He discovered he was ravenous, as he hadn't had much of an appetite for dinner after they'd left the Island of Shipwrecks. As the boys ate their lunches, they sank back into their individual thoughts: Alex devastated by the news of the coming attack and trying to sort out a plan from a jumbled mess of ideas, and Aaron feeling mixed about his immortality, combined with having to turn back to Artimé after he'd been so ready to go to his new home. Aaron's thoughts had taken him to consider the battle against Gondoleery, for he'd been immortal then, only he hadn't known it.

"If you think about it," Aaron said out of the blue, pausing before taking a bite, "it makes sense. The immortality, I mean. I got hit pretty hard in the battle with Gondoleery. I'd wondered about that—and I was really surprised I hadn't gotten knocked out or killed. I mean, look what her fireballs did to you."

Alex glared. "I was fine after a while."

Aaron raised an eyebrow. "Okay, if you say so. From my perspective you looked like a bonfire, but what do I know? I was only conscious *the entire time*."

Alex frowned and looked away.

"You're right, though," Aaron allowed after a minute. "You did pick yourself up pretty well."

Alex rolled his eyes and finished his meal. He folded his plate until it disappeared. "So you think the seaweed kept you from getting killed by Gondoleery?"

"She hit me dead-on with a fireball at close range," Aaron said, all traces of sarcasm now gone from his voice. "It stunned me, but I got up all right. Everybody else was getting killed or knocked out. I thought I just got lucky, like maybe her aim was bad that one time. But the seaweed explains it, don't you think?"

Alex shrugged and shook his head in wonder. "I guess it does," he said, looking up and catching his brother's gaze. "All I can say is that I'm glad. It'll make me worry less about you in this upcoming battle, that's for sure." He frowned and didn't say what else was going through his mind . . . that Aaron would also be doing some worrying. Now knowing the pirates were involved, Alex was certain they'd be coming for him— and they'd be extra vigilant in getting the right twin this time.

But Alex had so much more to consider than just his own life. There was Artimé, too.

Once they'd both finished eating, Alex sat up straight, pulled out his notebook and produced a pencil, and began to scribble down all the strategic ideas he could think of. He drew maps and made a list of his strongest fighters. He wished again for Florence, but knew he might have to do this without her, and it scared him to death.

When he ran out of ideas, he called on Charlie to communicate with Lani so he could run some plans by her. And every now and then he'd ask Lani's and Aaron's advice on something.

"This is crazy," Alex said at one point to both Charlie and Aaron, "but what do you think of our fighters meeting the enemies halfway? Battling it out at sea?"

Charlie soon relayed Lani's response, and Alex translated it so Aaron could hear. "Lani says, 'Nice idea against the Warblerans who can't swim, but maybe not the pirates since that's how they usually fight.' Hmm."

Aaron nodded. "Plus, we only have one ship. They have dozens, don't they?"

"Yes," said Alex. "Good point. Nix that." After a while he started scribbling again, and Aaron, feeling restless and unsettled, began to pace. Charlie sat down on the deck, but it wasn't long before he took on a slightly green tinge and held his stomach. When it seemed clear that Alex was done with him for the time being, he went back into the cabin to lie down.

Throughout the afternoon and evening the brothers strategized and mulled over ideas, sometimes bringing in Simber or Lani or Sky or Claire through Matilda and Charlie's telepathic connection. Alex knew that Artimé could put up a good fight. But the pirates were a different sort of enemy—they were trained fighters. It's what they did. Could Artimé withstand it? Especially now, with their ranks thinned from all the previous battles?

And what if Alex were captured and killed in the midst of battle? Artimé would disappear, and with it went the magic. It would put Artimé in terrible trouble. Even with Claire or Lani prepared to take over for him as mage, it would take time to bring the world back in order for the fighters' magic to be restored. First they'd have to get to the shack, grab a robe, stand on the back step without getting attacked . . . It was no easy spell, and it took a ton of concentration. Being without magic would leave all of Artimé helpless to defend themselves for however long it took to restore it. Possibly enough time to get them all killed.

It was during one lull in the strategic planning that the most incredibly ridiculous, yet totally brilliant idea came into Alex's head. And it wouldn't leave. He tried pushing it aside, but the more he thought about it, the more sense it made. He looked long and hard at Aaron, seeming to almost stare right through him as thoughts rushed around inside his head. He cringed. It made sense.

"Why in Quill are you staring and making faces at me like that?" asked Aaron. "It's unsettling."

Alex blinked. "What?"

"You're staring at me like you want to . . . I don't know . . . kill me or something." He nearly laughed at the irony, but Alex seemed stressed, and he didn't want to make light of such a serious situation.

"Sorry," said Alex. "It's just that . . ." He trailed off, thinking some more. "It's just that I have this idea. And . . ." His brows furrowed. "And I think you . . . can help me."

"Sure," said Aaron. "What is it? I'll do whatever I can."

Alex gave him another hard look. "Can I trust you? Completely, I mean. Fully, one hundred percent, no fears, no worries—"

Aaron sighed impatiently. "If you don't already, then I doubt you ever will," he said. "I can say yes all day but I can't change your mind."

"You're right, you're right," muttered Alex. "And I do. I just . . . this is going to sound strange. And likely insane."

Aaron watched Alex with growing interest. "Well? Go ahead and say it."

Alex studied Aaron's face a moment longer, and then he said, "I want you to be the head mage of Artimé."

A Secret Arrangement

Aaron stared at Alex. He sat up, opened his mouth, closed it again, and stared some more. "Have you lost your mind?" he asked presently.

"Seems so," muttered Alex. He paced to the bow of the boat and stood there for a moment, staring toward Artimé. A moment later he returned to Aaron's side. "No, I haven't. It's an excellent plan. Temporarily, I mean, of course, unless I die that is, and then it would clearly be for longer, I suppose. Hmm. Plus—and this is beside the fact—I think you'd be great at it."

"Perhaps you'd like to explain."

Alex nodded. "It's easy, really. You're immortal. If you're the mage of Artimé and you can't die, then Artimé will never disappear again like it did when you—" He stopped abruptly. "When you killed Mr. Today." He grimaced, and for an instant he thought he truly must have lost his mind to offer the head mage position to the person who had killed the very man who had created the magical world.

Aaron stared. He shook his head.

"Plus, to be honest, you're a stronger mage than I am, so you'd do well in the position in case you'd need to take it on long term."

"Wait. Stop." Aaron put up his hand to argue, but Alex waved him down.

"No, I'm serious," Alex said. "I've known it for a while—I just didn't like it all that much. But it's true. You're better at magic than most of us. *All* of us, maybe. And you have leadership skills—just look at how you handle the people of Quill."

"You're being ridiculous," said Aaron. But his eyes flickered, and his mind began to whir.

"No," said Alex, "I'm being unselfish for the sake of Artimé. Picture it: If the pirates kill me, Artimé will disappear until Lani or Claire has a chance to get to the shack, stand on the step with a robe . . ." He shook his head. "That spell is quite complicated, and if we're in the midst of battle, no one's magic will work until the world is brought back. And I doubt the pirates are going to sit idly by, waiting for Lani or Claire to do all the rigmarole, 'repeat times three,' et cetera, and for the magic to start working again. Anyone doing such an obvious thing will be tackled too, in an instant. And then what? Artimé will be defenseless if the mages keep dying. And it's not just Artimé now—it's all of Quill, too, that will disappear, leaving the Wanteds and Necessaries with no place to hide."

"Why not just appoint Claire or Lani now? So they don't have to restore the world?"

"The same thing will happen if they die fighting. That's why it's got to be you, don't you see?"

"Hide them away, then."

"No way. They're both way too strong, and both team leaders. I can't spare either one. We're going to need everyone fighting who is willing to fight." He knit his brow. "Plus, Artimé doesn't hide."

Aaron sat dumbfounded. He turned and looked back over

the water, thinking. It all made sense. But him, the head mage of Artimé? Even temporarily, what sort of uproar would that cause? He turned abruptly to look at Alex. "It won't work. No one will allow it. You know that well enough. Simber, Claire, Carina, Samheed—they'd throw me over the waterfall before they'd let me wear a robe in Artimé."

Alex grew troubled. "True," he said. He thought for a long moment. "But remember what Ishibashi said? He said not to tell anyone about the immortality. We don't want the news of the power of the seaweed to get into the wrong hands. We need to keep this information between us—at least for now. Since we can't explain why we're doing this, we won't actually tell anyone. We'll make the transition a secret."

"A secret?"

"Yes. And if I don't die, I'll just take the position of head mage back again after we win the battle, and no one will ever know. But in case I do, Artimé won't disappear. I'll appoint you tonight—I'll give you a robe and everything, just in case. Keep it with you, but don't wear it unless you hear of my death."

A myriad of emotions filled Aaron—more than he'd ever

let himself feel before. Anger and fear came out first. "You're not going to die," he said. "Stop talking like that!"

"Aaron, please. I've been in enough battles to know people die—even the ones you wouldn't expect to. As the leader of Artimé, I have to be practical. Don't you see?" He gripped Aaron's shoulder. "Say you'll do this. I need you to. For Artimé."

Aaron sighed, exasperated. He pulled away and walked to the front of the boat, letting the cool spray of the sea hit his face, his skin. He didn't know what to think. He didn't want to picture his brother dying. He didn't want to think about what Claire and Carina and Samheed and all the others would do or say if it happened—would they believe Alex had given him control? He doubted it. Simber would no doubt eat him immediately.

As if Alex could read his mind, he called out to Aaron, "I'll give you a letter of proof that explains everything so you can show the others. It'll be in my handwriting. Simber will know I mean it. He'll help you if I ask him to. So don't worry about that."

Aaron stared straight ahead over the water. Alex's plan would resolve the problem, he supposed. But something else was bothering Aaron. Something that stirred inside him. A dormant longing. A reawakening craving that was both thrilling and threatening.

Aaron clutched his vest, pressing his fist against the spot in his chest that stirred. It was almost painful. He thought about Quill. And he thought about Artimé. He thought of the stunning mansion and the majestic jungle and the beautiful lighthouse on the hill. He thought about all the magical abilities he'd already attained, and those yet to be discovered.

He pictured himself wearing the swishing, colorful robe, and sitting at the head mage's desk, and strolling over the entire island with the sun shining, the glorious green sea sparkling with whitecaps, and people—*his* people—fawning over him. It was everything he'd once dreamed about, and had finally given up hope of ever having. He didn't think he'd ever want it again. But now his mouth watered. A grimace crossed his face. He swallowed hard.

It pained Aaron to break away from the images. He dropped his hand to the railing and squeezed it until his knuckles turned white. He shut his eyes tightly, trying to block the images. "Applecorn," he muttered, opening his eyes.

The sun disappeared behind a cloud, turning the seawater gray. Aaron let out a breath. After a moment he let his grip slack on the railing. He looked over his shoulder at Alex, who was looking back earnestly, expectantly at him.

Aaron shifted his gaze. "Okay," he said lightly. "I'll do it."

When the boat reached Artimé's lagoon and the boys finally arrived back at the mansion, Alex brought Aaron up to his office. He chose a carefully hung robe from the rack in the corner, folded it, and placed it on his desk. Then he grabbed *The Triad* spell book from a drawer, gripped it tightly for a moment, and put it on top of the robe. From his pocket Alex pulled the letter that he'd written on the boat, which would explain everything in the event of his death, and slipped it inside the book. He picked them up and turned toward Aaron, who stood stiffly nearby.

"I'm not sure how to do this," Alex admitted. "I haven't found a book on transferring the duties of head mage yet, if there even is one." He glanced up at the ugly artwork that held the code to restoring Artimé. "But I declare here and now, in this magical office, in the presence of these magical pieces of art that hold the secret to this world, that I am hereby turning over the position of head mage of Artimé to my brother, Aaron Stowe."

With a solemn look, Alex held out the robe, the book, and the note to Aaron.

Aaron stared at them. He worked his jaw as he tried to control the desire that roiled inside him. And then he held out a quivering hand and took the items. "Okay," he said, in a voice not quite his own. "Is that it? Is it done?"

"I guess so," Alex said, feeling very weird. "I'll keep wearing my robe, of course. And you should just keep yours with you. If I die in battle, Artimé should continue on. But if Artimé ever disappears, the instructions for restoring it are in the book. Claire, Lani, and Sky all know the spell too."

Aaron finally dared look his brother in the eye. "Okay," he said. He gazed at the items Alex had given him, and then he rolled the robe tightly and bound it, and slid it inside his vest, tucking it out of sight. He clutched the book. "I'll memorize the spell tonight so I won't need the book, or help from anyone."

"Good plan," said Alex.

Aaron hesitated. "This is strange."

"Yes."

"I'm not sure I like it."

Alex looked at the floor. "I've been in too many fights and seen too many friends die. I'm prepared for the worst. You've actually eased my mind quite a bit with your immortality."

"That's strange too. Picturing my life going on when other people are gone. I don't know quite what to think. It's fine for now, but what about someday? You know?"

Alex nodded. "Yeah. It's almost too weird to imagine. But I guess there will always be the scientists for you."

"Maybe I can convince them to move here if I end up staying mage," Aaron murmured, more to himself than to Alex.

Alex frowned. "Hopefully that won't happen, though," he said. "Right?"

Aaron's eyes widened. "Oh, right—of course!" he exclaimed. "I . . . I shouldn't have said that."

They stayed together for a few more moments, working out the details of the plan and promising strict secrecy regarding their mage arrangement. They didn't need anything to detract from concentrating on the task at hand—preparing for the battle of a lifetime.

Getting Ready

That night, while Simber patrolled the skies, Aaron and Alex found Claire and Ms. Octavia at the octogator's desk in her classroom and sat down to discuss procedures for the coming attack. Claire and Alex talked through various strategies while Ms. Octavia drew detailed sketches of them. Everyone wished for Florence's expertise on the matter—they had never needed it more. But it was not to be had.

After a few hours of conversation deep into the night, Aaron, Claire, and Ms. Octavia retired to their rooms with plans to meet up again the next morning. They had a lot of

LISA McMANN

things to discuss, mainly what to do about Quill and whether they should enlist help from them or try to protect them somehow.

When Aaron reached his room, he pulled the robe out from inside his vest. Then he glanced at his blackboard and frowned. He went into his sleeping quarters and closed the door softly. There he unrolled the robe, shook it out gently, and placed it around his shoulders, securing it at his neck. He looked at himself this way and that, and then went over to his mirror and removed the paper he'd used to cover it. He stared at his reflection. "I'm the head mage of Artimé," he whispered.

He felt his spine straighten and his chest swell. The longing surged inside him until it felt like it was out of control. With tremendous effort, he batted it down. Slowly he removed the robe, folded it, then rolled it tight like a baton and tied it so it would be ready to stuff inside his vest in the morning. He set it down on his bedside table, within reach in case he needed it, and reluctantly put the paper up so it covered the mirror again.

When he climbed into bed, he lay on his side, staring at the bundled robe for a long while. And then he sighed and rolled over to face the wall instead.

» » « «

Before turning in, Alex went to the hospital ward and found Carina Holiday sitting with the young woman who had escaped from Warbler. Asleep in the bed next to the escapee's was Thatcher, the Warbler boy who'd been catapulted to Artimé's shores some time ago and had become quite good at spell casting.

Alex raised an eyebrow. "Why is he here?" he asked softly.

"They're siblings," said Carina. "She risked her life to warn us because of her brother."

"How is she?" Alex asked.

"She's exhausted," said Carina. "Dehydrated. Has a bit of a fever, too. I doubt she slept a wink as she paddled her way here."

"Did she arrive on a raft?"

"No, it was a canoe. Her paddle had a bite out of it."

Alex frowned. "What from?"

"We don't know."

Alex looked at the young woman. "Shall I take her thornament off?"

"Yes, if you're not too tired. I asked her when we were

LISA McMANN

assessing her if she'd like it removed, and she nodded quite emphatically. But Claire hasn't had a moment to do it yet."

"I'm not too tired," said Alex. He took a chair and sat next to the young woman. She was similar in age to him and Sky. Her skin was dark brown like Thatcher's, her face perfectly symmetrical and serene, and her black hair was trimmed close to her scalp. "Do we know her name?"

"It's Yazmin."

Alex studied Yazmin's necklace of thorns, then asked Carina to hold the girl's hands down to keep her from moving in her sleep while Alex was performing the spell. He didn't want to accidentally make anything besides the thornament disappear.

Carina held the girl's wrists, and Alex carefully touched the band of thorns. He concentrated for a long moment, then whispered, "Dissipate."

The thorns faded away.

Alex sat back and Carina released her grasp. "She'll have a nice surprise when she wakes up," Carina said.

"Will you let me know when she does?"

Carina smiled. "I will. Get some sleep. If what Yazmin says is true, we're in for a rough ride."

"I doubt she'd risk her life escaping if she wasn't certain," Alex said. "And the suspicious activities of the Warbler ships fall in line with her prediction. I'm afraid we're in for big trouble."

"Me too. I'm . . . I'm a little scared for us, Alex."

Alex gazed at the fearless fighter. If Carina was scared, the rest of Artimé had to be petrified. "We know what we're doing," he said. But they both knew that without Florence to guide them, they might be in for some unexpected trouble.

Alex left the hospital ward, said good night to Simber who'd returned from his night flight, and wearily climbed the stairs to the balcony. He went down the not secret hallway toward his room, but paused first at the door to the Museum of Large and went inside. He made his way past the library and the empty spaces where the ship and the whale skeleton had been, and went into the gray shack, which stored itself here when it wasn't in use. Alex wandered through the little house, remembering the terrible time Artimé had had here after Mr. Today's death.

"I'm so glad our island doesn't have to worry about that now," he murmured. The realization that he was no longer

LISA McMANN

head mage washed over him. It was hard to grasp. But he was convinced it was the right decision. Aaron's immortality was the main reason, of course, but the more Alex thought about it, the more sure he was that he'd appointed the right person in the event of his demise. Aaron knew how to lead. And he was so naturally talented with magic. There seemed to be no limit to what he could do. Now that Aaron had changed his ways, he would be perfect for Artimé if something happened to Alex. And he looked identical, so it would be an easy transition for all.

Of course, if Alex didn't die, all would go back to normal. And Aaron would go back to the Island of Shipwrecks to live his life . . . forever. And never die. The concept was unfathomable, especially now with so much else on Alex's mind.

In the kitchen of the little shack, Alex sought out the mini mansion, which was in its rightful spot in the cupboard, and then found the extra robe that he kept inside the shack. He very nearly took it since he had Aaron now, but then decided to leave it as a precaution. After all, Ishibashi had said no one really knew for sure if they were immortal because they couldn't test it. So just in case, Alex left the robe. Everything was in place.

Satisfied that everything was in order, Alex left the gray shack, walked past all the collected bits of airplanes and ships, and stopped next to Ol' Tater to pat the frozen mastodon statue on the tusk. After a moment, Alex headed back out of the museum and across the hall to his living quarters. It was a quiet night, and Alex couldn't help but wonder how many more nights like this he'd see.

He climbed into bed and began mentally preparing to somehow organize the people of Quill in the morning, and soon he drifted off to sleep.

Meanwhile on the Island of Shipwrecks, three lonely scientists lay awake in the dark and silent night, worrying as they often did about their friends in Artimé. Ishibashi wondered if he would ever find out what happened with the pirate attack. Perhaps he should have gone with the boys to help, though he didn't know what good a man his age might be. He reached under his pillow and grasped the tiny object he kept hidden there, rolling it between his thumb and forefinger, and made a wish on it. Then he closed his eyes and drifted into a restless sleep.

LISA McMANN

At the very same time on the Island of Legends, a giant, shimmering water dragon delivered somber news under the light of the moon, causing a frenzy of activity. Florence's body clanked against Talon's in a hasty embrace, and she climbed onto Pan's back and set off, while Henry ran to the island's mouth and met Spike there to have a final assessment and chat with Karkinos.

On the Island of Graves, seventy saber-toothed gorillas slept in silence under an empty tree, perhaps missing the mournful song of their pet American, Kaylee. And on the Island of Fire, only a few inhabitants too old or too young to fight remained, strapping themselves in and out of their drop-down seats as they robotically rode out the random plunging and resurfacing of their volcanic home.

Inside the Island of Dragons, the young orange female managed to flap her wings hard enough to soar up and out of the cylinder. She circled around it in the darkness and soared this way and that in pure delight. Moments later a second female followed, and then three more dragons appeared above the lip of the island and spread their wings wide, joyously riding the night breeze.

On the coast of Warbler, the Island of Silence, the lone voice of a hook-handed pirate captain rang out from aboard a ship. "Anchors aweigh!" he shouted. Twenty-four anchors rose up from the water, and slowly but surely twenty-four ships loaded with two island's worth of people moved eastward over the glimmering sea.

When Doubt and Fear Creep In

Simber woke Alex early.

"They'rrre coming," he said.

Alex opened his eyes and blinked at the ceiling, lost for a moment in a dream, and then he remembered. He sprang out of bed. "Already? How much time?" he asked.

"A few hourrrs," said Simber.

"And how many ships?"

Simber hesitated. "I counted twenty-fourrr."

Alex felt the blood leave his head, and he sat down on the edge of his bed. In an instant, the situation became alarmingly real, horribly immediate. Everything that had transpired between him and Aaron got pushed aside. It was all he could do to keep from hiding under the bed. "Twenty-four ships?" he whispered. He looked at Simber, aghast. "Twenty-four? We haven't got a chance against that."

Simber lifted his chin defiantly. "You may be rrright, but if I hearrr you speak like that in frrront of anyone else on this island, I may just kill you myself."

Alex sucked in a breath and then lifted a hand to his eyes. His thoughts were scrambled, and his heart sank deep into despair. There was no possible way Artimé could fend off twenty-four ships filled with pirates and Warblerans. He didn't have a plan in place yet. He barely had a handful of decent strategies worked out since he'd gotten the news. What was Artimé to do? What *could* they do against so many? They'd all die! Obliteration seemed like an understatement.

"Is Florence back yet?" Alex asked weakly through his fingers.

"Not yet."

"Of course not . . . it's too soon. Where's Claire?"

"I was planning to wake herrr next."

LISA McMANN

Alex dropped his hands, feeling overwhelmed and helpless. "Yes, do that. And if you could assemble my team . . . or wait. I'll have Clive do that." He shook his head. "I don't even know what I'm saying. I think I'm going to be sick. This is it for us, isn't it, Simber? The end?"

Simber gave Alex a stern look. "Alex, you'rrre the head mage, and we'rrre about to be attacked. You've handled it beforrre. Pull yourrrself togetherrr. Now."

"But . . ." Alex faltered. "Twenty-four ships . . ."

"Stop!" Simber growled under his breath, and then said, "You have battled and conquerrred two evil high prrriests and theirrr Quillitarrries, and you've defeated Warrrblerrr twice, once on theirrr island and once herrre. You've surrrvived a deadly hurrricane and a disastrrrous waterrrfall rrride arrround the worrrld, and you've fought off an enorrrmous eel and dozens of saberrr-toothed gorrrillas. You've brrrought Arrrtimé back frrrom the dead, rrrescued people in need, and set an ocean of sea crrreatures frrree. You took in people who didn't deserrrve forrrgiveness, and you accepted rrresponsibility forrr yourrr sisterrrs. The people of Arrrtimé and Quill believe in you. They trrrust you. You must not let them down."

The stone cheetah statue paused to make sure Alex was listening. "If you think you will fail now, afterrr all you have accomplished in your shorrrt life, then you arrre not the mage I thought you werrre."

Alex stared at the floor. It was true. He wasn't the mage Simber thought he was.

After a long moment, Simber turned and walked out the door, pausing just outside it. "I'll summon yourrr team to the lawn, and we'll meet you therrre in fifteen minutes. That should be plenty of time forrr you to rrrememberrr who you arrre and what you fight forrr, Alexanderrr Stowe. You arrre the head mage of the most powerrrful society in ourrr worrrld. And even when all appearrrs lost," said Simber, "you must fight with everrry-thing you have inside you, all the way until the bitterrr end."

With that, Simber loped down the hallway, shaking the mansion with every step.

Alex closed his eyes and sucked in a breath, letting it out slowly. And while he knew that Simber was right—mostly, anyway—Alex didn't know if he had it inside him to take on

LISA McMANN

yet another battle. Especially one that appeared impossible to win. So many lives were at stake. Would this be the demise of Artimé? Was this how Alex's life would finally end—in a fight with some of the same enemies he'd been fighting all along? How could Alex ask his people to fight one more time after all they had been through, when death appeared certain? This was more than just Alex's life on the line. This was an entire island's worth of people in danger. How could Alex possibly lead them into that?

"Perhaps we must surrender in order to survive," Alex whispered, hating himself for saying the words, but saying them nonetheless.

"Surrender?" shouted Clive, pushing his face out of Alex's blackboard. "You can't surrender. There is no such word in my vocabulary, so I'm afraid I can't share that kind of news."

Alex glanced up, but he didn't have the energy to deal with Clive right now. He shook his head sadly and looked away. "Go away," he said.

Clive's lips parted in hurt and surprise. He blinked and then he disappeared. But soon words appeared on the blackboard in place of his face.

Attention people of Artimé. We are under attack. A fleet
of ships is heading our way from Warbler and the Island of
Fire. It is with great humility that I ask you one last time for
your help in defending our world. As always, your refusal
will be met with acceptance and respect, for that has always
been the way of Artimé. Even if I find myself standing alone
on our lawn two hours hence, I will fight to the end for you.

Thank you for your many sacrifices,

Alexander Stowe

Head Mage of Artimé

Alex stood up and got dressed, ignoring the blackboard.

"Well?" said Clive, poking his nose and mouth out of the corner. "How does that sound? I was thinking of highlighting the border with yellow and green."

"I don't care what you do," Alex said. He went into his bathroom and splashed water on his face, then stared down at the sink, not really seeing it.

Clive smiled and disappeared, and soon the words had a flashing neon border surrounding them. A moment later they disappeared and Clive's face returned.

Alex came out of the bathroom, towel in hand and drying his face. When he was finished, he threw the towel at the blackboard. It landed, draped over the edge, partially covering Clive's face. Clive raised an eyebrow.

Alex loaded his component vest and filled his robe pockets with more components, not even sure if he'd use them. Perhaps he'd just give himself up—maybe the enemy would take him in exchange for leaving the rest of Artimé alone. At least Artimé would be safe with Aaron in charge.

He looked around his room one last time, making sure he had everything he needed, and then he went toward the door.

"Don't die," Clive said from behind the towel, so it came out slightly muffled. He bit at the towel and managed to pull it down and drop it on the floor.

Alex thought about that for a long moment. "Thanks, Clive," he said quietly, and went out, closing the door behind him.

A Meeting of the Minds

While Aaron got ready and tried to tame his thoughts, Alex blew out a breath, set his shoulders, and made his way downstairs. He went out the front door and found Simber on the lawn, staring to the west. Alex stood next to him and looked too. He could barely make out a few bumps on the water.

"I hope Florrrence and the otherrrs can get herrre safely without being attacked," Simber said. "I'm afrrraid they might be caught behind the ships."

Alex's mind didn't have room for more things to worry

LISA McMANN

about. "Sim," he said, "I'm thinking about surrendering. I don't want our people to have to fight again. That's all we've done since I came to Artimé, and things look especially bleak this time—you have to agree with me. If I give myself up, maybe the pirates and Warblerans will be satisfied with that."

A low growl came from deep within Simber and it turned into a roar.

Alex cringed and backed up. A few people came running out of the mansion to see what was happening, but Simber glared at them until they backed away and left.

"If you surrrenderrr," growled Simber with true anger in his voice, "who will lead this island when these enemies decide you werrren't enough to placate them afterrr all, and they come back again?"

Alex frowned. "I'm certain you'll be fine," he hedged.

"Well I'm cerrrtain we won't." Simber glanced at the team members coming toward them for their meeting and hissed to Alex, "No morrre of that talk. You must find yourrr confidence immediately, and defeat these enemies. Don't you see? Once they arrre overrrcome, no enemies rrremain. This is the final battle, Alex . . . but only if you fight it."

LISA McMANN

Alex didn't respond, and soon his team leaders ventured toward them. Alex turned to greet Aaron and Claire, the first to reach him. Aaron caught Alex's eye and patted the slight bulge in his vest. Alex nodded solemnly.

Soon Sean and Carina arrived with Ms. Octavia, and Sky came with Kaylee. Both of them appeared relieved to see Aaron back with them. The three stood together, Aaron a bit stiff around the shoulders, but on the surface he seemed pleased to see them as well, despite the circumstances.

Samheed and Lani came next, and then Mr. Appleblossom and Liam Healy arrived, talking earnestly together.

Alex glanced at Simber. "Is this everyone?"

Simber nodded. "Gunnarrr Haluki has been summoned and is on his way frrrom Quill as well."

"Th-that's correct," said Liam. "My, ah, my blackboard talked to his in Quill, and he got the message from Clive. He's coming."

Alex began to wonder what message Clive had sent out—perhaps he should have read it. He held up a hand to quiet the group, and they came to attention. "We have no time to waste," said Alex. "And while I'm devastated by this news and

LISA McMANN

have tried to come up with a way to keep this attack from happening, Simber has convinced me that our only option is to fight and defeat these enemies once and for all. So . . . anyone who wishes to join us in fighting should gather on the lawn within two hours. Does that sound about right?" He glanced at the tiny blobs on the water as if trying to determine their time of arrival.

"That's what Clive said," Liam told him.

"Oh," said Alex. "Well, then, let's go with that. I'd like each of you to lead a team as usual. Hopefully Florence, Spike, and Henry will be back soon to help us."

Mr. Appleblossom raised a hand.

"Yes, Mr. Appleblossom?" Alex studied the man. He looked a bit weary in the weak morning light.

Mr. Appleblossom offered a pained smile and cleared his throat. "If not these enemies at sea exist, our happy land would be at peace this day. But I should say to all who gather here that happy lands are such with strife to pay. 'Tis not till after hardship's won, we play." He looked around wisely, the eldest among them, and added, "I see the end of this, though some may not. But enemies are fully known this time. There are no others hiding round the bend. What's won is won for good, though rough the climb."

Alex nodded and glanced at Samheed, whose eyes held great respect for the theater teacher. "Quite right," Samheed murmured.

"Thank you, Mr. Appleblossom," said Alex. "Your words bring a very special comfort and they ring true with Simber's. I'm very glad you see the end to this, because I admit that for me, it's hard to look past this moment. We are all tired, it's true. And sometimes this cycle of fighting feels endless. So thank you. We take your words to heart."

Mr. Appleblossom bowed his head. "Your fearlessness and drive will lead this charge, and happy we will be to see the end. And in that hour of victory we'll meet in Artimé . . . and start the world again."

"That sounds like a good plan," said Alex warmly. How he wanted it! He was beginning to feel better. And even if he wasn't, he had to fake it for the sake of his team. He stood up a bit straighter. "Our final battle," he said to the group, with conviction. "Let's make this our final battle forever. And when it's over, like Mr. Appleblossom said, we'll start the world again.

With peace, and with family, and with friends." He looked at Aaron, and Aaron held his gaze.

Alex went on to everyone. "I must ask all of you to vote. As you have no doubt noticed, my brother Aaron chose to return with me from the shores of his future home once we heard the news of the pending attack. He has unselfishly agreed to fight with us again. So I ask of everyone here: May I offer him spell components? I will only do so with the consent of everybody present."

A murmur went up in the group, and Alex waited patiently while the people and creatures talked it over. Aaron stared at the ground.

Alex cleared his throat. "All in favor of offering spell components to Aaron, please say aye."

The group's voices rose up in a resounding "Aye!"

"Are there any opposed?" asked Alex. "If so, please speak now." He looked earnestly around the group, his eyes moving to the ones who had been suspicious of Aaron. Samheed and Carina both nodded their approval at Alex. Claire didn't meet Alex's gaze, but she remained silent.

"No," said Aaron suddenly, startling everyone. Perhaps even himself.

They turned to look at him.

"I don't want any," Aaron said. "It's true I know how to use them. But I can't bring myself to accept them. I would rather everyone in this community be entirely comfortable having me near them." He dared a glance at Claire. He'd barely spoken to her during his time in Artimé, knowing she must hate him for killing her father. But he also knew that if his new appointment as head mage were to be revealed, he'd need to strategize properly, and Claire would be his main hurdle. Claire looked up, and they both hurriedly looked away.

Alex shook his head, frustrated. "I'm sorry to hear that, Aaron, because you could be a big help to our spell-casting team."

"Take them," Claire said suddenly. "Please, Aaron. How would I feel if you were caught without any way to defend yourself? Your injury or death would be on my head then, wouldn't it? And it wouldn't do a thing to bring my father back. I don't wish death on you, no matter what has happened in the past. Let's put that aside for the sake of Artimé." She reached into her vest pockets and pulled out a handful of scatterclips and gave them to Aaron. "I don't have any heart attack components," she said.

LISA McMANN

Aaron took the scatterclips and looked at Claire. "Thank you," he said. "Are you sure?"

She held his gaze and nodded. "You've more than proven yourself to be a friend of Artimé."

Aaron put the scatterclips into his empty component vest pocket. "I am sorry," he said quietly.

"I know," said Claire. She looked up briskly. "Please continue, Alex."

"Thank you, everyone," said Alex. "Now, let's figure a few things out. First, we have one ship and one boat. Mr. Appleblossom, I'd like you to commission Captain Ahab to board our ship and take a crew with him. Sean, Carina, and Ms. Octavia, I want you and your teams fighting from the ship to protect it from takeover and help defend us and the mansion here on shore from approaching enemies."

They nodded.

Alex went on. "Claire, please take your team in the white boat and be our eyes around the island so we know where the ships are and where they intend to attack. You'll have first crack at taking out anyone who gets close enough. Got it?"

Claire nodded. "Excellent plan, Alex."

"Mr. Appleblossom, once you've got Captain Ahab convinced to board the ship, I'd like to have you and your team stationed at your *poste d'observateur* on top of the mansion. The squirrelicorns can help with communication between you on the roof, Claire in the white boat, and Sean, Carina, and Ms. Octavia in the ship, as well as having a few of them stationed with each team. Also, please send Kitten and Fox to see me. I'd like to have Kitten near me, and I want Fox on the ship—but have him check in here first, please."

Mr. Appleblossom nodded.

Alex went on, though his confidence faltered a bit—he wished he had Florence's guidance when it came to protecting the mansion. "I'd like Sky and Kaylee armed with your swords and stationed at the entrances to the mansion, at least until we understand what kind of attack we're dealing with. It's crucial no enemies get inside. I'll have those who are choosing not to engage in battle go to the lounge. In case there's a breach, the lounge will be a hard place for intruders to find since they won't know what to do with the tubes.

"I'll have a few teams line the Quill shoreline on the western side of the island since that might be where their ships land first. The rest of us and our teams will take our usual stations on the lawn, and if anything unexpected happens, I'll advise you on what to do via squirrelicorn message."

He took a breath and let it out, wondering if he'd thought of everything, and then continued. "I want all the fighting statues to be stationed facing the water all along the shore, ready to scare the stink out of anybody who makes it to land. The pirates won't have seen any living statues before, so have them focus their energies there and use distraction techniques with anyone else to buy the spell casters more time to prepare."

Alex shoved his hands in his pockets, his mind awhirl. "I think that's it for now. If you see Haluki, have him find me when he gets here so we can figure out what to do with Quill. I'll go write up some team instructions and send them to your blackboards. Grab some breakfast, fill your canteens, and I'll see you back here shortly."

He pressed his lips together. "This is going to be our most difficult battle yet, by far. And I honestly don't know how we're going to get through it. But I won't quit, and I won't surrender, and I won't back down, not for anything or anyone, no matter what they do to me." He shuffled his feet in the grass. "I guess

I just wanted you all to know that. You mean very much to me, all of you. And today I'm fighting for you."

After the moment of warmth, the team went to carry out their duties. Aaron, who'd been given no special assignment, slipped away with a determined look on his face and headed into Quill.

One by One, the Warriors (Reprise)

When Alex went back into the mansion, he stopped in the hospital ward to check on Yazmin, the brave young woman who had escaped from Warbler. She and her brother Thatcher were awake now, and he was sitting by her bed, talking with her.

"Hi there. Thatcher, right?"

Thatcher's eyes widened when he saw the head mage was talking to him. "Yes, how'd you know?"

"You're doing really great with your spells. Are you going to help us fight?"

Thatcher's eyes narrowed. "You bet I am. I'm going after Queen Eagala."

"Be careful," Alex warned. "Maybe start with a slow moving pirate or something." He looked at Yazmin. "Welcome. I'm Alex," he said. "We're grateful to you for the warning."

Her orange eyes were tired. "Hi," she whispered, and then she pointed to her neck. "Thank you."

"No problem. Is there anything you can tell me? We see the ships coming—the attack is imminent. But you should be safe in here."

"Queen Eagala has been meeting with the pirate captain for months," Yazmin whispered. "She built him a ship in exchange for help from them to defeat you." She struggled to sit up. "The pirates alone will make up the first several waves of attacks, but there will be Warblerans hiding on the ships, waiting to fight if the pirates fail."

"All pirates," said Alex. "I was afraid of that. Thank you. That helps."

"I want to help you fight," said Yazmin.

Alex frowned. "I don't think that's wise—Carina says you're quite sick. But you have helped us tremendously already.

You gave us days of warning. That made a huge difference in our preparation, and we're all very grateful." He glanced at Thatcher. "I hope you're pleased with how well your brother is turning out."

Yazmin smiled and put her hand on Thatcher's arm. "Our parents will be very happy to know that they made a good decision to send him here. They've been very worried."

"Perhaps you'll all be reunited soon," said Alex. He wished he believed it. He nodded briskly. "I've got to run now. Thatcher, your instructions will be on your blackboard." He headed out of the hospital ward into a bustle of activity as Artiméans moved throughout the mansion, preparing for battle or bringing possessions with them to the lounge. He saw Crow with Thisbe and Fifer heading for the tubes and stopped them.

"Stay safe," Alex said to his sisters. He kissed each of them on the forehead and looked at Crow. "I'm so glad they have you."

Crow smiled. "I'll take good care of them," he said. And with that, he and the girls slipped into the tube and disappeared.

Alex watched them go, then took the stairs two at a time and went to his living quarters. He quickly packed a bag of components for Aaron. "So you sent it," Alex said, knowing full well Clive was aware of his presence.

"You said you didn't care," said Clive.

"Well, thank you. And . . ." Alex thought for a long moment. "And if anybody gets inside the mansion, you and the other blackboards should do what you can to scare them back out."

Clive's face pushed out and his eyes flew open. "Like what?" he asked, incredulous. "We don't even have bodies."

"You'll think of something," Alex said. "Gotta go." He ran out of the room with Clive screaming "Don't die!" after him. And as Alex flew down the only-secret-to-intruders hallway past the Museum of Large, he skidded to a stop and stared at the door. He blinked a few times, shook his head, and mumbled something under his breath, followed by "No. Too dangerous." He continued on to finish up his meetings before it was time to defend their land.

At the bottom of the stairs he nearly collided with Fox, who was running around the entry area, dodging people's feet, and

LISA McMANN

trying not to get kicked or stepped on. Alex scooped him up and saw that Kitten was on Fox's head, hanging on with her tiny claws during the wild ride. Alex sidestepped down the hallway and darted into an empty classroom, setting Fox on a table.

"Whew," said Fox, trembling slightly.

"Mewmewmew," said Kitten.

Fox sat up to translate. "She says she is very happy to see you, her most especially good friend Alex, and she is delighted to be a part of this very special day of fighting."

Alex raised an eyebrow, but Kitten smiled so hard it made her eyes turn into slits. "Okay, quickly, I have jobs for you," said Alex. "Kitten, I want you to stay with me in case I need you. You can have a nice long nap in my pocket if you like. And Fox, I want you on board the ship. I have a special job for you."

Fox gasped. He sat up straighter. "A . . . special job?" he whispered. "For me? Is it top secret?"

"No," said Alex.

Fox's face fell.

"Or, um, *yes* is actually what I meant to say," said Alex.

Fox perked up again.

"Yes," Alex continued, "it's top secret. It's the tippy top of all the secrets that exist. It's so secret, I'm going to whisper it to you, and you must tell no one."

"Even in the face of death?" Fox asked, eyes shining.

"Even then," Alex said, and he nodded soberly. He bent down and whispered into Fox's ear.

Fox's face lit up, and when Alex was done he said, "That sounds very dangerous. And very clever, which is what I happen to be. Clever like a . . . cat."

"Yes, that's exactly why I picked you," said Alex. "No one else in Artimé can do it but you."

"Or the whole world," Fox said dreamily.

"Or the whole world," agreed Alex. He patted Fox and picked up Kitten. "I'll see you on the lawn, and when this is all over I'll want a full report, Fox."

"If I survive," said Fox.

"Right."

"And if I don't?"

"Well, then you'll die a hero, like Meghan."

Fox nodded. And then his face clouded over and his bottom jaw began to quiver. "I don't want to die," he whimpered.

LISA McMANN

"You won't," said Alex. "You're magic, remember? And you're a cat, so . . ."

"Oh, that's *right*," said Fox, panting in relief. "Phew. Nine lives."

Alex nodded. "Or something like that. I've got to go."

Alex left with Kitten snuggling up in his pocket. He went outside to find Simber, and discovered Gunnar Haluki there with him.

"Gunnar," said Alex in greeting. "What ideas do you have for keeping our Quillens safe?"

"I've got some Necessaries agreeing to help," said Gunnar. "I'll take them with me in my group—you can station me somewhere along the shore in Quill. I've told the rest of the Quillens to stay in their houses for now. If we're lucky, things won't make it that far inland to reach the housing quadrants."

"I'm going to put your team on the western shoreline with Aaron's and Liam's teams," said Alex. "You three know that terrain better than Artiméans would. Squirrelicorns will be circulating with updates." He looked out to sea. The ships were recognizable now. They stretched out across a wide portion of the water. "Any sign of Florence or Henry?"

"No," said Simber. "And I can't fly out to look forrr them, because I don't want the attackerrrs to see me. I want them to think they arrre surrrprising us."

"Good plan," said Alex, straining to see any sign of Pan or the returning Artiméans, but knowing if they were there, Simber would see them well before he did. "I really hope they get here soon." A familiar wave of dread rippled through Alex—it never went away, no matter how many times Artimé faced its enemies.

As Alex and Simber waited on the shore, the door to the mansion opened and Artiméans began streaming out and organizing themselves on the lawn like they'd done in the past. With very little guidance from any of the leaders, the people of Artimé stood poised and ready to hear their final instructions, as if they did this every day.

Sometimes it felt like they did.

A Word from a Leader

When those who wished to fight had assembled, Alex climbed on Simber's back and stood there so that everyone all the way across the lawn could see him.

It was a fairly large army of several hundred despite their losses against Gondoleery. Many of the Warbler children who had found success in Beginning Magical Warrior Training stood with the Artiméans for the first time. And at the last moment Aaron returned from Quill with a group of Necessaries following him, carrying makeshift weapons and standing in solidarity with the magical world.

Alex watched Aaron come in with the Quillens. When Aaron found a place to stand, he looked up at Alex. Alex tapped his fist to his chest, trying to express his heartfelt thanks to his brother for taking on the role of head mage, at least temporarily, as well as for finding more people to fight with them. Alex knew that if he didn't make it to the other side of this battle, Artimé would be in good hands.

Aaron lifted his chin, then repeated the fist gesture. He remembered it from the last battle. It was the Artiméan's symbol of support and courage and dedication. *I am with you.* Dozens of Artiméans around him had seen Alex do it and responded in kind.

The warriors quieted and turned their full attention to their leader. Alex, overcome with humility, looked back at them, so choked up he was unable to say a single word. They had been here time and time again. They had mourned enormous losses together, and they had celebrated tremendous victories together. They were the living. And as Alex looked from face to face in the crowd, he was determined to keep every last one of them alive. He wanted no one to suffer the way he'd suffered when Meghan had died.

"People of Artimé," Alex began, "you know how this works. You have your leaders. The squirrelicorns will act as messengers. Expect surprises, as always." He glanced at the growing line of ships, which seemed to be widening. "The territory we must cover is much larger now than it has been in the past, and the approaching ships appear to be spreading out. Our main enemy will be the pirates, and they know how to fight. I fear they will attack from multiple locations around the island so we must be ready for that. That means our ranks will seem thinner than they are. It means each one of you is more vulnerable than in the past. And it means your significance to Artimé has never been greater than it is today."

Alex looked over the crowd, and his eyes landed on Sky's mother, Copper. He hadn't expected to see her out here fighting. He nodded respectfully at her and continued. "Because we'll be spread thin along the shoreline around the western half of the island, we must be clever and resourceful. Use the new trees in Quill to hide in. If you're stationed in the west, utilize the lighthouse and hill to your advantage. And let's not forget the last time the Warblerans paid us a visit. Be ready for the catapults and steer clear of anything that comes by way of them."

Alex turned toward the group of Warbler children, and his eyes landed on Thatcher and Scarlet. "Warblerans and orange-eyed Artiméans, I believe these attackers are coming after you. You are welcome to change your mind about fighting. You may go inside and hide if you wish. I encourage you to do so, in fact. We don't want to lose you. But if you choose to stay and fight, please be extremely cautious and keep yourselves as safe as possible."

Thatcher glanced at Scarlet. Scarlet lifted her chin and nodded at Alex. She would fight, and so would Thatcher. He nodded at Alex too.

Alex continued with the usual instructions, finishing with a word of encouragement. "Most of all, people of Artimé and our friends from Quill and Warbler," he said, "I want to thank you for coming here today and being willing to fight, perhaps for the first time, and hopefully for the last. Let's split up now and go with our leaders. And may we fight with all we have in us to protect this magical land!"

An enormous cheer rose up, and Alex, heartened, lifted his fist in the air, then tapped his chest and held it there. "I am with you!" he shouted.

The people did the same and shouted back, "I am with you!"

After that, the groups began to break off from the crowd, and the leaders gave out their instructions.

Alex turned his focus to the sea, his brain whirring. His fingers moved absently to his pockets, making sure his components were in order, but of course they were. Every spell caster was well stocked with heart attack spells and scatterclips, as well as a variety of nonlethal spells. Everyone had water and knew where to get more.

Inside the mansion, Alex checked in with the hospital ward. Carina had prepped the nurses, and there was plenty of medicine, thanks to Henry's stockpiles. But it would still be nice to have Henry here. Where was he? And Florence and Spike? Had something happened to Pan?

Alex was forced to put the worry aside. When he saw Captain Ahab stumping toward the shore, Alex called to Simber. "Can you take Captain Ahab and his team to the ship?"

"Of courrrse," said Simber. He approached the team and knelt so Sean, Carina, and Ms. Octavia could climb onto his back, and then he scooped Captain Ahab up in his mouth, much to the captain's loud displeasure, and flew them out to the ship. Then Simber returned to shore to collect the rest of their team, including a slightly nervous Fox.

Claire, driving her namesake boat, came into view as she left the lagoon. She waved to Alex, and Alex lifted a hand in return. She drove slowly around the west half of the island. Inside the boat with Claire were Charlie and three other Artiméan spell casters who were learning how to control the white boat in case something should happen to Claire.

A moment later Matilda came running out of the mansion and dashed toward Alex.

"Ms. Morning has sighted Aaron's team heading for the spot where the palace used to be," Matilda signed.

"Exactly where I want him," said Alex. "Aaron knows that part of the shoreline well."

Matilda relayed the response, and then stood by the front door of the mansion to await further reports.

Restless, Alex went inside the mansion to check on Kaylee and Sky at their stations. Sky was at the front door with her hand on the hilt of her sword. She half drew it when Alex entered, then shoved it back in her belt when she saw who it was.

"Hi," said Alex. "Are you clear on what to do?"

Sky raised an eyebrow. "Chop up anybody who tries to get inside? Yes, I'm pretty clear. Except for the fact that I can't always see who's coming. Shouldn't we be stationed outside the door?"

Alex frowned and thought it through. "Yeah, you're probably right. I'd like you to do that—at least at first."

Sky nodded. "Good. I can't stand being stuck in here. Kaylee's going crazy too."

"I'm sorry—I'm not really sure what Florence usually does as far as protecting the mansion. I've always been outside. I wish . . ." Alex shook his head. "Never mind." He'd wished for Florence enough times already, but wishes wouldn't bring her back. He needed to figure out how to do this without her.

Sky smiled sympathetically and went outside, and Alex jogged to the back door of the mansion by the kitchen and told Kaylee about the change in plans.

"Thank goodness," said Kaylee, heading out. "I mean, I know it's crucial nobody gets inside the mansion, but it feels like prison being stuck in here when all we want to do is fight."

"I need you to stay alive," said Alex, "so if it gets too dangerous, please go back inside."

"It's a deal," said Kaylee. She drew her sword and lashed it through the air a few times as Alex went back into the mansion. He looked in the hospital ward where Yazmin lay sleeping and found a nurse.

"What do you normally do in here when we're in battle?" he asked. "Do you have a way to protect this room in case our enemies get inside?"

The nurse nodded. "We can close the doors and use a magical lock on them if we ever feel we're in danger," he said. "Henry came up with it and taught us all. He's not back yet, is he?"

"No," said Alex.

"I hope he comes back soon."

"So do I."

Alex left the hospital ward and went outside to the shore in front of the mansion where Simber stood.

"I guess you and I will have to work together this time, eh, Sim?" said Alex. "Can you stand it?"

"If I have to," Simber drawled. "I've got my team on the west side of the mansion, and I told yourrr team to stay on the east side and coverrr the lawn up to the jungle. Does that sound rrright?"

LISA McMANN

"It sounds sparse," said Alex. Usually the whole lawn was covered with warriors.

"Mrrr. Appleblossom's team is therrre too."

"Well, that helps. Where is Mr. A?"

"Alrrready stationed on the rrroof. We left his team on the grrround since they arrren't as adept with theirrr footing as Siggy is."

Alex looked up and spotted the man moving up and down the peaks of the roof without a moment's hesitation. Mr. Appleblossom climbed to the tallest peak and called out to the three teams in the area. "It won't be long before we see the start. The wind is on their side—be still my heart."

"You are among the finest and bravest, Mr. Appleblossom!" Alex called back to him, remembering how the theater instructor had so nimbly saved Samheed from the boy's own father in their first battle. "Are you afraid?" Alex asked him. The question was sincere, for Alex truly wanted to know.

Mr. Appleblossom looked down at Alex and said slowly, "I am afraid. It's true—this scene is stark. No greater enemy have we than this. We must go forward with a blinded faith that we will see the end of the abyss."

Alex gave Mr. Appleblossom a long, thoughtful look. *The abyss.* He hadn't thought of the years of constant battles as an abyss, but once the man said it, Alex could see it that way. Something to cross. Something that stood in the way of their ultimate goal for peace. The chance to end it all lay in their abilities and actions today, and the enemy was much larger than any they'd fought before.

"We win or die today," Alex said, more to himself than to anyone, but several Artiméans heard him and repeated the phrase to those around them. As the ships grew near, the island rippled with the words of their leader. "We win or die today."

When the phrase reached Aaron near the lighthouse, it meant something completely different to him. "I guess I can only win," he said grimly to himself. The gravity and fear of the war was combatting his desire for power and leadership, but it didn't disappear. His heart was with the people of this island—all of them. And he would fight his hardest against the enemy, and against the thoughts that continued to work their way around his brain. Still, now and then he

LISA McMANN

imagined what life might be like with him in charge, once all this was over.

To reach that, Alex would have to die, or at least become incapacitated. There certainly had been a time when Aaron had wished for this, but no longer. As he watched the ships grow close, Aaron clenched his jaw, trying to rid the thoughts from his mind. He didn't have time for them now. He needed to focus and lead. "Applecorn," he muttered. "Make Ishibashi proud."

He turned to his team, somewhat larger than the other teams because of the recruiting Aaron had done in Quill that morning. "Stand ready, soldiers!" he said to them. "Pay no regard to me if I fall in battle. Our ultimate loyalty is to the mansion. To our island as a whole. And to . . . to the head mage. Don't fail me in this. Quill and Artimé are one! Do you understand?"

The assorted group nodded.

"Then take your places," commanded Aaron.

They did so.

Oh, how good it felt to be in charge of something once more.

» » « «

Moments later in Artimé, a shout rang out from behind the mansion, and the ground began shuddering.

From the shore, Simber reared around with a growl in his throat, until he realized who was coming toward them at breakneck speed.

It was Florence. And she was dripping wet.

The Return of Florence

Florence!" exclaimed Alex, relief washing over him. "Thank goodness! What happened to you?" he asked as the lead warrior reached him and Simber at the shore.

"Pan and I got caught behind the line of ships," said Florence. "The only way to get past them without them seeing us was to go under them and stay underwater until we rounded the north side of Quill. Even then we weren't out of sight. I slipped off her back when we got close, walked ashore, and came through Quill. She stayed hidden under the water and continued home—she said she had things to take care of."

"Good grief," said Alex. "I'm so glad you made it. We were getting worried. But what about Spike and Henry? Where are they?"

"I don't know," said Florence. "I left with Pan immediately when she arrived on the Island of Legends. Henry and Spike went to do one last check on Karkinos—they were planning to follow us, but they never caught up. I'm worried they're stuck behind the ships just as we were, but unable to go underwater for that large amount of time because of Henry."

"Did you see any eels?" asked Simber.

"We fought one on the way to the Island of Legends several days ago. Luckily, after a major fight, we were okay—though we nearly lost the medicine. Pan bit the eel's head off. We haven't seen any since."

"That's great news," Alex said, but he was preoccupied. He'd forgotten about the potential for eels, and now Henry and Spike were possibly stranded. "Let's hope that was the last of them." He signaled to a squirrelicorn on the roof of the mansion.

The creature swooped down to Alex's side.

"Let our ship's team know that there could be eels prowling

about," Alex instructed, "and then tell Claire the same thing in the white boat."

"Yes, sir!" said the squirrelicorn, and she darted off to deliver the message.

"What did I miss here?" asked Florence, adjusting her quiver on her back and making sure she had all of her arrows after the ride underwater. "What's the plan?"

Alex pulled out the official battle chart that Ms. Octavia had sketched, showing the placement of all the teams in Artimé and part of Quill. He filled Florence in on all that had happened and the strategies in place.

"Basically," he explained, "I've got several teams stationed here on the south shore and all the way around to the west side of the island, facing the oncoming ships," he explained. "Mr. Appleblossom's team and mine are covering the lawn from the edge of the jungle to the mansion. Simber's team is on the west side of the mansion. Also with us in the mansion area are Sky, Kaylee, Matilda, Kitten, and now you. Our teams are small, some with as few as thirty fighters, but every team has a few statues and some squirrelicorns as messengers."

"Okay," said Florence. "Where's everybody else?"

Alex pointed to the chart. "Heading west along the shore in Quill you can see Lani's and Samheed's teams. I gave them a few extra members each because they have the most ground to cover. Then, rounding the curve near the lighthouse is Aaron's team—he recruited some Necessaries and I gave him some strong spell casters, as well as Jim the winged tortoise and the ostrich statue."

"So far so good," said Florence, glancing up to check the positions of the approaching ships before looking back at the charts. "Keep going."

"Beyond Aaron, stationed on the top of the hill at the west point, is Liam and his team. Rounding the island in the northwest curve is Gunnar Haluki and his team."

"That's it? No one on the north side?" asked Florence.

"No—I didn't see a need."

"And where are Sean and Carina?"

"They're on the ship with Ms. Octavia, Ahab, Fox, and a team of twenty or so," said Alex. "I've instructed them to stay closer inland than where I expect the ships to anchor. I want our ship to act as a barrier to the mansion. They'll attack anyone coming in straight on, or force the enemy to go around them.

LISA McMANN

"And Claire—is that her in the white boat roaming in the shallow water?" asked Florence.

"Yes, with a team of six, plus Charlie. She's covering the shoreline and will help out wherever needed."

"Good idea to have a mobile team," Florence said. "What about the Warbler children—are they fighting against their own people?"

"Many of them are," said Alex. "I've split them up evenly, just a few in each group so their teams can help protect them in case the attackers come ashore and try to capture them."

Florence nodded thoughtfully as she looked over the chart. "Hmm," she said. "Not bad work for a kid. You don't even need old Florence anymore."

Alex grinned. "Oh, yes we do. I'm extremely glad you're back," he said. "I did my best with the assignments, but if you want to change strategies, please do. You're the expert."

"You put a lot of thought into it," said Florence, growing serious, "and you did well. This is very close to what I would have done, except for one thing."

"What?" asked Alex.

"Well, from the looks of the line of ships as they draw closer around the island, and from the directions the outermost ships are heading in, I don't think they'll only stick to the south and west sides of our island."

"You don't?" asked Alex.

"No. Look how a few ships are fanning out as if they plan to continue past our island. I think they'll land on the north side, too. Once they reach the shore, it's not that far overland to reach the mansion."

"So we'll be surrrounded," said Simber. He began to pace.

"Time will tell," said Florence, looking at Alex's chart. "But I'm going to rearrange things a little to cover our vulnerable spots." She looked up. "And that means I need some more team leaders. Let's pull Carina off the ship and Sky and Kaylee off the mansion and have them take teams to the north side of the island."

"Whatever you think is best," said Alex.

Sky, standing nearby guarding the door, overheard. "But I'm not magical," she reminded Florence.

"You don't need to be magical to stop pirates," said Florence. "You thought about that, right, Alex? Pirates fight with swords and knives—close-range weapons. So even our best mages should be armed with some type of weapon."

Alex froze, then glanced at Simber. "Crud. We didn't think about that," he said. "I'm sorry."

Florence barked an order to three squirrelicorns on the roof to go into the mansion and find whatever swords they had and deliver them to Samheed's and Lani's teams, since they were the shortest on nonmagical weapons.

Then Florence turned back to Sky, who still appeared uncertain about being a team leader. "Okay, look. You fought off saber-toothed gorillas, didn't you?"

"Well, yes," said Sky.

"These attackers are much smaller," said Florence. "And they won't try to eat you. So this will be easy for you, especially with that sword you wield so well. I wish we had more close-range weapons for this enemy, but we can only make do with what we have. I'll be sure you have spell casters on your team as well. I think you'll make an excellent leader, because you're smart and you think well on your feet. Sound okay?"

Sky nodded. "I guess you've convinced me."

"Good." Florence went to get Kaylee, and Simber flew off to collect Carina, and by the time he was back, Florence had the three new teams identified. She instructed the squirrelicorns to fly out to each of the other teams and send a few members to one of three locations on the north side of the island. "Their team leaders will meet them there," she told them. The squirrelicorns were off.

With another glance at the ships, it appeared certain that the enemy was going exactly where Florence said they would. "They'll avoid the east side of the island because of the jungle," Florence said wisely to Carina, Kaylee, and Sky, "so we don't have to worry about that." She showed them the chart and the map, pointing out where she wanted each of them to go.

By now Alex was even more relieved that Florence had returned. He watched the planning over Sky's shoulder.

"The north side of the island is rocky, and there are only a few places to come ashore. I want the three of you to stay within sight of each other," Florence said. "Once the attackers make their move you'll be able to tell if you need to spread out to cover a wide area or concentrate in one place. Send a squirrelicorn to find me if you run into trouble."

"Why don't you think they'll land on the jungle side?" asked Alex.

"Too easy to get lost," said Florence, "and too thick to run through. They wouldn't be able to get here very handily. And even if they did, why—let them! It's a lot easier to fight them once they break through to the lawn than trying to throw spell components through brush and trees. I doubt they'll land there—pirates are seasoned fighters. They'll know better."

"But what about the mansion?" asked Kaylee. "Who's going to keep the people inside safe?"

Florence frowned. "Simber and I and the teams here will have to take care of it." She looked up. "Siggy?"

Mr. Appleblossom poked his head over the side of the mansion roof.

"If you see pirates getting past us and breaking in," said Florence, "strike them down."

Mr. Appleblossom nodded and went back to his observation area.

"Any more questions?" asked Florence.

Carina, Kaylee, and Sky said no, so Florence sent them and a few members of Alex's, Simber's, and Mr. Appleblossom's teams north. Sky glanced over her shoulder at Alex as she set out with the others toward Quill.

Alex held her gaze. He couldn't bear to think of this as their last moment together, but with the dire situation at hand, the thought wouldn't leave him. He wanted to run after her. He wanted to kiss her and tell her to be careful and tell her to come back to him and a hundred other things. But there was no time to waste. He lifted his hand, willing her to promise him all the unspoken things.

She smiled as if she understood and lifted her hand in return. Then she faced forward and didn't look back again.

With the new teams organized and on their way across the island to the north side, there was nothing to do but wait to see what would happen.

Alex returned to the shore, looking at the huge ships looming closer. Each one must be able to hold hundreds of people. And each of Alex's teams numbered fewer than fifty. He began to doubt again. Was it wrong to even attempt to fight? His people barely stood a chance against such force. The casualties would be immense. With an anxious heart, Alex went back to Simber's side and lay a hand on his neck. "Simber," he said, "I want to talk to them and see what they want. I have to try and stop this."

"Pirrrates don't comprrromise," Simber said.

Alex stood firm. "Please. I need to."

LISA McMANN

Simber regarded Alex for a long moment, and then wearily he nodded, knowing the mage wouldn't be satisfied until he had at least tried. "Let's fly out therrre, then."

Alex nodded. He let Florence know what he was about to do, and she agreed it couldn't hurt, though she, too, doubted anything could come of it.

The head mage of Artimé climbed onto Simber's back. Simber bounded along the shore and leaped into the air, flapping his mighty wings. They flew high over the ships, Simber using his keen sight to search for signs of Queen Eagala on the vessels.

They found her on a pirate ship straight out from the mansion, standing with a male pirate on deck.

Simber lowered himself slowly over the ship. Alex leaned to one side and looked down at them. "Queen Eagala!" he called out. "Will you speak with me?"

Queen Eagala rose to her full height, reminding Alex so much of Eagala's sister, the late high priest Justine. "Captain Baldhead and I warn you that there is no stopping this without full reparations for the wrongs you have done to our islands," she replied.

"What is it that you want?" asked Alex.

"The Island of Warbler demands the return of all Warblerans."

"Including the ones you so foolishly catapulted onto our shores?" asked Alex. "I thought they were a gift."

Eagala's face burned with rage. The golden Warbler pin on her garment flashed as it caught the sunlight. "Every last one of our children and our escapees, plus the two intruders, Lani and Samheed, whom you kidnapped."

Alex held his voice steady. "And the pirates? What do they want?"

The pirate captain growled in a deep voice, "We want our underwater glass cage fully repaired and all the sea creatures returned to us, plus ten million pieces of gold for the two eels you murdered."

Alex almost laughed at the impossible demands. There was no way Alex would send anyone back to live under the rule of the evil queen, and there was no way Alex would give the pirates the sea creatures that had been free and lived peacefully on the Island of Legends. As for gold, he didn't have a single piece to offer, much less ten million of them. "Anything else while you've got me here?" he asked sarcastically.

The pirate continued. "We want the hurricane restored to the Island of Shipwrecks, or we'll have to take control of it and find a new home for your little friends on the Island of Graves."

Alex's heart dropped at the threat of harming the scientists, and then his temper flared. "What else?" he barked at them through gritted teeth.

Queen Eagala snarled. "We want you."

"That's right," said the pirate captain, pulling a sword from his belt and brandishing it. "We want you. Dead." He turned to look over his shoulder. "First Mate Twitch, prepare the fleet."

The young man named Twitch pulled on a rope, which raised a black flag high in the air.

"What do you say, child?" asked Queen Eagala, her voice mocking.

"I don't agree to any of your demands," said Alex. "And you'll regret all of your decisions by the end of the day." Alex pressed his fingers hard against Simber's neck. "Simber," he said, pulling heart attack spells from his robe. "Attack!"

The Return of the Catapults

Captain Baldhead signaled the first mate, and suddenly the air was filled with the thwapping echo of catapults releasing all around the perimeter of the island.

"Heart attack!" Alex cried amid the din, pulling back his arm to fling a handful of spell components at the captain and Eagala. But just as he released the components, an orange flaming ball of tar came flying at them from close range, hitting Simber in the right flank, knocking the cheetah sideways in the air, and throwing Alex off balance. His legs jarred loose from Simber's sides, and Alex slipped off the statue's back and crashed to Eagala's ship below. One of his heart

LISA McMANN

attack spells hit a random pirate, dropping her, and the others went flying into the sea.

Alex lay on the deck for a moment, stunned, as Eagala barked out orders and silent Warbler men and women rushed over to capture him. But Simber dove down, plowing into the people and scattering them far and wide. He snatched Alex up in his jaws, with one orange-eyed woman grabbing on to Simber's open mouth and hanging by her fingertips as Simber soared out of reach. They rose higher and higher.

Alex lifted his head and looked over the edge of Simber's mouth. The woman's eyes were wide and frightened. Alex stared at her for a long moment, knowing she'd drown if she fell into the water, and then he grabbed her wrists and hung on as Simber carried them the short distance to land.

Facing the island, Alex discovered several tiny plumes of smoke rising from various places. From the front of the mansion, Florence was shouting out orders.

Simber landed, setting the woman down a bit roughly. Alex climbed shakily out of the cheetah's mouth as Florence grabbed the Warbler woman by the shirt and pulled her to her feet.

"That went well," Alex muttered to Florence.

"Clearly," said Florence. The Warbler woman began signing furiously, and Alex watched her, trying to understand what she was saying. "Stay . . . ," he interpreted. "Fight. You want to fight with us?"

The woman nodded profusely. She signed a bit more slowly.

Alex watched carefully, and then he looked at Florence. "She has a child here. She says she wants to fight and become an Artiméan. What should we do?"

Another round of thwaps punched the air.

"Look out, Siggy!" yelled Florence as a flaming ball of tar blasted through the mansion roof, just missing the theater instructor, and disappeared inside. Matilda dashed into the mansion to put out the fire it left in the upstairs girls' hallway.

Florence eyed the woman. "Who is your child?"

The woman spelled out a name.

"It's Scarlet," said Alex. "The blond girl. You know her?"

Florence nodded. "She's one of the best young warriors I have. Does she get that from you?"

The woman nodded profusely.

Florence thought for a second as the giant catapult arms wound back a third time. "Okay, fine. We can use all the help we can get. Scarlet is on Lani's team. Just follow the shore that way to the next team beyond Simber's." She looked up and called a squirrelicorn down to accompany the woman. "Make sure she doesn't try anything."

The woman's face was filled with gratitude.

"She won't try anything," Alex said as the woman left.

"I'm pretty sure you're right," said Florence. "Look out—incoming!"

Alex ducked, then jumped on Simber's back. "Come on, Sim," said Alex. "We need to figure out what's happening. Fly low to the water to stay out of the flaming fireballs. Are you okay, by the way? You got hit pretty hard."

"I'm fine," said Simber. "The orrrange flames arrren't hot enough to hurrrt me." Simber took off, and Alex instructed him to fly to their ship, where Captain Ahab was maneuvering it to a safe spot under the arches of the flaming tar balls, but also keeping it within spell-casting distance of one of the enemy ships.

"Fire at will!" shouted Sean, and he sent a handful of Lani's newest creation, smoke bomb spells, into the neighboring ship. Next he grabbed a bunch of heart attack spells and sent

LISA McMANN

them soaring. Ms. Octavia and the other spell casters on board the ship and Alex, from Simber's back, did the same with the heart attack spells, and together they took down five pirates. Fox cowered on deck near Captain Ahab.

"Thanks for the help, Al," said Sean. "We're doing well here. Under control so far, anyway." He reloaded.

"Hopefully they don't all come after you," said Alex.

"Something tells me they don't really need to take over our patched-up ship," said Sean. "They've got bigger goals in mind. I think we're safe. We'll just annoy the heck out of them as much as we can."

"That's the plan, then," said Alex. He looked at Fox. "Are you ready to do your special job for me, Fox?" he asked.

Fox lifted his head. "Is it time?" he asked.

"Absolutely. Go on anytime," said Alex. "It's that one, right next door." He pointed out the lead pirate ship, where Queen Eagala and Captain Baldhead were stationed.

Fox got up and shook himself, then tripped across the deck, hopped onto the railing, and fearlessly jumped over the side and into the water. He swam for the neighboring ship.

"Where did you send him?" asked Ms. Octavia.

"To eavesdrop on Eagala."

"Good idea." Ms. Octavia flung six tentacles full of heart attack spells at the neighboring ship, shouting "Heart attack!"

It was hard to tell with the smoke how many she took down.

Alex and Simber left the ship team to continue their attack, and flew to the white boat. Simber hovered over it while Alex checked in with Claire.

"I'm heading around the island to see where all the ships ended up," Claire said. "I saw you fall and hit the deck—are you hurt?"

"Just a little shaken up. I'm fine now. We're going to drop by all the teams and see what sort of damage these flaming tar balls are doing."

"At least Quill isn't made of desert-dry timber anymore," said Claire. "We don't need another fire."

"Agreed," said Alex. "The weather barrier is in place over the entire island now, but that can't stop the tar balls from getting through. It's definitely a concern."

A thwapping sound echoed around the island and everyone instinctively looked up and then ducked as flaming tar balls soared overhead and pelted Artimé and Quill. "Let me know if you need anything!" Alex shouted to Claire as he and Simber continued around the island to check on others.

"I will," replied Claire. She guided the boat and hit the throttle, speeding over the waves.

Simber flew to Lani's team next and found them stomping out a fire in the tree-lined area where the Quillitary yard once stood. "Get us some buckets, will you?" called Lani. "Then we can fill them from the sea and be ready for the next round of attacks."

"Great idea," Alex said. He directed Lani's squirrelicorns to follow him and Simber back to the mansion, where Mr. Appleblossom was anxiously trying to put out a fire from another flaming tar ball that had hit the roof. One of the main-floor mansion windows was smashed, and a tar ball smoked in the entryway.

Alex hurried to douse it with water from the kitchen and found a couple of chefs putting out another fire in the dining room. He grabbed as many buckets as he could stack and carry, and brought them outside, giving three to each squirrelicorn to take back to Lani, and then commissioning his own team's squirrelicorns to take two each and fill them with water to help Mr. Appleblossom put the roof fires out.

He went inside the mansion for more. Once outside again, he balanced them on Simber's back and hopped on behind so he could deliver them to the rest of the teams.

By the time Alex and Simber were off to make the rounds, Fox reached the ship that held Queen Eagala and Captain Baldhead. He scrabbled up the anchor chain so his ears were above the water, and hung on, listening carefully to the conversations on board like Alex had trusted him to do. It was a very important job, Fox knew, and he wasn't going to mess it up.

He strained his ears like a smart, sensitive cat would do, and tried to understand what the people on board were talking about. Tar balls? Melee? Fox didn't know what those things were, but they sounded like food and made Fox's stomach growl. But then he heard the voice of the scary woman from Warbler, which Fox remembered well, and she said the most horrifying words that Fox had ever known. "The giant eel."

Fox shuddered as the cool seawater dripped off his nose.

He had seen the giant eel before, and he never wanted to see it again. He had to report back to Alex right away! All of Artimé depended on him!

With a tiny splash, Fox slipped into the water and began swimming toward Artimé's pirate ship. But he didn't make it very far before a slithering tail wrapped around his whole body. By the time Fox figured out what was happening, he was jerked underwater, his screams for help muffled by the waves and the thwaps of the catapults. When Fox's eyes adjusted to the darkness, he saw the sinister face of the eel staring at him from just inches away.

The Battle Rages On

Over the course of the afternoon, Alex distributed water buckets to everyone and checked on the teams. There was only one injury so far—a Necessary on Aaron's team who'd been a little too close to an incoming flaming tar ball had gotten burned. Alex and Simber shuttled the injured Necessary to the hospital ward, and then continued on to check on Liam and Haluki.

One house in the quadrant nearest Haluki had suffered extensive damage, but no one inside was seriously hurt. On the north side of the island, the Ancients Sector took the brunt of the damage. Even the group of crotchety Wanteds, who lived crabbily on their little piece of sooty land, ran for cover. Carina's, Sky's, and Kaylee's teams kept the Ancients Sector from burning to the ground and helped the Ancients find safer places to stay farther inland. The teams were tired and hungry, but for the most part everything was under control.

"They're handling it," Alex said to Florence once he and Simber returned from checking in on the north-shore teams. "So far so good." Simber dropped Alex off on the roof so he could help Mr. Appleblossom put out the flaming tar balls that continued to hit it.

"Good," said Florence, filling six buckets at once at the edge of the sea and then handing them up to Alex and Mr. Appleblossom at the lowest section of the rooftop. "But I wonder what else they have in mind. They're tiring us out. I think that's part of their strategy."

"They'll have to run out of tar balls eventually," said Alex. Once the roof fires were extinguished, he poured water over the shingles to help keep them from catching fire when the inevitable next round came flying in. "Anyway, I'm feeling pretty good about it. This attack isn't as bad as I had pictured. They haven't even tried to come ashore."

LISA McMANN

"Not yet," warned Florence.

"Maybe Simber and I should join Ms. Octavia and Sean on the ship," said Alex. "They seem to be getting the most work accomplished since they're staying out of the direct line of fire and actually taking down some of the pirates and Warblerans. Have they disabled the ship nearest them yet?"

Simber craned his neck to look at the ship, and narrowed his eyes. "Definitely not. Therrre's still plenty of movement on boarrrd the enemy ship." He looked harder. "But something's strrrange on ourrrs. Sean and severrral otherrrs appearrr to be lying down."

"Are they hurt?"

"I don't think so. Now Octavia's waving."

"That seems . . . odd," said Alex, pausing to wipe the sweat off his brow. "Are their squirrelicorns all right?"

Simber frowned. "I don't see any squirrrelicorrrns." He sampled the air and rose up on his hindquarters to see better. "Wherrre's that annoying little mutt?"

"What?" asked Alex. "You mean Fox?"

"Yes, of courrrse," said Simber.

"I sent him to eavesdrop on the lead ship, remember?"

"I rrrememberrr," said Simber. "But he's not therrre, eitherrr."

Alex put a hand to his forehead to block the sun, which was turning orange and sitting low on the horizon by this time. "Where can he be?"

Simber lowered himself to the ground. "He's not therrre," he said again with a shrug. "Oh well. We should check on Octavia."

Alex frowned. "No, not *oh well*," he said, indignant. "Come up here and get me. We need to find Fox and see what's going on over at the ship. And where's Claire?"

Florence hoisted herself up onto the corner of the mansion roof and looked around the island, then let herself down again, not wanting to damage it. "The white boat is floating on the north side, directly opposite us."

Simber flew up to the mansion roof, balancing delicately on the edge of it and putting his wing out for Alex. Alex grabbed it and vaulted onto Simber's back as another round of flaming tar balls let loose from the catapults. Simber dodged them and flew to Artimé's ship.

When Ms. Octavia saw them coming, she began waving

with several of her arms. As Simber and Alex drew near, she cried out, "I thought you'd never notice us. I was about to swim in to get you, but I didn't want to leave the ship with everybody like this." She quickly fired half a dozen spell components at the ship next to them, but the pirates held up shields and only one component found its mark. The others plinked against the shields and fell into the water.

"What's wrong?" asked Alex, leaning forward, and then he gasped. Several humans were lying lifeless on the deck, and all of the ship's squirrelicorns were spread out on top of Captain Ahab's headless body. The captain's head rolled around in a corner with the ebb and flow of the waves.

Ms. Octavia looked wearily at Alex. "What's wrong? Clearly a lot of things, Alex. A lot of things."

As Darkness Falls

A s soon as Alex hopped off Simber's back to the deck of Artimé's ship, Warblerans from the nearby ship appeared at their railing with thin tubes, which they put to their mouths.

"Look out!" cried Ms. Octavia, shoving Alex out of the way as the Warblerans blew into their tubes. "Sleep darts!"

Alex ducked behind a stack of crates as a few of the darts pinged off Simber and landed on the deck.

"That's what happened," Ms. Octavia explained. "Captain Ahab brought us too close to the Warbler ship and they hit everybody on board except me with their sleep darts. The

LISA McMANN

squirrelicorns all took hits too, and fell off the mast. They landed deadweight on poor Ahab and broke his head clean off."

"Oh dear," muttered Alex. He called out to Simber, "Cover me while I try to steer this thing closer to shore."

Simber lowered himself in the air and hovered, giving Alex a chance to make a break for the ship's wheel. He was glad for his bit of experience at steering the great ship, even though at that time he'd been heading into a hurricane. But at least he'd gotten a taste of it. Now he guided the wheel properly, and then ran to adjust the sails so they could move away from the Warbler ship.

"What else is happening?" asked Alex.

"There are a mix of Warblerans and pirates aboard all the ships as far as I can tell," said Ms. Octavia. "The pirates have shields that must have some sort of magic treatment to them. I don't know what it is, but there's definitely a barrier that makes my components bounce off the shields without activating. I've been testing various spells while I've been trapped here in this corner, and just about all the component spells seem to be useless against the pirate shields. Watch."

Ms. Octavia threw a tentacle full of scatterclips at one of

the pirates in the nearby ship. He held up his shield and they bounced off and fell into the water. "I've managed to hit a few, though, when I've caught them unawares or if they turn around. It's just the shield that's helping them. The noncomponent spells are working pretty well, like the kind Meghan was good at—slam poetry, fire step, stinging soliloquy, and those sorts of things. But the freeze spell and the clay shackles aren't working either."

"I wonder if Queen Eagala's magic is protective or barrier based," said Alex. "You know, like Gondoleery's was elemental. Maybe the shields' power is similar to how Eagala keeps her island from having any sound at all—besides the sound of her own voice, of course."

"I don't know," said Ms. Octavia, "but clearly our initial strategy is no longer working."

"Well," growled Simber, "I forrr one am tirrred of this. I'm going afterrr them."

"Are you sure you want to do that?" asked Alex.

Simber didn't respond, and Alex dove behind the crates to hide and watch as the big cat flapped his mighty wings and flew to the nearby ship. Immediately the sailors all scattered down

LISA McMANN

the stairs and into tight corners that Simber couldn't reach. Simber slammed into the ship's cabin, but all it did was chip a bit of his wing and leave him furious and tripping over the catapult. Immediately someone released a flaming tar ball, hitting Simber square in the chest and sending the giant cheetah flipping head over tail through the air and plunging into the water. The splash was enormous and rained down on both ships.

Simber surfaced, spitting and flailing, until he finally composed himself enough to rise out of the water. He shook his body violently to free himself from the wet stuff.

Ms. Octavia hid her face behind a tentacle and eased from her hiding spot as the ship finally moved out of range of the blow darts. Alex reappeared from behind the crates, and Simber pretended like nothing had happened to him.

"Simber," Alex called. "There's nothing more we can do here. Octavia can abandon ship if she needs to, but she's a safe distance from the enemy ships now. The others will wake up eventually. We need to find Fox."

"Fox!" exclaimed Octavia. She looked all around in the water, alarmed. "He never came back," she said. "I didn't notice. Good heavens."

LISA McMANN

"He's not in the water around Queen Eagala's ship either," said Alex. "Not that Simber could see, anyway." He began dragging bodies off one another and laying them flat on their backs. "Sean got hit by a sleep dart," he said. "Again!" He rolled the sleeping young man onto his back. "Carina's not going to let him forget that."

"Carina might be in the same predicament before this is over," said Ms. Octavia.

"You're right, of course." He stood up straight. "I can spare you a squirrelicorn and a few people from my team until yours wake up. It'll be dark soon—are you all right here on your own for a bit?"

"I think so," said Octavia. "The other ships don't seem to want to follow us."

"Because it could put them in the line of firrre frrrom the catapults," observed Simber. "I think you'rrre safe forrr now."

Alex climbed on Simber's back. "You won't be alone for long, Ms. Octavia." He instructed Simber to go back to the shore. There Alex ordered a few Artiméans from his team to head out to the ship, carried by squirrelicorns, and then Alex and Simber flew back over the sea, dodging flaming tar balls and looking for Fox.

As the sun began to set in earnest, Simber rose up high in the air, out of range of the catapults. He flew over the ships, wishing he could safely catch the flying tar balls and drop them back onto the ships. But he didn't want to risk losing any claws to the heat.

Despite his dislike for Fox, who was definitely *not* a cat no matter how much he wanted to be, Simber scanned the water and the ships for signs of the creature. Over his shoulder, Alex searched anxiously. And as they were searching, Kitten pushed her way out of Alex's pocket and onto his thigh, and began to stretch.

Alex picked her up so she wouldn't be blasted off Simber's back by the wind.

"Mewmewmew?" asked Kitten.

"We'rrre looking forrr yourrr annoying frrriend," answered Simber.

Kitten's ears stiffened and she sat up. "Mewmewmew?"

"Alex sent him on an errrand and he disappearrred."

Kitten struggled against Alex's grasp, trying to see, and he held her out over the side of Simber's back so she could look too.

"Mewmewmew!" she said, pointing.

"No," said Alex, "that's just a piece of driftwood."

Kitten pointed the other way. "Mewmewmew!"

"No," said Alex patiently. "That's an oar."

Kitten frowned and stared harder, but after a time she stopped staring and began licking her porcelain fur, which was getting ruffled in the wind.

Simber soared over the ships one at a time, listening to the gruff shouts from the pirates below them and taking in the ship designs and vast number of pirates and Warblerans on board each one—the ships' top decks were jam-packed with sailors, and who knew how many more were belowdecks. Simber kept his worries to himself. They were in this. There was no use adding more gloom to the situation. Alex would figure it out soon enough.

When they'd looked over all the ships within a reasonable distance for Fox to swim to, Simber circled back, and in the waning light, he looked one last time at Queen Eagala's ship. Simber's ears twitched and rotated as the great cat took in a multitude of conversations below, listening for Fox.

And suddenly, as Kitten was finishing the grooming of her

left front paw, both she and Simber simultaneously jumped to attention.

"Mewmewmew!" said Kitten.

"Indeed," said Simber. He reduced his altitude near the lead ship where Queen Eagala and Captain Baldhead had been earlier in the day, and Alex strained along with the cats to listen for the voice of their missing comrade. And soon enough, Alex could make it out too.

"I am definitely not a delicious sort of animal," Fox was saying. "I'm basically made out of a tree stump. Do you really want a sliver in your gums? They can be very painful . . . or so I hear."

"What's happening?" Alex said, squinting as he tried to locate Fox on the ship.

"I see him," said Simber. "He's in a cage. I'm going in to grrrab it. Hang on."

Alex shoved Kitten back into his pocket and gripped the cheetah around the neck. Simber dove toward the deck, legs outstretched. He glided as shouts rose up from on board, and the zing of swords being pulled from scabbards rang through the air.

Alex flattened himself against Simber's back, his stomach sickened by the quick drop. As Simber reached his front legs out, he gave an enormous roar. He caught the roof of the cage where Fox was cowering and lifted up, but the bottom of the cage was attached to the deck. The top of it ripped off and the sides fell open, leaving Fox free but frozen in fear.

Simber threw the top panel of the cage at the sailors nearest Fox and lifted himself back in the air, then swooped around and headed back to snatch the canine. As he dove over the ship and picked him up, several Warblerans put tiny tubes to their mouths and sent darts flying. At the same time an enormous eel exploded from the water.

The eel wrapped its body around Simber's neck as a sleep dart stuck fast in Alex's back. Alex slumped lifeless against Simber, and all three Artiméans, plus Kitten in Alex's pocket, went crashing over the railing and plunged into the water.

A Watery Grave

Alex, unconscious from the sleep dart, slid off Simber's back and drifted toward the bottom of the sea. Fox bobbed in the water, unable to sink, and Simber thrashed and pawed at the eel, trying to loosen its grip around his neck. He chomped and bit at the creature and flapped his mighty wings trying to knock the eel away and free himself.

With a tremendous surge of effort, Simber's stone wing caught the eel in the head. The eel's body slacked, and Simber pulled himself loose. He kicked and bit at the eel, trying to kill it, but the eel was too fast. It slithered away into the dark water to nurse its wounds.

Simber continued to thrash his wings to keep from torpedoing downward. He managed to push himself above the surface. "Wherrre's Alex?" he roared at Fox.

"H-h-he sank!" cried Fox.

"Blast it!" Simber cried. He let gravity take over and dropped through the water as if he were falling through air. His head turned wildly this way and that, looking and listening for Alex. Had the eel taken off with him? If Alex sank, he must have been unconscious. Had he been injured when they crashed through the railing? Simber hadn't seen what happened. All he knew was that he had to find Alex fast.

After what seemed like far too long, Simber spotted movement. He swam toward it and saw it was Alex's robe, swishing in the cloudy water. Simber lunged for it, gripped Alex in his jaws, and used the sea floor to push off. Flapping his wings to project himself upward, Simber soon burst from the water. He snagged Fox with one paw before the pirates could fish him out of the water and continued flapping. Alex hung limp, facedown, from Simber's mouth, and Simber gently pressed on Alex's chest with his jaws. Water dribbled from Alex's mouth and nose, and he coughed and wretched violently, giving Simber hope. But the mage remained dead asleep.

Florence saw them coming.

Simber tossed Fox unceremoniously to the grass and landed on the shore by the mansion. Florence grabbed Alex and ran him inside, into the hospital ward. Simber followed close behind. Nurses gathered around and began working on him even before Simber had a chance to explain what had happened.

As darkness fell around them, the flaming tar balls continued to rattle the mansion, knocking out all but the strongest of windows. One especially large tar ball smashed into the side of the mansion, leaving a gaping hole in the second floor wall, straight through to Alex's private living quarters. Rubble flew everywhere, destroying a portion of Alex's bedroom and sending his dresser and blackboard crashing to the floor. The tar ball scorched the remains, but luck was with Artimé and it burned itself out.

Alex remained unaware. His unconscious body was focused

on expelling the rest of the water he'd breathed in, and the nurses were intent on keeping their mage alive, one minute at a time.

Finally, after an agonizing hour, Alex began to groan. He rolled onto his back and coughed and choked. "My throat," he rasped, and opened his eyes. He stared at the ceiling for a long, confused moment, and then looked at Florence and Simber. "What happened?"

Simber filled him in.

"Is Fox all right?"

"He's fine," said Simber. "Kitten is fine too. She crrrawled out of yourrr pocket a little while ago."

"What's happening out there?" Alex sat up and wiped his face with his damp sleeve as he began remembering everything that was going on. He struggled to his feet, waving off help from the nurses. "Thank you so much," he said to them. "But I need to get back out there."

The nurses shrugged at each other as Alex made his way through the hospital ward, fighting off the woozy blackness that washed over him. He stumbled. Florence reached out to catch him, and he grabbed on to the doorframe to steady himself and let the light-headedness pass. "What about Ms. Octavia?" he asked when he could see again. "And Sean and the others on the ship?"

"They're all awake and fine again," said Florence. "But we need to strategize about what to do with them. They're in a precarious position out there overnight."

"We can't leave the ship out there without anyone protecting it," said Alex.

"True," said Florence. "You could try transporting it to the Museum of Large."

Alex thought about it for a moment. "No," he said. "We may need it to be easily accessible. And there's no guarantee on placement with the transport spell—I don't want it to accidentally end up in the lounge, crushing everyone."

"I'll stay with the ship overrrrnight," said Simber. "I might not be able to attack an enemy ship prrroperrrrly, but I can prrrotect one of ourrr own without messing up. I think." The giant cat looked slightly disgusted with himself, which was rare indeed.

Alex flashed Simber a sympathetic look. "It's clear that they've prepared themselves for fighting you, Simber. That's one bad side to fighting enemies we've fought before—they've figured out how to handle you. We've lost the surprise factor."

"The shine has worn off," said Florence. "You're a has-been. Yesterday's news—"

"All rrright, I get it," said Simber, glaring at Florence.

Florence held her lips taut, not quite letting them curve up into a smile, and nodded in the direction of the front door. "Let's go," she said. "Back to work." The mansion shuddered as another tar ball struck.

They went outside. Simber left the other two in front of the mansion and flew out to the ship.

"Hoist me up to the roof, will you?" asked Alex. "I want to give Mr. Appleblossom a rest."

"Are you sure you're feeling okay?" asked Florence. "We don't need you falling off the roof to your death. That would just be embarrassing."

"I'm fine. Rested, even. Honest." It wasn't quite true, but it was close enough.

Florence gave in. She lifted Alex up onto the roof and, after a bit of coaxing on Alex's part, helped Mr. Appleblossom down to take a break. Alex sent him to the hospital ward to get his minor burns treated, and demanded he take a nap.

LISA McMANN

"Do we know what's going on around the island?" Alex asked Florence as she handed him a bucket of water.

"Squirrelicorn updates came in from almost all the stations. Everybody is holding up all right, just continuing to put out fires. Aaron's group has grown a bit over the course of the day. I guess some of the Wanteds and Necessaries whose homes were getting hit by tar balls decided they ought to pitch in and help."

"They're probably worried they'll get stuck back in Artimé again if the island burns down," muttered Alex. He stopped and stood up straight, and looked down at Florence as the whole ridiculous scenario of the attack played out before them. "What are we doing, Florence? Is this how it's going to be? Endless flaming tar balls? Isn't there anything else we can do?"

"Not unless they come ashore. We don't have the boats to go fight them in the water. Our one ship isn't making a dent—and if it were, they'd surround it and capture it. It's definitely telling that they haven't even tried to capture it—it means they find it insignificant enough to ignore."

"But should we consider attacking from the air?"

"I've thought about that a lot," said Florence, "and my conclusion is no. It's easy enough for the pirates and

Warblerans to hide from Simber and from any spells we cast from the air. They'd love for us to use up all our spell components without actually doing any harm to them. Add to that the risk of Simber having a wing broken off by a flaming tar ball, or the spell casters on his back being knocked down or shot with sleep darts and potentially captured . . . it's too much risk, and for what gain? We take out a few of their fighters? In the end, it's not worth it. I think our only move is to ride this out, Alex."

Alex sighed. "I suppose you're right. But it's maddening."

"That's exactly what they're counting on," said Florence. "Warbler might not be made up of the best fighters, which is why they'll keep them on the ships. But my guess is the pirates have done their fair share of fighting over the years. It's in their blood. They've got a plan in place, I'm sure of it. And they'll use it. Right now most of them are sleeping, and none of us are. That's exactly what they want. They're wearing us down."

Alex looked up wearily when he heard another round of thwaps, and ducked as a tar ball flew over his head and hit the lawn. Two of Alex's team members ran to extinguish it. "Unfortunately," he said, "it's working."

LISA McMANN

A Long, Lonely Night

As the night passed, Alex sent out squirrelicorns to instruct the teams to take turns resting if possible. The flaming tar ball attacks continued, but their frequency slowed a bit. In between, Alex found himself dozing off on the mansion rooftop, dreaming about Sky and the times they'd sat on the roof of the gray shack. But Alex always woke alone to the sound of the catapults. He wondered how Sky was holding up across the island, putting out fires.

After a while Mr. Appleblossom returned to the roof and urged Alex to take a break, so Alex went inside the mansion and surveyed the mess from the broken windows. He tried to

LISA McMANN

remember the broom spell that Lani had created, which would automatically sweep up the shards of glass that lined the walls. Eventually he gave up trying and found an actual broom. He began cleaning.

He stopped by the painted mural of Mr. Today on the doors that led to the hospital ward. The old mage would be horrified to see his beloved mansion in such a state. Windows blown out, tar balls littering the entryway. At least the mural hadn't been damaged.

Alex's eyes and nostrils burned from the smoldering tar odor that wouldn't leave even after the flames had been extinguished. When he finished sweeping, he took the tube to the lounge to check on the Artiméans who weren't fighting, and stood there in the dark for a moment, letting his eyes adjust to the soft light. Most of the people were sleeping. Alex spied Crow on the floor between Thisbe and Fifer, all three asleep, Fifer's thumb planted in her mouth. Alex stopped and watched them, then weaved his way to Earl, the lounge blackboard.

"Hello, Alex," said Earl in a low voice. "I think we're at capacity tonight. I haven't been this popular in years. How are things?"

Alex smiled wearily. "Under control so far, but you might

LISA McMANN

want to communicate with the kitchen blackboard to arrange for food down here in the morning in case the bar runs out. The battle rages on."

"You'd think Clive would have mentioned it to us," Earl said, a bit put out.

"I haven't had a chance to give him an update," Alex said. "It's my fault."

"Still, he could answer his page. Of course he's probably sleeping. *He* doesn't have a hundred people asking him questions all night long."

"Sorry, Earl."

"So did the boy return?"

Alex was puzzled by the abrupt change of subject. "What? Which one?"

"Henry. He's a nice kid. Very respectful. I heard he was missing."

Alex felt like Earl had hit him over the head with a bat. "Oh no," he whispered. How could Alex have forgotten about Henry and Spike? He found his voice. "No, he's not back yet." He ran a hand over his hair and turned away. "I . . . crud. I've got to go."

He ran back to the tube and hit the button that would take him to the entryway, where all was quiet for the moment. He rushed outside and found Florence tirelessly filling buckets and placing them on the edge of the roof for Mr. Appleblossom.

"I totally forgot about Spike and Henry!" Alex exclaimed. "Tell me again, Florence—were they right behind you? Did you see them leave the Island of Legends?"

Florence paused in her work. "I'm worried too," she said gently. "I don't know if Henry and Spike actually left. I didn't see them, but I assume they did shortly after Pan and me. That was the plan. Spike isn't quite as fast as Pan, but even if they left hours later, they should have been here by now."

Mr. Appleblossom set three empty buckets near Florence and took the full ones from her.

Florence went on. "I guess it could have happened that Karkinos took an unexpected turn for the worse and Henry had to stay back. But that seems so unlikely—the crab was steadily improving and actually doing quite well earlier that day. So based on that, I can only assume Spike and Henry are trapped on the other side of the line of ships and unable to pass them without being detected."

"Or maybe the eel found them," Alex said, his throat tight.

"Spike can outrun the eel," Florence said. "The only way she'd be in trouble is if the eel surprised her from the side or head-on. The eel would have to see Spike coming. But I'm sure Spike's intuition is on high alert—she'd most likely be able to detect the presence of the eel in time. I hope so, anyway."

Alex blew out a breath. "It's making me sick to think about it," he said.

Another round of flaming tar balls lit up the sky around the island. It was almost beautiful to watch them, so synchronized. Alex didn't have time to watch, though, as the one aimed at the mansion struck the side of the building near the top, right next to the existing hole. The tar ball vanished inside it.

Alex ran to the edge of the roof, lay on his stomach, and peered down at the gaping hole in his bedroom wall. He scooted back up to his feet and ran back to Florence. "There's a fire in my bedroom," he said. "Can you get me down from here?"

Alex grabbed two full buckets of water from the edge of the roof and Florence lowered him to the ground. He raced inside the mansion with them, trying to keep them from sloshing everywhere, and ran up the stairs. Florence thundered behind him with more water.

They turned at the balcony and ran down the not-a-secret hallway to Alex's living quarters. He set down a bucket to open the door, and then picked it up and rushed inside. Smoke billowed all around, and flames licked at the bedding. Alex threw the water on it from one bucket, then tossed the other bucketful on the tar ball, hoping to stop the fire from catching on.

Florence dumped her buckets of water over the fire as well, and stomped out stray embers with her feet. Steam rose up with an angry sizzle, which soon died down. The fire was out.

"Whew," said Alex, fanning the air. He set his buckets on the floor and climbed over the rubble to the hole in the wall. It was no less than six feet wide and taller than him. He peered out. He could barely make out Queen Eagala's ship and one other outlined by the dawn.

"That was a close one," Alex said. The thinning darkness played tricks on his eyes. He squinted toward the ships as moment by moment the sky gave off a fraction more light. "What the . . . ?" he muttered, and then beckoned Florence to come over and look. "Do you see something? Look alongside the ships."

Florence strode over and bent down to look out. "I don't have eyes like Simber," she said, "but I see something moving." She looked closer. "It looks like smaller boats being lowered to the water." She peered more closely. "And they're filling up with people."

Fear struck Alex's heart. He gripped the ragged edge of the opening. "This is it," he said. "They're coming ashore!" Immediately he whirled around. "Clive!" he barked. "Alert Earl in the lounge and all the other blackboards on the property to advise all nonfighters to stay hidden in the lounge! The enemy is approaching land!"

Clive didn't answer.

"Clive?" Alex frowned and turned around to look at the blackboard, but he couldn't see it in the dim light. He lit a highlighter and peered at the space where the blackboard normally stood, and then he gasped. "Oh no!"

Florence gasped too, and they rushed over to the pile of rubble that was topped with the second tar ball. Florence and Alex began dragging pieces of the wall away and flinging them out of the way, and then they shoved the dresser off to one side, and finally, at the bottom of everything, they uncovered the broken remains of the blackboard.

Clive's eyes were closed. He looked peaceful. But his face was deathly still.

"Clive!" cried Alex. He brushed some silt and mortar from the blackboard. Alongside Clive's face was scrawled one final message to the mage.

Don't die.

Pirates Ahoy

Alex dropped down next to the blackboard pieces, ignoring the crunch of broken glass under his knees. "Clive!" he shouted again. "Clive?"

Florence put a hand on Alex's shoulder. "Leave him," she said softly. "He's gone. There's nothing you can do."

Alex looked up at her, his face anguished. "But—"

"We'll take care of his remains later. Right now we need to get the word to the teams about the enemies coming ashore."

They heard what sounded like a stampede in the hallway. Alex immediately stood and pulled spell components from his pocket. A moment later, Simber skidded past the doorway.

LISA McMANN

"The pirrrates arrre coming ashorrre," he said, coming back and poking his head in. "Have you alerrrted the squirrrelicorns, Alex?"

Florence gave him a stressful glance.

Simber peered past the rubble. His stern look softened. "Oh," he said, and looked closer. "I'm sorrry. Who can take his place?"

Alex wrung his hands, distraught over Clive's death. "I can't even think about that! I mean . . . I didn't know this would happen. If only I'd thought to put him on the other side of the room when the tar balls began . . ."

"It's not your fault. I'll take care of him," said Florence. "Alex, go with Simber and handle the attack. Do it now."

Alex nodded, numb, and with one last look back, followed Simber out the door.

Simber regarded Alex carefully as they jogged through the mansion to get outside. "Sometimes you have to keep going," said the statue gently.

Alex nodded. He'd done it before, and he would do it again. Forcefully he pushed Clive's tragic ending to the back of his mind. "I'm okay," he said, feeling anything but. They went outside.

LISA McMANN

There were multiple tenders coming from each ship, and as the day brightened moment by moment, Alex could see they were packed full of pirates.

"Squirrelicorns!" Alex called out, his voice thick and a bit ragged. "Alert the west and north teams to the pirates' approach on land! Quickly!"

The squirrelicorns flew off immediately with their orders.

"Teams!" cried Alex next, to those on the south shore. "Fire at will as soon as they get within range!"

Alex's, Simber's, and Mr. Appleblossom's teams rushed to the shore and lined up, components in hand.

As two tenders left Eagala's ship and passed alongside Artimé's ship, the Artiméans on board rained spell components down on them, causing a flurry of confusion and a pileup of stricken pirates. "That's the way," Alex muttered.

Alex looked along the shore to the west, spotting Lani and her team doing the same thing his team was doing—protecting the shore and standing ready to take down as many of the pirates as they could before the boats had the chance to land. Alex raised a hand to Lani, and she signaled back. He hoped the other teams were doing something similar. The fewer pirates making it onshore, the better.

The boats that had come alongside Artimé's ship now veered wildly away from it. Instead of coming straight toward the mansion, they headed for the shore where Lani's and Samheed's teams were stationed. That meant two additional tenders full of pirates for those teams to defend against.

Alex frowned, and then ordered six members of his team to go up the shore to assist Lani and Samheed, worried that they were going to get the brunt of the attack. Simber and Florence would have to pick up the slack in front of the mansion. They were about to get very busy.

Before the first tenders made it to shore, more boats were lowered to the water alongside the ships. The pirates climbed into them and soon began rowing ashore. The waters were filled with them. Alex hadn't seen anything like it in his life.

Finally the first wave of boats came within spell-casting range. Alex, along with his team, began firing upon them.

Immediately the men and women seated in the front of the boats held their shields up. Most of the components bounced off them into the water. Alex remembered what Ms. Octavia had said the previous day about the protective spell.

"Try to get around their shields!" Alex shouted as the nearest boat struck the sandy bottom and stopped moving. "Or use spells that don't require components!" The pirates climbed out of the boat with amazing speed and agility, and ran the boat farther up the sand.

"None of those are lethal!" shouted one of Alex's frustrated fighters.

"Just do what you can!" replied Alex, flinging spells one after another.

The pirates rushed through the water toward the Artiméans at an alarming speed, holding their shields in front of them. Alex and his warriors continued pelting the pirates with spells, but only a few met their mark. As they reached land, the pirates drew their swords and ran at the Artiméans, and it was then that Alex finally realized just how big these enemies were, and how long and sharp their swords were, and how unprotected he and his people were. The Artiméans were forced back, casting spells as quickly as they could, but the pirates were too many, too fast, and too strong.

Rather than killing the pirates, which now seemed like an impossible task, Alex began casting glass spells between the two parties, trying to slow the enemy down and keep his team safer.

That definitely helped, as the pirates weren't expecting such a thing. Several of them smashed into the walls of glass, their weapons clanging against them. But each glass wall Alex put up took several seconds and a good amount of energy and concentration, and Alex wasn't nearly fast enough. Some pirates began to slam their shields against the glass, while others simply went around the panels and began swinging their swords wildly. Alex's team had nothing with which to protect themselves, and with only a small percentage of their spells causing any harm, they began to panic.

Some of them ran to the fountain in the middle of the lawn for cover, while others hid behind the mansion and cast spells from there, trying to find a better angle. Mr. Appleblossom on the roof was the most successful, for he could strike pirates on the head, but the pirates soon discovered him and moved out of range.

Alex, finding himself backed up against a shattered mansion window by a pirate twice his size, had no choice but to flip backward through the frame and scramble to his feet again in time to send a freeze spell at the pirate's ankles. It hit its mark, and the pirate froze in place. Alex jumped back out through the mansion window and finished off the brute from behind with a triple dose of heart attack spells, and soon the pirate fell over on his back, both frozen and dead. Alex grabbed the man's shield.

More boats arrived on shore. Alex looked up just in time to see thirty or more pirates with shields and swords running toward him, with none of his team around to help fight them off. Desperate, Alex began casting spells with all his might, but there was nothing he could do to stop them all.

Just then, Simber came swooping down from above and plowed into the line of pirates, knocking them flat. Swords and shields went flying. "Grab the shields to protect yourselves!" Alex screamed to his team. "Swords too, if you know how to use them!" The team descended on the items and armed themselves.

The next boat reached the shore, and the pirates piled out as before. Simber knocked them down as well, but the first row of flattened pirates was getting back up again.

"Into the mansion!" one of the pirates cried out.

Alex felt his heart throbbing, and his throat was parched. "No!" he yelled, and ran to pick up a sword. He brandished it awkwardly, then ran at the pirates. They knocked him aside like a feather. As they broke down the door, Alex, still prone, dropped the sword and found his extra stash of heart attack spells. He rolled to his side and pelted the pirates' backs with them one by one, and they toppled over, but it wasn't enough, and soon they were storming into the mansion.

Alex flopped back, exhausted, and then he struggled and scrambled to his feet and ran after them until he'd stopped every last one of them. He raced back past the hospital ward, shouting to the nurses, "Use the magic lock to protect yourselves—this is going to get very ugly!"

The Brunt of the Attack

Lani and her team took on the pirates the best way they knew how—by running past them into the water once they reached the shore and firing at the pirates' backs. It worked the first time, and seventeen pirates fell to their deaths. But all the rest of them whirled around, furious, and began brandishing their weapons. The pirates were big and they were strong and some of them were even smart, and Lani knew her team was in trouble.

But she'd also seen Alex put up glass spells, and while she had never been able to pull off that spell, she knew Samheed could do it, so in the midst of a high-speed chase with a lumbering pirate behind her, she ran toward Samheed's team. "Sam!" she cried. "Glass barriers!" She hoped he heard her. She circled around, three pirates on her tail now, and tried freezing them, but they blocked all of her attempts. She tossed heart attack spells over her shoulder, but they couldn't find their marks because of the shields.

She wished she'd grabbed a sword when her team had felled the first round of pirates, but those weapons were out of reach from where she was now. She knew that all she had to do was kill one of the pirates chasing her to get one. But it was proving impossible. She ran away from the water toward the rocky hill that led up to the road in Quill, now leading half a dozen pirates away from her team. Nimbly up the rocks she ran, and realized the pirates weren't quite as agile as she. She climbed faster, her legs burning, and the pirates fell farther behind. When she reached the top, she picked up a huge rock and threw it down at the first pirate, and because he was looking down at his footing, he didn't see it. It smashed into his head, sending him tumbling backward and knocking down the two women behind him.

Lani followed up with deadly scatterclips, one right after

the other, putting an end to all three before the pirates behind them could reach her. Heartened, she picked up the pace again, going down the rocky hill this time, leaping recklessly, but with no other choice. She ran past a few of her team who were struggling and managed to fire heart attack spells at their enemies' backs as she ran.

More tenders landed, putting Lani and her team in even bigger trouble. Lani managed to dodge the chasing pirates long enough to go back to one of the fallen ones and grab a shield and sword. She swung the sword wildly, finding it a good bit heavier than the swords Mr. Appleblossom trained them with in Actors' Studio, but she soon adjusted. And when she managed to knock the shield out of the hands of a pirate, she threw her own shield to the ground so she could grab a handful of heart attack components.

"Heart attack!" she cried, flinging them. They hit their mark, sending the pirate tumbling down the hill.

Lani lunged for the shield, but she'd lost concentration for a split second, and a burly pirate scooped her up from behind, then flung her over his shoulder. She kicked with all her might into the pirate's stomach and slammed her sword into the back of his leg. He spun around, roaring.

Lani wiggled a scatterclip from her vest pocket, and as he started pulling her off his shoulder, she shoved the clip deep into his ear and shouted, "Die a thousand deaths!"

The man went limp. He dropped Lani hard to the rocky hillside and fell on top of her. She was trapped.

"Get! Off! Me!" Lani yelled, struggling with all her might to push the pirate off, but one of her arms was trapped. She took a second to look out at her team, trying to see how many of them still stood, and counted fewer than half. She struggled again, and then realized the other pirates were ignoring her because she was on the ground. She eased her free hand under the pirate's smelly armpit and reached into her vest pocket, grabbing as many scatterclips as she could get her fingers around, and then laid them out on the dead pirate's back.

Whenever a pirate got close enough, Lani fired. She managed to take down eleven pirates over the course of her lengthy entrapment. But things were only getting worse instead of better, as a seemingly endless stream of pirates rushed ashore.

Soon Lani was the only living member of her team who hadn't taken to the trees in hiding or run into Quill for safety. The remaining band of pirates rushed toward the mansion.

"You stupid brute!" Lani yelled, pounding on the dead man's back. She pushed with all her might, but with only one hand free, she wasn't nearly strong enough. Finally she fell back, exhausted. Her trapped arm had lost feeling by now, and the rocks dug into her back. She closed her eyes, furious, and breathed heavily, trying to build strength. And then, out of immense frustration, Lani tried a spell she'd never done before.

She put her hand on the dead pirate's back, took a few calming breaths, and concentrated on an image in her mind of Queen Eagala's stupid face. When she felt good and calm and ready, Lani whispered, "Transport."

An instant later Lani was free, and almost simultaneously a hideous scream rose up from a nearby ship. Lani grinned. That voice was one of the very few sounds she'd heard when she and Samheed had been captive on Warbler Island—it was the unmistakable scream of Queen Eagala.

Lani eased up off the rocks and got to her feet. She shoved a sword in her belt, grabbed a shield, and shook out the prickling arm that had fallen asleep. "Yowch!" she muttered, half laughing and half crying as it came back to life. "Now *that* really hurts."

A moment later a stampede of pirates rushed along the shore below, coming from where Samheed had been fighting and heading toward the mansion. Lani knew that could mean only one thing . . . everybody on Samheed's team was down or gone.

"Oh no. Sam," Lani whispered. She peered to the west, then shouted for him. "Sam!" She started running toward his station like a mad person, searching the fallen bodies on the rocks.

"Where are you?" she said, her voice pitching higher with fear. "Sam!"

She scrambled up the rocky bank to the trees that lined the road. "Samheed!"

A body dropped out of a tree next to Lani, startling her. She reached for a component, ready to attack. And then she saw his face.

"Hi," whispered Samheed. "Are they gone?"

Lani blew out a breath of relief and nodded. "They're headed to the mansion."

LISA McMANN

Samheed whistled like a bird. "The coast is clear, everybody. Let's go help out Alex."

Seven or eight Artiméans dropped from the trees and gathered around Samheed, and they all began jogging toward Artimé, picking up a few of Lani's hiding teammates along the way. Samheed slipped his arm around Lani's neck as they fell in step. He wore a mischievous smile on his face and said, "Did you hear Eagala's deathly scream? I'd know that horrible sound anywhere. I wonder what that was all about."

"Hmm," said Lani with a grin. "I wonder."

Aaron Fights His Battles

On the west side of Quill, not far from the base of the new lighthouse where the palace used to stand, Aaron watched and waited with his mishmash team of Necessaries, displaced Wanteds, and a handful of Artiméan spell casters. Those with makeshift weapons stood at the top of the steep rise of rocky land, finding they had better footing there to stop the pirates from getting past them, and a better chance of knocking them off balance on the rocks.

The squirrelicorns had been by to deliver the news about the protective workings of the shields, so the spell casters set

LISA McMANN

themselves up in trees and in the windows of the lighthouse in hopes of staying out of range of the swords and perhaps having a better angle at which to fire their spells.

Seeing the pirate ship stationed in the water with the smaller tenders full of pirates coming toward them gave Aaron a particular sense of dread, for he'd witnessed this scene before—on the way out of the palace before the pirates had thrown him face-first into the smaller boat.

Aaron cringed, remembering the pain. He didn't want revenge. The truth was that he wanted to hide. It didn't matter that Aaron was immortal now—he could still feel pain. And with the number of pirates coming toward shore, Aaron assumed the worst.

He also expected the worst from his team. While they had grown to over fifty in number and were the largest of any team fighting for Quill and Artimé, many of the members had never fought before. True, Alex had given Aaron some especially strong spell casters, which was great. But if the spells were having as little effect as the squirrelicorns reported, Aaron wasn't sure what he was going to do.

The pirates reached the shore and climbed the rocky hillside. Aaron gripped his dagger tightly in one hand and some components in the other, and willed his hands not to sweat. When the enemy grew close, Aaron gathered his courage and rushed forward, tossing heart attack components and scatterclips and shouting the verbal components that went with them, trying to hit the pirate men and women before they had a chance to block the components with their shields.

He knocked down two with lethal components, and several others with the single component version of the heart attack, figuring he'd better conserve components and just try to stop the enemy first. He could kill them later.

His plan served to infuriate the mass of pirates, and several of them changed direction and came charging up the hill toward Aaron, determined to stop him. Aaron cast as many spells as he could, but aiming and throwing them individually and calling out the verbal part of the spell took more seconds than he had before the pirates reached the top of the hill. With one last "Die a thousand deaths!" Aaron turned his back and ran to the lighthouse, ducking inside as his team members came to his aid, swinging rusty makeshift swords, clubs, and even the water buckets that they'd been using all night to douse the flaming tar balls.

The pirates slashed and hollered, charged and stabbed, swung and connected, and soon the Necessaries and Wanteds who had joined Aaron either ran away in fear or lay dead on the road. Aaron and the other spell casters barred the door to the lighthouse and began pelting the pirates with spells from the windows above, taking out a few of them in the process. After concerted efforts to break through the door failed, the pirates grew annoyed by their thinning ranks, and most of them gave up.

"To the mansion!" one of the pirates cried. All but two turned and headed in the direction of Artimé's mansion, the roof of which was barely discernable through the trees, shining golden in the morning sunlight.

With the pirates fleeing, Aaron's confidence surged. Feeling emboldened and remembering his immortality, Aaron recklessly jumped from the window and landed on top of one of the two remaining pirates. She staggered and dropped to one knee. Aaron pummeled the woman until she flopped to the ground, then flung three heart attack spells at the other pirate's back, felling him.

Breathing heavily, he checked himself for wounds, finding a slice on his arm that barely emitted a trickle of blood before the skin came together again. While evidence of the injury clearly remained, it was certainly healing at an alarming rate. The pain, while present, was less than he expected. "Yes," he whispered. He could take some risks. At the moment, he couldn't imagine a better ability to possess than immortality.

He looked all around, and when he was certain the coast was clear, he called to his remaining team. "They're gone! Let's go!"

Aaron's team came running down the lighthouse steps and gathered around him. "What now?" one of them asked. Of the fifty, there were only six men and women left.

"Let's check on Liam and Gunnar and the teams on the north side of the island to see if any of them need help," said Aaron. "And then we'll head back to Artimé to protect the mansion."

Those remaining agreed and set out.

But soon another huge wave of pirates came from the

direction of Liam's station, also heading toward the mansion in Artimé. Knowing it would be crazy to take them on, Aaron and his group hid behind a stand of trees and waited for them to pass. As the last limping pirates passed by, Aaron and his team soundlessly took out the trailing ones, unbeknownst to the other pirates. When the enemies were out of sight, Aaron's team ran north toward Liam's station to see if anyone was alive.

"Liam!" Aaron called softly.

A few of Liam's team emerged from behind a group of rocks, Liam among them. "There were too many," Liam said, dazed. His pant leg hung in tatters, and there was a bright red bloodstain spreading on the remaining cloth. He limped out from behind the rocks, and his four remaining teammates followed.

Shouts rose up in the distance behind them, but they couldn't see anything. "Th-that's probably another shipload of them coming from Gunnar's station," said Liam. "We'd better check on them."

"We've got twelve of us now," said Aaron. "Let's stick together. We have to do something! I can't imagine what things are going to look like in Artimé. I hope . . . ," he said, thinking of Alex, thinking of *everything*. "I hope everyone is okay." He slipped his hand inside his vest to make sure the robe was still in place. It was. The battle inside his head returned while the one on the ground took a brief respite.

Aaron led the group toward Gunnar Haluki's post with Liam hobbling along behind, slowing them down. A short time later, Haluki came out from behind a section of houses. Seven women and men followed him sporting various injuries. Their faces were grim, and they barely spoke.

Gunnar flashed Aaron a defeated glance, and soon the group of twenty was moving along together, growing more fearful of what they would find with the teams on the north shore of the island.

Liam continued to lag, and finally Aaron sent him back to Artimé with one of Gunnar's injured team members, telling them to go to the hospital ward. That left eighteen. They began jogging eastward along the north shore of Quill, looking for signs of Artiméans, but for a long stretch they saw no one and feared the worst for Sky and her team.

LISA McMANN

"Perhaps Sky's team has already joined the others in Artimé," said Gunnar.

"I hope that's it," said Aaron. Neither of them believed it. They ran faster.

Finally they heard shouts and clangs of metal in the distance behind the Ancients Sector. Aaron and Gunnar's squirrelicorns rose up, spotted something, and pointed out the direction. The leaders pressed doggedly onward with their teams struggling to keep up.

When they emerged from behind the new building that housed the Ancients, they stopped to rest and take in the scene. Pirates and Artiméans lay lifeless on the ground, but unlike at the other posts, there were more dead pirates and fewer dead Artiméans here.

A small band of pirates was waging a full attack on Sky's team, with Sky keeping four of them at bay on her own. Carina was there too, with her team in the trees, as was Kaylee with hers. Kaylee had four or five pirates trying to best her, and she held them off, though it wasn't clear how long she'd be able to keep it up. Claire and her team were close in on the white boat, and as Aaron and his group looked on, Claire's team eased

LISA McMANN

their way off the white boat and came creeping up through the shallow water toward the shore.

"Stay quiet," Aaron whispered to his group, and pointed to Claire. "Let's take our cue from Ms. Morning. When her team attacks, and the pirates turn to see what's happening, we'll come in from behind them and strike where they are most defenseless. I think we've got a chance here to do some damage. Stay strong!"

Ms. Morning spotted them and lifted her chin, looking straight at Aaron between the attackers. Aaron lifted his as well, and pointed at her to tell her that he was going to follow her lead.

Aaron's team members crouched behind rocks and buildings, and when Ms. Morning signaled to her team to move, Aaron did the same to his.

Together they ran toward the melee from opposite sides, components drawn, and when the pirates turned to see Claire's team emerging from the sea, Aaron raised his dagger in the air. "Now!" he cried. With his other hand he flung three heart attack components at the biggest pirate near Kaylee. Wings sprouted from the heart-shaped components and they flew

LISA McMANN

straight and true, and struck the pirate in the back. His body jerked, and then his sword fell from his hands, and he hit the ground.

Everyone in Aaron's and Claire's teams dove into the fray. Aaron sent off another round of heart attack spells, hitting the next pirate near Kaylee, and then he did it once more, striking a third, his pockets emptying rapidly. Kaylee, realizing what was happening, focused on the fourth pirate. She kicked the woman's shield aside and stabbed her sword into the pirate's ample girth. Aaron saw it happen, and sent a single scatterclip flying at the pirate to finish her off, crying, "Die a thousand deaths!"

The woman fell, and all of Kaylee's opponents were down. Kaylee wiped the sweat from her forehead and took a breath or two before continuing on. Aaron pivoted and began to work on the next group of pirates. Soon out of heart attack components, Aaron switched to scatterclips.

The other Artiméans were quickly running out of their strongest components as well. The battle raged on, though the numbers grew to be much more even than they had been. With few components left, the Artiméans made use of the swords and shields strewn about, with varying degrees of success—some had never touched a sword until that moment, while others had taken several classes with Mr. Appleblossom. Still they struggled to fend off the remaining pirates, with Kaylee and Sky taking point and Claire consistently firing noncomponent spells until her concentration was shattered by lack of sleep and the intensity of the battle. But their efforts paid off, and the pirates dropped one by one.

Out of components, but armed with his immortality and swift healing, Aaron valiantly threw himself in front of several of his comrades in danger, taking the brunt of many swords and saving a few lives in the process. He cringed and fought off the pain, and checked to make sure the wounds were shedding little blood and closing up as swiftly as the first one had. They were.

Momentum grew on the side of Artimé, and finally the last of the pirates dropped. The north-side Artiméan teams had prevailed, but barely. There was little celebration. Everyone was exhausted, and no one noticed that Charlie the gargoyle had been waving from the boat for the past thirty minutes to try to get the attention of anyone who could understand him.

LISA McMANN

Finally, as Sky limped to the sea to wash the blood off her hands and face, she saw the gargoyle and signed back to him.

Charlie went on a tear, signing desperately, but Sky knew the language well and followed it all. After a quick response, she turned to the ragged crew of Artiméans.

"Everyone!" Sky shouted, her voice crackling with dust and fear. "We have to hurry! The head pirate, Captain Baldhead, is attempting to take over the mansion. He has hundreds of pirates still coming ashore!"

A Solemn
Discussion

The remaining members of the teams of Aaron, Liam, Gunnar, Sky, Kaylee, Carina, and Claire counted off. There were fewer than fifty of them in good enough shape to continue fighting. Several squirrelicorns circled above them, waiting for instructions.

Claire took everyone's canteens to the boat just offshore to refill them from the fountain. "I can take ten of you with me," said Claire, handing the full ones to one of her team members to distribute. "We'll go east around the jungle side of the island to the lagoon so we won't be seen, and then we can attack from that end of the lawn. The rest of you will have to cross the

LISA McMANN

island on foot. We're exactly straight across the island from the mansion right now—it shouldn't take you too long to get there. Then, if our timing is right, we can do the same thing we did here and attack from multiple directions."

Aaron frowned. "We need more components." He called out to a squirrelicorn. "Can you find a way to get us some spell components? I know Alex has sacks of them in his living quarters. Maybe you can figure out a way to get up there and bring them to us."

"Yes, sir!" said the squirrelicorn. "There's a hole in the side of the mansion that leads right into Alex's living quarters. Two of us can go. We'll deliver the ammunition to you before you arrive there."

"A hole in the mansion?" said Sky, eyes wide. "I'm afraid to know what else has happened."

Carina gave the squirrelicorn a grim smile. "That's perfect. Thank you," she said. "Scout out the situation and let us know if we should take a different approach."

"Yes, ma'am!" said the squirrelicorn. She called to one of the other squirrelicorns, and the two of them set off through the air to Artimé.

Aaron approached Ms. Morning. "How would you like to divide us up?"

Claire pressed her lips together. "I'll take Gunnar and Sky," she said, and picked eight others who would give her a variety of skills, both in close combat and in spell casting. "Everybody grab swords and shields. Take extras if you can carry them. Let's move."

Claire, Gunnar, Sky, and the rest of her team wasted no time and struck out for the boat, while Aaron, Kaylee, and the remaining warriors looked to Carina as their leader.

Carina shoved a sword in her belt and grabbed a shield. "All right. Let's go. We need to move fast if we're going to time this right and get it done before nightfall."

Carina set the pace at a jog. Aaron caught up with her and matched her stride, and soon Kaylee made her way to the front and moved in place next to Aaron.

Aaron was curious to know the details of the original north-shore attack. "How did you all end up together?" he asked Carina and Kaylee.

"We stayed in sight of each other," said Carina. "But there were really only a couple of natural places for the boats to reach land because of the rocks. So once we anticipated that the pirates would probably take smaller boats to shore, we talked through our plan. When the squirrelicorn delivered the news about the shields being magically protected, we decided the best option was to attack from multiple sides."

"It was going pretty well," said Kaylee, "especially at first, but then the pirates figured us out. We were in a pinch there for a while when you showed up." She poked Aaron with her elbow, startling him. "Thanks for helping me out. I'm glad you came back with Alex."

"Oh," said Aaron. "Sure. I didn't have a choice, really—I couldn't stay there wondering what was going on. It would have driven me crazy."

Kaylee looked sidelong at him. "I'm still glad," she said.

Aaron wasn't sure if the run was making him sweat or if it was Kaylee.

Kaylee looked closer at Aaron's various injuries. His clothing was mostly free of bloodstains, unlike most of the others. "You sure don't bleed much," she said.

Aaron shrugged. "Fast healer, I guess," he said. Feeling parched and winded, sore from his many healing wounds, and a bit bewildered by Kaylee's continued deep interest in him, he slowed a little, pulled his canteen from his belt and drank from it. Kaylee and Carina were moving along very briskly. It was painfully clear that Aaron was not nearly in the shape they were in. His lungs burned, and he checked on his wounds. They had all closed by now, but were by no means gone. He struggled to catch up.

"We've lost a lot of people," Carina said gravely. "I can't even think about it now. I'm scared to see what Artimé looks like. Who's at the mansion with Alex? Sean's in the ship with Ms. Octavia, I know."

"Simber's there with a team," said Kaylee. "And Florence, and a couple of the Warbler children. Mr. Appleblossom too. And a bunch of others."

"I'm glad Florence is back," said Carina.

"Lani's team is next to Simber's," said Aaron. "And Samheed is beyond her. Hopefully they'll be able to help protect the mansion."

"Yeah, if they haven't been totally demolished," said Kaylee, breathing hard. She shook her head. "I honestly think I was safer on the Island of Graves."

"All I know," said Carina as they ran across the desolate area of Quill and approached the road that led to Artimé, "is that we have to prevail. I don't care if we need to pull every human, statue, and creature out of the mansion to help us— if we fail, we may as well be dead. Because if the pirates and Warblerans take over, you know we'll be their slaves. We'll never be free again."

They ran without talking for the remaining stretch, and as a squirrelicorn approached with a small bag of spell components hanging from her mouth, all Aaron could think about was winning at all costs, because he and all of Quill were finally free of serving dictators. And while his future was uncertain, Aaron knew that there were only two possible options he wanted to pursue. Living out his quiet, peaceful life on the Island of Shipwrecks . . . or taking control of this island.

He couldn't decide which he wanted more.

When All Is Lost

A rtimé was in chaos. The mansion windows were all broken, tar balls and rubble littered the shore, and hundreds of pirates stormed across the lawn fighting every human, creature, and statue they could find. The ostrich statue lay on its side by a tree, missing its legs. The tiki statue was now three individual heads. The girrinos were battered and bruised, and Jim the winged tortoise could only hobble slowly through Quill as he returned from his post, his wing broken.

Florence stood near the front door of the mansion, picking up pirates whenever they ventured close enough and throwing them as far as she could onto a pile of frozen pirates, trying to knock them out. Her quiver and bow lay on the ground—all the magic arrows long gone by now since she'd had to use one every time Alex was about to get decapitated. She tried to stop the pirates from entering the mansion, but with the windows smashed, they had a dozen ways to get in. Finally she had to give up and focus on keeping people alive. And while most of the ships had stopped the flaming tar ball attacks now that their pirates were on shore and in the line of fire, the lead ship continued shooting them at the mansion. Florence could only guess they were trying to take out Simber and her.

Simber soared and dove, dodging the tar balls, picking up two or three pirates at a time and flinging them into the depths of the sea. But for every three he got rid of, six more arrived in a boat to take their place. Simber began to destroy the smaller boats so they couldn't be used to transport more pirates, but the task was made infinitely more difficult by the various rescues he had to make whenever an Artiméan nearby was about to die—which was often.

And Artimé's supply of lethal components had dwindled so low that Alex hadn't been able to give the squirrelicorns many

LISA McMANN

to deliver to the other teams around the island. In a desperate move, Alex sent Fox to bob in the shallow water along the shore to see if he could find any heart attack components that had bounced off the pirates' shields, unused.

Thus, the spell casters were stuck using temporary spells like fire step and slam poetry, causing even more chaos and confusion with the pirates running this way and that as a result. One helpful spell was the freeze spell because it stopped a pirate in his tracks, but the spell only worked if it wasn't blocked by the pirates' shields, which was less than half the time. Using a permanent version of the spell took a lot more concentration than the temporary version, and after the night they'd had, the Artiméans didn't have concentration to spare—especially when there was no guarantee the spell would hit its mark. So when it did, the effects wore off quickly.

It soon became abundantly clear: There were so many pirates, so few spell casters, and hardly any deadly spell components left, that the task of stopping the pirates with magic was impossible.

Alex was the first to realize Mr. Appleblossom hadn't been seen or heard from in quite some time. With the world fighting around him, Alex used a huge pile of rubble to climb to the roof of the mansion so he could check on him. Once he pulled himself up, he looked all around, then crawled up to the tallest peak. He searched the rooftop, and his eyes widened. Mr. Appleblossom was lying on the shingles, unconscious, with a huge bloody gash in his chest that looked like it came from a sword. Had pirates climbed up here to stop Mr. Appleblossom's aerial attack?

"Mr. Appleblossom!" Alex shouted, crawling over to him. He slapped the man's face trying to wake him up, but the theater instructor didn't respond. Alex scooped him up and slung him over his shoulder, then maneuvered sideways to the edge of the roof and looked down.

"Florence!" he called.

Alarmed, Florence bashed her current attacker in the face and turned to see where Alex's voice was coming from. When she saw him carrying Mr. Appleblossom, she ran over and reached up so Alex could lower the man into her arms.

"Oh, Siggy," she said, horrified. She vanished inside the mansion with him.

Alex stayed on the roof, fury rising up inside him at seeing

Mr. Appleblossom like that. With hot tears blurring his sight, he noticed all the tar balls in the gullies and on the flat parts of the roof that would make excellent weapons. Fueled by anger, he began flinging the heavy balls down on unsuspecting pirates.

Florence returned to find Alex. "The hospital ward is full!" she shouted to him. "I had to put him on the floor."

Alex, exhausted, could hardly process the horrible statement. *On the floor? The hospital ward full?* Alex's face was stained with sweat and dirt and blood. His clothes were ripped, and his body was covered in bruises and cuts. He looked down at the quickly deteriorating mansion, and at the masses of pirates tearing up Artimé and his people, and at all the dead and injured that littered the grounds, and at all the ships that surrounded the island with even more enemies still hiding aboard. He looked around for familiar faces of his friends, his team leaders, and he didn't see any of them. Not one. Were they dead? All of them? Where was Aaron? What if Ishibashi was wrong about the seaweed? He couldn't bear to consider it. How could he stand the grief of losing another friend? And then he choked on a ragged sob, and all the hope he'd ever held in his heart drained out in that moment.

LISA McMANN

That hope was replaced by the somber truth. Artimé was destroyed. There would be no prevailing this time. Soon there would be no more people for the pirates to kill, because they would all be dead, except maybe Aaron—and the pirates would just torture him until he finally outlived them all.

"Florence," Alex said, his voice anguished.

Florence turned again to face the mage. "What is it, Alex?"

"I think we need to surrender."

One More Try

Florence looked at Alex. And without blinking, without reacting, without arguing, she shouted in her loudest, most booming voice, "SIIIMBERRR!"

Alex looked at her, aghast. "What are you doing?"

Florence shook her head in disgust. "I want to see you make that suggestion to Simber. I could use a good laugh right now. SIIIMBERRR!" she called again.

"Stop!" said Alex. "Don't do that. He's busy."

Florence opened her mouth to call again, but Alex skittered down the slant of the roof.

"No!" he cried, and jumped on her, fists flailing. She caught

LISA McMANN

him and held him up with one hand. "Really, Alex? You want to break your fists punching *me*?" Quickly she stuck out her other arm and clotheslined a pirate who was running by. He hit the dirt, and Florence grabbed his sword. She stabbed it through his chest, barely taking the time to look at what she was doing.

Alex deflated. He'd lost his mind. He stopped punching the air and hung limply in Florence's grip until finally she set him down on the ground. She pulled the sword out from the pirate's chest, wiped it clean, and gave it to Alex.

"Moment of insanity," Alex mumbled, taking it. "Can we just pretend that didn't happen?"

"I'd certainly like to," said Florence. She saw Simber flying at full speed toward them.

"You're not going to tell him?" asked Alex anxiously.

"Not today."

"Good. Thank you. And sorry. I'm out of here." Alex ran off to start swinging his sword at pirates.

"What's wrrrong?" Simber asked Florence.

"Nothing," said Florence. "Only I see Claire and Sky at the edge of the lawn by the jungle. Do you see them?"

Simber turned to look. "I do now. And the rrrest of the teams arrre hiding on the otherrr side of the mansion, including Samheed and Lani, whose teams took some of the worrrst action. They just arrrived afterrr a skirrrmish with a group of pirrrates coming frrrom the lighthouse, and found the otherrrs setting up forrr an ambush." Simber snarled at a pirate, clamped her in his jaws, tossed her into the air, and batted her out to sea.

"Well then, let's go assist," said Florence.

"Wherrre's Alex?"

"Oh, he's around. Fighting hard."

"Does he know about this plan?"

"I don't think so, Sim. Let's surprise him. He could use it right about now."

Just then, a shrill whistle went up from the lawn where Claire and her team were standing. Automatically at least half of the pirates turned to see what was happening. With their backs turned, Carina and her team of forty rushed in and fired deadly spells at them, dropping a whole section on the lawn at once. They fired again and took down another group.

When the pirates realized what was happening, they all

turned toward Carina's team. With a roar, the pirates rushed at them, giving Claire's team open targets on their backs. Claire's team fired, once, twice, three times, until all their components were gone, and another thirty pirates went down. Then the team went in with swords drawn and continued the attack, with Sky leading the way.

Florence and Simber rushed in to clobber any pirates who had been struck dumbfounded by the attack.

At the sight of Carina, Aaron, Kaylee, Lani and Samheed, and Claire and Sky, Alex felt his heart refire. His friends weren't dead! Sky was alive! And Aaron! All of them! They were alive and fighting and not in any way looking like they wanted to give up. Maybe the tide was swinging just the least bit.

"We fight until we win!" Alex cried to the returning teams, who were equally glad to see him alive. But the returning teams were less glad to hear that there were still pirates and Warblerans on the ships, and no one quite knew what was coming next. They all dug in and kept going.

But the twenty-four-hour battle had taken its toll on their bodies, and slowly their euphoria at the momentary victory began to slip away.

They fought valiantly, but the pirates on land still out-numbered them four to one. It was only a matter of time before the Artiméans would collapse from exhaustion.

"We must win!" came Alex's ragged battle cry. "We must win *at all costs*! Every human, statue, and creature—fight for your life! Fight for our freedom!"

It was those words that stopped Aaron cold. First, seeing Alex alive brought a huge sense of relief, and not an ounce of disappointment. But beyond that, what Alex had said stirred a new idea in his mind. He turned and looked at his brother, taking in the words. *Every human, statue, and creature—fight for your life!* And then Aaron slowly looked the other way, across the lawn, past all the fighting, to the jungle beyond. He stared for a long moment, his sword going slack in his hand. And then he dropped it on the ground and moved stealthily away from the action, around to the west side of the mansion, where the gaping holes in Alex's room were.

Aaron climbed up the rubble, stepped on a broken window-pane, and shimmied up the side of the window, thinking little of falling. He reached high and grabbed on to the opening in the wall left by the tar balls, and pulled himself up and into

Alex's room. He dodged around the mess and the ransacked desk that had once held thousands of components, and ran out into the hallway. He tore down it to the kitchenette, and then stopped short. "Squirrelicorns," he muttered, and raced back to the gaping hole in Alex's wall.

"Squirrelicorns!" he shouted.

Three of them flew to him immediately.

"I need you to come with me," he said. "I've got a dangerous job, but I think you are the ones to do it."

"Yes, sir!" the three shouted.

"Follow me," said Aaron, starting toward the kitchenette once more. "Have you ever taken the tube before?"

The Call of the Wild

The squirrelicorns folded themselves up quite efficiently inside the tube, careful not to poke Aaron's eyes out with their long spiral horns, and there was room to spare.

Aaron explained his plan briefly, and then hit all the tube buttons at once. Soon they were transported to the quiet, dark jungle, smelling its earthy musk.

"I've been in the jungle before, but never this deep," said one of the squirrelicorns. "Sir."

"Well, you're in it now—this is the very deepest part. And it's dangerous. So stay close and do what I say."

LISA McMANN

The squirrelicorns agreed.

Aaron stepped out, twigs crackling under his feet. Within seconds, Panther came bounding toward them. She screamed at Aaron in delight, and sniffed at the squirrelicorns as if she might want to eat them. The squirrelicorns shrank back.

Then the ground shivered and the enormous rock caretaker moved into view.

"Oh good. I'm glad you're both here," said Aaron. Artimé is in a terrible spot, and we need your help. Rock, will you help us?"

The rock hesitated. "Of course I'll help you. But I don't know how."

"That's okay," said Aaron, anxious to get his plan in motion. "I've got that figured out. I'll tell you in a moment, but for now, can you find me some dropbears?"

The rock, which had learned to trust the mage of Artimé with his entire heart, went immediately without question, and soon disappeared into the jungle.

"Panther," Aaron said earnestly, kneeling down and stroking her on the head, "I need you to listen very carefully."

Panther nodded her head and impulsively licked Aaron's face, nearly knocking him over in his exhausted state.

"Good girl," said Aaron. "Please fetch me as many of the vine spiders as you can find and bring them right back to me. Quickly now, all right?"

Panther darted off and disappeared.

"Stay in the tube," Aaron ordered the squirrelicorns. "I'll be right back." He broke into a run down a small path in the jungle. "Where are you, you little terror?" he called out in a kind voice. He looked up in trees and down on the ground, trying to find the camouflaged dog with the deadly spiked teeth.

Finally the pup jumped out at him and bit his arm. Aaron was ready for it, and knocked the dog loose before his grip could take hold. Aaron picked the dog up and held him at an arm's length, then ran back to the tube where the squirrelicorns cowered. Panther stood over them. A pile of vine spiders sat next to the tube.

"Panther, please leave the squirrelicorns alone. They are not edible." Panther sat back on her haunches. Aaron held the dog up to show the squirrelicorns, leaving a safe distance between them. "One of you take this dog. If you hold him just right, he won't bite your leg off. Go straight through the tube and out of the mansion, and deposit the dog on the nearest enemy ship, and then come back immediately. Who is willing?"

All three of the brave squirrelicorns volunteered, so Aaron chose one and had the other two exit the tube. Aaron showed the chosen squirrelicorn the button he'd need to push, and then explained how to push all of the buttons at once in the mansion's tube in order to return.

Aaron carefully handed off the grinning dog, stood aside, and watched the squirrelicorn poke the button with his horn and disappear.

The ground shook again. Aaron, Panther, and the two squirrelicorns turned sharply to see what was coming, and they watched as the rock rolled into the area. Upon it sat six dropbears.

"That's perfect," Aaron said to the rock. "Hold tight there for a minute until our other squirrelicorn returns."

A moment later, the first squirrelicorn returned without the dog. "Job completed, sir," he said.

LISA McMANN

"Excellent work," said Aaron. "Okay, now this next part is going to be a little more difficult. I need each of you squirrelicorns to take two dropbears. They'll hold on to your bodies, but you need to hold on to them as well so they don't fall onto land. We need all six of these to go to the ship Queen Eagala is on. The way to do this is to fly overhead and hover there, and the dropbears will let go when they see a person they want to eat. Got it?"

The squirrelicorns contained their horror like professionals and confirmed that they understood completely.

Aaron set up the squirrelicorns with one dropbear clinging to each of their back legs. The squirrelicorns gripped the dropbears' fur with their claws, their wings flapping to keep them aloft. Aaron helped everyone squeeze inside the tube, and then said, "Once your bears have dropped, find Florence, tell her what we're doing, and ask her to come to the hole in the side of the mansion. I'm going to need some help."

"Yes, sir!" said the squirrelicorns. The dropbears were silent, but looked pleased to be going on an adventure. A moment later they all disappeared, and Aaron was left standing with Panther and the rock.

Aaron turned to the rock. "I'm going to take Panther with me. She's trained now. I think we'll be okay—I'm taking the vine spiders, too."

"And how can I help?" asked the rock. "Or . . . is my work finished?" He seemed sad to think it.

"Your work is definitely not finished," said Aaron. "If you're willing, I'd like you to go farther than you've ever ventured before," said Aaron. "Will you leave the jungle? Forge a path to the lawn and help Artimé?"

The rock seemed intensely excited about the proposition. "I—I will. If you think it's best."

"I do," said Aaron earnestly. "I believe you can help us a lot. We can use you to hide behind, and inside your mouth if you don't mind. And maybe if you find any other creatures along the journey who might do damage on board a ship, you could bring them along as well."

The rock rose up a little straighter. "I can certainly do all of those things," he said.

Aaron smiled and placed his hand on the side of the rock. "Thank you. And thank you for trusting me so willingly. You've been such a good friend to me, and, well, I don't . . . I don't actually deserve it." Aaron cringed, and realized he couldn't ask the rock to do such a major thing as this under false pretenses. His time to confess had come. He closed his eyes briefly, then opened them and forged ahead with it.

"You see," Aaron went on, "I'm not actually who you think I am. I'm not Alex. I'm Alex's twin brother, Aaron. And I've been . . . I've been lying to you. All this time. I'm dreadfully sorry, and I haven't found a good way to tell you once I knew I had to. I just hope that you will forgive me. And I understand if you don't want to be a part of this now. I truly do."

The rock rumbled loud and low. "I know," he said.

Aaron hazarded a glance. "You know . . . what?"

"I know that you are Aaron. Marcus told me about you, too."

Aaron stared. "How long have you known?"

The rock thought for a moment. "I suspected from the beginning when you knew absolutely nothing about fixing Panther's tail. And when you began playing fetch with Panther, I became certain. Marcus told me I'd know the difference between you boys because you are right-handed and Alex is left-handed."

Aaron was flabbergasted. "You let me lie to you all this time? Even though I was hated by all of Artimé?" he asked.

The rock smiled, revealing a glimpse inside his cavernous mouth. "Marcus didn't hate you. He said you were misunderstood. A misfit, just like us. I thought you probably belonged here in the jungle."

Aaron didn't know what to think. And there wasn't time to process.

"I'm sure you're needed back in battle. I'll be off now," said the rock. "I'll wait on the lawn until I'm needed." With that, the rock moved surprisingly fast over the paths, almost with a spring in his stride.

"Unbelievable," Aaron murmured. He piled the spiders inside the tube, stepped in, and looked at Panther. "Looks like it's just you and me and the spiders now," he said. "Can I trust you?"

Panther was ridiculously still, appearing to be frozen. For a horrible second, Aaron wondered if Alex had been killed and Artimé was gone, all the statues and creatures freezing in their tracks as they'd done before. But then Aaron remembered who was head mage. And Panther opened her mouth and screamed in his face.

When Aaron got over the shock of it, he called her to join him in the tube. Panther rose on her hind legs and put her front paws on Aaron's shoulders, and when she had squeezed fully inside the tube, Aaron pushed the button. Soon Panther was in Artimé once more.

Jungle Unleashed

aron and Panther nearly fell out of the tube into the kitchenette. It had been a tight squeeze. Aaron gathered up the spiders, and then he led Panther down the hallway to Alex's living quarters.

Florence stood outside the hole looking in at them. Her eyes widened when she saw the panther. "You're either brilliant or a total idiot, Aaron Stowe," she said brusquely. "I'm hoping for brilliant, but quite honestly we'll take anything right now." Florence eyed the killer panther warily. "Which ship does she go on?"

"I want to keep her here on land," said Aaron, trying to sound more confident than he was.

Florence looked at him. "Won't she kill randomly like she did Eva Fathom?"

Aaron hesitated. "I'm confident that she will follow my commands. I've been training her for quite some time now."

"Ah, so that's where you go off to when you head down the mage's hallway," said Florence. "Simber and I have a bet going, and neither one of us is right. I'm kind of mad about it."

"Yes," said Aaron. "That's where. Alex doesn't know . . . I still have to tell him, so if you could maybe not mention it . . ."

"There will be time for you to tell him after we win this war," said Florence. She reached up and stroked Panther's head. "Okay," she said with a sigh. "I guess I trust you."

She was looking at Panther but talking to Aaron. Or at least that's what Aaron thought. "I'll try not to let you down," Aaron said.

"Even if she kills randomly," muttered Florence, "she's got an eighty percent chance of getting a pirate." Florence helped Aaron down with his bundle of vine creations, then picked up Panther and set her beside him. "I'll go with you. We could really use a big distraction to give our people a minute to breathe."

They went around the mansion. Panther began to shake

with excitement at the activity on the lawn. She clearly recognized this place.

"Stay with me, Panther," said Aaron, and he began talking softly to her as they entered the fight scene. People moved out of the way when they saw them coming. Aaron dropped all the spiders at his feet except for one, and stroked Panther's neck at the same time. And then he started singling out the biggest, meanest pirates. He wound his arm back and let the first spider soar through the air, hitting a startled pirate in the shoulder with it.

"Attack!" he cried.

Panther needed no further urging. She took three powerful bounds and leaped at the pirate, shoving him to the ground. Her giant jaws opened wide, and her gleaming teeth dripped with saliva. It was lights out forever for the man.

"Panther!" Aaron commanded. Panther came bounding back with the spider daintily in her mouth and set it at Aaron's feet. He threw another spider at a pirate, commanding Panther to attack her. And another, and another, and another. With no one daring to come near him, Aaron realized he could probably play this game for as long as his arm held out.

By the time Alex noticed what was happening, Panther had

taken down nine pirates, the little dog had terrorized the entire top deck of one of the Warbler ships and had headed below-decks, and the dropbears were having a terrific lunch on board Queen Eagala's ship. By the time the enormous rock burst out of the jungle and rolled into Artimé, Alex was dashing into the mansion with an idea of his own.

The rock moved over the lawn toward Aaron and Panther, and several pirates ran in the other direction, holding their fighting to see what was happening this time.

"Aaron," said the rock, barely opening his mouth, "I brought a jungle friend to help."

Aaron's eyes widened. He tried to think of other creatures he'd met in the jungle, but his brain was fuzzy from lack of sleep. He shook his head dumbly. "Who is it?"

"It's the scorpion." The rock was clearly pleased with himself. He opened up his mouth, and there in the cavernous space was an enormous orange scorpion, tail swishing, pinchers waving. And with the rock's mouth open, it saw its chance for escape. The scorpion darted out and jumped down onto the lawn, squirming and charging unpredictably.

Screams resounded, and Aaron yelled louder than anyone.

LISA McMANN

"FLORENCE! SIMBER! HELP!" Valiantly he threw himself on the poisonous tail and held on, trying to avoid the deadly stinger and keep it from hitting anyone from Artimé. It didn't take long for the scorpion to buck Aaron off and send him sailing. Panther chased after him.

Florence came running and jumped on the beast's back. They twisted and fought over the torn up lawn, rolling over bodies and flipping through the air. The scorpion's tail slashed and struck out as Florence tried to pin the thing to the ground.

Simber swooped in, Florence rolled the scorpion on top of her, and Simber grabbed it with his claws and lifted it into the air. He flew straight out over the water to a ship that hadn't seen any exciting creatures yet and dropped it on board, just barely dodging the swinging catapult arm that all the ships had ready, like giant flyswatters, to keep Simber from getting too close.

A moment later, on the next ship over, an enormous mastodon statue appeared on deck, completely still, crushing the ship's catapult with his weight. Alex came running out of the mansion as Simber was returning to shore, and Simber, anticipating what was happening, swooped in low over land.

Alex jumped on the cheetah's back, and with barely an

explanation, Simber knew exactly what to do. He landed on top of the mastodon. Alex slid off him and crouched low on the stone beast to avoid the sleep darts that were being blown at him. The world watched, straining to hear what was happening.

Whispers of "It's Ol' Tater!" went around the lawn. Within seconds the mastodon came alive and began stomping around on the pirate ship. Simber grabbed Alex by the robe collar before he could get flung off Ol' Tater's back, and they cleared the area, flying over to Artimé's ship and pausing on board for a moment to see what would happen next.

In a mad rush from the four vessels nearest Artimé, pirates and Warblerans began to abandon ship at a remarkable pace. Once in the water, many of them cried out for help because they couldn't swim. The pirates on the lawn stopped fighting and watched what was happening, and as the sun set behind the ships, they began running for the small boats on shore that hadn't been crushed by Simber. Shoving off in a panic, they retreated to their ships to rescue their drowning people.

The Artiméans would sleep that night.

But the ships didn't go away.

LISA McMANN

Death Be Not Proud

When all the pirates had retreated, Aaron caught his breath and decided he'd pushed his luck with Panther about as far as it could go. As the other Artiméans moved slowly back to the mansion, Aaron made the trip back to the jungle with her. And with his arm aching and no longer fit to throw endless amounts of vine spiders, he thanked her and said goodbye, promising he'd visit again when the war was over.

When he returned to the mansion, he went straight to his room, completely exhausted. And with the absence of the adrenaline came the growth of the aching from his multitude of wounds. He hadn't died. But he hurt so badly he almost wished he could. At this moment he was especially glad not to be the head mage, with all the responsibilities that went with it. He poured himself a bath.

Alex's first duty once quiet had descended on the island was to extend the hospital ward to a size it had never been before, adding fifty more beds so those injured who'd been deposited in the entryway for lack of space would finally have one. Even with the extra beds, the ward was nearly filled, and all non-injured and visitors were sent out of the crowded ward so the overworked nurses could do their best to handle everyone who needed help.

Carina came into the mansion, dropped her sword and shield, cleaned up, and started a shift in the hospital ward with hardly a blink of an eye. She knew the hospital workers were in trouble without Henry there, and she dove in to help.

Samheed, having been banished by the nurses from sitting at Mr. Appleblossom's side, retreated to the grand marble staircase. Lani sat with him.

Alex, unable to retire to his disastrous private quarters, and frankly not wanting to be there without Clive, got cleaned up in his old room in the boys' hallway and then joined his friends on the stairs.

Before long Sky came in search of them and sat down too. Weary, all four eventually stretched out and fell asleep on the stairs. Sky slept on the stair below Alex, Lani on the one above, and Samheed on the stair above Lani. Simber watched over them, pacing through the rubble, going from window to window to watch for movement and checking in with Florence, who patrolled outside.

During the night, Carina, finishing her shift and heading for bed, stopped at Alex's side. She watched the sleeping mage for a moment, then slipped a folded piece of paper into his hand. She shook her head sadly and continued up the stairs.

The feeling of the paper in Alex's hand woke him a while later. He sat up, forgetting for a brief, blissful moment about all the tragedy that had struck Artimé. But his stiff, aching body soon reminded him.

Alex held the folded note up and studied it, bleary eyed, until the words on it came into focus.

Dear Alex,

I am so horribly sorry to tell you this . . . Mr. Appleblossom has died. He left the enclosed for Samheed. Stay strong, my friend.

Love, Carina

Alex couldn't comprehend it. He read the words again. It couldn't be true. He leaned forward and put his head in his hands. Mr. Appleblossom was gone. The genteel, sensitive, passionate, iambic pentameter poet and instructor. The writer of many plays and musicals, like *Perseus! Perseus!* and *And Then Everyone Dies, The End.* Now *he* was dead. Alex couldn't process it.

After a minute, Alex looked up at Simber, a question in his eyes.

Simber bowed his head. It was true.

Alex stood and moved up to where Samheed was sleeping. "Sam," he said, nudging his friend.

Samheed groaned. "What?"

"Wake up. I have some bad news."

Samheed's eyes fluttered open, and a moment later he was shoving himself upright, wide awake. "What happened?"

"It's Mr. Appleblossom," Alex said, his voice cracking. "Here." He handed Samheed the note, unable to find the words to tell him that his beloved theater instructor was dead.

Samheed stared at the folded paper for a minute, unmoving, barely breathing. And then he shook his head. Slowly at first, and then faster and faster he shook it, and began whispering. "No," he said. "No. No, no, no, no, no!" He sank back against the marble stairs and covered his face with his hands.

Alex wiped the moisture from his eyes and sat there, not sure how to help Samheed. Not sure it was even possible to do so. Like Mr. Today had been for Alex, Mr. Appleblossom had been a substitute father for Samheed when he needed it most. There was no comforting that loss.

After a while, Samheed sat up and looked at the paper again. The note was folded into fourths. He took in a steadying breath and unfolded it. Inside was another piece of paper, which had a barely noticeable pencil sketch of Mr. Today imprinted on it. "This is from Mr. Appleblossom's notebook," Samheed said. He looked at the words.

For Samheed, it read.

Below it, a few lines written in a shaky hand.

Good night, my son, and dream of victory. A man of greatest honor, you are he. Rise up and lead, and take these reins from me. A master of the theater you will be.

Samheed read the words. At "my son," the tears came and began to drip on the paper. Hastily he dried it so the ink wouldn't smear.

Alex, doing the only thing he could think of, reached into his nearly empty vest pocket and pulled out one of the few components he'd had no use for that day—a preserve spell.

"Shall I use this?" Alex asked quietly, showing Samheed the tiny ball of rubber.

Samheed stared numbly, then nodded.

"Preserve," said Alex, casting the component onto the note. It melted and spread, covering the paper in a nearly indestructible film, preserving the words forever.

"I wish there was a preserve spell for people," Samheed said after a while.

"Me too," said Alex.

Eventually their grief was overtaken by exhaustion, and they lay down on their steps and slept again.

Chaos Returns

J ust before dawn, Alex was having a weird dream about the chef slapping him in the face with a salmon. It was slimy and wet, and try as he might, Alex couldn't get away from it. He shook his head and brushed his cheek with his hand.

"Ax," said a little voice. "Ax!"

Alex vaulted from the tumultuous depths of sleep and opened his eyes.

"Hi, Ax," said Fifer. She was sitting on the step next to his head, slapping her jammy hand on his face.

Alex sat up, dazed. "Hey there, little Fife." He wiped his

LISA McMANN

face on his robe, trying to make sense of what was happening. "What are you doing here?"

She held up her fig-jam toast and grinned. "Toes," she said.

"Toast," said Alex automatically, emphasizing the *t* at the end of the word.

"Tote!" said Fifer.

"Close enough," said Alex. He gathered her onto his lap and looked around. Crow was nowhere to be seen. "How did you get here? You need to stay in the lounge."

"She came up thrrrough the tube," said Simber, whose head was completely outside the front window.

"All by herself?"

"Indeed," said the cheetah. "Made a beeline for the kitchen. I've had my eye on herrr."

"I didn't realize she could reach the buttons in the tube," said Alex, worried.

Simber backed up and swung his head around inside the mansion. He nodded at the nearest tube. "She had a little help."

On the floor of the tube was a small step stool that Kitten often sat on when playing her triangle in the lounge band.

"You're pretty tricky," Alex said to Fifer, shaking his head admiringly. He knew he should get her back down to the lounge for safety, but her presence was somehow comforting, so he held her a moment more.

Fifer munched happily on her toast.

"Has anything changed?" Alex asked Simber after a bit.

"Somewhat," said Simber. "All the ships that werrre stationed on the norrrth and west sides of the island have moved to this side. They eitherrr don't carrre about the Quillens, orrr they don't want them. They know we'rrre all herrre."

"They also know we're all that's left for them to kill," Alex said bitterly. He drew in a sharp breath, acknowledging the fact that the war would inevitably continue. He shook his head and absently smoothed Fifer's staticky hair. "I suppose I'd better get you back," he said to her. "Sunrise isn't far off."

Before Alex could get up, someone else arrived in one of the tubes. It was Crow, carrying Thisbe and looking fearful. "Simber," he said even before he stepped out of the tube, "have you seen—"

"She's with Alex," said Simber. "On the stairrrs."

Crow dashed over to the stairs, relief clear on his face. "I'm really sorry," he said to Alex, keeping his voice hushed because of the ones sleeping. "We were all asleep, and then I woke up and Fig was gone. How did she get here?"

"She used Kitten's stool to reach the tube buttons," said Alex. "I'm not sure if she pushed buttons randomly until she found the right place, or if she knew which one to push to get to her beloved jam and bread, but she found it."

Crow blew out a breath. "She's very clever. I'm afraid I taught her which one gets her closest to the kitchen, as I let them take turns pushing the buttons themselves. They love it so much." He smiled apologetically. "Sorry again. I'll take her down now."

"It's no problem," said Alex, reaching out and tickling Thisbe under the chin. "It's really nice to see them, actually." He considered telling Crow about Mr. Appleblossom's death, but he couldn't bear to. The news would travel soon enough once daybreak hit. He wanted to savor this moment—it would help him get through whatever was coming, he was sure of it.

Crow looked around. "Wow. This place is a mess," he said. "How did all of this happen?"

Alex gave him a rundown of the events of the previous day.

Before he could finish, Sky awoke. She sat up and stretched, and then added a few details that Alex had missed.

Crow stared, wide-eyed. "So is Ol' Tater still out there stomping around on that ship?"

"He is," said Simber from the window, "and enjoying himself immensely. I'm about to go out and do a flyoverrr to see what's going on. I expect something will happen since the pirrrates and Warrrblerrrans rrrefuse to leave."

"Go and check it out," Alex agreed. "They probably just needed sleep like we did."

Simber left, and soon Lani sat up, sleepy-eyed. After a moment she stood. "I'm getting food," she announced, and made her way down the steps. "I'll get some for everyone."

"Me too?" asked Crow.

"Of course," said Lani. "And Thisbe. Toast with jam all around."

A moment later, as the group talked quietly and Samheed woke up, Alex paused mid-sentence and listened. "Did you hear something?" he asked.

Everyone was quiet. From outside, they heard a low growl.

Sky grabbed her sword and stood up. "What was that?"

LISA McMANN

405 « Island of Dragons

"It sounded like Simber," said Alex. He reached automatically for spell components, but his pockets hung loose and empty. He shifted Fifer to his other arm and picked up his sword, then went cautiously to the window.

"Should I take the girls to the lounge?" said Crow nervously.

Alex peered outside. "It looks like storm clouds are rolling in. I don't see anything else." He turned and walked back to the stairs. "But I suppose we should say good-bye now," he said reluctantly. He propped his sword against the banister and planted a kiss on Fifer's cheek, and then leaned over Thisbe and kissed her, too. "It was very good to see you," he said softly to the girls, and brushed Thisbe's hair out of her face. "Thanks, Crow."

Crow smiled, and then he hugged Sky and took Fifer from Alex. "Stay strong," Crow said. "We need you."

Alex and Sky nodded solemnly. As Lani returned from the kitchen with a tray overflowing with food, Crow turned to let the girls pick up their toast so they could go back to safety.

From outside, Florence shouted. "Look out!" she yelled. "Incoming!"

Everyone turned to look outside, where the sky had turned

dark as night again. Before anyone could run for cover, a silent sea of black poured in through all the windows, filling the mansion.

Crow gasped and his face filled with horror. Everyone ducked and began yelling. The black mass separated into individual creatures that began flying all around Artimé and throughout the mansion, filling nearly every corner and space.

Lani's tray of food went flying. Sky, Alex, and Samheed grabbed their swords and began swinging them wildly through the air, trying to hit whatever it was that was flying at them. Crow dropped to the ground with the girls, trying to protect them, and then he began to scream in panic.

"It's the birds!" screeched Crow, his eyes filled with pure terror. "It's Queen Eagala's birds! They're here for us!"

The Birds

There were thousands of black ravens, and they were eerily silent, opening their mouths to screech but no sound ever coming out. Each wore a tiny gold collar of thorns.

Crow shook and cried hysterically, unable to do anything in his fear except crouch on the floor, covering his face. Thisbe escaped from his numb grasp and ran screaming to Alex, who hastily scooped her up and slipped her inside his robe, while Fifer stared at the birds, mesmerized, oblivious to the shouts and screams around her. She didn't make a sound. The ravens didn't touch her.

Sky battled the attacking birds with her sword, and Lani dove for the pile of shields, doling them out so the others could protect themselves from the pecking.

"Outside!" Samheed shouted. "Everyone, come on! They'll be less concentrated out there!" He picked up Crow and carried him out the front door. Alex, with Thisbe, grabbed Fifer and followed, hoping Samheed was right.

It was dark as pitch outside, though the sun had been rising thirty minutes before. The air was thick with ravens circling Artimé and diving down to peck at anything they saw moving. Florence was fighting off a hundred or more, and Simber was flying erratically above, trying to get them off him. Only Fifer continued to watch them, unaffected.

Soon the birds permeated the residential hallways, pecking at the doors until curious Artiméans opened them to see what was happening. They were pelted by seas of ravens swarming in. The birds filled the tubes and pecked at the buttons, which sent them to all sorts of places the pirates hadn't discovered yet. They flooded the lounge and the theater and library, sending the nonfighters running for the tubes to escape the confines of the mansion.

Over the course of the next hour, every last Artiméan who was able to move found his way outside to the lawn, trying to get some reprieve from the attacking birds. Most found that there was little they could do to stop it, so they crouched on the ground like Crow had done, making themselves as small as possible. But then the ravens began to try to lift the orange-eyed Warbler children into the air.

"Help!" the children cried, wresting themselves free. "They're taking us away!"

Aaron dashed out of the mansion, his wounds and pain so vastly improved from a night of sleep that he was almost like new. Desperately he searched the crowd. Finally he found Alex and his sisters amid the chaos. "This way!" he said. He guided them toward the rock, taking Crow from Samheed along the way. When there was a moment of peace, the rock opened his mouth, and Alex and Aaron quickly shoved Crow and the girls inside before any birds got in. Then they set out to gather up the smallest of the Warbler children and put them inside the rock's mouth too before they got carried off to the ships.

Sky and her mother, Copper, refused to go into the rock, preferring instead to fight, though they were being harshly attacked. Thatcher and Scarlet stayed outside of the rock as well. They beat off the ravens quite desperately at times to keep the birds from lifting and carrying them off.

On Artimé's ship, Sean and Ms. Octavia and the rest of their team took on the fewest ravens, for they'd hidden their orange-eyed Warbler fighters in the lower cabins overnight for safekeeping. But from their vantage point they could only watch helplessly and try to use freeze spells on as many of them as they could. It was such a small number of spells compared to the thousands of birds that it barely made a dent in the population. But they, too, had run out of deadly spells, leaving them with little in the way of ammunition.

Now that every Artiméan was fully occupied outside the mansion except for the helpless injured and nurses in the hospital ward, the ships emptied out into their tenders once more, and this time both pirates and Warbleran people filled them. They began rowing to shore without anybody in Artimé noticing. When they reached land, they streamed out of their boats and began to make a human wall all the way around the bird-fighting Artiméans.

Soon every tender had reached the shore and unloaded, and

Warblerans and pirates stood armed in a giant circle around the panicked people of Artimé, watching the birds do their work for them.

A single raven managed to get inside the rock's mouth. It went straight for Crow's face and began pecking. Fifer reached out, grabbed the bird, and screamed at it.

The scream rose above all other sounds in Artimé and reverberated through the land. Everyone, even the birds, froze and listened.

"That's one of the twins," whispered Alex, eyes wide.

Within seconds, the scream ended and all of the thousands of ravens turned to smoke.

A Familiar Face

The blackness billowed and lifted into the sky, forming streams of smoke like giant black snakes slithering back to the ships, weaving through their sails and entering through their portholes and pouring down their staircases.

"Who—what—?" cried Alex. "Was that Fifer?"

"It sounded like her," said Sky, breathless and incredulous.

The pirates and Warblerans watched wide-eyed, then looked at each other, concerned. And that's when the Artiméans realized what had transpired during the raven attack. They looked around the lawn as the morning light returned, and realized with dread that they were entirely surrounded by rows and rows of pirates, and now Warblerans, too. There were twice the number of enemies than they'd seen the day before. Unfortunately, most of the Artiméans had fled the mansion without their weapons.

Captain Baldhead, looking pristine and unblemished, and only slightly fazed by the unplanned disappearance of their secret weapon, stepped forward to address the ragged, rapidly shrinking crowd of Artiméans. "We've got you surrounded," he said in an ominous voice. "Hand over the Warblerans, or we will end every last one of you." He drew his sword, and everyone around the circle, including the Warblerans, drew swords as well.

The Warblerans of Artimé looked surprised to see their people holding weapons, and doing so quite expertly.

That's why they waited so many months to attack, thought Alex. *They were training the Warblerans to fight.* Alex tried not to show his panic. He didn't know what to do.

The Artiméans, looking small on the torn-up lawn, gazed with false bravado into the eyes of their enemies, knowing it was only a matter of time before they'd meet their tragic ends. Even

Florence and Simber knew they were vastly outnumbered—a wrong move now could cost the rest of the Artiméans' lives.

The orange-eyed among them who weren't hidden inside the rock—Copper, Sky, Lani, Samheed, and Scarlet and Thatcher—stood together, surrounded and protected by their friends. Copper glanced at Sky, knowing Artimé would never give them up. She and Sky had talked privately about this day, and what they would do if and when it came. Sky looked at Alex with love and sorrow and apologies in her eyes, and Alex looked back at her, alarmed, worried that she was going to give herself up for the sake of Artimé.

"Don't," Alex mouthed. He shook his head, eyes pleading. "Please don't."

Sky's chin quivered, and after a moment she turned her face away.

Copper looked at the pirates, her gaze moving slowly over the ranks. She recognized some of them, having slaved for them before her rescue from the Island of Fire. They stared back at her with contempt. She held her head higher. And then her gaze landed on another familiar face.

Her eyes flickered.

His eyes narrowed. And then he tilted his head the slightest bit, revealing the thorn necklace below his pirate-shirt collar. He looked away, and in doing so reminded Copper not to let her gaze rest too long on him.

Alongside the fear grew a tiny sprout of hope, for the man she recognized was her old friend and fellow slave, Daxel.

When All Is Lost
(Reprise)

Copper's fingers brushed the back of Sky's hand, and when Sky glanced her way, Copper shook her head.

Sky breathed a quiet sigh of relief. She didn't know what had changed her mother's mind, but clearly something had happened. And then she, too, noticed Daxel, the pirate slave who had helped them escape with Copper from the Island of Fire. Soon she realized there were a number of pirates she hadn't seen yesterday, all wearing white, high-collared shirts that bulged suspiciously at the neck, and all with the telltale orange eyes. More slaves like her mother.

Captain Baldhead lifted his sword. "Pirates, prepare to

destroy the rock and remove the hidden children!"

A small band of pirates stepped over to the rock, while others filled in their spots in the circle to keep it strong. The pirates raised their swords and began hacking at the rock's mouth. The rock's yellow eyes flinched.

"Stop!" shouted Aaron, horrified. He ran forward, lifted his sword, and sliced it across the back of the nearest pirate who was attacking the rock. The pirate screamed, dropped his sword, and fell to the ground. Aaron took a second swing at the next pirate.

And then the lawn exploded into battle once more. Simber ran at the small band of pirates, knocking them away from the rock with his mighty wings, trying not to hit any Artiméans by accident. Florence grabbed the dead pirate's sword and began swinging, striking down pirates in the circle, two and three at a time. Simber turned and charged toward the circle as well, running a length of it and plowing down pirates and Warblerans in a long row.

Alex pulled his sword and ran toward Captain Baldhead, but a dozen pirates jumped in the way. Determined, Alex vowed to fight his way to the captain or die trying. He swung blindly with all his might, felling one after another, but there was always one more to take his place.

Meanwhile Daxel lifted his finger to his lips, and at first Copper thought he was asking her to be quiet, but then she realized it was a signal. Forty or fifty pirate slaves threw off their jackets and ripped open their shirt collars, revealing their thornaments. And then several dozen Warblerans removed golden Warbler bird emblems from their shirts and tossed them to the ground, and pulled colorful ribbons from their pockets and put them around their necks, distinguishing themselves from the rest of the Warblerans. Copper watched as one of them signed to her.

"The Warblerans with ribbons are fighting with Artimé!" she cried out. "They're fighting for their children!"

Sky's heart surged as she joined ranks with nearly a hundred orange-eyed people from both islands. She pulled out her sword, hoping the extra help was enough to give Artimé a chance.

And now, with all the pirate ships seemingly emptied, Simber flew out to Artimé's ship to transport Sean, Ms. Octavia, and the others to shore to help in the fight, leaving the ship unprotected,

LISA McMANN

but having no other choice—they needed all the help they could get on land.

Artimé surged, their numbers nearly doubled by the turn of events. But they were still vastly outnumbered, and the pirates and Warblerans fighting against them were bigger, stronger, and had more training for this kind of battle than the Artiméans. The magical land began to falter again.

In the intensity of the battle, no one noticed the eel lifting its head up out of the water and assessing the potential damage it could do on land.

And nobody noticed the other enormous sea creature coming toward Artimé at a fast clip.

It was only when Lani heard a familiar shout that she glanced up. Others around her turned as well, and their mouths dropped open. Many of them gasped. The pirates fighting them stopped and stared, leading still others to look out to the water. And soon the entire lawn of pirates, Warblerans, and Artiméans focused all of their attention on the strange sight in the lagoon.

First came Spike the whale. Sitting on her back was Henry Haluki, shouting, his hands raised in a triumphant pose. On one side of Spike was a giant squid, and on the other was a sea monster. And together the three of them were leading a very large, very alive giant crab island named Karkinos, which gave home to a strange assortment of armed inhabitants standing all along the edge of his shell, waiting to come charging ashore.

Florence nearly dropped her sword at the sight of them. But then she saw a familiar, sinister ripple under the water and cried, "Wait! Look out!"

Some Very Special Guests

Captain Baldhead ordered his pirates to return to fighting, and as the Artiméans continued their battle on land, the eel slithered around Issie the sea monster and yanked her under the water.

Karkinos whirled around, his claws clacking furiously as the giant squid dove for cover underneath him. A second later the crab's pincer connected with the eel. He lifted it up out of the water and shook it until it let go of Issie, and then Karkinos clipped the eel in half. Both ends slithered all the way into Karkinos's gaping mouth and disappeared.

The inhabitants of the Island of Legends cheered and

rushed down the crab's reeflike claws all the way to the shore of Artimé. They didn't wait for orders. Henry, Talon, Lhasa the snow lion, Bock the golden-horned deer, and the blurry, smelly hibagon all began fighting in very special and unique ways.

Henry noted that all the Artiméans were strangely fighting with nonmagical weapons, and he soon figured out that they must have run out of components. He had gobs of deadly spell components left in the crate on Spike's back, having used none of them on his journey. He ran ashore with them and handed them out to the spell casters as quickly as he could, and then at Carina's urging, he went inside the mansion to see how he could help in the hospital ward.

Talon the bronze giant made fists and began punching pirates in the face and throwing their shields into the sea. Their weapons had little effect on him, though the clanging was a bit hard on everyone's ears.

Lhasa showed a vicious side of her no one had ever seen before, and she bared her teeth and began biting pirates in the bum very hard at every turn, and dodging their swipes at her. Bock used his golden horns to ram into the enemy fighters, sending them flying through the air quite precisely in front of Karkinos, who crushed them soundly with his claws.

The hibagon, who was extremely nervous but wanting to help, went over to blend in near the rock, and the mere odor of his presence made pirates run away from the hidden Warbler children just to get some distance from the rotten stench . . . except for one unfortunate pirate who made the mistake of looking at the hibagon for a little too long, and fell in love.

Issie the sea monster lumbered onto land, swinging her tail and knocking pirates down, and yowling her familiar noise, demanding the pirates give back her missing baby. Ms. Octavia jumped on the opportunity to follow in her wake, casting lethal spells on the fallen pirates to keep them down permanently.

Even Vido the golden rooster left his perch and fluttered around the pirates' heads just out of reach. He uttered disconcerting prophecies and made-up proverbs, like "Those who follow Captain Baldhead lose much more than just their hair." At the end of the phrase he drew the tip of his wing across his neck, cutthroat style. Another favorite he recited was "A stitch in time saves NOBODY—YOU WILL ALL DIE! TRUST ME I KNOW!" which made no sense at all but still managed to unnerve several pirates and completely throw the most superstitious of them off their game.

Spike spent her time along the shore as close in as she could get without beaching herself. She scanned the sea for eels, then she circled in and out among the twenty-four ships, keeping close watch and even speaking with Ol' Tater for a moment in whatever language he spoke.

And then on the Island of Legends, in one grand, furry migration, hundreds of dropbears descended from the trees. Like a small sea of gray paint, they poured out of the wooded area of Karkinos, across the beach, down the claw reefs, and onto the shore of Artimé. They surged around the fighters and spread out to the trees, scores of them climbing up each tree and spreading to the ends of the sagging branches, waiting for just the right moment to do what they did best.

Slowly but surely over the course of the day, the pirate and Warbleran ranks thinned until their numbers were merely two to one against Artimé. And at one particular moment when the enemy was concentrated on the lawn under overhanging branches, the dropbears went to work. Without a sound, they dropped from the trees onto the pirates, covering them in layers upon layers of gray fur. The pirates screamed and slid to the ground in shock. Some tried to fight them off, but no manner of flailing or clawing could get the pirates free from the dropbears.

Talon noticed the act, and though he was tempted to tell the dropbears to go ahead and eat the pirates, he refrained for the sake of a safe land to return home to. "Good work, dropbears!" he called out. "Keep them covered."

Now Artimé was closing in, and for the first time the sides were almost equal. But the people of Artimé had been fighting an uphill battle since dawn. They were tired. Most hadn't had breakfast, much less lunch—Alex's breakfast was still on the floor in the mansion where Lani had dropped it after being attacked by the birds. He was sorely aware of his own hunger and weakness, and couldn't imagine how the young children were holding up, stuck inside the rock's mouth. With the hibagon's great stink keeping the pirates away from it, Alex knew he had to get them out of there and back to the mansion so Crow could get them some food and water. When Alex had a moment of reprieve, he wiped the sweat from his forehead and pulled Kitten from his pocket.

Kitten stretched and yawned, having slept through most of the war. "Mewmewmew," she said sweetly.

"Hi, Kitten," said Alex, crouching behind a tree for safety. "I need you to do a very important thing for me. Can you go over to that giant rock right there, sneak between the cracks into his mouth, and get Crow to understand that it's time to take the Warbler kids back to the mansion? I'll get some others, and we'll run with them to make sure they're safe."

"Mewmewmew," said Kitten. She hopped off Alex's hand and landed in the dirt, then scampered around the giant feet of the fighters, dodging and twisting to avoid getting stepped on.

Alex stood up, peered around the tree, and pulled out some more components that he'd gotten from Henry. He eyed his next opponent, choosing only ones in the path the children would need to take to the mansion. Many of them had had their shields knocked away by Talon, so Alex's chances of successful throws were high. He took aim and waited for his moment to strike.

"Behind you, Al!" Samheed shouted.

Alex whirled around a second too late as a sword lashed into his side. He stumbled and cried out while Samheed

LISA McMANN

rushed to his aid and took the pirate down. Samheed's shirt was covered in blood.

"You okay?" Samheed huffed, going over to Alex.

Alex steadied himself on one knee. "I think so," he said, gripping his sword like a cane and leaning on it. The ground swirled before his eyes, and he tried to breathe through it and focus. "Crow . . . ," he said, breathing shallowly between phrases, "is coming . . . out of the rock . . . with the children . . . and taking them . . . to the mansion." He dropped the sword and put one hand on the ground, checking the wound in his side with the other. It came away wet with blood. Was this how it would end? "Aaron," he whispered.

"I'll help you cover the children," said Samheed, taking a moment to rest. "Are you sure you're okay?" He waved Lani and Sean over.

Alex closed his eyes, feeling nauseous.

Samheed frowned. "You'd better go inside with the children, Alex. Have Henry patch you up and get yourself something to eat and drink."

Alex nodded, pressing hard on his wound to stop the bleeding. He rallied, then told Lani and Sean to go to the cave's mouth to help the children out and lead them to the mansion.

Moments later the rock's mouth slowly opened. Crow peered out, looked around, and then jumped to the ground. He turned around and reached inside the rock's mouth, pulling children out and handing them to Sean and Lani, who began running with them toward the mansion, the rest of the children following. Samheed stood halfway between, holding off the attackers. Crow pulled Thisbe and Fifer out last and hitched their legs around his waist while Kitten ran down the rock's side to the ground and led the three around the fighting. Samheed had his hands full when another group of pirates rushed toward them.

"Keep going!" shouted Sean to the children. "Straight to the lounge!" He and Lani stopped to help fight off the attackers. The Warbler children ran for the mansion. Crow lagged behind with Thisbe and Fifer, trying to go as fast as he could, but he was weak with hunger like everyone else.

"Here comes Crow," Samheed shouted over his shoulder to Alex, who was still on his knees trying to get his breath back. "Do you need help walking?"

"No, I'm okay," said Alex. He opened his eyes and stumbled

to his feet, then tripped and fell to his hands and knees.

"I'll cover you," said Samheed. "But get moving, will you?"

Alex got up once more, ran a few steps, and fell again.

"That's their leader!" shouted Captain Baldhead, fighting his way over. "He's down. Kill him!"

Five pirates nearby stopped what they were doing and surrounded Alex. Sean and Lani came running and blasted two of them out of the way, and Samheed slammed his sword over the top of one's head.

"There go the Warbler children!" shouted a pirate. "They're escaping inside the mansion!"

More and more pirates rushed toward the running children. Alex pushed through the chaos and got to his feet, his fear for the children giving him the renewed strength he desperately needed. He ran toward Crow, who was falling behind carrying the twins, and tried stopping Captain Baldhead by shoving his shoulder into the man's chest.

Captain Baldhead swung his sword, hitting Alex in the arm, but then tripped over a body on the ground.

Alex absorbed the pain and continued on.

Captain Baldhead regained his footing and pushed forward,

cutting off Crow and the girls and grabbing Crow by the neck with his hook hand. He whirled the children around to check their eyes, and laughed viciously. "Three for the price of one. I'll take these two little black-eyed ones in exchange for the orange-eyed ones we don't get," he said. "Black-eyed children sell for a premium in the market." His laughter rumbled.

White-hot with fury, Alex swung his sword, but the captain blocked it. He held Crow in front of him as a human shield and began moving toward the boats with his prisoners.

"Stop!" yelled Alex, pushing through dizziness and pain. He doggedly ran after them, trying to get a clean shot at the captain without endangering his sisters or Crow.

"Drop the girls!" Alex called to Crow, knowing the boy was completely terrorized with the hook at his throat and unable to think clearly. "Crow! Drop them! They'll be fine!" Alex stumbled again and fell to one knee, feeling about to faint and fighting it with everything he had.

Crow's glassy eyes cleared for a moment, and he let the girls slide down to the ground. But they didn't like what was happening and ran screaming after their favorite friend.

Captain Baldhead roared his displeasure at Crow and

clutched him tighter, his hook digging deeper into Crow's neck. Crow's eyes bulged, and a trickle of blood rolled down to his collarbone. The captain switched directions, swatting at Fifer, who was closest. He reached her and yanked her up under his free arm.

"Mewmewmew!" Kitten howled, trying her best to assist Alex, but there was nothing she could do.

Fifer wailed. Thisbe screamed at the pirate. Crow's eyes rolled back in his head and he went limp. Alex revived, pulled himself to his feet, and started running after the man again, but seconds later a Warbler enemy plowed into him, knocking him flat.

Thisbe, red faced and furious, pointed her finger at the captain. "Boom!" she shouted.

Captain Baldhead's face turned gray. He shuddered and took an unexpected step back, his boot landing on top of Kitten and crushing her porcelain body to bits. Crow sank to the grass. Fifer tumbled to the ground. And with a loud boom, the captain's body cracked from head to toe. His appendages separated, like broken pieces of a toy, and went flying in different directions.

Alex rolled and got to his hands and knees, then crawled over the dirt and grass to gather his sisters. He held them tightly, unable to believe what he'd just witnessed from Thisbe.

Scarlet, who'd seen everything from afar, came running. She saw Crow on the ground, knelt next to him, and helped him sit up.

"Are you okay, Crow?" she asked, her white-blond hair swishing close to his face.

Crow's eyelids fluttered and opened. He stared at her, dazed.

Scarlet gently pressed her sleeve to the cut on Crow's neck and wiped the blood away. "You'd better have that looked at," she said.

"Hi," said Crow.

Scarlet smiled. "Hi. I think you might be in shock. Come on, let's help Alex and get you checked out." She took Crow's hand and helped him to his feet, then put his arm around her neck and led him to where Alex and the girls were. She picked up Thisbe and handed her to Crow.

"Can you hold her until we get inside?"

Crow nodded numbly and took the girl.

Scarlet picked up Fifer and gave Alex a hand so he could get to his feet. Together they limped and stumbled safely to the mansion.

Kitten's crushed body lay still on the ground for a moment. Then all her porcelain pieces magically came back together. When she was in one perfect piece again, she jumped up and down, gingerly at first, and then less so, testing her body out. Everything felt as good as new.

"Mewmewmew," she said before heading back into the fight. *Seven lives left.*

A Short Reprieve

What?" asked Henry as he stitched up the ugly gash in Alex's side. "You're saying *Thisbe* killed the pirate captain?"

"I'm not sure killed is the right word," Alex said. "Dismantled. Scrambled and flung about, maybe." He winced. "Ouch. Unless I'm delusional, which is entirely possible."

"How did she do it, though? Here, drink some more juice." Henry shoved Alex's glass at him with his free hand and finished his stitching, then fetched some ointment to put on it. "You'll feel good as new by tomorrow."

"I have no idea how she did it," said Alex. "She didn't have a component or anything—not that we have a spell that does what she did anyway. She just got mad because the captain was running off with Fifer, and she yelled 'Boom!' at him and it just happened."

"Yikes," said Henry. "Can we get her to stop saying that word? If she starts saying it randomly to our people, I'm not sure I'll know how to fix them."

"That's just it—she's said the word lots of times, like when she's knocking down sand castles and piles of stones and stuff like that. She never blew anyone to pieces before, though."

"Maybe it was different this time because she was mad." Henry reached for a roll of bandages and lifted Alex's arms into the air, then wrapped his chest. "Try not to get hit in that same place, all right? Otherwise you're good to go if you feel strong enough. Did you eat?"

"Yes, I ate. I'm fine now, thanks to you. How's Liam, by the way?"

"He snuck out to fight after the whole bird incident. He was limping but feeling okay, last I saw him."

"So you heard about the birds?"

"Yeah. Crazy." Henry shook his head. "I'm sorry Spike and I didn't get here sooner. After Florence and Pan left and Spike and I were getting ready to leave, Talon suggested we all go. I couldn't turn the offer down. Are they helping?"

"Immensely. We'd be defeated by now without them. I'm just glad you're not dead. When you didn't show up, Florence and I feared the worst."

"Spike and Issie and the giant squid all pulled Karkinos along," said Henry, "so we made pretty good time. And we came into sight of Artimé at dawn, right when all the ships were emptying, so we just kept rolling in. We saw the black smoke."

Crow piped up from a nearby bed. "That was Fifer," he said. "She screamed and crushed a raven in her hand, and it turned them all to smoke."

"So it *was* Fifer," Alex said, shaking his head in wonder. "We could hear her scream. It about broke our eardrums."

"Wow," said Henry. "You've got your hands full with those two."

"I'm suddenly worried for my own safety," said Alex. "Thanks, Henry."

"No problem. I've got to keep moving—good luck out there." Henry turned to assist the next injured person.

Alex smiled and slid off the bed, then picked up a pile of sandwiches that the kitchen staff had made for him to take out to the others. He headed to the lawn, feeling re-energized.

"Oh good—you're okay!" exclaimed Kaylee when she saw him coming. "Things are falling apart a bit out here. Can I have one of those? I'm starving." She grabbed a sandwich and shoved half of it into her mouth.

"Sure," said Alex. "What's happening?"

"The Loch Ness Monster got stabbed," she said, her mouth full. "She's okay though."

"The . . . what?"

"The Loch—" Kaylee began, then rolled her eyes. "Oh, forget it. Culture gap. The sea monster thing. Nessie."

"You mean Issie?"

"Yeah, whatever you call her in this world. No wonder nobody in Scotland can find her. Anyway, thanks for the sandwich." She grabbed two more and ran off toward Sky and Carina.

Alex was mystified by Kaylee's words, but there wasn't

time for questions now. Half a dozen Artiméans were writhing on the battlefield. He tossed the remaining sandwiches at Samheed and Lani so they could pass them around, and ran to help the injured. Soon he was dragging people into the hospital ward.

The pirates rallied, and their size and experience began to get the best of Artimé yet again. And though they'd been strong for so long, Alex's friends began to fall. Lani took an especially hard hit to the back that sent her flying into the air and landing hard, knocking her out cold, and she wouldn't wake up. Carina got backed into a tree and took a shallow stab to the stomach. Thatcher had a deep slice across his forehead and cheek that wouldn't stop bleeding, but he refused to quit fighting and eventually passed out on the lawn.

One by one, Alex carried them all in, his body and heart aching. Why couldn't they just win and be done with this? Things were looking desperate again. Some of Alex's best spell casters were forced into the hospital ward, leaving the Artiméans struggling to hold their own.

When Alex returned to the lawn after bringing Thatcher inside, he saw a pirate leveling Claire Morning with his fist.

From the ground, Claire kicked the pirate hard, and the pirate slammed his shield into Claire's head, knocking her out. Alex gasped. The pirate lifted his sword up over her chest.

"Stop!" Alex yelled, and tore over the lawn toward Claire, but he was too far away to reach her in time. As the pirate prepared to stab his sword down, Liam came out of nowhere like a bull and slammed his head into the pirate's gut, sending them both reeling back. They scrabbled on the ground, fistfighting. The pirate slipped from Liam's clutches, grabbed his sword, and dove at Liam, pinning him to the ground. He lifted his body off Liam, and before the former governor could move, the pirate ran him through.

Horrified, Alex drew his sword and came up behind the pirate, but before he could attack, Kaylee rushed over and brought her blade down over the enemy's head as hard as she could. The pirate wobbled and crashed to the ground in a heap. Alex and Kaylee pushed him aside and knelt next to Liam, then pulled the sword from his body. But Liam was already dead.

Feeling sick, Alex turned away. He went to check Claire for a pulse and found she was still alive. "Keep fighting!" Alex said to Kaylee as she ran off to do just that. Alex lifted Claire into his aching arms and slogged with her back to the mansion, hoping there was something Henry could do to help her pull through.

With the tide turning sharply in the pirates' favor, Alex needed more than a miracle to get through the rest of the day.

To the Rescue

Aaron limped into the mansion on Ms. Octavia's orders because he was bleeding everywhere. Since he couldn't explain that he'd be fine soon enough, he went. Sky was looking battered and bruised too. Samheed's shirt was in tatters, with cuts all over his chest. The pirates had heard about their captain's death, and they reared up stronger than ever, determined to finish the fight.

Alex began thinking about surrendering again. His people were falling left and right, and the pirates were still standing. If Simber could just finish them off, they could end this. But the fighting was so close that if Simber tried to plow into a

LISA McMANN

group, he'd certainly hit just as many Artiméans as pirates. So the cheetah was forced to pluck them up one by one whenever he had a chance—whenever he wasn't helping Alex bring the injured to the mansion. Artimé was losing fighters twice as often as the pirates.

The day was waning, and so was everyone's spirits. But when the battle seemed endless, pointless, and senseless, and Alex was ready to give up, Simber swooped down and landed next to him.

"Alex," he said.

"Please don't tell me someone's dead," said Alex. "I can't take any more."

"All rrright," said Simber. "I won't. Just look up."

Alex frowned. "What?"

"Look up. And out towarrrd the lagoon. And then up again."

Alex obeyed. In the sky he saw five dots growing bigger. And just beyond the lagoon, he saw something black and shimmering, coming toward them at top speed. "No!" he cried in disbelief. "It's Pan!"

"And herrr childrrren," said Simber. "They'rrre flying."

443 « Island of Dragons

"Are they . . . are they flying here? To help us?" Alex looked at Simber, his weary eyes bright. "Maybe we can win this after all," he said.

"Believe it," said Simber. And with that, he was thundering off to grab another pirate.

Alex ran back into the mansion and went inside the hospital ward. "Attention!" he called. "If any of you are able to return to the lawn, we need you now more than ever. And with any luck," he said fervently, "this war will be over soon. Reinforcements of the grandest nature are on their way. Join me if you are able."

Alex didn't wait to see if anyone would follow. He ran back out to the lawn, picked up a sword, and began fighting with everything he had in him. Aaron joined him immediately, and other Artiméans trickled out of the mansion, limping and bandaged, ready to make a final go of it for Alex's sake.

Minutes later, Pan reached the shore. Alex and Aaron ran toward her, fighting off pirates as they went. Pan saw them coming and curled her tail around them, lifting them up in the air, out of reach of the enemy. With a flaming roar, she got everyone's attention.

The fighting halted abruptly, and the pirates began to grow frightened. A small band of them drew their swords, and in a concerted effort they ran at the dragon, trying to get to Artimé's leader. They swung and connected with Pan's chest, and she watched them in their attempt to hurt her.

When she did nothing in response, more pirates came running to attack. They surrounded the dragon, and some even climbed on her tail and ran up it, trying to fight Alex and Aaron. The brothers fought back, knocking the pirates down, and all the while Pan just glowered at the ones trying to hurt her.

"What's happening?" whispered the Artiméans to one another. "Why isn't she fighting them?"

No one knew the answer, but they were grateful for the chance to rest and watch in awe as the young dragons flew in and circled above their mother's head.

"I hope this isn't a trick," murmured Sean to some others. "Are we sure the dragons are on our side?"

"They'd better be," said Samheed under his breath. He'd done plenty to make them stronger.

Pan looked up at her young, signaling them to pay attention

LISA McMANN

as more pirates grew brave enough to join their comrades and help attack her.

"Watch," said Ms. Octavia to Sean and Samheed and the Artiméans around them. "She's teaching her children."

When fifty or so pirates had gathered to beat on her with their swords, Pan took a deep breath, then flamed them with the heat of a thousand suns, burning them to a crisp in an instant.

Stunned silence was followed by an uproar from the enemy, and new vigor in their attacks. But the pirates were smart. They left the dragon alone and turned once more against the ones they knew they could beat—the people of Artimé.

With the pirates changing focus, Pan began moving Alex and Aaron around over the lawn with her tail, wherever they were needed the most, while at the same time fighting off pirate and Warbleran attackers with her jaws and her fiery breath.

The Artiméans dug in with renewed strength but kept their distance from the dragon for their own safety. Pan's children soared overhead, spreading out, then each found a spot on the lawn to land. Pan called to them in the language of the dragons, and they began sniffing the people, determining which of them

LISA McMANN

contained more evil than good, and going after them one at a time.

Some of the pirates tried to capture the young dragons and drag them away, their greed taking over their senses. Others tried to fight the creatures. But their swords wouldn't cut them, nor would they penetrate their scaly skin, for the dragons' new wings had been protected by preserve spells, which covered them all the way to their extremities.

Pan let Alex and Aaron down so she could use her tail to protect her young. The brothers didn't falter. Instead they herded the pirates toward Pan so she could finish them off.

Arabis the orange and the ice-blue dragon played tug-of-war with one pirate, while the two purples teamed up against a small band of pirates and practiced using their ropelike tails to lasso them. When they reined in a pirate, they tried out their fire-breathing skills. And Ivis the green took to the trees, flushing out the pirates who had gone into hiding.

Pan moved toward another group of pirates and began picking them up with her tail and flinging them like torpedoes onto the ship where Ol' Tater was stomping around. And if the pirates were lucky enough to avoid being stomped on and dove overboard, Spike was there to bat them back on board so Ol' Tater could try again.

The pirate ranks thinned, and one by one the exhausted Artiméans dropped back, both to get out of the way as the dragons had fun playing with the pirates before putting an end to them, and to give themselves a chance to rest. Soon Alex had no other pirates or enemy Warblerans facing him, and he actually had to search to find some. He looked around, determined to fight to the very end, but then dove out of the way of Pan, who was coming farther and farther on land. Some of the pirates gave up and started to run away, but Pan's tail brought them back in. She wasn't about to let any of them escape.

The young dragons began to chase the pirates around the lawn.

Pan spoke sharply to her children, and then the six of them began herding the enemies to one central location, gently pushing the fighting Artiméans out of the way. Soon they moved to make a tight circle around the remaining enemies.

Alex backed off and saw that many of his friends had stopped fighting as well. They moved slowly toward the mansion, watching what was happening, almost unable to believe that the dragons had arrived to help them.

And then Alex remembered. "Has anyone seen Eagala?" he asked.

Samheed looked up wearily. "Lani took her out early on with a transport spell." He looked around. "Where is Lani, anyway?"

"She's hurt," Alex told him. "Pretty badly, I think. Henry's working on her."

Samheed's face filled with concern. He glanced at the enemies, and then back at Alex.

"Go," Alex said. "See how she's doing."

Samheed didn't hesitate. He jogged to the mansion.

Alex looked around for Sky, his heart leaping into his throat. He hadn't seen her in a long time. Finally he spied her, still alive, and his throat tightened. She limped to the mansion, her exhaustion clear, but she lifted a hand at Alex to let him know she was okay. She went inside to the hospital ward.

The rest of the Artiméans and their Quill and Warbler friends backed away from the battle, awestruck by the size of

Pan and the beauty of the young dragons, and thrilled not to have to be fighting against them.

They watched as the young dragons gently pushed the more-good-than-evil Warblerans and pirate slaves to the outskirts of the lawn, and corralled the more-evil-than-good pirates, herding them with their fiery bursts of breath toward the center of the lawn.

Soon all of the remaining attackers were surrounded.

Alex retreated for safety to the front steps of the mansion, with Simber, Florence, and Talon standing behind him. Together in silence they watched Pan demonstrate to her children once more how to decimate an enemy group in quick fashion. And soon there were no more pirates.

When the dragons had finished their lesson, they returned to the water to cool down and play, and Pan joined them there, praising them for their work in detecting the mostly good from the mostly bad.

The remaining defenders let their weapons fall from their hands. Some of them wept. Others fell to their knees, overcome by the intensity of the battle, or the fact that they had made it through alive. None of them felt like cheering.

They had overcome the enemy at last, but it came at a tremendous cost. Alex wasn't sure how many Artiméans remained alive, but evidence of their struggle was strewn about the entire island. How many had they lost? The numbers seemed extraordinary. Clive. Liam. Mr. Appleblossom. And Alex spotted Bock the golden-horned deer lying on his side, dead too. Hundreds more, gone for the sake of Artimé. It was almost too much to bear. But the hospital ward, with ninety full beds, was buzzing with the news of the dragons. There was life in there. The bodies would heal. And Artimé was at peace at last. Was it worth it?

Alex knew that was an impossible question. Would he have done better by surrendering and saving everyone's life, but forcing them to become slaves to the pirates? In Alex's mind, there was no choice—he'd done the right thing. And though he'd faltered, he'd always had people, creatures, and statues to back him up and set him on track again.

Aaron came up to Alex in the crowd, a hint of a grin working

LISA McMANN

at the corner of his mouth. "You made it through," he said.

Alex held his brother's gaze and nodded. "Amazing. And you—you look . . . good, actually."

"Fast healer," said Aaron. His tired eyes lit up, making Alex laugh. "I'm half-dead inside, though. I don't care if it's still daytime. I'm going straight to bed. Wake me up if you need anything."

"I will," said Alex.

Aaron went inside.

While others filed into the mansion to collapse from exhaustion, Florence, Simber, and Alex remained outside looking at the destruction.

"It's over," said Alex. "I can't believe it."

"I hope we never see anything like this again," said Florence.

"Me too," said Simber. "I'm rrready to rrretirrre."

Just then, there was a bit of commotion around the corner of the mansion behind them. Alarmed, they turned to look. Alex's heart sank, fearing the worst—that someone had been hiding, lying in wait to attack. But then three figures rounded the corner, and a familiar voice pealed as they came closer. "What has happened here? Did we miss our chance to help you, Alex-san?"

Alex, Florence, and Simber could barely contain their shock.

"Ishibashi-san!" exclaimed Alex. "Is it really you? Ito-san and Sato-san!" He was caught speechless for a moment, and then found his voice. "How in the world did you get here? Did you build a boat?"

Ishibashi shrugged and smiled his toothless smile, his eyes twinkling behind his cat-eye glasses. "I fixed the tube," he said.

A Little Help

LISA McMANN

fter their arrival, the scientists discovered they'd just missed Aaron and didn't want to wake him. They'd wait until morning to surprise him. In the meantime they helped clean up the mansion and looked forward to retiring to their newly assigned rooms to enjoy the comforts of home: bubble baths, soft beds, and room service. It wasn't too much of a hardship.

Henry and Carina and the nurses continued to help the injured, who still streamed into the hospital ward. Simber, Talon, and the young dragons began to transport the dead pirates and Warblerans to some empty Warbler ships, piling

them up high on the deck. Pan promised to give them a respectful burial at sea.

The herbivorous dropbears from the Island of Legends
returned in a mini stampede to their island and disappeared
into the woods, and the hibagon and Vido the rooster returned
home as well. Lhasa retired to her favorite spot on Karkinos
to mourn the loss of Bock, who had died valiantly protecting
a group of Warbler parents who were fighting for Artimé.
No doubt Bock had wanted them to fulfill their wish of being
reunited with their children again.

The squirrelicorns transported the Artiméan dropbears
and the little dog from the ships to the rock. The rock put
them inside his mouth and delivered them to the jungle to
be with Panther, with plans to return for the scorpion when
Simber was finished collecting pirates.

Alex rode on Spike to the pirate ship where Ol' Tater was
still stomping around and crushing things. Standing on Spike's
back and looking into the very happy mastodon's eyes, Alex
sang the song that put Ol' Tater to sleep.

Once Ol' Tater was in dreamland, Alex climbed aboard
the ship. He pressed his hand against the mastodon's side and

closed his eyes, breathing deeply for a moment, ignoring the pain all over his body. With all the concentration he could muster, Alex focused on the giant empty space in the Museum of Large and whispered, "Transport."

Ol' Tater vanished.

Alex listened for a moment. "Do you hear any screaming, Spike?" he asked.

"No I do not, the Alex," said Spike.

"Good. I think Ol' Tater made it to the right place, then."

"I knew he would." Spike was silent for a moment, perhaps in contemplation over the fate of a fellow magical creature. And then he said, "He was happy to stomp around and scare all the pirates away."

"Yes," said Alex. "I definitely think he was finally happy. If there was any good in this battle, it was giving Ol' Tater a ship and some pirates to stomp on for a couple of days." He climbed down the side of the ship and dropped to Spike's back, feeling like he just wanted to lie down and take a nap. But he stayed stoic, wanting to get as much taken care of as he could before nightfall. "Okay, Spike. Now we've got to get Captain Ahab and his head from our ship so Ms. Octavia can put him back together."

Spike traveled the short distance to the patchwork ship, weaving around the bevy of empty boats that floated untethered in the sea.

Alex climbed aboard and looked around at the mess of a ship. It would take weeks to repair the damage inflicted by the pirates. But it was still floating safe and sound, thanks to Florence and Copper's excellent work rebuilding it on the Island of Shipwrecks—not to mention the preserve spell that covered the exterior from stem to stern.

"You did well, little ship," Alex said, placing his hand on the mast. "Thank you for your excellent service through the years of battle."

Alex smiled at himself, a bit sheepish after talking to the ship like it was a person. But it had been his home for a good portion of the past few years, and it had served him and Artimé well. He thought back to the first time he'd seen the ship, whispering nonsensically in the Museum of Large. And he remembered all the journeys it had taken him on. The uncontrollable trip to the Island of Fire, then to the Island of Silence to rescue Samheed and Lani. The first eel attack that left Florence crashing through the deck and disappearing over the side, to rescuing Sky's mother, Copper. The days of rest and mayhem on the Island of Legends. And then there was the violent trip down the waterfall and around the world; who could ever forget that? And the hurricane . . .

Alex sighed. He was amazed by all that had taken place. Amazed by all he had accomplished since that day in the Commons of Quill when he had been sentenced to die.

Little did Alex know back then that he'd see his brother again. Little did he know that life was just about to begin, and that it hadn't ended for him, after all. Little did he know, on the bus to the Death Farm, that the blue-eyed girl connected to him by a rusty chain would become his fierce friend. That Samheed, whom Alex never liked in school, would become one of his closest confidants. And that Meghan, Alex's best friend from early childhood, would die fighting for a land no one in Quill could have dreamed up . . . except for a man named Mr. Today.

"Is everything okay, the Alex?" asked Spike.

Alex pulled out of his reverie and looked over the edge. "It will be," he said with a languid sigh. "Very soon it will be. I'll get Captain Ahab."

"Good, because something seems strange here."

"Something strange?" Alex almost laughed. "Do you really think so?" He looked around at the twenty-four foreign ships in the water, the Island of Legends sitting off the coast of Artimé, and six water dragons not far from that. Nah. Not strange at all.

Spike circled the ship as Alex gathered up Captain Ahab's body. Then Alex brought it to the side of the ship where Spike had settled and lowered it over the side, letting it drop gently into the shallow water that covered Spike's broad back. The whale rose up slightly to ground it.

"Something is not right," Spike said.

Alex frowned. "Something new, you mean?"

"Yes."

Alex groaned. "Okay, let me grab the head and we'll go figure it out."

"You should come right now," said Spike.

"Okay. One second." Alex quickly went to get Captain Ahab's head. He picked it up and tucked it under his arm, and then hurried back to the side of the ship. He tossed Captain Ahab's head to Spike, who caught it gently with her tail so it wouldn't break.

But just as Alex reached for the rope to climb overboard onto Spike's back, he heard the horribly familiar zing of swords being pulled from their scabbards. He froze for a split second. His heart raced, and without turning around, he lunged for the railing. A second later he was jerked back, choked by the robe around his neck. Somebody was pulling him.

He stumbled and tried to yell as the unknown attacker grabbed him around the chest from behind and pinned his arms down. Soon Alex felt the cool edge of a sword sliding across his neck. Alex closed his eyes and swallowed reflexively, and then he was being turned around.

His eyes flew open. In front of him on the right was Twitch, the pirate captain's first mate. And on the left was another pirate, a woman he didn't recognize. Standing directly in front of him was Queen Eagala herself. Alive and well.

Alex's heart sank.

Eagala folded her hands around the hilt of her sword and held it in front of her, pointing upward, like a prized possession, guarded by her strange, long, curling fingernails that snaked through the air.

Alex opened his mouth to tell Spike to go for help, but

Eagala pressed her sword to his lips, silencing him.

In her most sinister voice, she said, "Your creature had better stay still and silent, or I'll kill you right now." It was loud enough for Spike to hear, and Spike didn't move.

Alex blinked. He didn't dare speak with the blade against his mouth. All he could do now that he'd gotten over the shock of seeing Eagala was curse himself for not making sure she was dead. But how did she get from her ship to this one if she, like all Warblerans, couldn't swim?

Out of the corner of his eye, one of the tenders floated into view, and Alex had his answer. His stomach twisted. Maybe somebody on land would look this way. Was he visible to land? With his back turned to them, he wasn't sure. Certainly Simber would notice if he was anywhere nearby. But who knew where Simber could be, collecting pirate bodies from all over Quill.

Slowly Alex moved his left hand a fraction of an inch at a time, closer to the hilt of his sword. Eagala had apparently begun talking to him, as she was spitting in his face. Alex tuned in.

". . . my count, you have eighty-seven of my people on your island. You will have your creature bring them to me

LISA McMANN

now—all of them, including your friends who caused me so much trouble. But the one I want the most is the child who shattered my raven curse. If you return them all, including that one, I may let you live."

Had Eagala seen the twins? Did she know who they were? Alex was furious, but he knew he couldn't show it. There was no way he'd let Fifer anywhere near Eagala, or any of the Warblerans who had fought for Artimé. He'd never give them up.

Eagala leaned forward, putting her face directly in front of his. Alex leaned back, but was immediately punished for it by First Mate Twitch, who stuck the point of his sword into Alex's neck and flicked it away, leaving a cut. Eagala's sword slid across Alex's lips and left blood trickling from the bottom one. Sweat mingled with the cuts and stung him. He couldn't speak. He couldn't move. His hand was still inches away from his sword.

After a long moment of Queen Eagala staring into Alex's eyes and Alex trying not to flinch, she finally pulled her sword away from his face. Slowly and deliberately she withdrew a handkerchief from her pocket and wiped the blade clean of his blood. "Tell your creature to fetch my people."

Alex could barely breathe. He closed his eyes, and when Twitch returned his sword's blade to Alex's neck and pressed down, Alex lifted his chin. "Spike," he said.

"Yes, the Alex?" said Spike.

Alex swallowed, his Adam's apple bobbing over Twitch's blade. His mind whirred. "Did you hear what the queen said?"

"Yes."

"I'm in some pretty big trouble here," said Alex, his voice quivering, "so let's do what we need to do to get me out of it, then."

"Are you sure you want that, the Alex?" asked Spike.

"I'm sure," Alex said, trying to sound very unsure.

Spike hesitated. "All right. I will go . . . right . . . now."

Alex's eyes widened at the way Spike responded. He held deathly still as Spike shot away from the ship, and then, after a moment of suspended silence, something slammed hard against the hull, and Alex's world began shaking and rocking uncontrollably. The sword pierced Alex's neck a second time before the pirates lost their balance and their grip on him.

Alex pulled from their grasp. He shoved the female pirate into Queen Eagala, sending them both sprawling and tangling

LISA McMANN

in a pile of ropes, and he unsheathed his sword, lifting it up and swinging wildly. He caught Twitch off balance as the ship rolled and bounced, and flipped the pirate to the deck. Twitch kicked Alex's sword into the air and got back up, but the ship lurched again, throwing them both down. Alex's sword clattered nearby, and Twitch kicked it away again, out of reach.

Alex had no time to search for a component. He slammed his fist into Twitch's face as the other pirate returned, slicing Alex across the shoulder, just missing his neck thanks to the rocking boat. Alex lit into her and knocked her sword overboard as Eagala came running at him. Alex sidestepped her and grabbed for her sword, wresting it from her and ripping off two of her fingernails in the process, making her scream out in pain.

Alex threw the disgusting fingernails to the deck and ran at Twitch, who was struggling to get to his feet. Alex didn't flinch. He stabbed the sword into Twitch's stomach and ran him through. Twitch wavered on his knees, then clattered to the deck. Alex tugged at the sword, trying to pull it out, but it was stuck fast. He whirled about, looking frantically for his own sword, and dodged the other pirate, who was running at him. He shoved her into Queen Eagala again, and when she came rebounding back, he grabbed the pirate by the jacket and ran her to the railing, her fingers digging at his eyes and throat. With all his might he lifted her up and threw her over the side of the ship into the water.

Queen Eagala regained her footing and grabbed Alex's sword from the deck. When Alex turned to fight her, she slammed the sword down hard on Alex's already injured left shoulder. The pain sparked and burned through Alex, and he cried out as his left arm flopped uselessly to his side. He kicked Queen Eagala's hands with all his might, sending the sword flying into the air.

"Jump now, the Alex!" cried Spike.

"She's not dead yet!" Alex screamed. He couldn't feel his left arm. He dove for the sword, retrieved it with his right hand and swung, hitting Queen Eagala awkwardly, just hard enough to throw her off balance.

"Jump now, the Alex!" said Spike again, more insistent this time.

Alex frowned and tried gripping the sword with both hands for a final swing, but his left arm wasn't working at all. He couldn't hold it.

"JUMP NOW, THE ALEX!" shouted Spike.

Alex stopped questioning Spike. He threw the sword in Eagala's face and kicked her in the stomach, giving himself enough time to dive blindly over the side of the ship. He sucked in a breath, landed in the water, and sank down, all the while hoping that Simber was on his way to finish the job.

With his good arm, he pulled himself to the surface, and soon Spike was pushing him up and sliding him onto her back. When Alex broke the surface, he opened his eyes and twisted around to see Eagala cackling madly above him. It was all he could do to stare in horrified silence.

And that's when he heard it.

And that's when he saw it.

The pirate ship was whispering. It began tugging against the anchor.

Alex's eyes widened. The ship was whispering. Alex knew the story behind that now—it only whispered when someone on board had died, and then it automatically headed home to the Island of Fire. To the volcano island that randomly spewed fire, then plunged under the surface of the ocean, dragging everything nearby it into its watery, cavernous mouth.

LISA McMANN

"It says it wants to go home now," said Spike, who could understand all languages, apparently even the language of ships.

"I know!" said Alex. "Oh, Spike, this is perfect! Can you break the anchor chain?"

"Yes, I can," said Spike. She swam over to it, slid the point of her faux diamond–encrusted spike into a link, and began sawing back and forth. After a moment the chain snapped. The ship lurched and began heading in the direction of the pirate island.

"There it goes," said Alex, gripping his useless arm, almost mad with joy.

On board, Queen Eagala's laughter died in her throat. "What's happening?" she cried out. "Where is this ship taking me? Who's driving this thing?" She ran over to the ship's wheel and tried to steer, but that didn't affect its direction. The ship had a mission that it had to complete, and it wouldn't change course for anything—Alex and all of Artimé knew that well enough.

As the ship grew smaller, Alex watched with giddy satisfaction. He wasn't worried about her jumping overboard. She

467 « Island of Dragons

couldn't swim. She'd ride that ship all the way down into the volcano, and then be covered by tons and tons of water. "Good-bye, Queen Eagala," he said, holding his lifeless arm closer to him, trying to ignore the increasing pain in his shoulder. "Not gonna miss you."

After a moment the giant squid surfaced next to Spike.

Spike spoke to it in a strange language, and then the squid disappeared.

"What was that about?" asked Alex. "And how did you get the ship to rock so much? Did you do that all by yourself?"

"No," said Spike. "I called to the squid underwater so nobody would hear, and she came to help me."

"That was so smart of you," Alex said. He grimaced with pain, and readjusted his body to take the pressure off his arm. "And did you know I didn't really want you to go get the Warbler people?"

"Oh yes," said Spike. "I am intuitive. And you have taught me your different voices. The voice you used was not your voice of truth."

Alex smiled and shook his head, amazed by the creature he'd created. "And where did the squid go now?"

"He is giving Queen Eagala a little push to help her along and to make sure she arrives at her destination. The squid knows all about the workings of the volcano after being trapped in the aquarium for so long."

Alex marveled once more. "Thank you, Spike. You never stop amazing me."

"You are welcome, the Alex. I am just doing the job you gave me."

"Well, I have one more job for you," said Alex wearily.

"Taking you home," said Spike.

Alex's voice grew faint. "Yes, please."

So Much to Do

When Spike dropped Alex off in Artimé, the mage gathered up his strength and stumbled ashore. He stopped and looked at the island. It was a disaster. The mansion was in ruins. The lawn was a mess with very little grass left, and all of Henry's greenhouse plants were destroyed. The fountain was dismantled and water sprayed everywhere. And Issie the sea monster roamed the land, calling out in her strange, forlorn voice.

Pan floated in the water next to the Island of Legends with her children, all coiled up, teaching them to use their tails to fish as dusk gathered around them. Alex lifted his good hand to the great dragon in thanks for her help. The dragons had saved them.

Pan nodded and looked at Issie. "She continues to look for her child," she said.

"Yes," said Alex. "She sounds terribly sad."

"Perhaps one day someone will find her."

"I hope so," said Alex.

"May we stay here for a while?" asked Pan. "I'd like the children to practice their fishing and flying and get to know the people of Artimé and Karkinos as friends, so they don't forget you."

"Of course! But won't we always be friends?" asked Alex.

Pan frowned and didn't answer.

"Sorry," said Alex. He cringed and shifted his arm. "We'll be grateful for the peace of mind your added protection will bring us. Stay as long as you like if you feel the waters are safe."

Pan glanced at Issie again. "My children will be moving on soon," she said, a hint of sadness in her voice.

Alex had no idea what that meant—moving on. But he knew better than to ask. He began feeling faint from the pain. "You're welcome here anytime," Alex said. "If you get lonely . . .

or whatever. Maybe we can convince Karkinos to stay nearby so you can check on Talon and the sea creatures more easily. And," he added, "don't forget my promise about making new wings for your children when they grow too large for these."

Pan bowed her regal head. "Thank you. I will not forget." She turned back to her children as Arabis caught a fish. She looked at it in surprise, then joyfully gulped it down. Pan stroked the young dragon's back with the tip of her tail.

Alex braced himself against the mansion's doorway as a wave of pain washed through him, and then he walked heavily inside, where those who could move about were rapidly cleaning and repairing. He could hear Florence and Simber up in the not secret hallway, having an argument about how to fix Alex's wall.

Sky saw Alex on her way out of the hospital ward and hobbled over. "Your clothes are soaking wet. Did you go for a swim?" she asked.

Alex looked at her and laughed weakly. "Yeah. Something like that." He didn't want to talk about Eagala right now. He didn't want to talk about anything. He slipped his good arm around Sky and kissed her full on the mouth. And then he pulled back and stroked her dirty cheek, and looked into her bloodshot orange eyes, and pulled a twig out of her hair and threw it outside through the broken window. "I'm so glad you're okay," he whispered. "I love you."

Sky frowned at his swollen bottom lip. "You'd better have that cut looked at. And this slash on your shoulder—you're bleeding pretty badly, and your arm is swelling up like a balloon. It looks serious."

Alex sighed. "I know." He started toward the hospital ward.

"Hey," Sky said, grabbing his wrist.

Alex winced and turned, his eyesight dimming. "Yeah?" he asked. Sky's face swam in front of him.

Sky smiled. "I love you, too."

They kissed again. And then everything went black and Alex slumped to the floor.

Facing the Truth

When Alex awoke a short time later, he couldn't focus on the face above him. Everything was fuzzy. He closed his eyes and groaned, and then opened them and tried again.

"Who's there? Henry?" he whispered. His mouth was parched, and it tasted like stale seawater.

"Hey," said Henry. "How do you feel?"

Alex concentrated on the question. He wasn't sure how he felt. After a while he remembered he hadn't answered yet. "Not great," he said.

"The medicine will be working soon," Henry promised.

Alex closed his eyes again and fell into a black cavern of sleep.

The next time he opened his eyes, Henry's face was easier to recognize. Sky was there too, looking terribly concerned.

Alex tried to sit up, but his left shoulder was heavily bandaged, and his arm wouldn't move.

Henry stopped him from trying. "Just stay still for a bit. How do you feel now?"

Alex blinked. "I feel okay," he said, sinking back into the pillows. "Better."

"Good," said Henry. A shadow crossed his face, and he glanced at Sky, then back at Alex. "I have some bad news."

Alex stared, still a bit dazed. "What is it?"

"Your shoulder was injured badly. *Severely.*" Henry spoke in a soft, firm voice. "We were able to patch you up and stop the bleeding, but I'm afraid . . . " Henry swallowed hard and continued. "I'm afraid you won't be able to use that arm or hand anymore. I'm sorry, Alex."

Alex let the words sink in. He shook his head slightly, trying to comprehend. "You mean just for a while, right? Until it heals?"

LISA McMANN

Henry pressed his lips together. "I mean forever. It's damaged beyond repair."

A breath escaped Alex's lungs as his whole body went numb. "Forever?"

Henry nodded. "I'm so sorry."

Sky put her hand on Alex's good arm and massaged it, her face awash with emotion.

Alex hardly noticed. He stared at Henry in disbelief. And then, a little at a time, he began to realize the devastating consequences of the prognosis.

"But . . . ," he whispered, "that's my drawing hand. My spell-casting hand."

"There's a chance you might regain a tiny bit of movement once the swelling goes down," said Henry, "but it won't be much."

Alex was quiet for a moment. "I do *everything* with this arm. It's . . . it's . . . Don't you see? It's what this arm can do that makes me the person I am! How can this be happening?" He struggled to move it, trying to prove Henry wrong. But as much as he could feel himself putting forth the effort, his arm wouldn't budge, not even a tiny bit. Not even a tremor.

"You're wrong, Alex," said Sky. 'Your arm doesn't define you. This doesn't change who you are."

Alex closed his eyes. He didn't have the strength to argue. Sky had no idea what this meant to him. What if he could never draw or paint again? How could he ever fight again? His lashes grew thick, and silent tears escaped. After a minute, he asked, "Does Aaron know?"

"Not yet," said Sky.

Alex opened his eyes. "Where is he?"

"He's still sleeping—it's not midnight yet. I'll wake him up if you want."

"No," said Alex. "Send a note to his blackboard. That way he'll see it when he wakes up." He turned his head listlessly. "Tell him everything . . . that way I don't have to."

Sky glanced at Henry, and they both stood up. "Of course," said Sky, leaning over and kissing a tear on his cheek. "I'll do it now."

"Thanks." He squeezed her hand. "Get some sleep." Alex closed his eyes again, dismissing them. He needed to be alone to absorb the news. Without waiting for sleep, he dove head-first into his worst nightmare.

He'd never considered how much he depended on his left arm. And now he couldn't help but think he'd lost a giant piece of his identity. His creativity, once unlimited, was practically shut down. He thought of the 3-D drawing of the young dragon that had popped up out of his notebook, and realized he'd never be able to do anything like that again. It tore him up inside.

He thought about spell casting. With his left hand, he was a near-guaranteed shot. Sure, he could cast spells with his right hand in a pinch, but he could never count on them to be perfectly accurate. And he'd never tried drawing with his right hand. Alex pictured himself in the future, once the bandages were gone. He'd wander about the mansion feeling useless, unable to work on his art. Not even able to create precise spell components with only one hand to shape them. If Artimé was ever attacked again, he'd have to opt out of fighting and sentence himself to spending the duration of the war in the lounge. It sounded horrible. His stomach churned thinking about it. Everything had become utterly foreign in an instant.

He thought of Sky, and how he'd never be able to wrap both arms around her again, and a sob welled up in his throat.

People would have to help him do everything. He wouldn't even be able to put his own mage robe on by himself. He swallowed hard and opened his eyes, staring at the ceiling. What kind of head mage would he be if he couldn't even fasten his own robe?

Turning his head to look at his bandaged shoulder, his limp arm, his lifeless fingers that wouldn't move no matter how hard he strained, he thought about Artimé and his beloved people, and what it was that *they* needed most.

He knew the answer without having to think at all.

Sometime after midnight, Aaron awoke to the message. Quickly he dressed and went down to the hospital ward, and found his brother awake. He sat down beside Alex's bed. "I heard what happened," he said quietly. "Are you okay?"

"Not really," said Alex.

"I'm sorry."

Alex couldn't answer.

They sat together in silence for a while, and then Aaron pulled the rolled-up robe from inside his vest. He looked at it for a long moment, then held it out to Alex. "Maybe this will cheer you up," he said, ignoring the pang in his chest. "Me handing this back to you means you're alive. That was the goal, wasn't it? You defied the odds." He smiled gently. "I'll bring the Triad spells book to you in a bit. Or I can put it on your desk if that would be easier for you."

Alex looked at his brother and didn't take the robe. He shook his head. "No," he said. "You're it."

Aaron frowned. "I'm . . . what?"

"You're the mage of Artimé. And you're staying that way. I need you to keep the robe. I . . ." Alex's voice faltered. "I can't be what Artimé needs me to be anymore."

Aaron stared, shocked by the resolution in his brother's voice. His eyes widened. "That's ridiculous." He shook the robe at his brother halfheartedly.

"No," said Alex. "I mean it."

A forbidden thrill passed through Aaron, and he immediately tried to stamp it out. He'd made his peace with this. He knew he should object. He knew he should reason with Alex. He knew it wasn't right. But the tiny thrill wouldn't die. Instead, it grew.

Aaron's grip slowly tightened around the robe. His hands

began to sweat, and his pulse pounded in his eardrums. He stared at Alex, feeling his body sort of hovering outside itself for a moment, as if he were split in two pieces—inside and out. He watched his own hand slowly withdraw, still clutching the robe, and he heard his own voice say almost breathlessly, "Are you sure?" The silky fabric sizzled and sang luxuriously beneath his fingertips.

"I'm sure," said Alex dully. "I'll make the announcement in the morning."

The Longest Night

Alex refused to stay in bed once Aaron had gone back to his room. He had too much on his mind to sleep. The magical medicine had worked quickly and done its job to take away the pain, leaving only his bandaged left arm hanging numb and useless at his side. Henry reluctantly agreed to let Alex get up, and fashioned a sling for him. Soon Alex was moving gingerly around the mansion, trying to get a grip on his thoughts.

Outside, the friendly dragons were protecting the island overnight, but there was little to worry about now. No enemies remained. The atmosphere throughout the sleepy mansion felt lighter somehow because of it, and Artimé's residents benefitted greatly from it as they enjoyed their first delightfully deep sleep in several days.

By now, all of the Warbler parents had reunited with their children and were only in need of rooms of their own to sleep in. As Mr. Today had often said, there was plenty of room for all who wished to be in Artimé—all Alex had to do was extend the hallways a bit.

He managed that much right-handed, for it was mostly a verbal spell. He wasn't entirely useless, which gave him a bit of comfort. But it wasn't much.

He taught the Warbleran parents how to access their new rooms, and he promised to take off their thornaments as soon as he was able so they could experience true freedom from Eagala's reign, like their children had. But first he had to work up the courage to try it with his right hand. Secretly he hoped Claire would heal quickly so he could ask her to do it instead. He didn't trust himself to be steady with it.

As Alex prowled the hallways, he ran across Florence, Talon, Simber, Ms. Octavia, and Fox and Kitten working through the night to clean up the glass and repair all the windows. It was quite amazing what Ms. Octavia and Florence could do magically to make things feel like home again. Kitten wasn't much help at all, but she played her tiny triangle and sang a little song for entertainment, which amused at least one of the others.

After surveying the damage to the mage's living quarters, Alex knew no one would be sleeping in there for a few days. Clive's remains had been removed, but the apartment was still a mess. Alex packed up a few necessities and made his way to his old room in the boys' hallway, where he'd soon be living permanently.

Alex cleaned himself up the best he could in his old room, but he didn't stay. It was too quiet in there, which only reminded him that Clive was gone. He didn't want think about how empty his life would be now without Clive. Without his art. Without his job as head mage. Instead he returned to the hospital ward, where he felt less alone among the disfigured.

Seeing that Henry was running on fumes, Alex worked alongside him and the nurses until all the injured were stable.

When everyone was quiet in the hospital ward, Henry finally sent the nurses to bed, and at Alex's urging, he sat down to rest in a chair between some of the most critically injured—Claire Morning, whose head was wrapped in bandages, and Thatcher, whose face Henry had stitched up, but who had lost a lot of blood and hadn't woken up yet.

Alex kept busy, awkwardly rolling bandages and refilling medicine bottles, watching Henry as he did so. The young healer didn't take his eyes off Thatcher's face until slowly his lids drooped and closed, and he slept.

Lani was across the room. Surprisingly, after having taken that spectacularly awful hit in the back from a pirate, she was awake, but completely unable to walk and had no feeling in her legs. No one knew how long that would last, or if she would ever get better. As with Alex's arm, Henry didn't have medicine that could fix that.

Alex and Lani exchanged heartbreaking looks from afar, but neither could stand to talk about their fates—not yet. So Alex stayed a safe distance way. Samheed slept in a chair on one side of her bed, holding her hand, and her father slept on the other. Henry and Carina had done all they could for her. Now they had to wait and see if she healed.

Eventually Alex found comfort in going quietly from bed

LISA McMANN

to bed, assisting those who stirred and perhaps needed a sip of water or an encouraging word. Alex wasn't the only one facing difficulties—that was obvious. They'd struggle together.

And then there was Aaron, the only one left still fighting a war. After his visit with Alex he'd returned to his room, but was unable to get back to sleep because of the battle raging in his head. First he sat and thought. Then he paced inside his room. When his blackboard got too nosy and started asking questions, he left and began to roam the quiet mansion instead.

He kept the robe hidden away inside his vest, but touched it now and then, alternately planning out his reign and then cursing himself for doing so, until he nearly drove himself mad.

"It's what Alex wants!" Aaron found himself saying in the now empty lounge. He sat on a barstool in the darkness, the very stool that Will Blair had once sat upon, though of course Aaron didn't know that. The only light in the lounge was a bluish glow coming from Earl the blackboard, who was asleep.

Aaron pulled the robe from his vest and looked at it, then he pressed it to his face and breathed in. The fabric was still silky and soft against his skin, but it smelled like sweat from being trapped inside his vest for days. Aaron shoved it back in place with a frustrated groan that woke Earl.

"What's your problem?" asked Earl, a bit grumpily. "Lounge is closed for the night."

"Sorry," said Aaron. He fled to the tubes and went to the mansion entryway, where a glance out the shiny new windows gave proof of the sun rising on a new day. Artimé began to stir.

Aaron turned to look into the hospital ward, expecting to see Alex asleep in his bed, but instead found him up and about, doing what he could to help the people of Artimé.

Aaron watched them for a long time—the way the injured people's faces lit up when Alex came by their beds. The way he comforted them and soothed their fears. The way they responded to him and worried over his injury as if . . . as if they were all family.

Aaron slipped his hand inside his vest and his face cracked in pain. Something inside him fussed and roiled and wouldn't settle.

"Good morning, Aaron-san," said a soft voice from the stairs.

Pain spiked inside his chest as Aaron whirled around. "Ishibashi-san," he said, incredulous. "You're here!"

"I fixed the tube," said Ishibashi with a grin.

"I can't believe it," said Aaron. He tried to smile, but his face was strained and his lips trembled. He jerked his fingers away from his vest and shoved his hands in his pants pockets, his heart engulfed in warring emotions. "I'm really glad to see you." His voice was thin.

Ishibashi came toward Aaron. He squinted, searching the young man's face. "Something is troubling you," the scientist said.

Aaron's vision blurred. He couldn't deny it. He turned his gaze away.

Ishibashi tilted his head an inch, studying Aaron. His eyes were filled with compassion as he seemed to read Aaron's expression. After a moment he said quietly, "Your applecorn is exploding."

Aaron stared at him. And then he broke down and launched himself into Ishibashi's arms.

A Grand Reunion

After a while, Ito and Sato joined Ishibashi and Aaron, and word of the scientists' arrival began to spread. Kaylee came running when she heard the news, for she had often thought of the men since her short visit to their island. They were glad to find Kaylee alive and well and in such good company.

The five of them spent a good part of the morning at the kitchen bar, eating breakfast and drinking tea that Aaron made for them—real tea this time. Aaron and Kaylee filled the scientists in on everything that had happened since they last saw them, from Kaylee's extended stay on the Island of Graves,

LISA McMANN

to the battle and win over Gondoleery, to Aaron constructing dragon wings.

And then it was Aaron's turn to ask Ishibashi a question. "I worked so hard trying to get that tube to work, and I couldn't figure it out. How in the world did you manage to fix it?"

Ishibashi smiled. "You had it mostly fixed. All it needed was a spring." Which was entirely true, though Ishibashi decided not to mention that it was he who had the missing spring all along.

Kaylee leaned forward. "And how did you get from the tube in the kitchenette into the rest of the mansion? Could you see the balcony from the hallway? I've only ever seen a wall there. If you could see the balcony, you must be very magical."

Ishibashi translated the question to Ito and Sato, and all three men had a hearty belly laugh. Ishibashi turned back to Kaylee to answer. "We did not see the balcony. But we did see a large hole in the wall of a bedroom, so we climbed down that way."

Kaylee and Aaron laughed. "Well, don't worry if they patch that hole up," said Kaylee. "There's another way in through a 3-D door that I'll show you later."

Aaron grew somber. "We haven't found a way back to your original world, though," he said, and then he looked down. "I hope you don't mind that I know the truth. Kaylee figured out where we are. It's called the Dragon's Triangle."

Kaylee nodded, a sad look in her eyes.

Ishibashi pressed his lips together and then spoke to his friends for a moment. "It is as we suspected all these many years," he said after he told Ito and Sato. "But now that we are no longer stranded by the hurricane, we have renewed hope that we may be able to find a way out. Perhaps we could borrow one of your many extra ships? Ito, Sato, and I would like to take a journey and see what we can find to the north and south."

Aaron looked up. "And me. Right?"

Ishibashi's eyes burned into Aaron's. "Do you wish to abandon this island?"

Aaron held his gaze. After a moment he nodded. "I do."

Ishibashi smiled and patted Aaron's arm.

Sato said something to Ishibashi. Ishibashi laughed and translated for him. "Sato wants to know why you would want to leave now that you have found . . . a friend?" He smiled,

LISA McMANN

indicating Kaylee, and Aaron could feel his face heat up.

"I want to go with you," Kaylee declared. "Even if Aaron doesn't. I want to find a way home too, if there is one. Will you take me, Ishi? Please? I'm an excellent sailor. Well, I mean, obviously I ended up here, but . . ."

"We ended up here too," Ishibashi reminded her. "The storms are insurmountable in the Dragon's Triangle. It is nothing to feel shame for." He turned to speak to Ito and Sato, and the men nodded emphatically. Turning back to Kaylee, he said, "We would be honored to have your expertise on board our ship. I am sure you will bring us luck."

Kaylee pumped her fist. "Yes!" she said. And then she realized Aaron was quiet. She looked at him. "Is that okay with you? I mean, I don't want to intrude. I know you have a special relationship with the scientists, and I know how much you like to be quiet and alone and—"

"I think it would be okay," said Aaron, feeling suddenly bold. The turmoil in his mind about being the head mage had turned to turmoil of the heart over the proposition of Kaylee being around indefinitely. He definitely preferred this kind. "It might even be nice."

LISA McMANN

Kaylee raised an eyebrow. "Dude," she said. "You have no idea just how, ahem, *nice*, it's going to be. Ishi," she said, looking up, "we have a lot of work to do with this one. Good thing you're patient."

Aaron frowned. "What are you trying to say?" But then he thought he knew, and he couldn't help the silly grin that crossed his face. He leaned to the side and made another bold move, lightly bumping shoulders with Kaylee.

Kaylee looked sidelong at him. "What did you just do there? Are you flirting with me?"

Aaron looked back, suddenly suspicious. "What does that mean?"

Ishibashi laughed loudly and shook his finger at the teenagers. "This is going to be a very interesting trip," he said.

Proper Paths

While Aaron was catching up with the scientists, Alex abandoned all intentions of rest in favor of savoring his last moments acting as head mage to his people.

It was a decent run, he thought. He'd been a good mage, for the most part. He was happy with his time as their leader, once he'd found his footing, at least. But now they needed someone who could actually fight in a battle. Someone who wouldn't struggle to cast spells. Someone whose creativity hadn't been yanked away for good.

Yes, Aaron was the right mage for the job. And his immortality made him the perfect leader for the magical world. With Aaron in place, the island of Quill and Artimé might never have to see another transition of leadership again. There was some relief in that kind of stability.

Once Alex had visited with all the patients, he kept working to keep his mind occupied, scrubbing and cleaning until his good arm felt like rubber. Finally Simber ordered him to take a break and get something to eat. Wearily, Alex decided to listen for once.

Aaron's party eventually broke up to help clean up the lawn. But Aaron had one thing he needed to do first. Tired, but feeling much relieved, he ran up to his room, then went in search of Alex. He found him in the dining room, slumped over a table in the corner away from everyone else, fast asleep. Next to him were the remains of what looked to be a hastily eaten meal. The room was filling up with people eating breakfast, but they were uncharacteristically quiet out of respect for their exhausted mage.

That expression of respect didn't go unnoticed by Aaron. He gave a sad, crooked smile at the sight of Alex's limp arm in the sling. His heart broke for his brother and the difficulties he would face learning to work with his new set of circumstances. But Alex was the most creative person Aaron knew. He'd figure it out in time.

Aaron sat down across the table from Alex, hesitating to wake his identical twin. "Identical," he murmured ruefully. "Not so much anymore." With Aaron's permanently scarred forehead and Alex's useless arm, it was easy to tell the two boys apart now.

"Alex," Aaron whispered.

Alex didn't move.

"Alex," Aaron said, a little louder.

Alex's head popped up and his eyes shot open. "What? What happened?"

"Nothing happened," said Aaron. "Take it easy."

Alex blinked a few times, took a deep breath, and relaxed. He looked down at his arm, and his face fell as he remembered. "Oh," he said.

"Does it hurt?" asked Aaron.

"Not anymore. It's . . . it'll be fine." He looked at Aaron. "I think we should do the announcement this morning, don't you? I really just . . . ," he sighed. "I want to get it over with, to be honest. I'm going to tell Simber first, of course, and some of the others—"

"Alex," said Aaron. He reached across the table to his brother. "Listen. About that—I have to tell you something."

Alex looked up. "What?"

Aaron glanced over his shoulder to make sure nobody was watching or listening too closely, then reached into his vest and pulled out the robe and the Triad spells book. He put them firmly in front of Alex and sat back. Without faltering, he said, "I don't want to be head mage."

"What?" Alex's face fell. "Aaron, why would you say that? You're perfect—"

"No, I'm not. I'm not perfect for it. I would be bad at it, actually. It's a terrible idea. And it's just . . . it's not something I should do. For my own personal reasons. So I declare—"

"Stop!" said Alex, alarmed. "What are you talking about? Who am I supposed to appoint, if not you?"

An incredulous look crossed Aaron's face. "No one," he said. "You are the clear leader of this island, Alex, and the head mage of Artimé."

"But I can't do anything anymore!" Tears sprang to Alex's tired eyes, and he appeared even more frustrated by their unexpected presence. He leaned forward and lowered his voice. "I'm not fit for this job. Artimé needs someone with incredible magical abilities and strong leadership experience. With my arm like this, I'll never . . ." He faltered, then sniffed and forged ahead. "I'll never be what I was. And even then, I'm not as good as you. That's what makes you so perfect. Don't you see?"

Aaron's face softened. His heart ached for his brother. But he also knew the truth. "The people of Artimé would never follow me," he said softly. "Nor should they. Being the head mage, the leader of a place like this—it's an all-encompassing job that takes way more than just some dumb luck with magic like I've had in order to succeed. It takes the kind of person who can lead people unselfishly, with goodness and love and the best intentions for them. The kind of person who cares deeply about them, no matter if he's in the depths of personal misery, or at the height of mutual harmony and peace."

Aaron leaned forward. "And that person is you, Alex. I've been watching you for years—seeing how your people respect you. How they'd do anything for you. They'll fight anyone you ask them to fight, and they'll work tirelessly together to build a stronghold of a nation just to hear one word of praise from you, and that word stays with them for a lifetime."

Aaron gripped Alex's wrist and spoke with his heart wide open for perhaps the first time, but certainly not the last. "I used to be jealous of your relationship with your people. But now I'm just proud to be your brother. And that's all I want to be when it comes to this island. You could lose all your limbs, Alex, and you would still hold more esteem and authority with the Artiméans than anyone else here, because you've built it. Don't you see that you'd only hurt them by stepping down, after all they've done for you? Do you want to give up like this, right in front of them? And try to explain that you, Alexander Stowe, can't overcome this setback after that impossible victory you just managed to pull off?"

Alex's jaw slacked. He wet his lips and closed his mouth, then swallowed hard and looked down at Aaron's hand on his arm. After a moment he turned his gaze to the robe and the book in front of him.

His brother was right. What kind of example would Alex

be if he stepped down now? His people had lost friends and family and had suffered just as many injuries as Alex and his friends had, but they weren't giving up. They were stronger than ever in their loyalty—to him and to Artimé. And now they were finally at peace.

"You deserve to lead in a time of peace, Alex," said Aaron, as if he could read Alex's mind. "You have to at least try."

Alex's eyes remained on the robe and book. Slowly he nodded. "You're right," he said softly.

Aaron smiled. "I declare," he began again, and this time Alex didn't stop him, "that Alexander Stowe is now the head mage of Artimé."

Alex slid his hand out from under Aaron's grasp and picked up the robe and book. After a moment he looked up at his brother, whose expression was sober but whose eyes were bright. Alex pressed his lips together, then held the items to his chest and closed his eyes. He took in a solid breath and let it out slowly, then opened his eyes. "Thank you," he said.

The End of the End

The scientists decided to go home for a while before embarking on their great adventure, though they didn't know which tube button to push to get there. Alex explained that there was no book in the Museum of Large that addressed the subject, not that he'd ever found anyway, but clearly he hadn't made it through all of them yet. He warned the men to be very careful, though, for no one knew where most of the buttons went—if anywhere.

Aaron and Kaylee puzzled over it with the scientists for a while, and then Ito said something to the others and pointed at the blue button.

Ishibashi looked at Aaron. "Ito thinks it's this blue one because the button in our tube on the island is also blue."

"That makes sense," said Aaron. He thought about the other remote tubes he'd been in. The button in the jungle's tube was white, but there were no white buttons in the kitchenette tube—they were the colors of the spectrum. Aaron frowned. Pushing all the buttons at once would be akin to mixing all the colors of the spectrum, and doing that most certainly would result in white—Aaron had learned that much about color and light in his short time in Artimé. So perhaps there was something to the color matching.

Aaron tried to remember what color the button had been in the tube in Haluki's closet, but it had always been so dark in there that he'd never noticed it. Was it red, like the first button in the kitchenette's tube? He had no idea. And that tube had been destroyed by fire, so there was no way to check.

Ito spoke again, and Ishibashi translated. "Ito says he's willing to risk it." He grinned, and he and Sato stepped aside to let Ito get into the tube. Ito smiled brightly and waved, and then pushed the blue button. He disappeared.

Kaylee looked at the others. "Aren't you nervous for him?" she asked, incredulous.

"Nah," said Ishibashi. "He's one hundred and eleven years old. Good time to die." He and Sato began laughing uproariously. Aaron joined in, as if he were in on some sort of joke. Kaylee looked on in confusion.

A moment later Ito returned. He spoke to Ishibashi, and Ishibashi looked at Aaron. "He says he found the right button!"

With promises to return in a month to join Aaron and Kaylee and set out on their journey, the three scientists went home, leaving Kaylee shaking her head in wonder at the bravery of the three old gentlemen.

She and Aaron left the kitchenette and walked down the hallway. When they reached the 3-D door, Kaylee said goodbye to Aaron and disappeared through it just as Alex exited his partially repaired private quarters.

Alex closed his door and looked up, seeing Aaron. "Did they make it back to the Island of Shipwrecks?"

"They did—it's the blue button. How's the construction going?"

"It's coming along," said Alex. The brothers walked together past the two doors that had never been seen open as long as Alex had been accessing this hallway.

"Do you think you'll ever figure out how to get in there?" asked Aaron, pointing at one.

"I hope so," said Alex. "Now that life is settling down I'll have time to try, at least." And then he chuckled. "And if not, we'll just have to bring Thisbe or Fifer up here."

"Yes," said Aaron with a wry smile. "Either a 'boom' or a piercing scream ought to bring the doors down, I'll bet."

With everyone on the island pitching in, even the Wanteds and Necessaries, it didn't take more than a few weeks for the entire island of Quill to be restored, and soon Artimé was back to looking its best, too. The fountain was flowing properly, the lawn was lush, Henry's greenhouse garden had been replanted, and the mansion appeared even better than new. Alex's living quarters now included a circular glass door where the hole had been, leading to a private balcony where he could sit and enjoy the sunsets. Sky often joined him to watch.

The jungle residents settled back to life as usual. While

Aaron waited for the scientists' return, he introduced Alex to the creatures there and explained how to handle the toothy dog, how to fix Panther's tail, and how to make the rock feel important now and then to boost his spirits. He reminded Alex that the six dropbears in the jungle were carnivores, not herbivores like the ones on the Island of Legends, and suggested it might not be a good idea to let them mingle—at least until things settled down and the island needed a bit of excitement.

Karkinos decided to stay nearby, which made it very easy for the Artiméans to visit whenever they wanted to—and for the inhabitants of the Island of Legends to visit Artimé. That suited Talon and Florence perfectly.

And all but one of the Warbler ships that hadn't been destroyed had been moved to the lagoon, near the *Claire*, until they were needed. It was a very impressive fleet. Alex had instructed Captain Ahab, who had been put back together, to leave one of the ships out front so Aaron and Kaylee could paint and decorate it to their liking and supply it with all sorts of comforts for their upcoming journey.

The hospital ward slowly emptied out one last time. Alex was able to shrink it back to the size Henry liked. The only

LISA McMANN

frequent visitor was Lani, who still couldn't walk or move her legs at all. She kept a brave face and a strong attitude about it with her brother and her friends, and she wasn't in pain. But when she was alone or with her father and she let herself think about it, she cried quite a bit, especially at first. But then she pulled renewed strength from somewhere deep inside her—perhaps it was the spirit of Meghan that propelled it—and she carried on with her life, discovering new ways to live it, though not without immense frustrations.

Watching Lani figure out life in a new way helped Alex tremendously, and it reaffirmed his decision to remain head mage. What was Artimé if not creative enough to thrive with change? They were a people who had survived against the odds since their first infractions under High Priest Justine's rule.

And while Henry, Carina, and the nurses puzzled over Lani's injury, as they'd done with Alex's, they could come up with no way to heal her. But Aaron, ever the designer, was struck with an idea. Inspired by Lhasa the snow lion, Ms. Octavia, and the contraption Ms. Octavia had made for Sean Ranger back when he'd had a broken leg, Aaron began tinkering. With a little help from the octogator, he designed and built Lani an intricate but minimalistic contraption, which she wore like a belt at her waist. It allowed her to move about Artimé in a standing or sitting position, floating just slightly above the ground like Lhasa did. Ms. Octavia added magic to it so that Lani could control it with a few key commands. The contraption could even help her climb the stairs to her room. As Lani got used to it, she began buzzing around Artimé almost as often and as speedily as she used to, just in a different way. And once that happened, it was back to work for her—which was exactly what she wanted.

Often she and the group of friends gathered together in the dining room or the hospital ward to work together. Henry, Carina, and Sean experimented with medicine. Alex, Samheed, and Lani created the concepts for new spells, and Sky, Kaylee, and Aaron executed the designs of the components. Thatcher joined them now too, interested in learning more about how to create spells. It didn't hurt that he and Henry had become close friends in the time since the war ended, and they were often seen having deep, philosophical talks together.

Soon Claire was well enough to remove the thornaments on all the Warblerans who had survived the great battle.

Thatcher's sister, Yazmin, had recovered nicely and was on her feet not long after the battle ended. Their parents were among the Warblerans who had switched sides during the fighting, and both made it through, scarred but alive. Scarlet's mother, who'd grabbed on to Simber's mouth from Queen Eagala's ship, had fought alongside her daughter. Both Scarlet's and Thatcher's families decided to stay in Artimé.

Copper and Daxel, along with several other Warblerans, chose to take one of the ships back to their home island and start life anew with Copper in charge of things. To their great joy upon returning home, they discovered that Fifer's spell-breaking scream had not only turned the ravens to smoke, but it had also broken the silence spell that had covered Warbler for years. With all the thornaments removed, the Warblerans were well on their way to peace within their own vast caves. And Copper, Sky, and Crow made plans for frequent visits between the two islands.

The Island of Fire never saw the return of its pirates. Spike went to check on the inhabitants, and she returned to report that the few elderly people and young children who hadn't joined the attackers continued to live on without trouble in the reverse aquarium, riding the whim of the plunging volcano with no way to escape. Alex decided that once things were under control at home, he'd pay a visit to the residents of the Island of Fire to see if anyone wanted to leave their home and join them in the outside world, living in peace in Artimé. But that time had not yet come.

Life in Quill was back to normal—the only thing missing was the threat of attack. Gunnar Haluki strolled around the almost pleasant streets of Quill, often with Claire Morning at his side for company, making sure the people there had what they needed. Well, most of the people, anyway. He left the few ornery Wanteds alone on their patch of soot.

Crow thrived in his role as caretaker to the twin girls, and his secret admiration for Scarlet grew. He was thrilled to discover that she was staying in Artimé, though of course he said nothing to anyone about his feelings. He liked to day-dream that she stayed because she liked him, even though he knew that wasn't the reason. Once in a while she smiled his way, and that alone energized him for days.

Sean and Carina grew closer than ever and decided to stay together, wherever life would lead them. They hoped for some quiet before they took on any new adventures, though. And Carina's son Seth began to think of Sean like a father. Sean thought that was the greatest thing since magic was invented.

Claire Morning and Ms. Octavia were back in their class-rooms as usual, teaching those who wished to be taught, both young and old. The library buzzed with frequent visitors, and the lounge was much less crowded than it had been during the final battle. Kitten and Fox rejoined the lounge band, and Earl the blackboard was slightly less grumpy than before.

But the theater was dark for now. Former students scribbled poems and stories in iambic pentameter on tissue paper and brought them in to place them on the stage, under a single spotlight. The papers fluttered about at the slightest breeze in butterfly-like tribute to Mr. Appleblossom. And mounted on the walls all the way around the auditorium were the many hundreds of swords and shields left by the pirates—for dec-oration, but easily accessible just in case they should ever be needed again.

Florence and Simber were most often found perched on their glorious pedestals inside the front door to the mansion, as they were meant to be. New to the entryway was Talon, who often came for his morning visit to gaze upon Florence's great beauty and be charmed by her wit. Sometimes the gazing and charming was more than Simber could take, so he went for frequent walks. Once he even ventured into the deepest, darkest part of the jungle to say hello to Panther, whom he thought was quite striking, though he had his reservations about her violent impulses.

Panther screamed in his face.

Spike was thrilled to have underwater friends nearby, and she spent her days as the great communicator between crab, giant squid, and sea monster. She delivered the squid's report to Alex that Queen Eagala had indeed ridden the whispering ship straight into the volcano and disappeared, hollering most of the way.

Sometimes Spike helped Issie look for her baby, though the sea monster mostly kept to herself. Every now and then Issie would disappear for several days at a time, but she always returned. No one ever learned where she went—or if they did, they kept silent about it. Kaylee had a pretty good guess, though.

Pan and her children roamed the sea and airspace around

the islands. Pan made sure all five of the young dragons had met the people and creatures of Artimé and Karkinos and understood that they were friends.

Thisbe, Fifer, and Seth grew very fond of the young dragons, and quite vociferously wished they would visit more often. The girls especially took to Arabis the orange, who was the calmest among the five, and who even let them ride upon her back as she floated gently in the shallow water.

On the morning that Aaron and Kaylee were to depart with the scientists, Alex and Sky sat on the lawn with Samheed and Lani, all of them working on projects of some sort. Samheed ignored everyone as he desperately wrote the last scene of the play he'd been working on so that he could reopen the theater and get the new young students to test it out. It was a daunting task, but Samheed was determined to fulfill his mentor's dying wishes, and he could think of nothing else.

Sky studied the ship's logbooks that Kaylee had recovered from the Island of Graves, wondering if there were any clues inside that would help them understand how people from the outside world first came to be here in the Dragon's

Triangle—and if there was any way out. As an added bonus, she learned a lot of strange things about circus people.

Lani was penning a book of her own. "It's for the library," she explained, "like Mr. Today's journals. So one day after we're all gone, people will know what happened here. And even though I'm writing it down, we have to promise to tell the stories about our battles and adventures and about the way life used to be on the seven islands. We must tell them over and over again," Lani implored, "so they aren't forgotten. Maybe if we tell the stories, things won't ever get as bad as they have been."

Sky and Alex nodded and promised to communicate them to everyone who would listen, starting with Thisbe and Fifer. Secretly Alex wasn't worried—he knew the stories would live forever with Aaron. Samheed grunted in agreement, but didn't look up from his work. Lani watched him, laughing softly. She'd have plenty of time to remind him once he was finished writing his play.

Alex sorted spell components in front of him so he'd have something to give Aaron to magically protect the ship from whatever unknown enemies still lurked in the waters.

LISA McMANN

Thisbe, who was playing with Fifer and Seth Holiday, saw what Alex was doing and sidled up to him. "Dat?" she asked, bending over and picking up a heart attack component.

"Hmm?" said Alex. He looked up at her, and his eyes widened in fear. "No, no, no! Don't throw that!" He lunged for her chubby fist, trying to get the component away from her, and she giggled and threw it at him. Wings sprouted from it, and it sailed at Alex, hitting him in the chest. "Aaauuugh!" he cried, shuddering and falling back on the lawn.

Sky gasped. Lani and Samheed looked up from their work. Thisbe came closer, still giggling, to see what Alex was doing, and Lani quickly realized what had happened. She released the spell.

Alex sucked in a ragged breath and opened his eyes, finding Thisbe, Lani, Samheed, and Sky all looking down at him. "Ouch," he said, clutching his chest with his good hand and giving Thisbe a look. "No more spell components for you!" He coughed weakly and sat up, and quickly grabbed Thisbe when she reached for the sack of scatterclips. "Oh no you don't." He snatched it away and looked at his friends. "This kid is dangerous," he said, shaking his head in wonder. "She didn't even have to say the verbal component—did you notice that?"

"I sure did." Lani nodded and scribbled furiously in her notebook.

Sky leaned over her. "What are you writing now?"

"I'm making sure that if we all wind up dead," said Lani, "people will know it was Thisbe who did it."

"This is going to be very interesting, raising these two," Alex muttered. He put all of Aaron's components into one sack and all the rest into another, and looked around very carefully to make sure he hadn't left any on the lawn.

A short while later, Aaron and Kaylee came out of the mansion, each carrying a few crates. Simber flew them out to load the supplies onto the ship, which was anchored in front of the mansion between Artimé and Karkinos.

When the two returned to shore, Alex got up and took the girls with him to the front of the mansion. Ishibashi, Ito, and Sato emerged from it, having come from their island through the tube and the magical 3-D door, all packed for their first adventure.

Alex looked at their excited faces. "Are you ready?" he asked.

"Yes, we are ready," said Ishibashi. "Thank you again for your hospitality and the use of your ship."

Ito and Sato smiled. "Thank you," they repeated.

"We have more than enough ships to spare," said Alex. He shook hands with each of the men. "Thank you for giving me my brother back."

"He was not ours to give," said Ishibashi modestly. "He gave himself back to you."

"With a lot of help," Alex said.

Ishibashi conceded the point with a toothless grin. "And with Kaylee aboard, I am quite sure we will return Aaron to you somewhat changed again."

Alex snickered. "I'm excited to see what he learns along the way," he said. "I wish you all the luck in finding what you are looking for."

"Thank you," said Ishibashi. "I do not hold out hope, though it's true the pirates were selling sea creatures *somewhere*. Perhaps we will find the hidden land, perhaps not. But it will be a good adventure for us, and one we never thought we'd get to take until you came along." He adjusted his suitcase and looked eagerly at the ship.

"Someone will check on your island a couple times a week,
Alex promised. "And Henry's going to take care of your greenhouse plants and your new outdoor garden. He can't wait."

"We are most grateful," said Ishibashi. He leaned in.
"Henry is a special young man. He is a grand prize."

"Yes," said Alex. "He's quite something. I'm very proud of
him."

By now a small crowd had gathered to wish the explorers well.
The scientists said good-bye to everyone, and then they climbed
onto Simber's back for their first exciting cheetah flight ever.

Aaron and Kaylee hugged people all around, until only
Alex was left. Kaylee leaned in and kissed Alex on the cheek.
"Thanks for saving me," she said.

"Thanks for fighting with us," said Alex. "We needed you.
Stay safe. And take care of the scientists for me. And this one,"
he said, pointing at Aaron.

"I will."

"I can take care of myself," said Aaron.

"Oh, believe me, I'm quite aware," said Kaylee. She gave
Alex a look. "This is either going to be amazing or awful. I
can't quite tell which yet."

LISA McMANN

you two would stop talking about me like I'm not ...... Aaron.

...y because we care," Alex replied with a grin.

Kaylee ignored Aaron and said one last good-bye all around, then left Aaron and Alex face-to-face, with their sisters on either side. Aaron knelt down to hug the girls and say good-bye. Then he stood up again. The brothers looked at each other.

"I'll miss you," said Alex. He hesitated, then added with a secretive look, "Don't die."

Aaron smiled and dropped his gaze. "That's what Clive used to tell you."

"Yes," said Alex.

"I guess it worked."

"Not for Clive, though." Alex thought about that for a moment. "I hope that doesn't mean I'll kick the bucket before you return."

"What bucket?"

Alex laughed. "Ask Kaylee." He reached out to hug his brother. The two embraced, and when Alex tried to pull away, Aaron hung on.

"Thank you," said Aaron quietly as Simber returned to the shore.

"Thank you," said Alex. He blinked hard.

When they finally pulled apart, Aaron's eyes were wet. He flashed a sad half smile, and then pressed his fist to his chest.

Alex did the same. And then Aaron was off.

Alex stayed with his sisters. Sky, Lani, Samheed, and Simber rejoined them on the lawn to watch the ship take sail.

"Do you wish you were going?" Alex asked.

"No stinking way," said Samheed vehemently. "I'm still tired."

"I'm good right here, thanks," said Sky.

"No, I guess not," said Lani with a little sigh. "Though we never found the big mass of land on the pirate map." She glanced at Alex. "Why do you ask, Alex? Do you wish you were going?"

Alex shook his head. "Not even a little." He was done with exploring and done with rescuing and done with fighting. He had new challenges to face. "This peace we have here now? This is what I've always wanted. I hope it stays this way forever."

"So do I," said Simber.

"It will," said Lani. "At least until the next ship or airplane from Kaylee's world gets caught in the terrible storms of the Dragon's Triangle."

They all thought about that for a while. And while they sat there, Pan's enormous body moved into view on the water, her five children flying above her in V formation. Arabis the orange led the way to the west, her wings flapping elegantly and her scales sparkling. They weren't stopping.

"Dat!" cried Fifer, pointing. She jumped to her feet.

"Dat!" echoed Thisbe, and the girls ran down the shoreline, chasing after the dragons.

Pan looked back at Alex, her face full of sorrow, and then she nodded regally. This was her good-bye day too. She would return alone.

Coming from a long walk around the island, Florence and Talon saw the twin girls running toward them. They each caught one and held them up high so the girls could see their precious dragons one last time, and perhaps pretend that they were flying too. Sky watched teary-eyed as the beautiful creatures disappeared in the distance. "I wonder where they're going?" she said.

But no one knew, and the question hung in the air unanswered. Pan's secret remained a mystery, perhaps to be solved another day by a very different pair of young magical twins.

Acknowledgments

I'm using this space to thank you, dear reader, for coming with me on this journey all the way to the end. Finally book seven is here! Thank you from the depths of my heart for caring about this story. Thank you for telling your friends and parents and grandparents and teachers and students and children about it. Thank you for finding me on social media to tell me about the moments that mean something extra special to you.

Thank you for loving these characters as much as I do. Your love for them keeps me going on the difficult writing days. Thank you for being Unwanted too, and for demonstrating it by using your creative abilities in all sorts of amazing ways. You are magical to me.

If you're feeling a little sad or bittersweet after reading this book, you are not alone! I was feeling that way too, so I decided to do something about it. I want to let you know that while this particular story of Alex and Lani and Samheed and Sky ends with this book, there are more stories coming soon about the world of Artimé and the characters you love, as well as some new ones. I can't wait for you to see all the fun surprises I will have for you in my new series, The Unwanteds Quests! The first book comes out in Spring 2017.

I hope you enjoyed reading *Island of Dragons* as much as I enjoyed writing it. And let me know if you're excited about the new series. You can find me on Instagram, Snapchat, and Twitter at @lisa_mcmann, and on Facebook at facebook.com/mcmannfan.

Thank you again for everything you have done to make the Unwanteds series something special. These books wouldn't exist without you.

All my love,
Lisa McMann

P.S. Now that you've reached the end and you've had a chance to think or cry or do whatever you usually do when you finish a book series, keep turning the pages. I've included a special sneak peek of the first book in the new Quests series. A new adventure awaits!

The Quests begin here. . . .

Sneaking Off

The moon was high in the night sky when Thisbe propped herself up on one elbow and peeked under the curtain. The outline of the two dragons filled the lagoon. Thisbe turned to her twin across the room. "Are you sure, Fifer?" she whispered. "Alex will be so mad if he finds out."

Fifer's eyes shone in the darkness. "He'll get over it." She climbed out of her bed and slipped on some clothes. "I wish we had component vests," she grumbled.

Thisbe fell back into her pillow and rested there a moment, then hoisted herself to the floor and started getting dressed. "What about Seth?"

"We'll send him a seek spell."

"You know how to do that?"

"How hard can it be? Kitten did it once and she can't even say the right word." Fifer patted her pocket. "I've got that scene Seth gave me—the one that he wrote in Mr. Burkesh's class. That should do the trick." She hopped onto Thisbe's bed and drew the curtains aside. Then she put her hand on the glass windowpane, concentrated, and whispered, "Release." The windowpane disappeared. Fifer looked over her shoulder. "Ready with the rope?"

Thisbe frowned, then reached behind the wardrobe and grabbed a rope. "Can't we just go the normal way?" she asked. Even though she'd climbed down the side of the mansion a dozen times or more, her stomach flipped at the thought of it.

"You mean so Desdemona sees us and reports us to Alex's blackboard? I don't think so. Plus, we'd have to walk right past Simber."

Fifer had a point. The girls had often found themselves in odd predicaments, and their blackboard, Desdemona, was a major tattletale. And there was no way Simber would keep a secret from the head mage of Artimé.

"Not the back door either?" Thisbe pleaded.

"The chefs will see us. Come on, Thiz," Fifer said impatiently. She glanced at her sister and turned sympathetic. "Aw, I know you're scared. But you can do it. It's the only way."

Thisbe sighed. "All right, fine. Catch me if I fall?"

"I'll turn you into a bird so you can soar to the ground," promised Fifer.

"Ugh. No thanks. Can't you just catch me?"

"Sure," said Fifer, growing impatient again. "Just hurry up."

Thisbe tossed the coiled rope to Fifer, who, balancing on the sill, attached one end of it to an invisible hook outside the window, which one of the girls had installed years before for the first of many escapes.

As Thisbe put on her boots and tied them, Fifer slipped out and rappelled down the side of the mansion. Thisbe reached for her backpack, and not knowing how long they'd be gone, quickly stuffed it with their canteens and a few snacks they had in the room. She climbed on the bed and peered out the window at the ground below. With a grimace she grabbed the rope, took a breath, and swung out, hanging suspended above the ground from a dizzying height. She found her footing against the mansion wall and began descending. A few feet down, she stopped, and with a shaky hand, cast a new glass spell in the opening.

Once on the lawn, Thisbe breathed a sigh of relief. Now that the scary part was over, she grew excited for their adventure. Muttering a spell under her breath, she released the hook's hold on the rope so it landed in a heap at her feet, then coiled it up and put it in her backpack.

Nearby, Fifer was concentrating on the bit of script that Seth had given her. She held it pinched between her fingers, and when she felt ready, whispered, "Seek." A flash of light exploded from the paper and shot up to the second level of the mansion and in through a window, leaving a softly glowing line behind it. The girls waited breathlessly, hoping Seth was sleeping lightly enough that he would notice the spell.

Finally their best friend appeared at the glass. The girls waved frantically and jumped up and down, and after a moment Seth saw them. He waved back, then disappeared. A few minutes later he exited the back door of the mansion and closed it softly behind him. He was wearing his new component vest, its pockets bulging. Fifer smiled approvingly.

"What's this all about?" he whispered. "How'd you do that seek spell?"

"Never mind that," said Thisbe. "Did anybody see you?"

"Just the night chefs. They don't pay much attention to me."

"Let's hope not." Fifer scowled. "We need to move before Simber finds out what we're doing out here. Come on." She took off running across the lawn, toward the jungle. Thisbe and Seth jogged behind.

"Where are we going?" whispered Seth.

Thisbe glanced sidelong at him, her backpack jouncing on her back. She flashed a mischievous grin. "We're going to rescue the young dragon."